The Viper Contract

A Colin Pearce Adventure

Chris Broyhill

SECOND EDITION

Published by
Citadel Publishing LLC
Dover, Delaware, USA
2017

ISBN-13: 978-0-9988250-4-5
ISBN-10: 0-9988250-4-2

Paperback

Cover Design By: Robin E. Vuchnich

Acknowledgements for the Second Edition

As my first venture into professional writing, *The Viper Contract* has been more successful than I ever could have imagined. It has created a league of Colin Pearce fans and inspired a series of Colin Pearce adventures that will continue for many years.

First and foremost, I must thank you, my readers, for the dedication you've shown to Colin Pearce and the inspiration that you have provided me. When I find myself struggling to finish a chapter or make my way through yet another edit of a new Colin Pearce adventure, all I need to do is read an email, a Facebook comment or a review on Amazon and I find the fuel I need to "turn and burn." Perhaps the highest compliment I've been given came from a former Viper driver who told me that when someone asks him what it was like to fly the Viper, he tells that person to read *The Viper Contract*. It doesn't get any better than that.

Secondly, I need to thank my personal friends, my friends in the aviation industry, and my family members for their continued support of my writing "habit." In the years since The Viper Contract was first published, I've built a new flight department for a Fortune 100 company, finished a course of study and dissertation for a Ph.D. degree and written three more Colin Pearce books. Without the support of my friends and loved ones, none of these endeavors would have been possible.

As you may have noticed in the pages above, this version of *The Viper Contract* features a new publisher. While my previous publisher was very supportive of my work, it limited the formats for the book and the venues in which the book could be presented. My new publisher, Citadel, offers a much more flexible approach and allows me more control in the process.

This second edition of The Viper Contract is nearly identical to the first edition. It has been reformatted, proofread an additional time, and slightly edited to improve readability. If you're a previous reader of the book, I hope you find the changes an enhancement. If you're a new reader, welcome to the world of Colin Pearce!

Thanks again to everyone who has supported Colin Pearce and me through our literary sojourn together. Onward and upward!

Chris Broyhill
Irving, Texas
December, 2017

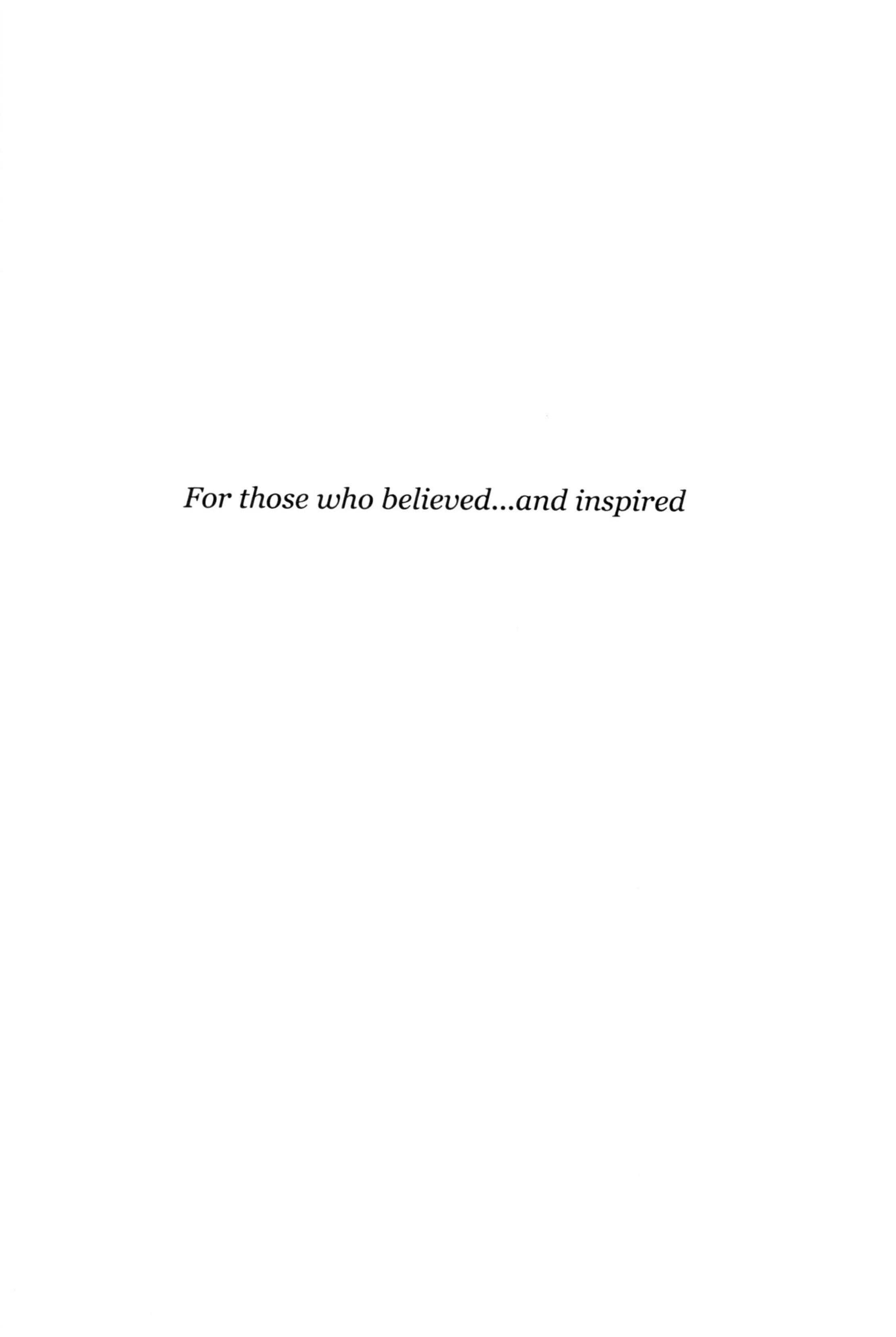

For those who believed...and inspired

PROLOGUE

At some point, I'm going to have to write all this shit down. As if anyone will ever believe it. I'm nearly fifty years old and sitting in the cockpit of an F-16. Our formation is about to launch and drop the equivalent of forty-five Hiroshima bombs on a target near one of the most densely-populated areas in the world.

I've got one group of people paying me to do it. I've got another group paying me to stop it. And I've got pretty damn good reasons to be pissed at both of them.

How in the hell did it all come to this? I'm a contractor. The only thing I'm supposed to care about is my own ass.

The Viper is humming around me, the powerful GE engine whistling in the sleek airframe. Like a falcon, quivering in anticipation atop his handler's gauntlet, the deadly jet seems anxious to take to the skies and seek its prey. I feel a grim sense of expectation as I sit here in the air-conditioned cockpit, the plastic oxygen mask clamped to my face and the lightweight helmet cushioning my head. The performance-enhancing drugs are coursing through my system, increasing the angst. And the anticipation. I look at the jets around me through the tinted visor as I gently caress the buttons and switches on the Viper's side-stick controller and throttle. I'm eager to unleash the jet's full fury—to get into the sky and kick some ass.

I just hope I'm good enough to survive the next twenty minutes.

But I'd rather be lucky than good.

CHAPTER ONE

Friday, 4 September
1900 Hours Local Time
Hartsfield International Airport
Atlanta, Georgia, USA

It all started with a phone call that turned my life upside down.

The first sip of twelve-year-old Macallan was easing its way down my throat when I felt the vibration of my BlackBerry in its holster, followed closely by the opening bars of AC/DC's *Dirty Deeds, Done Dirt Cheap*. The strains of Angus Young's guitar were barely audible above the din of background noise in the bar at the Atlanta International Airport. I silently thanked the cell phone gods for the vibration feature again. After twenty-seven years of flying jet aircraft for a living, my high-frequency hearing isn't all it should be.

I pulled the BlackBerry from the holster and looked at the screen. The caller ID came in as 'Unknown' and I briefly considered not taking the call. I had just come off a five-day trip as captain of a Falcon 900EX business jet. The trip had not gone well and I was hoping I hadn't lost a regular client as a result. In the contract pilot game, regular clients are the 'bread and butter.' Losing one is serious business. I was looking forward to forgetting the last few days by putting on a nice whiskey-induced buzz, riding Delta back to Philadelphia, and getting sloshed on my own single-malt collection when I made it home.

But I'm a contractor and contractors answer their phones or they don't work. It's as simple as that. I hit the green button. "Colin Pearce," I said.

"Mr. Pearce." It was a statement, not a question. The voice was flat with no inflection. Like a machine. "Contractor."

"That's me," I replied. "Eight thousand fifty hours total time, type-rated and current in the Falcon 900EX and the Gulfstream Four, with over 2,000 hours pilot in command time in each."

The machine voice was unimpressed with my spiel and remained flat. "We have a job to discuss with you. It pays $1,000 a day. Are you interested?"

"What's the equipment?"

"We'll talk about that when we interview you. When can you make it to Atlanta?"

I could have made a show of putting him on hold for a second or two while I checked my calendar, but I just didn't feel like making the effort. I knew my schedule was clear for the upcoming week.

"Well, probably within the next few days, unless," I laughed quietly, "you'd like to interview me tonight or tomorrow. As luck would have it, I'm in the Atlanta airport right now, making a flight connection."

"Tonight will be fine," the voice said as if it were unsurprised by that coincidence. "We're in a hurry. We'll pay you a grand for your time tonight, put you up at a suite in the Airport Marriott, and give you a first-class seat on a morning flight to Philly tomorrow. What do you say?"

I quickly reviewed my options. It didn't take long. The date with my scotch collection notwithstanding, there was no reason to hurry back to my empty townhouse in Wilmington, Delaware, and a thousand bucks was a thousand bucks.

"Where and when do you want to meet?" I asked.

"Take the Marriott courtesy van to the hotel and check in. You can meet us in the lobby bar in about an hour."

"How will I find you?"

"Don't worry, Mr. Pearce. We'll find you."

The call was dropped and I spent a good thirty seconds staring at my phone before I re-holstered it. I contemplated the conversation for another five minutes while I finished the Macallan. As the glow took hold of me, I found myself grateful that a new client lead had materialized, especially considering the trip I had just finished. In my career as a contractor, every time I made the interview, I was offered the job. I sat there feeling damn pleased with myself.

##

I walked into the lobby bar at the Marriott about an hour later, after checking into my surprisingly sumptuous suite and tidying myself up, to include the usual freshly-pressed navy-blue suit, white button-down shirt, and maroon tie. I prided myself on being professional and, despite the fact that I wasn't sure where this interview was going, I felt I at least needed to look the part.

The lobby bar was typical of most bars found in the nicer airport hotels - a lot of wood, a variety of plants, and nearly empty of customers at nine o'clock on a Friday night. I walked up to the bar itself and looked over its selection of single-malt, knowing full well it wouldn't create a good impression to walk into a job interview with a scotch in my hand, but thinking I might have a glass or two afterward. The bar had the standard two: Glenlivet and Glenfiddich, but then there was an unexpected bottle of eighteen-year-old Glenmorangie.

As if on cue, an attractive and well-put-together thirty-something blonde showed up behind the bar and took my order, an innocuous glass of club soda. As she turned to get the glass, I inspected her superb rear end and briefly considered attempting to make some small talk. But it quickly occurred to me that she was probably accosted several times per week by guys like me. She placed the glass on the bar and I reached for my wallet, fished out a few singles for a tip, and slid it into the tip glass on the bar.

"Thanks," I said.

"There are two gentlemen over there waiting for you," she nodded toward the rear of the bar. "It's too bad you didn't want anything more expensive. They told me to expect you and to place your drinks on their tab."

"I'll keep that in mind for later," I said, intrigued. "How did they tell you to recognize me?"

She smiled at me. "They just told me to watch for a tall, good-looking guy in a business suit with a tired expression on his face."

It was a nice compliment - if you forgot that she worked for tips. I instinctively looked into the mirror mounted on the wall behind her and saw an average middle-aged man-face looking back at me, with hazel eyes and enough lines to make it look "rugged, but not old," or so I've been told. I'm fortunate enough to still have a full head of brown hair, although it is going gray at the temples. The bad news is that I weigh about two-hundred-forty-five pounds, at least thirty-five pounds more than I should, thanks to a job which has me perpetually sitting on my ass in airports or airplanes. I don't look too bad in my clothes, due to a lot of time spent in the gym when I was younger, but there's less muscle there than there used to be, and I've gotten to the point where I don't care much. I contemplated the image in the mirror and decided for the thousandth time that there was nothing special there to look at.

But the bartender smiled at me again and it seemed genuine enough, so I nodded, thanked her again, and began to make my way to the rear of the bar.

I waded through the few rows of tables, went around a divider composed of a half-wall of wood with a planter built into it and found several more rows of tables. It didn't take long to find the men I was there to meet; they were the only other occupants in this section of the bar. They sat behind a round table in the corner of the lounge area and watched me approach. I was immediately on my guard. These guys didn't look like typical pilots, owners, or clients. They had a different look, one I knew well.

In my business aviation career, I have flown former presidents a few times and they were surrounded by an entourage of tough and competent-looking Secret Service agents who exuded a similar professional look. But there was something these guys had that the Secret Service did not. These guys were professional killers. Thanks to some exploits in a previous 'life,' I'd spent enough time around their kind to know them when I see them.

I quickly realized there was no coincidence about our meeting in Atlanta and it also occurred to me that the girl behind the bar must have been provided a full description of my appearance. I felt the back of my throat go a little dry and I instinctively raised the glass of soda to my lips and took a good slug of it, instantly regretting there was no scotch in there.

I neared the table and the two men stood, presumably to shake my hand. They rose with a practiced sort of slow motion, as if they didn't want to convey how quickly they could really move.

The man on my left was slightly shorter than me, but stockier. He had a thick mane of blonde hair, almost like a surfer's, and had an earring in his left ear. His brown eyes looked me over closely and I did my best to appear non-threatening. I got the feeling from the way his clothes hung on him that a business suit wasn't his normal garb. I could also see his muscles ripple beneath the fabric. He looked like he'd burst out of the thing if he laughed too hard.

The other guy was about the same height as his associate but slimmer. He had nondescript brown hair and a growth of beard on his face that indicated he was at least a day out of a good shave. His eyes got my attention though. They were dark green, like the color of jade, and they bored right into me. He had an oval face and a distinct dimple on his chin. I guessed that he'd have a bitch of a time disguising it if he did any undercover work. He also had long, manicured fingers and I had the feeling that he was the more dangerous of the two. here was something vaguely familiar about him, but I couldn't quite retrieve it.

I extended my hand toward him and flashed both men my best 'damn glad to meet you' smile. "Colin Pearce," I offered. "I presume you two are the gentlemen who are treating me to a night in a suite?"

"Dave Smith," the skinnier one answered as he took my hand in his with a firm, comfortable grip. He released my hand and motioned to the blonde guy. "My partner here is John Amrine." I shook the blonde's hand and was surprised that he shook with another firm, comfortable grip and didn't try to show his strength with his handshake the way a lot of muscleheads do. But I suppose when you kill people for a living, proving your masculinity with your handshake is a bit redundant.

"Please, Mr. Pearce," Smith said, "have a seat. The party paying for your suite," he continued, "is the United States government. Would you like to know why?"

"I thought it was something like that as I was walking over here," I replied after a moment. You two don't look like aircraft owners, managers, or chief pilots."

Smith flashed me an unsurprised smile. "Really? And what do those types of people look like?"

"They look like me," I replied. "Soft, out of shape." I changed gears with them right away because the suspense was killing me. "Do I need a lawyer before we continue this conversation?"

Smith glanced over at Amrine and they exchanged an indecipherable look between them. Then Smith looked at me again. "Why? Do you think you need one? Have you done anything wrong?"

Damn Feds, I thought. *Answering questions with questions.*

"Not that I'm aware of," I said, "but the last time I talked to federal agents without a lawyer present I got my pee-pee whacked for my trouble. I don't intend to make the same mistake again unless you can convince me that it's in my best interest to do so."

Smith nodded and reached inside his coat pocket. "If we were here to do that, we wouldn't be giving you this." He produced a thick business-letter-sized envelope and tossed it on the table in front of me. "All we want you to do is listen to what we have to say."

I retrieved the envelope and looked inside. There, as promised, were a first-class plane ticket to Philly booked on the mid-morning flight and ten $100 bills. I thumbed through them quickly and stowed the envelope in my coat pocket. "Well, you're good to your word, so now I have to really wonder if you're the US government. I'd like to see some credentials please."

Smith reached into his jacket pocket again and retrieved the standard credential wallet, which I'd previously seen Secret Service guys display. He did it the way they all do, with his left hand so he could keep his right hand free. He opened the wallet awkwardly with one hand and laid it on the table in front of me. You'll have to forgive me," he said. "We don't display these often."

I stared down at the blue, laminated ID card and shook my head slightly. There was Smith's picture, and then a series of numbers which didn't seem to have a pattern. About that time, Amrine's ID appeared on the table next to Smith's and

I made a show of looking it over, but by that time, my eyes weren't even in focus.

"These cards don't..."

"Don't have names?" Smith asked. "That's how you know they're genuine. If someone claims to be from the CIA and shows you an ID with a name on, run for the hills."

"Especially if he claims to be from the NCS," Amrine chimed in. "National Clandestine Service," he added for my benefit. "That's our directorate."

I knew the creds were genuine. Because I had seen similar ones before. A long time ago. I was seated at a bar table in the Atlanta Airport Marriott with two genuine CIA operatives and my head was swimming. I looked up at both of them and tried to appear calm as I sat back in my seat and brought my glass of soda to my lips. My hands were shaking and I dribbled a little of the liquid down my chin as I sipped it.

"Okay, you've got my attention. What could the CIA possibly want with me?"

"You're a contractor, right?" Smith asked.

I nodded.

"We want to hire you, at your rate of $1,000 per day, to do some work for us."

"Okay," I said after a second, "I'll bite. What kind of airplane?"

"Well there's a little more to it than just flying, but the jet is one you've flown before," Amrine answered, "an airplane you've got a lot of experience in."

"Fine," I replied, feeling like the conversation was settling into a reasonably comfortable area, "which one?"

"The General Dynamics F-16C, although now I understand it's built by Lockheed Martin. The 'Viper,' I think you guys call it."

I almost spit out the remaining water in my mouth. "The Viper?"

Amrine looked over at me flatly, his nonchalance belying his surfer-boy appearance. "You've got a few hours in that jet, haven't you?"

I nodded slowly. "Almost 2,000."

"And you were a fighter weapons instructor in it, right?"

I nodded again. "I attended Weapons School in the A-10 and went back again in the F-16."

Amrine nodded as though he knew all that, which he obviously did.

I set my glass on the table and carefully put my hands in my lap so neither Smith nor Amrine could see that they were shaking. "Since when," I asked at last, "does the CIA have F-16s?"

Smith looked like he had been waiting for that question. "We don't," he said as he pulled a file from a briefcase on the floor next to him and laid it on the table in front of me. "Someone else does. And they're going to make you a job offer sometime in the coming week. We just wanted to make sure we got to you first."

"What?" I was convinced I hadn't heard him clearly.

"There's a mercenary group out there flying Vipers and using them to attack ground targets," Amrine added. "We have hard intel that they will be approaching you sometime in the next few days to offer you a job. We want you to take the job so we can get some eyes and ears inside their organization and stop them from executing the raid they're currently planning."

So, I heard correctly. And I had heard enough. "Guys," I said as I pushed my chair back, "I imagine that you've done some pretty extensive research on me; and if you have, then you know how I got to where I am."

They looked back at me and I could tell both knew what I was talking about. I should mention that I'm a retired Air Force Lieutenant Colonel. My departure from the service wasn't pretty and I held the entire USAF responsible for it, although most of the blame rested squarely on the shoulders of an organization known as the Air Force Office of Special Investigations or OSI for short, the USAF's answer to the

Keystone Kops.

"Funny thing is," I continued, "for about the last seven years or so, where all this 'service to country' shit is concerned, my 'give-a- damn' has been flat-out busted." I patted the coat pocket where the envelope was and stood to leave. "I thank you for this opportunity," I said, "but I don't think this will be a good fit."

It was almost funny. Neither of them moved. Neither showed the slightest indication that they were the least bit surprised by my outburst.

Smith just looked up at me casually and said, "Two words. Burt Magnusson."

Suddenly, I heard a ringing in my ears as if the background noise in the bar had been instantly blotted out.

Smith did me the courtesy of not requiring me to speak. Instead, he showed the first indication of the evening that he might be a mere mortal. He shrugged and I saw him struggle to not let his face change expression as he looked down at the file in front of him. "He was working for us and now he's disappeared."

Amrine broke eye contact with me as well and looked at the far end of the bar. "We're not here to solicit you to serve your country. We're here because we thought you might want to find out what the hell happened to your best friend."

Smith broke in and his voice was softer but firmer now. "We don't have time for this shit, Pearce. We're going to talk and you're going to want to hear what we have to say." He inclined his chin toward my chair. "Sit," he said.

I sat.

CHAPTER TWO

Saturday, 5 September
1030 Hours Local Time
Flight Level 370 and Mach .80
Somewhere between Atlanta, GA & Philadelphia, PA, USA

"*I said* would you care for something to drink, sir?" The flight attendant was pert and brunette and obviously annoyed that I had not answered her question the first several times she had asked it. I was tucked into my first-class seat on the Delta flight to Philadelphia and staring out the window.

I glanced at her tray, determined to choose something that would get her out of my face as quickly as possible. "Champagne, please."

She took a glass off her tray, set it on my armrest with the usual bowl of mixed nuts, and turned to serve the much more attentive guy across the aisle. We had just leveled off after our departure from Atlanta and my head was still recovering from the events of the previous evening. After my discussion with Smith and Amrine had ended, I returned to the bar and finished the bottle of eighteen-year-old Glenmorangie, glad that it was on the government's dollar. I had hoped that the booze would erase the thoughts that were careening around inside my head and push them back into their place, but that didn't happen and I spent a sleepless night tossing and turning on the decadently comfortable pillow-top bed in my opulent suite.

The news about Burt Magnusson had been devastating, but Smith and Amrine had one detail wrong in their pitch. Burt, or 'Boomer' as we used to call him in the USAF, wasn't my best friend. He had been my only friend. Since we were roommates at the Air Force Academy - over thirty years ago.

Before he and I were assigned to same room when our class rotated squadrons, in the fall of our junior year, my record with roommates wasn't terribly consistent. I was an exemplary 'team member' when it came to room inspections and duties, but I steadfastly refused any forays into my personal life and made myself scarce whenever possible, studying alone in a solitary carrel in the Academy's vast library or in an empty corner of the recreation hall. And of course, at the end of every semester, when the option to swap roommates was presented, I always found myself with a new one. I even remembered overhearing a conversation once in which one of my former roommates was speaking to another. "I spent a whole semester with the guy," one of them said, "and I don't have a clue who he is." The other former roommate had nodded in understanding. "He's a nice enough guy. But it's just a little creepy."

I guess I should have been insulted, but I the truth was I didn't care. Keeping people at a distance was important.

After growing up in a miserable small town in Florida with a father that was never home, a mother who wallowed in alcoholic self-pity, and two younger brothers I was charged to raise and who hated me for it, I had no desire to get close to anyone.

But somehow Burt, with his easygoing manner and infectious laugh, had crept under my sullenness. He was from Minnesota and sported the Scandinavian looks so common there. Taller than I was at 6 feet 4 inches, he had impossibly blonde hair, a Nordic complexion, and a thin, athletic build. I was his opposite, the dark, brooding one from the South, slightly shorter, definitely stockier, and much more introspective.

Yet, despite our differences, somehow, we had clicked. Maybe it was his understanding of my reserved demeanor and his refusal to be put off by it. He said once that Scandinavians were masters at understated emotions and he had long ago refused to live that way. After the first semester of our junior year, he didn't sign up to change roommates and the bond between us was cemented for our remaining time at the Academy. We shared class notes and textbooks and spent several 'all-nighters' awake at our desks, pumping coffee into ourselves and exchanging jokes as we prepared for exams or wrote research papers.

I was also lucky enough to benefit from his appeal to the ladies. The women he dated often had friends who wanted to be fixed up with a cadet and I enjoyed many double dates and couples ski-trips thanks to his insistence that I be included. One of the more memorable ski-trips began with me paired with a young beauty named Amanda Peters, and ended with her and Burt as a couple. He married her a few years later and I stood by his side as best man and felt ridiculously happy for the two of them.

Since graduation, while our careers had overlapped on several occasions, we often went long periods without communicating, so the silence over the last year had not been surprising or alarming, but as the information had flowed last evening, I began feeling like a part of me had been ripped away.

I looked out the window of the airliner and sipped the crisp champagne. The cool liquid swept across my tongue, and as I felt its familiar bite on the back of my throat, I also sensed the growing emptiness inside me and along with the emptiness, the first stirrings of something I hadn't felt in a long, long time - the lust for blood. I closed my eyes and let the "hair of the dog" do its work while last night replayed in my head.

##

"We'll start with the background," Smith had said.

It's refreshing to work with guys in the government who are on the 'business end' of things. They don't stand on ceremony, formality, or bureaucracy. Instead, they just do what they have to do.

Smith had opened a file of photographs stamped with acronyms like TS, SCI, and SSI. "This first group of photos is satellite imagery of a drug laboratory in the mountains of Colombia," he'd said. "These were taken about eleven months ago. One of our satellites was re-tasked after the DEA reported that the lab had been destroyed. The local field office had no idea how it happened and knew that none of the soldiers from any of the local contenders for the throne had been involved. They were at a complete loss to explain it and turned to us." He'd pushed the first photograph into my hands. "This is a file photo taken several months prior to the incident."

The photograph was a satellite image with resolution so good it looked as if the viewer was in a balloon or something just above the complex. The lab was in a large clearing on a plateau on the side of a heavily-forested mountain. There were four long buildings and several smaller ones. The buildings were solidly constructed with concrete walls and steel roofs. The place was teeming with activity. Vehicles were everywhere and scores of people, most of them armed, could be seen throughout the area. A formidable fence surrounded the entire complex and was patrolled by both vehicles and men on foot. At regular intervals along the fence were concrete guard towers, and just outside the fence there was a deep trench filled with metal spikes. On the other side of the trench was a cleared, flat area, obviously both a minefield and a clear field of fire for the guard towers. I had seen prisons that weren't as well constructed. The place would have been nearly impregnable to ground assault. Those who owned this place must have spent a huge sum building it and were obviously determined to protect it.

Smith had pushed the rest of the photographs in that group across the table to me.

"These," he'd said, "were taken...after."

Armageddon had come to the mountainside. The buildings were flattened. Charred pieces of vehicles and people were scattered all over the clearing. There was no sign of life. To someone who had never seen the damage from an airstrike, the destruction would have looked thorough, but random. To me though, it looked systematic. There were no craters, but it was clear that the destruction had emanated out in a series of circular systems. Here and there, the charring was manifested in arcs and the earth itself showed the evidence of rounded shock waves throughout the clearing.

I could feel Amrine's eyes on me as he had asked, "What sort of ordnance do you think was used here?"

I had swallowed hard. Only one thing I knew of that made a pattern like this. "Fuel-air explosives," I said at last.

Fuel-air explosives, or FAEs, were a gruesome weapon developed by the guys in the Coke-bottle glasses in the latter stages of the Vietnam War. During that war, napalm had gotten all the attention, but napalm was to fuel-air explosives what firecrackers were to six-packs of dynamite. FAEs contained a fuel mixture in a canister that had an airburst fuse and was activated fifty to one hundred feet above the ground. When the canister opened, the fuel was propelled out as an aerosol in a circular radius and ignited after a fraction of a second. At the moment of detonation, all the oxygen in the radius of the weapon was instantly sucked out of the atmosphere. Then a shock wave, equal in force to a tactical nuclear weapon but smaller in size, was generated, flattening everything in the effective radius. Finally, the area became a raging inferno with temperatures in the range of 5,000 degrees Fahrenheit.

I had looked at the rest of the photographs in the first group and took another gulp of club soda. "Holy shit," I had said. "It obviously wasn't us; those things were out of the inventory a long time before I retired."

"How do you think they did it?" Amrine had asked, quietly.

I had shuffled through the photographs. "If I had planned it, I would have used four jets with two weapons each. Two-thousand-pound class weapons, like BLU-96s or the equivalent. I'd drop them in pairs from low-altitude deliveries."

Smith had sat back in his chair. "Why low-altitude?" he had asked.

"Assuming they're using off-the-shelf weapons and not something I don't know about, the canisters are highly subject to wind drift when released at high-altitude. They were designed for low-altitude delivery for just that reason."

I had looked up at Smith and Amrine and they had nodded back at me, apparently satisfied with my observation. "You've got a serious problem," I'd said. "These guys are good. They would have had to get four jets on and off target before the first weapon detonated. They're professionals."

Amrine had nodded and smiled grimly. "It only gets worse."

For the next hour, they showed me four more sets of before and after photographs. A refinery on the Malaysian coast was obliterated - combined effects cluster bombs had been used on that one. A power plant in Kenya leveled - conventional high-explosive bombs there. A cache of tanks and armored personnel carriers in Somalia ripped to shreds - combined effects cluster bombs again. The attack on the last target was a work of art. The structure was a reinforced bunker built into the side of a mountain in eastern Turkey. There was a series of black holes on the mountainside, each about two feet in diameter. That was the only external evidence of the attack.

But the inside of the bunker would have been devastated. The weapons there were probably multiple BLU-109s, hard-target-penetrating 2,000-pound bombs. The attackers would have had to perform an extremely precise low-altitude, low-angle delivery to get the correct penetration angle, and that spoke of a high degree of proficiency indeed.

I had pushed the last set of photographs back across the table at Smith and leaned back, impressed against my will. These guys were easily on a par with the most experienced USAF pilots I had flown with. "I can't believe there hasn't been something in the news about this stuff," I had muttered.

"There has been," Smith said, as he'd collected the photographs and replaced them in the file, leaving one pile, which I had not seen, in front of him. "They were all passed off as random incidents. The Colombian thing was an explosion created by the chemicals used to produce the drugs. The refinery in Malaysia was a venting issue that went catastrophic. The power plant in Kenya was a fuel explosion. The Somali thing, no one really cared about, and the Turkey thing was never mentioned because no one wanted to admit the complex had been there in the first place. Let's just say that a certain international arms dealer had built the complex as a place in which to hole-up and the Turkish government looked the other way. These events just stayed in the 'noise level' of things."

"So, who are these guys?" I had asked. "Sort of an 'Airstrikes-R-Us?'"

Smith and Amrine had exchanged a quick glance between them and Amrine smiled. "Actually," he said, "that's almost what we called them."

My jaw dropped. "You've got to be kidding me."

"Nope," Smith said. "Since we were the first to confirm their existence, we should have been able to code-name them. But our supervisor didn't like it. The name we ended up with was MAG for mercenary air group. You have to admit, it has a certain ring to it."

I smiled in appreciation. "So, who are they and where'd they get the jets?"

Smith had pushed the last stack of photographs toward me. "You're not even going to believe this," he'd said. These photographs were of the Aerospace Maintenance and Regeneration Center at Davis-Monthan Air Force Base in Tucson, Arizona, otherwise known as the "Boneyard." There was a row of F-16s parked along a section of fence. Several jets from the row were obviously missing.

"No way," I'd said, looking down at the photograph then up at them."

"Yes," Amrine had said quietly, "they stole the jets. From us."

"That's how we got involved in this business," Smith had interjected. "This was way beyond the capability of the Air Force OSI to investigate, so the FBI was called in. The FBI special agent in charge of the case readily saw the implications for external security and he called us. Sometimes, this Homeland Security cooperation shit actually works."

I was shaking my head. "How the hell did they—"

"Sadly," Amrine had interrupted, "it was easier than you think. It happened about 18 months ago and was the subject of one of the largest hush-ups I've ever been a part of. As classified as the rest of this stuff is, this last bit is classified at the Director and National Staff level. Smith and I had to sign release forms to even be allowed to briefyou."

The impact of that had taken a second or two to hit home. After my highly-visible departure from the Air Force several years ago, I was again the subject of conversations in the halls of leadership. The thought didn't thrill me.

Amrine had continued. "It happened in the middle of the night. They used a group of commandos to knock out the power to that section of the facility and to tranquilize the entire night shift. Then, they used a crane and lifted eight jets out of the row parked along the east fence, placed them onto a series of flat-bed trucks and simply drove away with them. We later found the flatbed trucks abandoned several hundred miles away. We had no idea where the jets went until...later."

"What kind of Vipers did they get? Not Block 40s or 50s?" Block 40 F-16s and the later models had the plumbing for precision weapons delivery, like laser or GPS-guided bombs. Block 50s had a sophisticated avionics suite and more advanced radar.

"No, thank God," Amrine had said. "There aren't any of those in the Boneyard yet. They got Block 30s."

"Let me guess. They got the big-inlet, GE-engined jets."

They'd both nodded.

"Great."

The F-16 was the most prolific jet fighter in the world and came in many models and variants, but of the older vintage jets, the Block 30 F-16 with the enlarged air-intake was a first among equals. In full afterburner, its General Electric engine emitted 3,000 pounds more thrust than the same engine in a small inlet airframe or the Pratt and Whitney engine did in either airframe. The Block 30 accelerated so fast on takeoff roll that it could exceed the limiting airspeed for the landing gear. That's zero to 300 knots in a little less than three quarters of a mile. Once airborne, it was a 'g-machine' and did not lose energy at all if correctly managed in a visual fight. I knew the jet well. My first Viper tour was in the big-inlet Block 30 at Kunsan Air Base in the Republic of Korea.

"I guess I'm kind of surprised they didn't buy Mig-29s or something else a little easier to obtain on the open market instead of resorting to something like this."

"The former Soviet equipment is just too unreliable," Smith had said, "and spare parts are scarce."

"Also," Amrine had added, "because the F-16 is so common all over the world, it doesn't draw too much attention when extra ones show up in certain places from time to time."

"It sounds like they really thought this through," I'd said.

He nodded.

"So how did Burt get mixed up in all of this?"

"When was the last time you saw him?" Smith had asked.

"I had dinner at his house in Florida a little over a year ago."

"Did you know what was going on with him at the time?"

"I assumed he was running his aircraft business; he didn't discuss it much."

"That's because he was getting ready to file bankruptcy. His business had crashed and he was in debt several hundred thousand dollars."

I'd sat back in my chair and put my hands over my face. "Oh my God!" I'd said in exasperation. "That's what she meant!"

"What do you mean?" Amrine had asked.

"Mandy, his wife, told me that Burt needed me to be around more. That's why. She wanted him to have someone to confide in."

"She probably also wanted you to be around so he could ask you for money," Smith had added. "How much money do you have stowed away in that offshore account in Bermuda? Six hundred thousand or so?"

No use denying it. I made anywhere from $1,000 to $1,200 per day depending on the terms of the contract. It's not like I have some sort of master financial plan; I just have no life. The money piles up.

"Yes," I'd said at last, "but I would have given him anything he needed."

"Well, sometime shortly after he met with you, MAG hired him and offered him a ticket out of his financial crisis. He had no choice but to take it. They paid him enough up front to keep his house from the creditors and to keep his family taken care of and promised him enough when his contract was completed to put him back to where he was, financially.

I'm sure he felt like he didn't have a choice."

I'd nodded. That was the Burt I knew. Always thinking of others. Particularly his family.

"How'd they contact him?" I'd asked. "It's not like you answer a job ad for out-of-work F-16 pilots."

"When he was attempting to get some capital for his business, he ran into another Air Force Academy graduate named Ronald Phillips, who at least on paper, represents a company called Fieldstone Capital. He knew Phillips at the Academy, and although Phillips couldn't or wouldn't help him with business capital, he evidently was the person who presented Burt with the job a few months later. It is apparent now that the company thing was a cover."

I'd raised my eyebrows.

"We got that lead from his wife," Amrine had said, "when we took her and the family into protective custody. Phillips came to Burt's house a few days before Burt left for the job. Burt told his wife that Phillips had presented him with an opportunity to get them out of debt and that he had to take advantage of it. She remembered Phillips distinctly when we debriefed her. She said he was way too 'pretty.'"

"Who is this guy?" I'd asked.

Smith had pulled another photograph out of the pile in front of him and slid it across to me. "Ronald Allen Phillips, USAF Academy class of 1980. Rhodes Scholar. F-15 pilot."

I studied the photograph. It was obviously taken while he was flying the Eagle because he was dressed up in full pilot gear, with helmet bag in hand. And yes, he was a little too pretty. He had brilliant blue eyes, immaculately coiffed and combed blonde hair, perfect teeth, and the kind of face normally seen on movie posters. His smile was brilliant and looked like he could re-create it on demand.

"He was fluent in Russian, thanks to his extended studies in the language," Smith had said, "so he became an Air-Attaché at the embassy in Moscow after his F-15 assignment and spent two tours there. After that, he had the pick of any high-powered job in the USAF he wanted, but he suddenly resigned and just sort of disappeared off the grid. A few years ago, he reappeared as the Chairman of Fieldstone Venture Capital, a company with a lot of money, headquartered in the Cayman Islands. One day he wasn't there and the next day he was. At the time, we had no idea where he was, or the money he controlled, came from."

"We still don't know where he was," Amrine had chimed in, "but now we know what he was up to."

"So, what happened with Burt?" I'd asked them. "Was he working for you all along, or what?"

Smith had answered, with a shake of his head, "Not at all. He contacted us, specifically me, about two months ago, using a secure email account. The message just popped up on my BlackBerry. By that time, he had been working for them for nearly eight months and you could say that his conscience was getting the better of him. It was *our* friend Burt," Smith had gestured to the stack of photographs, "who planned every one of these strikes."

Suddenly, the reason Smith had looked familiar to me gelled in my head.

"You're the spook!" I'd said.

Smith had nodded. "So that's what he called me, huh?"

It was my turn to nod. "You're the guy he knew from the parachute team while we were at the Academy! He told me that one of the guys he used to jump with had joined the CIA."

"That was a long time ago, after I finished my commitment to the USAF," Smith had said. "I thought there had to be more to life than the OSI."

I allowed myself a begrudging amount of respect for Smith. At least he had seen the OSI for the clowns they were. But there was something else about him that gnawed at me.

"Anyway, John and I had been working on this MAG thing for several months and were getting absolutely nowhere. They had made the five strikes we showed you and we still had no clue who or what they were, other than the fact that they flew F-16s and were highly proficient. Then, two months ago, Burt's email pops up and he starts feeding us information. Suddenly, all the pieces began to fall into place."

"How'd he correspond with you for that long without someone getting wise to it?"

"He used one of those online encrypted email sites and changed his address weekly. I managed to give him some different addresses as well, addresses that didn't look like they were encrypted but were. Obviously, though, someone eventually figured it out, because we haven't heard from him in two weeks."

My throat had gone dry again. I took another sip of the club soda and waited until I could trust my voice. "That sucks," I'd said.

"Yes, it does."

"Here's the kicker, though," Amrine had interjected. "In the last email we got, he mentioned that they were preparing for an upcoming 'project,' to use their vernacular, which was going to have devastating consequences. He asked us to take his family into protective custody and to find you."

"Me? What was that about?"

"Evidently, MAG keeps a short list of 'talent' which they can draw from if they need a quick replacement. They get the names of potential candidates from the people they hire and then do the preliminary background checks. Even if Burt hadn't given them your name, they would have eventually gotten to you. They've undoubtedly already done the initial background work on you. You fit their profile."

"Really?"

"Really," Smith had answered. "You were a highly-proficient fighter pilot who maintained no contact with the military for the last several years. In your case, you were an even better candidate than Burt was, because you have no family to speak of and you already do contract work as your livelihood."

"I see. So after all this time, why did he suddenly tell you to look for me?"

Smith glanced over at Amrine, who had picked up the narrative. "We think he knew they were on to him. He was actually trying to protect you. He thought that if something happened to him, they'd come after you next."

Yet again, Burt's humanity shined through. I had always thought that he was a better friend than I deserved. My guts began to twist.

"So, what it comes down to is this, Mr. Pearce," Amrine had continued, "although you may not give a shit about your country, do you care enough about your best friend to finish what he started?"

I'd barely heard him. I could feel my face getting warm and the blood coursing in my veins. I had to fight to keep the discussion on familiar turf.

"This is gonna cost you and Uncle Sam. The rate will be $2,000 per day, six-month minimum," I'd said, struggling to keep my voice flat. "Half in advance, the remaining half upon completion or at the six-month point, whatever comes first. If additional months are required, they are billed at the same rate and payment is due in advance on the first day of the new month."

They'd both sat there and I swear to God, they looked right through me. I wasn't fooling them.

"I need payment in my account when these guys show themselves, or I'll turn them down and the whole thing is no deal."

Smith and Amrine had looked at each other and some sort of unspoken conversation occurred between them. Then Smith had looked at me. "Done," he'd said. "One thing though. We need to be absolutely clear about what we're hiring you for. If we can't stop this upcoming operation, you'll have to.

Somehow. Some way."

My eyes had narrowed. Suddenly, I knew the other reason Smith was familiar. He had been with the SEAL Team which had gotten me out of Iraq when I was shot down during the first Gulf War. That's when I first seen the strange blue badge.

"That's the other reason we're here," Smith had said. "There aren't many people who know what you're capable of. We do."

Smith's face swam in front of me, morphing into a vision with face paint and a black watch cap as I felt the world spin and time was reversed to a place several years in the past.

I was sitting against a wall somewhere and Smith was kneeling next to me, talking to me. "Captain Pearce, are you all right? Are you hurt?"

I must have answered him satisfactorily because he nodded at me. "The blood all over him isn't his," he said to the other men who were with him.

Then, I could see them too. They were all in black tactical gear, with blackened faces as well.

"I'll bet it's on that big, fucking knife he's got in his hand," one of them whispered.

Then I heard another voice behind me. "They're all dead, the entire platoon," it said.

"How?" Smith asked them.

"You're looking at him," the voice said. "They all had their throats cut, and I mean ripped fucking open."

"You need to keep tabs on this guy, Mr. Smith," another voice chimed in. "He does just your kind of work."

Suddenly, the Delta jet's landing gear thumped down and I was brought back to the present. As we made our approach to the airport over the Delaware River, I watched the Philly skyline go by and the words that had been echoing in my head since last night rang out again.

What the fuck have you gotten yourself into?

CHAPTER THREE

Sunday, 6 September
1700 Hours Local Time
My Townhouse
Wilmington, Delaware, USA

The next day, Sunday, was typically boring. I did my laundry, paid my bills and caught up on my housework. Four years in a military academy instead of a real college and an entire adult life living by myself have made me a bit anal about keeping things clean.

My townhouse is a compact two-bedroom model in a nondescript part of North Wilmington and never requires much time to clean. It's located just off Route 202 in a small development of similar townhomes arrayed in a square around a common area with a pool and small clubhouse. They are all colonial in style, with brick facades, shutters of varying colors (mine are brown) and vinyl siding. My house is three stories, with a two-car garage and storage room on the bottom level; a kitchen, living room, and dining room on the middle level; and a master suite and guest suite on the upper level. My living room is outfitted as a library and I have my books, desk, recliner, and a comfortable sofa all grouped around a brick fireplace with a fifty-inch LCD TV hanging over the mantle. Maplewood bookshelves take up most of my wall space because my book collection is extensive. I spend my nights on the road reading instead of partying, and my tastes extend from the classics to John D. McDonald, Nelson DeMille, Lee Child, Lawrence Block, and John Sanford. The library was my favorite room in the house and I often stayed up until the wee hours of the morning engrossed in a book in front of the fire, sipping a good single-malt.

Speaking of single-malt, in the dining area I have a wooden bar set up with all my bottles of the luscious stuff arrayed by region, distillery and by age - about fifty in number. I have a nice dining table with a buffet as well, although I rarely use them.

My neighborhood tends to be quiet, with just enough 'kid sounds' to keep it from getting boring. Most of my fellow residents are young adults, some with children, some without. About half of us are in the 'over forty' crowd.

I managed to avoid thinking about Burt until late in the afternoon. I barbequed myself a huge porterhouse steak and ate my favorite meal: steak and homemade Caesar salad. I polished off a bottle of Shiraz with the meal, and then did the dishes. Afterward, I poured a healthy shot of twenty-five-year-old Macallan in a crystal tumbler and retired to the study.

I found the photo album I was looking for without too much difficulty, sat on the sofa and opened it up on the coffee table. Then for the next hour or so, I turned the pages and relived the past with my only friend on earth.

The first photographs were of Burt and me at the Academy during our junior and senior years, hanging out in our dorm room in Sijan Hall, on squadron trips, at squadron parties, and then with our dates at the Graduation Ball. He married his date. I ditched mine before departing for pilot training. Then there we were hugging each other as the jets flew overhead after the graduation ceremony.

The next set of pictures was of us together during the Gulf War. I was still flying A-10s then. We had some hard miles on us and it showed on our faces.

Then there were the pictures from our two F-16 tours together. He had gone directly to the F-16 out of pilot training where I had done two tours in the A-10 first. By the time I got to the Viper, I had a lot of catching up to do; and Burt, who was a Fighter Weapons Instructor, made it his business to make me as good as he was. He was ruthless with me, constantly drilling me on numbers, tactics, and radar mechanics.

After a particularly grueling ride, we'd been drinking beer in the squadron bar and he'd told me something I never forgot. I remembered the look in his eyes and the way his jaw was set when he said it.

"There are two types of fighter pilots out there," he'd begun. "Some are *technicians*. They understand the mechanics of what we do. Some of them understand it exceptionally well. But when they fly a sortie, it's always like a series of problems for which they find solutions. Their ability to react to new problems is limited by their ability to compare it to a problem they've already seen and select an appropriate solution. But then there are *the artists* and their understanding goes way beyond mechanics. It's even beyond a conceptual understanding. They just *get it*. At a glance, they see the big picture of a developing situation and their response just flows out of them without any real conscious effort."

He'd stopped and took a long draught of his beer and then looked at me directly as he swallowed it.

"Today's sortie was the fifth time we've flown together and while I suspected that was who you were before we took off; you proved it in the air today. You're an artist, TC. You *get it*."

I'd been stunned by his declaration and it had taken me several moments to respond.

"Well, you've got to be one too," I'd replied slowly. "You're a hell of an instructor and you're better than I am."

He shook his blonde head.

"No," he'd said quietly. "I'm a technician. I'm a damn good

technician and one who can kick your ass on a regular basis at this particular moment in time. But I'm not an artist. Soon, you'll be kicking my ass on a regular basis and doing so with far less effort then it takes me to kick yours now."

I'd grinned at him. "That'll be the day," I'd said.

He'd grinned back, but his expression was more wise than mirthful. "It won't be long," he'd said.

He was right. I quickly climbed the upgrade ladder from wingman to two-ship flight leader, to four-ship flight leader, to instructor pilot. Then, thanks to Burt's influence with the leadership in the F-16 Division, I was allowed to return to Fighter Weapons School and go through the entire F-16 Fighter Weapons Instructor Course as a major, even though I had already attended the same course as a captain in the A-10. I was the outstanding graduate of my Viper class and Burt was at my graduation to see it happen.

The last two pages of the scrapbook featured the pictures we took the last time I visited him and family a little over a year ago. With the context of Smith and Amrine's words floating in my mind, I saw something in the pictures I hadn't seen before. While there were smiles for the camera, there was an undertone of strain on Burt's and Mandy's features.

I closed the book and extinguished the lamp next to me. Then I sat and sipped the Macallan as I stared into the gloom, cursing myself for my ignorance of Burt's travails and wondering if my soul was as murky as the darkening room.

##

I awoke on my sofa Monday morning with scotch-breath and a rip-roaring headache. After a shower, I made some breakfast and retrieved the paper from my front stoop. As I chewed my egg sandwich, I read a headline about the IRS and offshore banking and that keyed a thought in my head. I put down the sandwich and raced into the library. Quickly, I fired up my computer and logged into my offshore bank account at the Bermuda Branch of the Hong Kong Beijing Bank.

A few years ago, I had the fortunate experience of flying a contract job for a Bermuda-based company for an extended period and my employers assisted me in establishing a corporate bank account there. Bermuda is a tax-free country, so every penny I make is wired there. Then I pump it into the US as required. I pay my share of taxes on my earnings when they come into the US, but I pay Uncle Sam on my schedule, not his. Also, thanks to the fact that HSBB's interest rates are higher than those found in the US, the funds that stayed in Bermuda grew at a healthy rate.

As the positions page of the account came up in my browser, I saw something that filled me with excitement and dread at the same time. My account balance had been increased by $180,000 - the first-half payment for the six-month minimum. Smith and Amrine were good to their word.

I spent the next two days in a state of tense anticipation. I went grocery shopping, got the oil in my Ford Explorer changed and got out of the house for dinner at the local Applebee's. When I was home, I'd find myself staring at my BlackBerry for hours on end. It did ring twice with potential jobs, both from current clients.

One was a month-long contract to fly a G-IV for a Fortune 500 flight department based at Trenton, NJ. I took the job because it didn't start for about seven months. By that time, I'd either be finished with the CIA thing or dead. The other job was a Falcon contract for a week-long trip early next month. I told that client that I had another offer pending for that same period and I had to call them back.

##

The call I was dreading came when I was in the bookstore at the local mall. I was doing my usual thing, browsing through the titles in the clearance stack, looking for the ever-elusive bargain, when the BlackBerry vibrated in its holster. I pulled it out and looked at the display. I was surprised to see a local area code and number displayed.

"Colin Pearce," I said after I keyed the green button.

"Good day, Mr. Pearce. I'd like to interview you personally regarding some contract flying work." The voice seemed friendly enough.

"That's what I do," I said, "I fly the Falcon 900EX and Gulfstream Four."

"Fine," the voice said, as though the aircraft didn't matter. "When would you be available for an interview?"

"My next trip starts on Monday," I said, trying to sound nonchalant, "I'm free until then. Where will you be conducting the interview?"

"We'd like to come to you. At your home. Is that satisfactory?"

I'd never had this request before, but there was nothing wrong with it. Unless it was coming from a secret company who bombed people for a living and might not want someone who turned down its offer to live to talk about it.

"This is rather unusual," I stammered. "I don't normally meet clients at my home."

"I see," the voice said.

Suddenly, the BlackBerry beeped, indicating that there was another incoming call. Normally, I would have ignored it, but it happened to be the same number that had called me at the Atlanta airport. "Excuse me," I said to my caller, "I have a call I have to take on the other line. I'll be right back." I clicked over to the other line.

"Colin Pearce."

"Nod your head and say, 'Hello, Mr. Andrews,' louder than you would normally speak." Smith's voice was so soft I could barely hear it.

"Hello, Mr. Andrews," I said dutifully, loudly enough so

nearby people glanced at me.

"We don't know whether they have distance mics on you. Accept the interview at your house. We can cover you more easily there. Now say, 'I'm sorry Mr. Andrews, I'm already committed for that weekend.'"

"I'm sorry, Mr. Andrews, I'm already committed for that weekend."

"The Mr. Andrews you're speaking about is the head of Unisys' Flight Department. He wanted you to fly for them next weekend, but you've already got a job on the books. He will verify the call. Now say 'Maybe next time, sir,' and go back to your other call."

I did as I was told and clicked back over to the other line.

"Sorry about that, sir," I said. "In my business, you can't afford to miss a single call."

"Another potential client?" the voice asked, conversationally.

"Actually a previous one who wanted to use me again," I said, more easily than I felt. "I happened to be committed on the dates he needed me though. Now where were we, sir?"

"I was asking if it would be satisfactory for us to come to your house to interview you."

I paused again, trying to play hard to get.

"Mr. Pearce, this job is extremely sensitive and we don't want to discuss it in public. Our offices are in another country and we don't have access to a secure facility here. Your home would really be most convenient. We'll pay you $1,000 US for your time."

Well, it was my lucky week. Another interview fee. If this kept up, I might never have to fly again.

"That will be fine, sir. When can I expect you?"

"At 1300 hours local time tomorrow. Can you give us directions to your house?"

I gave succinct directions and he grunted perfunctorily. He already knew where I lived. The question was: how long had they been watching me? More disconcerting was the realization that the CIA was watching me and watching them at the same time and I never had an indication that anything was going on at all.

Holy shit, I thought.

"By the way," my caller said as he prepared to end the call, "my name is Ron Phillips. And there will be two of us. Our chief pilot will be there to interview you as well."

The BlackBerry went dead. I took it away from my ear and stared at it for a few minutes. Then, I slowly re-holstered it.

As I began to walk to the mall's nearest exit, I saw her. She was sitting on the edge of a planter with a magazine in her lap and she was staring directly at me. The stare was openly appraising and generated an odd sense of discomfort inside me. I took a step backward into a bench. Without thinking, I sat slowly, all while continuing to stare back at her.

The woman was breathtaking and she exuded an intensity that I could feel even at a distance. She had piercing brown eyes and a slightly olive complexion with facial features that seemed to imply some Italian blood. Her face was framed with luxurious brunette hair that fell to her shoulders in long, wavy locks. I couldn't see much of her figure, but what I could see looked enticing. She was trim, but with some meat and muscle on her, not like so many of the icons that Hollywood was propagating these days.

She nodded at me slowly, then looked down at some sort of handheld device and pressed a button. I nearly jumped when my BlackBerry vibrated. I reached down for it to find a one-word text message waiting for me.

"Tomorrow," it said.

Then, I looked up and she was gone.

##

Later, I found my way back home again. It took me an

inordinately long time, considering that the mall was about five miles from my house. I couldn't decide what I wanted to do.

Eventually I ended up in my garage, sitting in my SUV in the dark after the garage door closed behind me, and wondering how I got there, or more importantly, *why* I was there. I exited the car, entered the downstairs hallway, and stopped to disarm the alarm. I hung my coat on the rack next to the door and climbed the stairs to the main level. The stairs from the bottom level open into the dining room and I found myself looking at my bar, illuminated by the moonlight coming through the windows in the rear of the house. I poured myself about three fingers of Laphroaig and went into my study.

It was well after sunset and the rest of the house was dark. I sat in my desk chair and took a long pull at my drink. Then, I fumbled for the switch on my desk light, wondering why the room was so dark when I usually left the curtains on the front windows open.

The light came on, and I was startled for the second time that evening. Smith and Amrine were seated on my sofa, looking at me with twin amused expressions on their faces. They had bottles of water in front of them on the coffee table and had removed their jackets. I was surprised not to see guns in either hip or shoulder holsters. I had assumed they were armed.

Amrine ran his hands through his hair and made a show of stretching and yawning. "Took you long enough, Pearce," he said. "We were starting to get worried about you. What were you doing with all that driving around?"

I had been followed, of course. I sat back in my chair and sighed. "I was thinking," I said after a long pause.

"You weren't thinking about running, were you Colin?" Smith's voice was just louder than a whisper and it sounded like he was hissing.

"Actually, I was," I admitted. "But something stopped me."

I took another pull at my scotch and leaned back in my desk chair, trying to remain calm as I contemplated the fact that I had two CIA agents seated on my sofa.

"Which was?" Smith asked me, motioning for me to continue.

"You know what," I said. I took another sip of the Laphroaig. It was beginning to build that nice warm place inside me.

Smith smiled grimly and nodded.

I leaned forward. "Do I have to buy a new alarm or get something fixed? You guys were in here and the alarm was still armed which means you bypassed it or disabled something."

"Our backup team handled that," Smith said. "I'm sure it will be fine after we leave. As you might expect, when we have occasion to break into someone's house, we don't want them to have any clue we were there."

"Great," I said, "so why are you here?"

"To brief you, of course," Amrine said. "We couldn't exactly meet you in public after MAG had made contact with you."

"I guess not," I said slowly. "So how long have they been watching me?" I asked, not really sure if I wanted to hear the answer.

"They were in place late Monday and watched you through Wednesday before they made contact."

"I guess that means they're pretty thorough."

"Possibly," Smith said. "Don't forget, they've undoubtedly done a full background check on you and may have been performing spot surveillance for a while as well. When they meet you tomorrow, they'll know everything about you."

"What about the money you guys put in my bank account? Will they be able to see that?"

"Actually," Amrine said, "that money was never there. Our IT guys intercepted your inquiries and directed you to a phony web site which showed the deposit."

I raised my eyebrows at him.

"We didn't want to argue with you at the interview, but we knew that bank activity of any size just prior to their interview with you would spook MAG, but Uncle Sam pays his debts." He lifted a brief case off the floor and opened it. Then he extracted an envelope and walked over to hand it to me.

I opened the envelope and inside was a cashier's check from Bank of America made out to me in the amount of $360,000. The payer was a company I'd never heard of: International Trading Consortium, Inc.

"Six months, paid in advance. Better than you asked for. You can stow that in your touch safe with the Colt .45 in your desk, if you'd like." Amrine said as sat again. "They won't look for it there. They've already searched your house."

"When did they..." It only took me a second. "Tuesday night while I was at Applebee's." I took another gulp of scotch, suddenly realizing that I tended to drink a lot when I was around these guys. "What's the briefing?"

"Simple," Smith said, "just be yourself. The only piece of information you have that might make them suspicious is what we told you about Burt Magnusson. You'll need to act surprised if they mention him. And we're betting they won't. Other than that, be yourself. And you'll be fine."

"What happens if they interview me and decide they don't want me?"

Smith looked at me. "You're going to have to sell them. Give them the same speech you gave us about your lack of patriotism. They'll buy it. They're behind schedule right now because they don't have Burt and they need a brain and pair of hands like his. They need you, although they won't want to show it."

At the mention of Burt's name, I felt the warmth of the rage begin to rise again.

"You're looking at this the wrong way," Amrine said as he and Smith both rose to leave and turned to retrieve their coats.

They weren't unarmed after all. The grip of a semi-automatic pistol was just visible above Amrine's belt in the small of his back. A quick glance at Smith confirmed that his weapon was stowed in a similar fashion.

"They think they have all the cards," Amrine continued. "They think they're luring you to them. When really," he paused as he put his coat back on, "you're luring them to you. Like those unfortunate intruders in your house in Phoenix. Remember?" He looked right into my eyes. "This is like Phoenix. Sell them. Lure them. You know you want to kill them all. Just get yourself inside so you can do it."

The Laphroaig was the only thing that brought me sleep that night. And it took nearly the entire bottle to do that.

CHAPTER FOUR

Thursday, 10 September
1200 Hours Local Time
My Townhouse
Wilmington, Delaware, USA

Yet again, I awoke with a roaring hangover. One of the problems with getting old is losing the ability to recover quickly from a night of drinking. When I was in my twenties and thirties, I could drink well into the night and wake the next morning, raring to go. Hell, I could even service the woman I'd spent the night with in the morning. But once I got into my forties, hangovers became increasingly harsh, and the ability to get over them took longer and longer. Once I got upright, I looked at my watch and realized with a degree of horror that it was nearly noon.

They'11 be here in an hour!

I went into the kitchen and gobbled a handful of aspirin and Advil and washed it down with two glasses of water. Then I forced down a quick breakfast of microwaved dried beef gravy and toast. I was upstairs and in the shower shortly soon after.

I was out of the shower in ten minutes and shaved and dressed in another fifteen. I wore my standard navy-blue interview suit, although I chose the one made by Brooks

Brothers instead of something less expensive. I had found that paying more for high-quality clothes in my line of work made sense. I spent a little more time in front of the mirror than I normally did and I'm not sure why. Maybe I wanted to see if I could look in the mirror and figure out why the hell I was going to do this.

But I already knew.

The main floor smelled a little stale when I got back down there, so I cracked the windows in the front of the house to let some air in. I quickly tidied up my desk and ensured that the coffee table was dusted off. After that, I went into the kitchen and started a pot of coffee. Then I had a seat at the counter and watched the coffee brew.

I must have lost track of time because I suddenly heard the coffee maker sputter the way it does when the last few drops of water are passing through it. Then I heard the doorbell ring and felt my heart skip a beat.

In the most bizarre slow-motion, I watched my legs walk me to the front door. I could almost feel the pile of the carpet through my shoes. I recall thinking the carpet was a lot bluer than I had noticed before. When my door swung open and I saw who was on the other side, my mind zoomed into the moment.

It was the man with the movie-star face. His hair was impeccably coiffed and the suit was Armani. I don't own one, but I've seen it enough to recognize it. He smiled at me and extended a perfectly-manicured right hand.

"Ron Phillips," he said in a pleasant voice. "May I come in?"

"Colin Pearce," I said with a confidence I didn't feel, "please do." I stepped back and he strode in confidently and did a slow three-sixty.

"Very nice," he said and seemed to mean it, "very nice. Did you do all this yourself?"

I stared at him for a moment, with my hand still resting

on the doorknob. “Uh, yes,” I said, eloquently. “Weren’t there going to be two of you?”

“The chief pilot will be along in a few minutes. I wanted to talk to you alone for a few moments first.”

I closed the door. “Would you care for some coffee?”

“Absolutely,” Phillips said. “Do you mind if I look at your books while you get it?”

“Help yourself,” I said, motioning toward the bookcase. I began to walk into the kitchen. “How do you take your coffee?”

“Black, please.”

“Roger that. I’ll be right back.”

I went into the kitchen and retrieved two of my china cups and saucers and poured two cups of coffee. I put some half and half and a little sugar in mine and then carried both out into the living room. Phillips seated himself on the sofa with his briefcase on the coffee table in front of him. He popped the catches on the case and opened it as I approached him.

“Here you are,” I said offering him his coffee.

“Thank you,” he said, taking the coffee with his left hand. Simultaneously, his right hand reached into the briefcase obviously looking for something. Then it emerged. I was a little surprised that there was a document in it instead of something else. Like a gun, for example.

“Before we discuss anything about our proposed contract, I need you to review and sign this document.”

“Okay.” I took the document from him and sat down in my recliner. I sipped my coffee as I read and was grateful for this moment of pause to gather my wits. I stole a glance at Phillips across the narrow room, but he was engrossed with something inside his briefcase. I heard a quiet ‘beep’ and realized that he probably had a PDA and was checking his e-mail.

The document was a nondisclosure agreement. I saw a lot of them in this business, although this was the first one ever presented to me before the interview began. The crew of a business aircraft sees and hears many things the average person doesn't. They see inside the business of Fortune 500 corporations and into the private lives of celebrities and extremely wealthy individuals. Paperwork to ensure that employees, even contractors, keep their mouths shut is commonplace. This agreement was a little more draconian than what I'd previously encountered though. The gist was that my potential employer, Fieldstone Venture Capital, Ltd., would financially ruin me if I breathed a word about this interview or my potential employment, if we got that far. I had to look on the bright side; at least there wasn't a lot of fine print.

I signed both copies of the agreement, kept one, and walked over to Phillips to hand him the other, all the while hoping like hell that Uncle Sam would pay my attorney's fees if these guys ever made good on their threats.

Phillips stood to take the document from me, and then sat again, making certain I couldn't see inside his briefcase.

"I'm assuming one of those copies was mine," I said.

He nodded and motioned me back to my seat. After a few moments more, he spoke. "Before we begin, Mr. Pearce, I have to ask you a question."

"Okay."

"Do you make it a practice to record interviews from potential employers?"

I was stunned. No one had asked me that question before, and had two CIA agents not been seated last evening exactly where Phillips was now, it wouldn't have fazed me. I wondered if Phillips had been sweeping the room for listening devices.

"I've never taped an interview in my life," I said truthfully, hoping that would be enough.

I guess the CIA's technology was good, because he smiled and shut his briefcase with two decisive clicks. "Good," he said. He picked up his coffee cup and saucer, stood and walked over to my bookshelves.

"Your library is extensive," he said. "There's everything

here from Chaucer and Dickens to Ian Fleming. I also see that you're a student of military history. There's Thucydides' *The History of the Peloponnesian War*, Sun Tzu, Clausewitz, Patton, and quite a few others."

Phillips was good. While setting me at ease by complimenting me on my library, he had made his way behind my desk and now, with me sitting on my recliner in front of the desk and him standing behind it, he had created an atmosphere which left no doubt who was in control here. I also noticed that he moved very gracefully and smoothly, almost with an air of restrained power. *This is a dangerous man,* I thought.

He looked at me, apparently waiting for an acknowledgement.

"I was a professional military officer for twenty years," I said at last. "One studies one's profession."

He nodded. "How did you like the military?"

"I liked flying the jets and I liked the people I worked with, but I was ready to go when I left, and I haven't looked back."

"Twenty years is a long time to stay with something and then give it up," Phillips said thoughtfully.

"That's true, but retiring at the twenty-year point is pretty common. Longer careers aren't for everyone. A lot of my friends went on to higher ranks and more responsibility, but that's not what I wanted. As I said, I was ready to get out."

"And why were you so ready?"

"I think I had arrived at the point where the flying and camaraderie had taken a backseat to the politics. I liked to fly and take care of the people who were assigned to me. I also liked teaching younger pilots the tricks of the trade. I had no desire to be a general. Unfortunately, above the rank of Lieutenant Colonel, the career path only has one lane. It became apparent that any further time spent in the USAF was going to more about politics that it was about flying and leadership. So, I left."

Phillips grunted in acknowledgement. "So how did you get into flying corporate jets?"

"About six years before I retired, I was assigned to do a year of school at the Army Command and General Staff College. I met a guy in Kansas City who owned a Lear 24, and he asked if I'd help him out by flying the right seat from time to time. I flew off and on for him until I retired. He sold the 24 for a 25, and eventually sold that and bought a 35. He even paid to get me typed in the jet. That was my first look at business aviation. I liked the fact that the decision making was left to the pilot, and the flying was dynamic. When it came time to retire, a lot of my fellow pilots were getting hired by Southwest Airlines, but that gig didn't appeal to me. I got hired by a company in New York, which typed me in the Falcon and the Gulfstream Four, and I flew for them long enough to get some experience. Then I went out on my own as a contractor and have been doing it ever since."

"Don't you miss flying fighters?"

"I see you've gotten a copy of my résumé."

He nodded and smiled.

"I'm not going to lie to you. Flying fighters was great. The A-10 was raw fun and the F-16 was the most demanding flying I've ever done. There's absolutely nothing like it. It's funny, though. Occasionally I'll fly a client into an airport that's joint use with an Air National Guard or Air Reserve wing, and I'll see the Vipers taking off in full afterburner; and for a second or two I'll wish I was back in that cockpit with all that power in my hands again. But in a few seconds, I'll remember the military BS and the desire passes." I hoped I wasn't laying it on too thick here. It all happened to be 100% true, but sometimes the truth can sound terribly banal to the wrong person.

"I see. So are you completely happy flying business aircraft after a career in fighters?"

The truth was that a career flying business jets after a

career flying fighters is like having mind-blowing sex nonstop for years, then being sentenced to masturbate for the rest of your life.

"It pays the bills," I said, diplomatically. "And that's pretty much what my life is about these days. Besides, I like flying airplanes, and I take a measure of pride in being able to do it better than the average guy."

"Are you a patriotic man, Mr. Pearce?"

"Not particularly," I said.

Phillips turned to me with raised eyebrows although I could tell he wasn't surprised by my answer. "But you stayed in the Air Force for 20 years!"

"People don't stay in the Air Force or any military branch for patriotic reasons. That's a load of propaganda foisted by recruiters and Republicans. People stay in because they like the work, they like the people, and it's a guaranteed paycheck. And for some, it's a way to scratch the ambition itch. Anyone who says differently is either brainwashed or lying."

Phillips chuckled. "I was in the Air Force," he said.

I wondered when we'd get to this. "Really," I said, trying my best to sound surprised. "I'm sorry if I offended you, but I still believe what I said is the truth."

"So do I," Phillips said. "I stayed in for as long as it suited my needs, and then I got out when I got a better offer."

"Well, that's about where I am," I said. "As a contract pilot, I make about double what I made in the USAF, and I have a lot less to worry about when I come home at night."

"Then if I hear you correctly, money is your major motivating factor these days."

"It's pretty much the only factor," I said.

"But what about principles and ethics and honor and that sort of thing? Like they taught us in the Air Force?"

"That shit is overrated," I said bluntly, "and it doesn't pay the bills or get me a villa in the Caribbean with a view of the beach and a blonde with big tits. Do you remember the line from Ernie Hudson, the black guy in the movie Ghost Busters? The secretary, Annie Potts, is asking him if he believes in all this paranormal stuff, and he looks at her and says: 'As long as there's a steady paycheck in it, I'll believe anything you say.' That's me all over. I'm scrupulously loyal to the people who hire me, and I meticulously abide by the terms of the contracts I sign. Apart from that, I really don't care about the 'who,' the 'why,' or the 'what,' only the 'how much.'"

Phillips smiled at me. "It's time that you met our chief pilot," he said. He pulled a cell phone from his pocket and hit the send key. "I think it's time for your questions," he said into the phone.

A knock came at the door a few moments later. Phillips motioned me to stay in my seat and went to the door. He opened it and stepped outside for a few minutes. I heard some whispers, and then he came back inside, holding the door open for the person who followed him.

It was her.

She strode confidently into the room and her eyes locked on to me like I was a potential target. She wore a Burberry overcoat on top of a black business suit and carried a black portfolio. Without taking her eyes off me, she handed Phillips her portfolio, then slipped out of her coat in a move that was the epitome of unselfconscious grace. She gently shook her long brunette hair to allow it to fall to her neck and shoulders and retrieved her portfolio from Phillips. Then she walked, or more precisely, floated, over to my chair.

She was a little shorter than I anticipated, but it did not detract from her presence. She was wearing heels, and I put her height without them at a little under five-foot-six. As I had noticed before, her figure was trim and attractive but not too skinny, and I could tell at once that she was extremely fit. At this distance, I got a much better view of her face and her flawless Mediterranean complexion.

She wore only a touch of makeup on her skin, a little

mascara on her eyes and some magenta lipstick. I didn't dare take my eyes from her face, but since I was gazing up at her, I couldn't help but notice that her breasts were perfectly proportioned to her figure and stood forth from her body firmly.

I rose from the recliner to greet her and she extended her hand.

"My name is Ruth Shalev," she said in voice that was professional and even-toned. "I'm the chief pilot for Fieldstone."

"Colin Pearce," I said, damn proud that I could even get those words out. We shook hands and there was a spark from the static electricity she had incurred in her walk across the carpet. We both laughed it off, and the tension was broken.

She motioned toward the couch. "Would you care to join me on the sofa? You and I have a lot to talk about and I hate talking across a room or across a desk."

"Sure," I said.

"Is that coffee I smell?"

I suddenly remembered my manners. "Yes, it is. Forgive me for not offering. Would you care for a cup?"

"Please. With cream and sugar."

"Mr. Phillips?" I asked. "Would you care for a refill or a top off?"

"No," he said with a knowing smile. "I'm fine."

I felt my face flush. I quickly retrieved my own cup and exited the room.

In the kitchen, I gulped the rest of my coffee, quickly filled a new cup for Ruth, and gave myself some more. I eyed the bottle of Bailey's sitting on the counter next to the coffee pot and briefly considered spiking my coffee with a shot of it to calm my nerves. Probably not the best move to pass a flying interview, though. I poured half and half into both cups and added a little sugar. Then, carefully noting which cup belonged to whom, I went back into the living room/study.

As I entered the room, I noticed that Phillips had seated himself next to Ruth on the sofa and that they were reviewing some paperwork. She had her hand on his arm as she explained something to him, and for some reason, I felt a tinge of something that might have been jealousy. I wasn't sure.

Phillips stood and moved aside as I approached. Ruth glanced up at me and flashed a quick, but brilliant smile. I smiled stupidly back.

"Colin," she said, "would you sit down here?" She patted the now vacant sofa next to her. Phillips had vanished, at least for the moment.

I walked around the coffee table, doing my best not to stumble over my feet and sat where she indicated. She leaned back into the sofa, crossed her legs, and opened the portfolio on her lap.

"I know you probably have a lot of questions," she said apologetically. "And the time will come when you'll get your answers, either directly on or paper. But first, I need to see how much you remember about an airplane we saw on your resume, the F-16. Okay?"

I did my best to create a surprised expression on my face. "Sure," I said. "There aren't many things I like talking about more than the Viper."

She took a sip of her coffee and made a sound of approval. "That's very good."

"Thanks."

She sat back against the cushion on her side of the sofa and became all business. "What versions of the Viper did you fly?"

"Blocks 25, 30, 40, and 42."

"When was your last flight?"

"Just over seven years ago, in July."

"Where?"

"Luke Air Force Base, Arizona."

"What squadron were you flying with?

"The 309th, 'The Mighty Ducks.'" I couldn't say it without

a snicker.

"Do you remember what kind of mission you flew?"

"Surface attack," I said confidently, "on Range Three at Gila Bend."

"Do you remember what events you flew?"

"Not specifically, but if it was a normal profile, we did two high-altitude, high-release deliveries, two dive bomb deliveries, two pop-ups to low-angle, low-drag deliveries, three pop-ups to low-angle, high-drag deliveries and two passes of low-angle strafe."

"Great," she said, marking something down on her pad. "Now, I want you to hold up your right and left hands and talk me through the switches on the F-16 throttle and stick."

"Wow," I said, "it's been a while, but I'll try." I held my left hand in front of me and to my left, like I was resting it on the throttle in the F-16. "As I recall, your thumb and index finger did all the work."

I closed my eyes and placed my index finger and thumb on my imaginary throttle as I talked my way through the switches. Extending my left index finger, I began. "On the throttle. Furthest outboard was the mic button and as I recall, you pulled to talk on UHF and pushed to talk on VHF. Then there was the missile reject/uncage switch which doubled as the gain adjustment knob for the radar." I retracted and extended my thumb. "Your thumb rests very close to the Dogfight switch." I moved my thumb down slightly and could almost feel the knurled, plastic edges of the switches. "Under that was the speedbrake switch." I moved my thumb down a little further and pulled in slightly. "Below and slightly aft of the speedbrake switch was the cursor slew control, and it could be depressed for certain functions as well. And," I kept my thumb on the same level and extended it slightly, "ahead of that was the elevation control knob for the radar, the EL Strobe."

"Do you remember the three modes of the Dogfight

switch?"

I opened my eyes and frowned in concentration. "I think so. I remember that they were programmable. Inboard was whatever you had programmed for the master mode you had selected. It could be air-to-air or air-to-ground. Middle position was sort of a neutral position. In air-to-air rides, guys used to put a different radar mode in that position. For air-to-ground, guys would leave it in the Navigation Mode so they could use the timing functions. Outboard was dogfight, of course, which brought up the AIM-9 and the cannon and their associated symbology."

"Good," she said. "Tell me about the stick controls."

I placed my right hand on an imaginary control stick in front of me. I flexed my index finger. "The trigger of course, was under the index finger." Then I straightened the finger. "Alongside the stick, outboard, was the missile step switch, which allowed us to select which air-to-air missile would fire next if we were in the air-to-air mode and allowed us to step between weapons release modes in the air-to-ground modes. It also turned on the nose wheel steering and recycled the air refueling system." I straightened my thumb and began to trace the four corners of a square. "In the upper left is the weapons release or 'pickle' button, upper right the china-hat switch for the trim, lower right, display-management switch, and lower left target-management switch." My thumb dropped to the lower third of my imaginary stick. "There was a countermeasures switch here in the Block 40 and onward," I said. "I think that's it." My right pinky finger twitched involuntarily and I remembered something else. "Oh yeah, at the base of the stick, where your pinky finger could actuate it, was the field of view control switch for the Maverick missile."

She nodded briefly then grilled me on the avionics and weapons systems controls on the Viper for a long time. She was very knowledgeable, but she merely guided the discussion and let me do most of the talking. She asked me questions on air-to-ground weapons employment including modes of delivery, effects of different ordnance on various target types, and fusing options. We discussed air-to-air weapons employment and radar modes, choices of formations, intercept tactics, and visual fight methodology. All the while, my hands performed a ballet of their own, demonstrating switch positions, formation and attack geometry and basic fighter maneuvers. She watched me closely. I became obsessed with getting a favorable reaction from her, and I felt like a schoolboy trying to impress a girl on the playground.

"Okay," she said at last. "I want to do one last thing. I want you to sit back on the sofa with your back against the cushions, your feet on your floor, and your hands resting on your legs."

I did as I was told.

"Now shut your eyes."

I was totally under her spell and complied.

"You're flying a Viper at 500 feet and about 480 knots groundspeed and all of the sudden you feel a sudden loss of thrust. The cockpit lights up like a Christmas tree and the RPM and ITT roll back."

In a microsecond, I was back in the cockpit of the Viper and my hands went through the appropriate motions as I spat out the memory items.

"Zoom." I pulled back on an imaginary stick. "Throttle off, then midrange." I moved my left hand back and even remembered to actuate the pinky switch to move the imaginary throttle over the detent from idle to off. Then I moved my hand forward again to the middle of the sub-AB range. "Stores jettison, if required." My left hand moved forward to push the imaginary STORES JETTISON button on the left auxiliary console. "If no relight before RPM decays to less than 50% or if below 10,000 feet, then engine control switch to SEC." I reached forward of the imaginary throttle to lift the imaginary switch guard and throw the engine control switch to the secondary position. "JFS start two if below 20,000 feet and

420 knots." I reached just in front of the imaginary engine control switch to grasp the switch for the Jet Fuel Starter and pulled in back to the 'Start2' position.

"That's good enough. Now keep your eyes closed."

I smiled stupidly, still with my eyes closed.

"Now, you're the defender in a visual fight. Your adversary is trying to gun you, but you force the overshoot and reverse into him. Before you know it, you're in a flat scissors, about 70 degrees nose high in full AB. You see him sliding slightly forward on the three-nine line, and you figure it's time to make your move. So you roll into him and apply full back pressure on the stick. Suddenly the nose comes up and then it drops and the jet starts to spin. What do you do?"

"Controls release," I said, opening my right hand. "Throttle idle." I moved my left hand back again. "If in an inverted deep stall, rudder opposite yaw direction."

"You're upright," she said.

"If still out-of-control, then MPO switch override and hold; stick cycle in phase." I reached forward of where my imaginary JFS switch was and grabbed the imaginary Manual Pitch Override switch, even pretending to place one of my fingers around one of the finger rings next to the switch as I did so. Then I rhythmically moved the imaginary stick fore and aft.

"That will do," she said, flatly.

I opened my eyes and looked over at her. For a second, I thought I could see cogs turning in those deep, brown eyes.

"Why'd you choose the memory items for a Block 30?" she asked.

"I don't know," I mumbled, still mesmerized by her. "I guess because it was the first Viper I flew. The oldest knowledge must go the deepest."

She nodded but there was a look on her face that I couldn't quite identify. "Stand up and take your coat off please."

"What?" I was a little stunned.

"We're almost done. I just need to assess your physical condition."

I got to my feet and reluctantly removed my jacket, folding it carefully and laying it carefully across the arm of my side of the sofa. I wasn't looking forward to this.

"Do I have your permission to touch you?" she asked politely.

"Sure," I said grimacing. "I guess so."

She laughed. "Relax, I'm not going to hurt you."

I don't think I had ever been so embarrassed in my adult life. If I had been expecting anything tender, my hopes were quickly dashed. She stood in front of me and felt my shoulders, then ran her hands down my upper arms, obviously attempting to judge how much muscle was left there.

"Put your arms out and turn around please."

I did as I was told and her hands started on the underside of my arms and traced my body down my lat muscles to my waist. Even though her touch felt strictly professional or as professional as it possibly could have been, considering I'd never experienced anything like this in a job interview, there was still electricity to it that affected me. I sensed myself beginning to stir below the waist and wondered what the hell was wrong with me.

"Okay," she said. "You can put your coat back on again. Thank you for your patience."

I kept my back to her while I donned my jacket and hoped like hell that things below my waist would settle down. Fortunately, they did, and I turned around.

"What did you weigh before you retired from the Air Force?" she asked.

"Two twenty on my retirement physical," I answered with embarrassment, knowing full well where this conversation was going.

"And what do you weigh now?"

"Two forty-five," I sighed.

She nodded. "Ron," she called.

Phillips appeared in the door from my kitchen. "Your verdict?" he asked.

She stood next to me but it was like I wasn't there. "He'll do."

"How long?"

"Four weeks," she said, eyeing me like I was a cow she needed to fatten up before butchering.

Phillips nodded. "Okay," he said. "That will work. I'll inform the client."

She retrieved her coat and walked to the door. As she touched the doorknob, she looked me in the eyes. "Be ready," she said with a hard voice. "I'm going to have to kick your ass to get you to where I need you to be."

I nodded dumbly as she turned and exited the house.

Phillips walked over to me pumped my hand enthusiastically. "Congratulations!" he said. "You passed!"

He let go and returned to his briefcase, snapped open the catches, raised the lid and retrieved a document before snapping it shut again. Then he walked over to my desk and tossed the document on the blotter.

"That's the contract," he said. "It is covered by the confidentiality agreement you signed and is strictly for your eyes only. The terms are nonnegotiable, but I think you'll find the pay commensurate with the terms. You have until tomorrow at noon to accept the offer. If you do, fax the signature page to the number indicated, and we'll send a plane for you. You can give us a signed original copy of the contract then." He turned to walk toward the door.

"But wait," I said, "what will I be flying?"

Phillips looked at me with a disappointed expression on his face. "The F-16," he said, "wasn't that obvious?"

"What will I be doing with it?"

"Projects," he said. "Projects which clients hire us to do."

"Will I have to kill anybody with it?"

"Maybe," he said, "but read the contract. There's a generous bonus if that's required. Will that be a problem?"

A part of me felt an ambivalence that was shocking. I couldn't decide whether I was playing a role or playing myself. Maybe a person with a little more depth or even a little more conscience might have had some sort of epiphany. But that person wasn't me. It wasn't me now. It might not have ever been me.

"I guess not," I answered.

Phillips nodded and walked out the door.

I walked over to my desk and looked down at the contract there. I knew I needed to read it. But I needed something else first. I headed into my dining room to the bar and grabbed the first bottle ofscotch I could find. I didn't even look at the label before I poured a liberal shot into a glass and slammed it down.

CHAPTER FIVE

Thursday, 10 September
1800 Hours Local Time
Applebee's Restaurant
Wilmington, Delaware, USA

About four hours later, I was seated at the bar of my local Applebee's, waiting for my dinner to arrive. Staring sightlessly at the shapely ass of the lovely bartender, I nursed my beer and ruminated on the day's events. The dinner at Applebee's wasn't my idea. If it had been up to me, I probably would have stayed in my house and made a meal of single-malt. The idea for the dinner was the CIA's.

Shortly after Phillips left my BlackBerry buzzed. The title of the new email was "You've Won!" and although it looked like a typical junk email, something about the timing told me it wasn't. I opened it and it said "You've won a dinner at your local Applebee's! Go to our web site and enter promo code 3432200 to claim your free coupon!" Even if I hadn't been playing spy games, I would have done what it said. I eat there a lot, and anything I can do to reduce my bill is welcome. I should buy stock in the place.

I turned on my computer, went to the web site, and entered the promotional code. The browser went into a secure mode and produced a single web page with a few lines on it.

"You are under surveillance. Leave the contract on your desk. Be at Applebee's at 1800 hours and sit at the bar to have your meal. Don't come home before 2000 hours. S & A."

I sat back in my chair. I didn't want to think how the CIA could get inside my internet connection and divert my browser as it went to Applebee's website. I just shook my head in silent amazement. These guys were good.

I clicked on a link under the message and found myself staring at an apparently genuine Applebee's coupon for $10 off my next meal there. I silently thanked the CIA for their generosity and printed the coupon. And now here I was, waiting for the imminent arrival of my favorite item on their menu, the Bourbon Street Steak, and wondering how many beers I was going to get to enjoy tonight. Especially considering I was departing for my new 'job' tomorrow.

I had signed the contract per the instructions and the faxed the signature page to the number provided. The terms were generous: $100,000 per month with a six-month minimum. Full medical and dental coverage while I was with them. And a $50,000 signing bonus for my immediate availability. I also noted a bonus of $100,000 for each project successfully completed, the bonus to which Phillips had referred.

They must have been waiting for the contract, because my fax machine rang about five minutes later and spit out two sheets of paper. The first page was a copy of the signature page of the contract, countersigned by Ron Phillips. I noticed that his title was "Director of Operations, Fieldstone Aviation, LLC."

The next page was a typed note from good old Ron. "Dear Colin," it began. "Glad to have you aboard. We'll send our corporate jet for you tomorrow at 1200 hours. The tail number will be VP-CFD. You can meet it at Atlantic Aviation at the New Castle County Airport. We'll need you for at least six months. We'll be providing all your uniforms and equipment so pack very lightly please. See you soon!" It was signed in

Phillips' distinctive scrawl. More documentation for the CIA's files.

My Caesar side salad arrived in typically speedy fashion and I began to dig into it with my fork. As I crunched away on my croutons and lettuce, a man sat next to me and ordered a beer in a distinctly southern accent. I don't normally inspect people when they sit next to me, but I'd become a little more aware lately. About my height but thinner, he was dressed in jeans and some sort of flannel shirt.

"So, what's good here?" he asked me with a twang.

I turned to him. "Just about everything," I said, "but I always tend to order the Bourbon Street Steak."

"Sounds like a good meal to have before flying," he said softly, in Smith's voice.

Some undercover operative I am. I almost spit out my lettuce. There in front of me, the man turned into Smith. I couldn't believe I didn't notice it was him before.

"You okay, buddy?" he asked me.

"Yes," I said, turning back to my salad, "sorry about that."

"No problem."

As I began to eat again, Smith's beer came. He thanked the bartender and began to sip it. "Could you turn up the volume on this TV?" he asked the bartender, gesturing at the TV directly over our heads.

The bartender nodded and hit the remote control until the sounds of the basketball game on the TV set above us were loud enough to drown out a lot of the background noise in the restaurant.

"We had to get you away from your house so they'd follow you," Smith said into his beer while staring up at the TV overhead. "We copied the contract and dusted the original for fingerprints. We also ran the registration number of that jet through our database. It's a Gulfstream 550 registered in the Cayman Islands under Fieldstone Venture Capital, so that part fits the cover. The problem is that Fieldstone's address is a P.O. Box in the Caymans, so we don't have any idea where they're taking you. We planted several GPS transmitters in your luggage. They will only respond with a position when we interrogate them from one of our satellites and they can't be detected by any sort sweeping gear. So, you can relax; we'll be tracking you every step of the way."

"Didn't you ever find out where Burt was when he was communicating with you?" I was careful to not look at him and keep food in my mouth or my mug in front of my face. It had occurred to me that he was deliberately obscuring his mouth, possibly to prevent someone from reading his lips.

"No," he answered into his beer after a moment or two. "All Burt knew was that he was on an island somewhere. They always transported the pilots and the F-16s from the Island, the training and operations base, to the launch location and back by air freighter. Boeing 747s, to be precise. That's about all he could convey."

"Boy," I wondered out loud, "some of those transport flights had to be fairly long. You'd sure think they'd be able to steal a glance out a window or something."

"Evidently not," Smith said.

I thought for a moment. "This is not a low-rent operation."

"No, it's not. It appears they've thought of everything."

"Except me, hopefully."

Smith smiled at me and smacked me on the back, motioning to the TV above us as one of teams scored a three-pointer. "Except you," he said. "By the way, in one of the emails Burt sent, he wrote something that intrigued me. He said 'They've tried to make it like a normal fighter squadron here but instead it's like a whole different world. There are parts that make sense and other parts that don't any make sense at all.' I don't know what that means, but I thought you should know about it."

"Thanks," I said as I filled my mouth with another forkful of salad. "I'll keep that in mind. So how do I contact you?"

"In your desk drawer, you'll find a new BlackBerry. It looks exactly like the one on your hip and has all the same information. We've modified it to dramatically increase its range and transmitting power and we've given it SATCOM and encryption capability. When you want to get information to us, send an email to Phil Collins. His name and contact info have been added to your address book. It will be automatically encrypted and sent out with more power than any others you send. We'll get it. We want you to send us an update at least once a day."

I stared up at the TV and drank my beer. "Won't they be able to detect the transmissions?"

"No. The BlackBerry is data-burst capable and will switch frequencies every time you send one of those emails. It will also delete the email after you send it."

"Aren't you afraid they'll take it from me?"

"It's a calculated risk. If they made it a practice to collect cell phones from their employees, they'd create a little panic in the ranks, don't you think? Besides where they're taking you is either beyond cell phone coverage or they have hardware to block cell phone transmissions. It doesn't matter. When you send to us, they won't know it and won't be able to stop it. For your first transmission when you arrive, we need to know the local time at your location. That's critical."

I nodded. Compare that against Greenwich Mean Time and you'll at least know what time zone I'm in."

"Or what time zone they want you to think you're in."

My second beer and my steak arrived at about the same time, the latter sizzling loudly on its iron skillet.

"Wow," Smith said, slipping into his Southern twang again, "that's a helluva steak, son! Wish I had time to have me one."

"Maybe some other time," I answered, and then whispered under my breath, "was there any other info Burt provided which might help me out?"

Smith looked back up at the TV and raised his beer to his lips. "He said that the target location or grid kept changing. He also said that they kept changing their minds about weapons and tactics for this imminent project. They were trying to achieve a specific effect."

"Hmmm," I said. The Weapons and Tactics officer portion of my brain was slowly spinning into gear after several years of disuse. "I wonder what they were after."

"Burt didn't spend a lot of words on that in his last message because there was so much else he was trying to communicate. All he said was something like, 'This is bad. They're looking at maximum-range, loft deliveries. Will discuss with Phillips.'"

I nearly choked on the bite of steak I had just put in my mouth. "Holy shit!" I swallowed the chunk of meat rapidly and reached for my beer.

Smith looked at me curiously. "You okay, buddy?" he said with the twang again. "You're havin' some problems tonight."

I nodded and raised the glass to my lips and took a huge gulp of beer. "Do you have any idea what that could mean?"

He looked at me blankly. "We haven't had a lot of time to ruminate over it," he said. "We've been focused on getting you in place."

I put my beer glass on the bar, my right hand shaking so badly I had trouble controlling it.

"What's the big deal?" he asked.

I reached for my napkin, ostensibly to wipe my face and ensured my mouth was completely covered. "When I was flying the Viper, we typically practiced maximum-range loft deliveries for only one type of ordnance."

For the first time in our brief acquaintance, I got a visible reaction out of Smith. His eyes grew discernibly wider. It was only about a microsecond and he was back in character again.

"Oh, my God," he whispered, "how could we have missed that?"

He knew the ordnance I was referring to, but I said it

anyway. "Nukes," I said into my napkin. "Odds are it's a parachute-retarded, B61 nuclear bomb delivery."

Smith grabbed his beer and drank the remainder of it. Then he laid some bills on the bar. He smacked me on the back again. "Good luck, Buddy," he said loudly, "enjoy the game." He turned to leave, but then sat down at the bar once more. "I need to ask you something," he said softly. He lowered the volume of his voice even further and looked me directly in the eye. "That conversation you had with Phillips. Were you playing the role or is that how you really feel? The stakes just got pretty fucking high here."

I turned back to my steak and my beer and deliberately avoided his eyes. Then I told him the truth. "I don't know," I said, cutting a symmetrical piece from my steak.

"Jesus," Smith whispered behind my back.

When I looked over my shoulder, he was gone.

CHAPTER SIX

Contract Day One
Friday, 11 September
1130 Hours Local Time
New Castle County Airport (KILG)
Wilmington, Delaware, USA

About fifteen hours and one more hangover later, I sat nursing a bottle of water in the waiting area of the Atlantic Aviation FBO at the New Castle County Airport, about thirty minutes from my house. The customer service representative behind the counter, an attractive blonde woman about my age, had informed me that VP-CFD had made a 'twenty minutes out' radio call to the FBO just before I walked in and graciously encouraged me to have a seat on the sofa. I accepted her invitation gladly and sank down on the comfortable leather cushions, gobbling a few more ibuprofen pills with my water.

The FBO, or Fixed Base Operator, is a standard feature of business aviation. It is a combination executive terminal and aircraft service station and can be found in many different variants, some lavish in accommodation and others less so. Atlantic Aviation was my personal favorite of the several national chains, largely because of the quality of the people they hired and the fact that they didn't try to gouge their customers with fees and exorbitant fuel prices like some of the competition. Atlantic had purchased this facility from a small-time, local operator who didn't put much money into it. I hadn't been in the place since Atlantic bought it and it was obvious Atlantic had spent some serious dollars here. The improvements were impressive.

I put my head back on the sofa cushion and stared at the ceiling, trying to strain my recovering brain to see if I had forgotten anything. This morning, I had run the 'Long Contract Checklist' and it had taken me nearly all morning to do it. As usual, all the utilities were turned down and all windows and doors were locked and double-checked.

I have all my bills paid automatically, so I didn't need to make any special arrangements there; and fortunately, my checking account was rather fat so there wasn't any danger of running out of funds there for several months. Additionally, I called all my clients with whom I had trips scheduled for the next three months, expressed my regrets, and told them I'd be back in touch when I was back in town. Nearly all of them were understanding. Some were not. Contract piloting is an uncertain business, and the big paycheck in the hand today is worth a lot more than the possible paycheck next week or next month. I've had trips cancel on me with as little notice as when I was walking out the door to catch a plane, so I didn't feel too badly about canceling on clients at the last minute if a better offer came up.

I had packed lightly as requested, with just a roller bag and a computer bag/briefcase. I also had the CIA BlackBerry on my hip and my normal one safely locked away in one of my gun safes. I wore my standard traveling attire for these trips, which consisted of the navy-blue Brooks Brothers suit, light-blue dress shirt, and appropriately conservative tie, as well as a comfortable pair of Rockport dress shoes. I didn't know how long my flight was going to be, so I had packed three paperback novels I could read on the aircraft. I also had the original copy of the contract with me, and I hoped the fingerprint stuff the CIA had used wouldn't be detectable.

There are moments in life that have an air of destiny. The pounding in my chest and the sweat on my palms told me that this was one of them. In a few minutes, a jet was going to pull up on the asphalt ramp outside the FBO's generic glass doors and I was going to board it and go wherever it took me. I had no clue what I would do when I got there and no idea whether I'd be back alive.

I found my mind wandering to Burt's family and I wondered how difficult it must have been for him to leave them behind. The whole concept of having someone waiting for me was so totally foreign that I couldn't comprehend it. Even now, well over thirty years after leaving home and long after I buried both my parents, the wasteland that was their marriage lived in my mind like an image permanently burned into a computer monitor. As a result, when I needed female companionship, I made it very clear that I was interested in friendship and sex, nothing more. It was a system that had worked.

And it was, of course, the reason I sat here alone as I pondered my life.

But there had been one time when the system hadn't worked and I had been okay with that.

It had begun at this airport, at another FBO across the field. I had picked up a G-IV just out of a pre-buy inspection for its new owner, the flamboyant publisher of Bachelor Magazine. Then, I was retained to fly him around the US for nearly three weeks along with his newly-hired Chief Pilot, the delectable Sarah Morton, a stunning redhead with hair like silk and impossibly deep, green eyes. Sarah was a highly-capable pilot and not so coincidently, a former "monthly mistress" for the magazine.

For reasons that are still a mystery, Sarah's interest in me quickly went beyond professional and we spent the majority of those three weeks fucking our brains out in a variety of hotels throughout the country as her boss went about his business. But somewhere in all the professional and physical interaction and the carefully erected fences between us, we got through to each other and it scared the shit out of both of us. When the contract ended, she took me to the Burbank airport to put me on a plane back to Philadelphia and on the sidewalk, there in front of God and everyone, she kissed me passionately under the clear, blue California sky. Then, as I lifted my lips from hers, I saw moisture in her eyes and felt an odd burning in my own. She quickly got back into her little sports car and shot off into traffic, leaving me standing on the sidewalk watching her go.

A part of me had always wondered what became of her. But I had made no attempt to contact her after our episode and she had not contacted me. We both knew the code.

That incident had taught me something about myself that terrified me. After everything that had happened in my life, I *believed*. Not that it had done me any good. Not that it would *ever* do me any good.

"Mister Pearce?"

I looked up to see a clone of myself in a corporate pilot uniform looking down at me. He was about my age, weight and build. He had the pleasantly tired look that all of us have in the middle of a long day of flying.

"Yes?"

"I'm Joe Taber, the captain of Victor Papa Charlie Foxtrot Delta. We're ready for you. Can I help you with your bags?"

Before I could answer, he grabbed my roller bag and computer case and gestured toward the door of the FBO. We walked outside to find a beautiful, sparkling white Gulfstream G-550 with blue and gold stripes parked there, APU running and ready for departure.

I felt a little weird stepping onboard an aircraft like this and turning aft toward the cabin, not left toward the cockpit, but I did so, after stopping to shake hands with the co-pilot.

An attractive and businesslike flight attendant seated me and asked me what I wanted to drink. I briefly considered a scotch but settled on a glass of Perrier.

She had it in my hand before the pilot got the door shut and before he had the engines started I had guzzled it down, barely noticing that it had a slight aftertaste to it. I sat back in my seat and contemplated the next few months of my life as we began to taxi, suddenly feeling very tired. As I felt my eyes begin to close, I remembered that the pilot, for all his professionalism, had not given me an important piece of information before he retired to the cockpit.

He never told me where we were going.

TOP SECRET / SPECIAL
COMPARTMENTALIZED INFORMATION
CLASSIFIED BY: US Central Intelligence Agency
DECLASSIFY ON: OADR

From: Special Projects Group [NCS]
Sent: Saturday, 12 September 2009, 2351 EDT (13 September 2009, 0351Z)
To: Director, NCS
Cc: Special Projects Group [NCS]; damrine@cmail.cia.gov; dsmith3@cmail.cia.gov

SUBJECT: Update, Case File: 08-434A (MAG)

(TS) Narrative:

1. (TS) Contractor 09-017 (Pearce, Colin M.) departed New Castle County Airport, DE (KILG) on Gulfstream G-550, registration VP-CFD at 1552Z (1152 EDT), 11 September 2009. He had 3 MK-303 CGUs placed in his luggage and a BlackBerry with the standard operative package installed.

2. (TS) At 2259Z (1359 AKDT), VP-CFD landed at Ted Stevens Anchorage International Airport, AK (PANC). After remaining on the ground for almost 17 hours, VP-CFD departed PANC at 1600Z (0700 AKDT), 12 September with a flight plan filed to Hong Kong International Airport, People's Republic of China (VHHH).

3. (TS) At 0222Z (1022 HKDT), 13 September 2009, VP-CFD arrived at VHHH and in-processed customs and immigration at the Signature FBO on the field. A person matching Pearce's description disembarked, accompanied by three crewmembers. Close inspection by local field office

personnel indicate that while the passport information matched the crewmembers and Pearce, they are not the same persons. Multiple GPS interrogations produced no response.

(TS) CONCLUSION: A large portion of VP-CLD's flight-planned route from PANC to VHHH is outside of radar control. We believe a decoy G-550 assumed the original VP-CFD's flight plan while the original VP-CLD continued to an unknown destination. Pearce's whereabouts are currently unknown.

(TS) ACTION: We will continue to interrogate Pearce's MK 303s and await his contact via e-mail.

(TS) RECOMMENDATION: None. Information Only.

TOP SECRET / SPECIAL
COMPARTMENTALIZED INFORMATION
CLASSIFIED BY: US Central Intelligence Agency
DECLASSIFY ON: OADR

CHAPTER SEVEN

Contract Day Three
Sunday, 13 September
1400 Hours Local Time
Island Training Base

I don't remember exactly what woke me. It might have been the 'thud' and air noise as the landing gear deployed. Or it might have been the gentle impact of the gear on the runway as we landed. Or maybe it was the silence after the engines and APU were shut down. What I do remember is the flight attendant gently shaking my shoulder and telling me it was time for me to disembark. I just looked at her, trying to shake the grogginess off.

"Have I been asleep for the whole flight?" I asked her as I forced the haze aside.

The flight attendant looked at me sympathetically. "We drugged you," she said. "Security precaution."

I looked out the window next to my seat and saw that the G-550 was under some sort of awning just outside a hangar. Then I saw something that made my heart stop.

"Oh, my God," I muttered.

I rose from my seat and stumbled toward the door of the Gulfstream.

"We'll have your bags sent to your quarters," the flight

attendant said as I brushed passed her and alit from the jet.

I stood at the foot of the boarding stairs and gazed into the cavernous hangar, transfixed by what lay before me. There they were, neatly parked in two rows, the nose wheels aligned with military precision along the painted yellow lines on the floor: eight Block 30 F-16Cs, their gray-blue paint schemes gently illuminated by the overhead light bars. Even with the safety covers installed and gear pinned, they looked eager for flight, ready to leap into the sky and take command of it.

I fell in love with the airplane all over again.

There's never been an airplane like the Viper. From the compact size and sleek lines of its airframe to the agility of its fly-by-wire flight controls to it its exceptional thrust-to-weight ratio; it's more like the brainchild of a mad sports-car designer than a restrained aeronautical engineer. And like a Ferrari, Porsche, or Lamborghini, the Viper is something you strapped on, not something you strapped into. It was a work of art, and you became part of it.

I couldn't help myself. I walked toward the nearest jet and put my hands on the smooth metal skin on the side of it. Then, I ran my hand around the nose and down to the wing. After nearly seven years, I was finally touching a Viper again, and it felt good. I felt an uncharacteristic lump in my throat.

"Were you wondering if they were real?" Her voice came from a few feet behind me.

"I was," I said after a long moment.

I turned around slowly and found myself face to face with Ruth Shalev, who looked every inch the fighter pilot. She was attired in a desert tan flightsuit just tight enough to reveal the curves in her body, but not so tight as to be unprofessional. She had her hair pulled back into a taut ponytail and wore minimal makeup. She couldn't have looked more different from our interview a few days ago.

"Ms. Shalev," I said, extending my right hand.

"*Major* Shalev, Colonel Pearce," she said, taking my hand

for the requisite shake.

"I haven't been called Colonel in a long time, and I was only a Lieutenant Colonel so I was never really comfortable with that. Israeli Air Force?"

She nodded. "How did you know?"

"Well, if you have Viper on you and a name like Shalev you're either in the USAF or the IAF; and if you'd been in the USAF when I was still wearing one of those things," I said, gesturing to her flightsuit, "I would have heard about you."

"I take it there weren't a lot of female F-16 pilots in your Air Force then?"

I shook my head. "No, and at the risk of possibly offending you, there weren't any that looked like you."

She smiled politely.

"Okay, so moving on, why the nap on the way in here? Aren't I going to see where I am when we do our training?"

"Yes and no," she said, "but I'll let your instructor tell you how that works. You have to understand," she said, tilting her head slightly, "our location is a closely-guarded secret so that we don't suffer reprisal attacks. In the event you were shot down during a project and captured, you couldn't reveal our location because you wouldn't know it. It's for your own protection and ours."

"I guess that makes sense," I mumbled while my head reeled with the implications of her words. No one here knew where they were and no one could get away. The island was essentially a prison and she and Phillips were the wardens. For the foreseeable future, my fate was totally under her control. It took all my self-control to not swallow audibly. So, I guess you've got your own little 'world' here," I said, as the words from Burt Magnusson's email rang in my ears.

"Yes," she replied firmly, looking me right in the eyes, "we do." She motioned toward the back of the hangar, where a small reception committee was forming. "Shall we begin your in-processing and get you settled? Your training starts tomorrow and we need to get all the admin items completed today."

"Not wasting any time, are we?"

"No, we're not," she said. "Time is one commodity we never have enough of around here."

She turned and headed toward the back of the hangar. I inspected the Vipers as we walked between them. Despite the fact they were at least twenty years old, they were in outstanding shape and looked like they were meticulously maintained. Every jet showed the signs of being fussed over: perfect paint, unmarred canopies, landing gear axles free of excessive grease, and wheels that were clean and polished.

Damned impressive, I thought.

We reached the small crowd of people who were waiting for us and Ruth made a gesture of introduction. "Ladies and gentlemen, Colin Pearce, our replacement pilot. He's a retired USAF Lieutenant Colonel with nearly 2,000 hours in the jet and is also a graduate of the USAF's Fighter Weapons School." She turned to me. "You actually went twice, right?"

"Yes," I said, "I was a glutton for punishment. I went in the A-10 and in the F-16."

"Wow," one of the pilots in the group said, "that's probably the most masochistic thing I've ever heard of." He stepped forward and extended his hand. "Fred Burns," he said. "You can call me Rug."

I smiled and shook his hand. I'd known a few guys in the USAF with the last name of Burns and nearly all of them went by the handle 'Rug.' Fred was a few inches shorter than me and obviously in much better shape. He had hair that was so dark brown it was nearly black, showing some gray at the temples. His eyes were widely spaced apart and bright blue. Judging by the lines on his face, I guessed we were close to the same age. He pumped my hand once and released.

"Fred is my assistant chief pilot and training officer," Ruth said. "You can call me," I started to say, stopping as Fred held up his hand.

"You're FNG until we name you," he said. "That will occur at the end of your training.

"Some things never change," I said. FNG was short for 'Fucking New Guy' - the standard name for a new arrival in any fighter squadron.

"We try to keep some of the traditions."

I nodded. Many units made a practice of formally 'naming' their new arrivals after they were mission-ready. Burt had been right. This was weird.

Ruth took me by the elbow and led me toward the other pilots. The next one in line was short and swarthy and looked very young. His name was Dan Fielstrom and he was Belgian. He shook my hand and flashed me a friendly smile. "I go by VB, short for Viper Baby. Glad to have you aboard, sir!" he said with a mild Flemish accent.

I accepted his handshake and smiled back. The 'baby' part of his moniker was accurate. He couldn't have been more than thirty.

The next pilot was Niels Petersen, a Dane. He was very slightly built and blonde. Trying to make up for his lack of physical stature, he tried to crush my hand with his handshake and seemed surprised when I showed no sign that he had expended the effort. "Hello dere," he said, "I'm Niels, but you can call me Pete." I smiled and allowed him to end the masculinity contest by releasing my hand first.

The last pilot was Hans Briel, from the Netherlands. "Brinker," he said, barely troubling himself to acknowledge my existence. "I hope you last longer than the last American." His handshake was loose and limp, belying his physique. He was nearly white-blonde but he wasn't slightly built like Petersen. Muscles bulged under a flightsuit which appeared to be intentionally just a little too small on him. His eyes were pools, limpid and gray.

Ruth then turned me toward the remaining three people;

all women, I was surprised to see. "These are the key personnel of our support staff. This is Natasha Rasletin. She was a maintenance officer in the Russian Air Force working with MiG-29s and SU-27s."

Natasha was in her mid-thirties and looked like an ad from a 'brides by mail' catalogue. She had a plain face and stringy black hair which hung from a loose bun on the top of her head. Her complexion was pasty white and she had deep-set green eyes. She was wearing coveralls, so her body was not on display, but I could detect no unsightly bulges anywhere. As Ruth introduced me, Natasha stepped forward and underwent a transformation. She flashed a very radiant smile and her eyes lit up. In a second, she was attractive and vibrant. She extended her hand and I shook it.

"You are most welcome, Colonel," she said in heavily accented English. "I must greet you in the Russian way."

And with that, she embraced me and placed a wet kiss on both of my cheeks. The second kiss lingered slightly longer than the first and there was a barely discernable touch of her tongue on my cheek. In my peripheral vision, I saw Briel smirk and Ruth roll her eyes.

I flushed and gently pushed her away. "Thank you, Ms. Rasletin. Good maintenance officers are difficult to find. If you could keep the MiG-29 and SU-27 flying, I'm sure the Viper is easy."

She nodded. "Piece of cake," she said, licking her lips. "Come to hangar anytime and Natasha will give you grand tour."

"I'd like that," I said.

I felt forceful pressure on my elbow guiding me to the next person in the line. Her name was Brianna Blenhem and she was an Australian. Brianna was the administrative officer and I guessed that she was somewhere in her mid-thirties, as well. She stood about five-foot-two and had flowing black hair that cascaded to her shoulders. She wore a flightsuit, like the pilots, and filled it out superbly with breasts jutting forth, barely contained by the fabric. She looked up at me with huge brown eyes, all professional in their gaze.

"Colonel Pearce," she said, shaking my hand firmly, "glad to meet you."

"Likewise," I said. "Are you the one who handles the payment process?"

She nodded with a tired smile.

"Then we'll be seeing lots of each other," I said.

"Looking forward to it," she said in a well-practiced monotone.

When I turned to focus my eyes on the last woman in line, I inhaled suddenly and felt an unexplained warmth inside me. Her name was Samantha Everhart and she sported a mane of strawberry-blonde hair, the most piercing blue eyes, and a mature beauty that made pinpointing her age impossible. She was about five-foot-nine, and the way her flightsuit clung to her left no doubt that she was exceptionally fit. She looked me right in the eyes as she reached for my hand.

When our fingers touched, something passed between us that seemed to take us both by surprise.

"Glad to meet you," she said quickly, with the barest trace of a high-class English accent. "I'm afraid you're going to hate me because I'm going to be your personal trainer."

"Well," I said, "I guess it's good to know the threat up front." She nodded and smiled, her eyes never leaving mine.

"Okay, ladies and gentlemen," Ruth said in conclusion, "let's let Colonel Pearce get settled and through his processing. Rug, he's all yours. Please show him to his quarters." She turned to me. "Get your gear stowed quickly. We need to get you through admin, physical, and life support tonight before the evening meal."

"Roger that," I said.

Rug extended his arm and motioned that I should follow him. He took a few steps, opened one of the double metal doors at the rear of the hangar, and held it for me. I went through it and into a carpeted hallway which paralleled the hangar's rear wall.

"Here's the nickel tour," Rug said, "not that there is much to it. To the right is the admin section. Here you'll find the orderly room, commander's office, chow hall, and clinic. If you go through admin, you'll be into the technicians' quarters and maintenance, where 'Natasha the Insatiable' and her minions live."

"Okay, I have to ask. What's her story?"

"She's Russian," he said, chuckling. "That should explain everything." Then his voice turned more serious. "After we get your gear stowed and get you into some suitable clothes, you'll see Brianna in admin before you see Sammy."

"Sammy?"

"Dr. Samantha. Her handle is 'Igor' but no one ever calls her that."

"Interesting handle for a woman who is an absolute knockout."

"Well, that's a nickname that's easy. She spends all her time in the clinic or the gym changing peoples' bodies. It just fit."

He led me to the left. The first room we came to on the right was obviously a mission planning room and featured a large map table in the center and several computers on other tables nearby. The inevitable rack of data transfer cartridges, or DTCs, metal cartridges about the size of a big paperback book with a handle on the end, was next to the computers.

"Mission planning," I said redundantly.

Rug nodded. "And let me tell you, they spent some money here. Latest software, maps, computers, everything. I've never seen a better facility, even in the USAF. And this isn't even the best of it."

"Where'd you fly the Viper?" I asked. "You and I seem to be about the same age, so I'm surprised I haven't run into you before."

"I was mainly a Block 50/52 guy," he said simply.

That explained it. The Block 50 was the most sophisticated Viper in the USAF inventory when I retired and was specifically outfitted for the suppression-of-enemy-air-defenses mission, often shortened to SEAD. The skill-set for that mission was so refined that it became a sub-community within the Viper world.

"Where'd you fly it?"

"Shaw, Misawa, and Spangdalem," he said. "I retired out of Shaw, got out right before 9/11." He stopped at a series of three doors, two single doors on either side of a set of double doors. He pushed the double doors open and said, "Lights on."

Instantly the room was bathed in fluorescent light. It was a small amphitheater with three large screens and a podium in front. Comfortable-looking stadium seats for about one hundred people were aligned in several rows, and a rack of sophisticated video equipment on a rack was built into the wall next to the podium.

"This is the main briefing room," Rug said. "Any mass gatherings will take place in here as well as the formal mission briefs for the projects. We also debrief air-to-air missions in here."

"Works like an ACMI facility?" I asked, referring to Air Combat Maneuvering Instrumentation, a computer system which takes the aircraft parameters from a telemetry pod mounted on the aircraft and transmits them to a computer system on the ground. It makes debriefing air-to-air sorties precise because the computer provides animation showing the exact parameters of each jet in the system and its relationship to any one of the other jets in the system.

"Yeah," Rug said, "and it's damn good. By the time you're out of your jet, your mission will be cued up and ready for debrief. And there's no fiddling with settings to determine what view you want. You just speak it and it happens."

"Wow," I said.

"Lights off," Rug said, and the room went dark. "This is also where you'll have your academics when you're not in one of the flight briefing rooms." He motioned to the two smaller doors, one of which was set on each side of the double doors. "I don't know why we have two," he said. "We only ever use one. Oh well."

We walked a little further and found that constant fixture in every operations squadron, the operations desk. This one had two LCD TV screens behind it, both dark.

"The ops desk," Rug said. "Don't worry; you won't have to work behind it. That's just for Major S or me."

"What's her handle?" I asked.

Rug smirked. "Blade," he said flatly.

"Okay, I have to ask."

"Wait until you fly a BFM sortie against her."

"She likes to knife fight, I take it."

Rug nodded. "They must teach those Israeli pilots something different," he said. "We were taught never to get slow in visual fight. That's her whole game plan. You swear you won't let her do it to you and somehow she manages to get you slow and then get you in the phone booth and then she sticks it to you."

"Wow," I said, "I'll be on the lookout for that."

"No one has beaten her," Rug said. "And it pisses all of them off that they can't. Me, I'm old and I've just accepted my limitations."

Rug led me a little further. "That was the work part of our side of the building. This is our off-duty part."

We came to the other constant in a fighter squadron, the bar. This one was roomy and featured a solid cherry counter with a mirror that ran the entire length of the wall behind it. Bar stools were lined up in front of the counter next to the inevitable pool table, modified for the sport of fighter pilots - a game called Crud. On one side, there were several big-screen

TVs, two sofas, and several recliners. On the other side, there were several arcade-style games, and on the floor in between, several tables and chairs.

"Wow, what a bar," I said.

"They spent a lot of money on it and they built it large enough for us to have unit parties here from time to time."

We continued along the corridor to a place where there were two hallways branching off to the right about twenty feet apart.

"This is 'officer country' and it's just us up here. The girls are in the second hallway and we're in the first. At the end of each hallway there is a door to the common shower."

"Common shower?" I asked.

He smiled. "Major S' idea," he said. "Apparently, it's the norm in the Israeli Armed Forces; and frankly, after spending a good portion of my career in Germany where a lot of saunas, pools, and showers are the same way, I can tell you it's no big deal. Besides there are so few of us, we're rarely in there at the same time anyway."

He took me down the guys' corridor, which had three rooms on each side and past all the rooms with small name plates on the door. Rug. VB. Brinker. Pete. Mine was the one on the end on the left. It had FNG on the door, of course.

"This is yours," Rug explained. "Make sure your bags made it in here and lose the street clothes. There should be some flightsuits in your room. We need to get you into admin."

I nodded and opened the door.

The room was nicer than I expected and was about the size of a British hotel room, that is to say, cozy. To the right was a small washroom with a sink and john and a clothes closet built into the wall next to it. The bed was queen-sized and was centered on the opposite wall with a nightstand on either side. A blue wingback reading chair rested on the carpet between the bed and the left wall with a floor lamp nearby. To my immediate left was a built-in unit mounted to the wall which had a desk with a computer, a TV with an internal DVD player, a small stereo boom box, bookshelves, cabinets, and drawers. The furniture was all highly polished cherry wood.

I opened the closet to find several desert tan flightsuits hanging inside and a new pair of desert flying boots on the shoe rack below them. I expected both would be the right size. My roller bag was neatly stowed on a rack in the closet. I pulled it out, opened it, and found that my clothes had been put away for me. I smiled to myself. This had probably been the opportunity they needed to search it. My computer bag was sitting on the desk. A quick inspection of it revealed that the contents were still all there, but not quite in the order in which I had packed them. That bag had been searched as well.

Returning to the closet, I kicked my shoes off and hastily shed my suit. With the possibility of a physical exam later, I also went into the bathroom and used a washcloth and soap to wash a few areas of my body quickly and thoroughly. Then I put on a fresh pair of boxer briefs, clean undershirt, and socks, and donned a flightsuit. I placed my legs into it, slid my arms in, and zipped it up in a motion that was as natural as if I had done it just yesterday. I sat on the bed and laced the boots up and then stood to examine my reflection in the mirror. Apart from the roundness in my face and my middle, I looked like the same guy who had flown his last sortie in the Viper years ago. I shook my head. Time was a strange thing.

I noticed that the flightsuit did not have the usual Velcro squares sewn onto the upper arms or right chest area for unit patches to be affixed to. It did, however, have a rectangular Velcro area on the left side of my chest where a black, leather name tag was placed. The tag had command pilot's wings on it and the letters FNG stenciled below.

"Cute," I said to the empty room.

I retrieved the original copy of my contract and left the room to find an empty hallway. "Rug?"

His head popped out of a door two rooms down. "That

was fast," he said. "It's just as well. The quicker we get you into Sammy's hands, the better she'll like it."

I gave him a questioning look.

"You're a challenge for her," he said. "She doesn't have a lot of time to work with you, and she wants to see what she's up against. It's what she does."

We walked back through the hallway. This time when we passed the bar, the TV was on and the other pilots, less the inscrutable Major Shalev, were in there watching something. Rug waved at them and led me toward the admin section where he dropped me off.

"See Brianna in the orderly room first and then go to the clinic to see Igor. When Igor's finished with you, come find me in the bar and we'll get you through your life support fitting."

My visit with Brianna was an exposition of her efficiency. I gave her the original contract and found that nearly all my paperwork was filled out to include address, bank information, and next of kin. They had pulled nearly all my relevant information without my knowledge but I made no mention of it. I also made no mention of the fact that somehow, during my travel, I had lost two days of time. Her calendar showed the 13th of September. I was betting I was somewhere on the other side of the International Date Line, perhaps eastern Asia or the western Pacific Ocean.

Brianna showed me a printed copy of a wire transfer confirmation.

"Here's proof that your signing bonus has been wired to your account in Bermuda," she said with her pleasant Aussie lilt. "You will be paid your salary promptly on the last day of each month along with any bonuses for successful projects flown during that month."

I nodded.

"You also have a death benefit of six months' salary to be paid in the event you," she paused to choose her words carefully, "are unsuccessful in servicing one of the projects.

Who would you like it paid to?"

I was tempted to put Burt Magnusson's widow's name on the beneficiary line but that would have been too transparent. Instead I listed the names and addresses of my two brothers, neither of whom I had seen for several years. I smiled to myself. This would be quite the windfall for them if it happened. Of course, they'd both blow it, but I wouldn't be around to care about that.

Brianna gave me copies of all my paperwork in a neat folder and shook my hand again. The process took maybe twenty minutes.

"You need to go see Dr. Everhart now," she said. She pointed to the door of her office. "Out the door and right. Go past the dining area and then enter the first door on the left. Have fun."

"Is there a joke here that I'm not getting?" I asked.

"The joke is on everyone," Brianna said. "We've all had to go through this. It's just your turn." She paused and tried to keep a smirk from forming on her face. "She's just a little tougher on the guys than the girls."

"Great."

I walked out of her office and turned right down the corridor. I passed the dining facility, a small kitchen with a buffet line and seating for about one hundred or so. By the lights, smells and activity, I deduced the crew was gearing up for the evening meal.

After I passed the dining facility, I came to a glass door with the word 'Clinic' stenciled on the upper portion of it at eye level.

"Here goes," I mumbled to myself.

I entered the clinic and found myself in a small waiting area with seating for about five. "Hello?" I said timidly.

"Back here," came Dr. Everhart's voice. "Left of the counter; the exam room is at the end of the hall."

I walked back and found her placing a series of hypodermic

needles on a tray that rested on a cabinet near the back of the room. The exam room was like all the others I've seen. Cushioned table covered with paper, an X-ray viewer, and cabinet space for the tools and drugs of the trade. An EKG machine, vision tester, and scale were lined up along one wall.

"Glad you made it," she said as she flashed me a winning smile. "Now strip off."

"Excuse me?"

"Take off your clothes. All of them, including your shorts."

I just stood there.

"Well?" She asked.

"Aren't you going to leave or get me a gown or something?"

"No. We're very relaxed around here and it's just me anyway. Besides, I'm going to see all you've got so it doesn't matter if it's now or later."

I sat down on the table and began unlacing my boots. "This is a first. It's a good thing I'm getting paid well."

"You're making more than I am."

I dropped the first boot and sock on the floor and started working on the second. She picked them up and put them in a plastic bin which she had for that purpose. The rest of my clothes followed and in a few minutes, I was completely naked with my butt resting on the paper of the examination table.

I'm not a modest person. I've done the nude beach thing several times, although I was in much better shape then. Even now, carrying about thirty extra pounds, I wasn't self-conscious, but I had never experienced anything like this before. She had watched my every move and had taken every scrap of clothing I had shed and collected them in the container. Her gaze wasn't sexual. I t wasn't even professional, from a medical perspective. If I had to sum it up, I'd say it was suspicious.

Samantha took the tray of clothes, which included the CIA-issued BlackBerry, and placed it outside the exam room door without explanation. Then she closed the door.

"Stand up please."

I did as I was instructed. Thus, began the most thorough medical exam I've ever been given in my life.

In addition to the standard tests common to a physical, I was poked, prodded, and felt in places I never had been before. I provided blood, urine, and even a stool sample, all of which were immediately given to a young male technician who ran off to process them. I was x-rayed multiple times and vaccinated against more things than I could count. I had every muscle in my body analyzed and had her gloved finger in my ass for an excruciatingly long time while she did a prostate check and, I suspect, looked for anything that might be concealed there.

I might mention here that she was incredibly strong. Her hands kneaded every muscle in my body like a combination of doctor and masseuse as she worked to ascertain my physical condition. I was certain I'd be sore in the morning.

There were too many embarrassing moments to recount, but probably the worst one was while she was on her knees in front of me feeling the muscles of my upper quads. With no notice whatsoever, she transitioned into a hernia check and the light touch of her gloved hand on my balls gave me a nearly instantaneous erection. I think my whole body turned red with embarrassment.

"Nice," she commented. Then she looked up at me with her first concession to humanity that day.

"Happens to all the guys. Something about a blonde with big tits playing with their balls. Don't sweat it. We used to measure guys when they were in this state, but the data wasn't useful."

I had no idea whether she was kidding and had no intention of asking her.

Finally, my clothes were returned and I was allowed to dress. She finished making her notes and looking over my lab paperwork as I zipped up my flightsuit.

"Now, do you want the good news or the bad news first?" she asked.

"Let's start with the good."

"You're in good health. Your heart is strong and all your fluids are normal. You're free of parasites and your musculature is sound. You don't have any STDs, something we're really concerned about in a close environment like this. In short, the foundation we have to build upon is very good."

"Okay, now what's the bad news?"

She sighed. "You could stand to drop between thirty and forty pounds. Your body fat level is close to thirty percent when it should be fifteen or less and your testosterone levels are low."

"I suppose we'll begin working on that tomorrow."

She nodded. "You're going to hate me. But in a month you won't recognize your body. I'll have you buffed out like you wouldn't believe. But it's going to hurt."

"Bring it on," I said defiantly. "I've trained before, I can train again."

"You haven't had a deadline before. Now you do, and for the next month I am going to run your life. You won't have a morsel of food without my approval and I'm going to work you until you drop from exhaustion." She turned away for a second to grab a plastic cup with a dark, purple fluid it in from the counter behind her. Then she handed it to me. "And it starts right now. Drink this."

I sipped obediently. The liquid tasted like thick, syrupy, grape Kool-Aid. I finished and handed the glass back to her.

"What is that stuff?"

"A mixture of things that would never be legal for me to dispense anywhere in the US or the UK. It'll speed up your metabolism, give you a lot more energy and allow your body to function like it did about twenty years ago. I'll stock your room with a supply of this stuff, pre-measured in individually sealed cups. You'll drink one dose every morning."

"Any long term damage?"

"No idea," she said, turning to place the cup back on the counter. As she returned her gaze to me, she must have seen the slightly shocked expression on my face. "The truth is, we don't really care," she continued. "This stuff allows us to train you more quickly and intensely and gives you the mental acuity and reflexes of a much younger man. It makes you more useful now. And that's what matters to us."

I nodded. It was the military way, more or less. No one ever did any research on the possible long-term damage on the human body of intense high-g force when the recipient was sitting in the thirty-degree tilted seat of the F-16. But I had heard rumors about torn intrathoracic muscles and permanent injury to the heart and lungs.

I looked at her. "You know when you provide fuel like this to let the 'warrior instinct' loose, there are predictable side effects." I motioned to the area around us. "Doesn't that make things difficult to manage in an environment like this where men and women work closely together?"

She allowed herself a thin smile. "That's one of reasons why the ratio of males and females is relatively even. We account for that. We allow for 'events' but we discourage 'relationships.'"

"And the boss isn't concerned about the effect of all that possible fucking around on 'good order and discipline'?"

"Let me ask you a question," she said. "What's the one drive in the human animal that rivals the urge for sex?"

I nodded and smiled. "Greed," I answered. "Everyone behaves because they want the money. That's fucking brilliant." I turned toward the door. "Are we done?"

She reached into a drawer and pulled out a handful of condoms. She unzipped the breast pocket of my flightsuit and shoved them in there. "Natasha will come on to you. Do yourself a favor. Don't fuck her," she said. "But if you have to, use one of these things or your penis just might fall off. That chick has had more men inside her than a Piccadilly pisser. She's been tested, like all of us have, but it's still just gross."

"I'll keep that in mind."

"You do that," she said. "You're free to go."

She turned her back on me and returned to her notes. I heard her pick up the phone as I walked out of the room and slowed my pace so I could overhear her.

"Boss? Sammy." There was a pause. "It went well, he's a good specimen... nothing hidden actually... yes, me as well."

I could hear her footsteps as she walked to the exam room door to shut it. "You were right; he does look like Trevor. It's a little spooky. I have to say though, he's 'equipped' a little better than Trevor was." I heard her sigh as the door began to close. "Now if only he played the drums."

CHAPTER EIGHT

Contract Day Three
Sunday, 13 September
1700 Hours Local Time
Island Training Base

After the ignominy of my physical exam, my life support fitting was quick and painless. It was handled by the lone life support technician, a retired Royal Air Force enlisted man named John Blair. He went about his work briskly and precisely, and I was fitted with a flying helmet, oxygen mask, anti-g suit, and survival vest in about thirty minutes. The equipment was new out of the bag in every case, and I assumed they purchased it commercially.

Shortly thereafter, I made my way to the bar and joined the pilots and other 'officers' who were having a few beers before dinner. As I entered the bar, the conversation died down for a moment, then resumed quickly. 'VB' Fielstrom, 'Pete' Petersen, and 'Brinker' Briel sat at the bar while 'Rug' Burns played bartender. Ruth, Samantha, Brianna, and Natasha sat at a table, engrossed in conversation. Rug motioned me over to where the guys were and raised a beer mug in greeting.

"That looks good," I said.

At the sound of my voice, Samantha turned around in her chair. "Drink up tonight, chap," she said. "Tomorrow we go at it, starting bright and early at 0600."

"Yes, dear," I replied.

She smirked at me, and then leaned forward to whisper something to her table mates. A few moments later, a round of giggles emanated from the table. I could only imagine what they were talking about.

I walked up to the bar and Rug handed me a cold mug of draft beer. I gulped a large slug of it down, savoring the flavor.

"Wow, that's good," I said. "Stella?"

Rug nodded. "Stella Artois, indeed. Life's too short to drink cheap beer. Especially when the good stuff is free. By the way," he motioned toward the table where the girls were still giggling, "five will get you ten that they're talking about your tackle. Sammy's like a guy, and she talks about the stuff on guys like guys talk about the things on girls. I wouldn't be surprised if she hasn't passed out a chart that rates our equipment."

"That's a new take."

"Yes, it is. By the way," he said as he leaned across the bar and rested his weight on his forearms, "when Major S first mentioned your name to me, I thought it sounded familiar but I couldn't place it."

I tensed, expecting the inevitable questions about the circumstances of my departure from the Air Force. It wasn't exactly a secret. But he went somewhere else instead. Fortunately.

"Weren't you the guy who got mixed up in some gang-related thing in Phoenix?" He nodded toward the other three pilots. "The boys and I were discussing it before you came in. I was trying to explain it to them, but I'm not sure I understood it correctly."

"There's not much to understand," I said. "When I was stationed at Luke, I lived off base in a west-valley town called Avondale. Three guys broke into my house, looking for trouble. They found it."

"Who were they?" VB asked.

"Members of a Latino gang called *Los Diablos*. They had been burglarizing houses in the neighborhood where I lived, stealing electronic equipment to sell on the street. They also tended to mess with any people they found in the houses at the time. The cops couldn't stop them. And they made the mistake of trying it in my house."

"What did you do?"

"My burglar alarm went off in the middle of the night, and I woke up and got the shotgun which I kept under my bed."

"A shotgun?" Brinker said in disdain. "The only thing we use those for in Holland is bird control."

I looked over at Rug who rolled his eyes obligingly.

"This gun was built for killing only one thing, and birds aren't it. It was a Mossberg Model 500 pump shotgun with an 18-inch barrel, a five-round magazine, and a collapsible combat stock."

"So, what happened?" Pete asked, now eager to hear the story. I noticed that the conversation from the girls' table had ebbed.

I shrugged and fought to control the rising warmth in my blood as the incident played through my mind. "I waited for the first one to come into the bedroom, and when he stuck his head around the corner, I blew it off. One of his pals came running in a moment after that, and he got the same treatment. The last guy decided to try to run out of my house through the garage." I took a sip of beer. "He didn't make it."

Brinker snorted. "Typical American. You shot him in the back."

"Actually, even though the law in Arizona didn't require him to be a direct threat for me to apply deadly force, I did tell him to halt first." The memories were playing back quickly now, coming from the places where they had been long stowed. It wasn't about giving him a chance to surrender at all, not that he would have. It was about me pulling the trigger and seeing the expression on his face, or what was left of it.

"You still ambushed him."

"Yes, I did," I said with a shrug and looked at him over the top of my beer mug. "Those guys were animals and they got what was coming to them. I was just glad to be the one to do it."

"What was all that stink in the papers afterward?" Rug asked. "What you did was obviously self-defense."

"The legality of it was never the issue, only the political correctness. I was Anglo and the three invaders were Latino, so obviously I was a racist. But the heat got a lot worse when a rumor was leaked to the media about something I allegedly did during the Gulf War."

I had their complete attention now. The girls had left their table and I could feel them behind me as I faced the bar.

Rug's eyes lit up immediately. "You're T.C?" he asked incredulously. "You're T.C.? I thought that was a myth! Holy Shit!"

I nodded.

"T.C.?" VB asked. "What, who's T.C.?"

"It was a story we all heard during the Gulf War and afterward," Rug said, "about a US pilot who had been captured and escaped by killing several of his guards."

Brinker shrugged, communicating his disinterest.

"So where did the T.C. come from?" Pete asked, repeating VB's question.

"It was the way they were killed," Rug said looking at Pete and drawing an imaginary line across his throat with his index finger. He looked at me with new respect in his eyes. "How many?"

"I don't remember much about it," I said. "I was just trying to get out of there as fast as I could."

That was a lie. I knew how many there were. I could still remember the terrified expressions on ten faces and reveling in the sensation of their warm blood spattering on my skin, again and again. The same feelings which were reawakened when I blew the brains of my home invaders all over the textured drywall of my home in Avondale. The same feelings that Burt's disappearance had revived.

Goddamn it, I thought. Smith and Amrine knew this would happen to me. *They fucking knew it.*

The silence was palpable.

"So why was there an uproar over this when you killed the gang people?" Pete asked. "I just don't understand the American press."

"It turns out that killing your captors during an escape attempt is a violation of the Geneva Convention, which makes me a war criminal," I said taking a sip from my beer. "After the story was leaked, the press tried to use that to show that I was some sort of 'rabid-dog' type killer."

"What happened?"

"Nothing," I said, slowly finishing my beer. "What I had done to the gang members was in fact self-defense, and in spite of the involvement of the Air Force's answer to the Gestapo, the OSI, there was nothing concrete to link me to the Gulf War rumor. It all just sort of went away."

"Throat cutter," VB said in realization, "T.C. stands for throat cutter."

I nodded again.

"Why did you cut their throats?" It was Brianna's voice. Her Aussie-accented voice was clearly quavering. I found it ironic that someone engaged in the business of killing people by the hundreds was having difficulty dealing with the death of a few Iraqi soldiers during an actual war.

I turned toward her slowly and looked down at her. "You do the best you can do with what you have available. While a few of the guards were giving me the usual 'new-prisoner beating,' one of them kept brandishing this big shiny knife with a jeweled handle, which he was obviously very proud of. Later, I got tired of the beating and faked unconsciousness.

Thinking that I was out of it, the guards tied my hands very loosely to a pipe on the wall. I worked the ropes loose, and when I was left alone with two of them, one of whom was the guy with the knife, I surprised them. They were sitting at a table playing cards, and I grabbed the table and pinned them against the wall with it. When I did, the knife fell off the table into my hand. Without even thinking about it, I ran it across both of their throats."

"Quickest, surest kill," Ruth said matter-of-factly.

I shook my head. "I'd love to tell you that it was a flash of good tactical decision making, but the truth is that I couldn't get to their bodies because they were blocked by the table I was pinning them with, and I couldn't have them crying out to warn anyone else."

"But why did you keep doing it?" Brianna asked.

I just looked at her. "Because it worked," I said. That was a lie too. The truth was that I liked it.

She shivered in revulsion and left the bar, obviously sick to her stomach.

"Well, we won't be seeing her at the mess," Rug said sardonically.

The group broke up then. Pete, Brinker, and VB started discussing 'crazy Americans,' and Samantha went around the bar, filling her beer mug at the tap before perching herself next to Rug and grabbing a solid handful of his ass. He smiled at her and grabbed her ass in return. I glanced over at Ruth and she rolled her eyes.

"The theory is that they're just good friends," she said. "She's the one who got me his résumé."

"Really?" I said, leaning against the bar. I was grateful for the change in subject matter.

"Yes," Samantha said. "I was an exchange Medical Officer with Rug's unit at Shaw before he retired. After I got back to the UK and was contacted about this job, and I made sure he got a call."

"That's pretty cool," I said, thinking it was about time to test the water. "I'm still wondering why I got a call. There have to a lot of Viper drivers out there who would love a gig like this."

"Our criteria are demanding," Ruth said, just a little too quickly. "You were the only one available who fit them."

I was looking directly at Rug and Samantha when Ruth spoke, and both of them broke eye contact with me.

"Whatever gets me back in the cockpit of that machine," I said, pointing my empty mug at a large Viper photo on the wall, "and the sooner the better. Flying business jets is a little like playing with yourself. It's fun and can be done with one hand, but it's not something you brag about, and it's not completely satisfying."

The small talk continued for a little while and then we filed into the mess hall for dinner. That's when I got my first look at the full complement of staff. Besides the officers, there were about one hundred support personnel. This seemed like a lot of people, but it really isn't. A jet as complex as the F-16 requires several maintenance specialties to keep it flying. Crew chiefs take care of the daily 'care and feeding' of the jets. Avionics troops are responsible for the computers and gadgets that control it. Then there are all the specialists who deal with the individual aircraft systems, to include airframe and flight controls, hydraulics, electrical systems, and power plant. Last, but not least, personnel who assembled the ordnance and loaded it on the jets were required. Looking out over the crowd, I surmised that each person there had multiple specialties, and that luring them away from hourly-wage jobs wasn't difficult with the large salaries MAG had offered them.

I went through the buffet line and helped myself to some spaghetti and meatballs, bread, and salad. I also filled a huge glass with ice and Diet Coke from of a very American-looking soda fountain. The 'officers' sat at two tables against the far wall of the room, so I walked over and sat in the only available spot left, right between Natasha and Ruth. Brianna was absent, as Rug had predicted. I had no sooner sat down when Natasha pushed her leg up against mine. Trying to discourage her, I turned to Ruth. "So," I said, "at the risk of possibly sticking my nose where it doesn't belong, what happened to the pilot I'm replacing?"

Where there had been an undertone of conversation at the table, suddenly it was silent and I congratulated myself for dominating the conversation twice in less than an hour. Instantly, there was a tension in the air which came out of nowhere and every face at the table stole a glance at Ruth. I felt a lessening of Natasha's pressure against my leg.

Ruth was smooth, though. She only allowed the tension to last a second or two before she volunteered the answer. "He left," she said flatly.

"I see," I said at last.

"We were very sorry to lose him," she continued. "He was a great guy and an outstanding pilot. His name was Andy Dickson. Did you know him?"

"The name sounds familiar," I said. "But I can't picture the face.

Do you have a photo of him anywhere?"

Ruth nodded. "Brianna has the file. But I want to be there when you see it...just to answer any questions."

"That works for me," I said after a moment, "when it fits into the schedule." I made a point of deliberately returning to my food to defuse the tension.

"Just let me know," Ruth said.

The conversation resumed, as did Natasha's pressure against my leg. As the air relaxed, I made a mental note not to be in a hurry to see the file in question. There was something about this that just wasn't right. The hair on the back of my neck was itching, and it was one of the few things in my life I trusted.

After dinner, we all returned to the bar and spent the

balance of the evening telling stories, drinking beer, and telling the requisite dirty fighter pilot jokes. They were doing their best to bring me into their fold. To make me one of them. I laughed and played along, keenly aware that I was being observed the entire time. I even allowed Natasha to teach me to tango. She was a decent teacher, although I'm sure the body contact was overdone. As the evening wore on, I made a production of yawning and excused myself to get some rest. Predictably, Natasha followed me to my room to 'tuck me in.' She backed me up against the door to my room in the hallway, repeatedly telling me I needed a 'Russian-style massage' to ensure I slept well. I diplomatically resisted and made excuses for jet lag, alcohol, fatigue level, and anything else I could think of. I managed to escape with a full-body hug that reeked of body-odor and a kiss that tasted a little like flavored vodka.

Once safely inside my room, I brushed my teeth profusely and stripped off for bed. As I lay down on the surprisingly comfortable bed, I typed a quick arrival message to Smith and Amrine on the CIA BlackBerry and hit the send button. I included the local time as I had been instructed. Wondering how the message would get to them, I turned out the light.

With all that was going through my mind, I expected the gears to turn in my head for several hours. But my body knew what it needed. I was asleep in seconds.

TOP SECRET / SPECIAL
COMPARTMENTALIZED INFORMATION
CLASSIFIED BY: US Central Intelligence Agency
DECLASSIFY ON: OADR

From: Special Projects Group [NCS]
Sent: Sunday, 13 September 2009, 0937 EDT (14 September 2009, 1337Z)
To: Director, NCS
Cc: Special Projects Group [NCS]; damrine@cmail.cia.gov; dsmith3@cmail.cia.gov

SUBJECT: Update, Case File: 08-434A (MAG)

(TS) Narrative:

1. (TS) At 1139Z, 13 September 2009, an e-mail message was received from Contractor 09-017 (Pearce, Colin M). The message arrived via internet, apparently via the BlackBerry's clandestine worm utility, through an open Wi-Fi connection at Pearce's location. He has successfully arrived at MAG's training base. The local time at which the message was sent was 2335 hours. Assuming normal internet delays, the originating location lies in the GMT+12 time zone.

2. (TS) IP address trace was inconclusive as the message was routed through multiple servers and false addresses. Pearce's GPS gear is still unresponsive.

3. (TS) Pearce had a complete physical exam, including body cavity search, upon arrival. His baggage was also searched. He expects to begin academic and physical training tomorrow.

4. (TS) So far, Pearce has heard nothing about the upcoming 'major strike.'

(TS) CONCLUSION: Pearce's whereabouts, although presumably somewhat localized, remain unknown.

(TS) ACTION: We will await further contact via e-mail.

(TS) RECOMMENDATION: None. Information only.

TOP SECRET / SPECIAL
COMPARTMENTALIZED INFORMATION
CLASSIFIED BY: US Central Intelligence Agency
DECLASSIFY ON: OADR

CHAPTER NINE

Contract Day Four
Monday, 14 September
0600 Hours Local Time
Island Training Base

Hey, FNG!" Samantha's voice wafted in from the hallway, far too cheerfully. "Let's hit it!"

My eyes scarcely opened but somehow, I forced my legs onto the carpeted floor and padded over to the door of my room. I had barely turned the knob on the door when she came barreling into my room, standing before me in a tight, cotton workout ensemble which accentuated every curve of her body.

"You look like shit!" she said brightly. "I told you not to fuck Natasha."

"I didn't," I replied, probably a little too defensively. "I sent her out of here."

"All I know is that she came back to her room late last night, humming a happy little Russian tune."

"I wouldn't have been any good to her anyway. My body has no idea what time it is."

"It's not going to get any better until we get you on the program. Here, drink this." She handed me a plastic cup with the purple concoction inside. I drank it without thinking, and as a drop of the syrupy stuff landed on my chest, I suddenly realized I was naked. The living alone thing catches up with you sometimes. I was too tired to care, though. I handed the cup back to her.

"Guess I should get dressed," I said, raising my eyes to hers.

"Well, I personally don't mind," she replied playfully, "but it might set people talking if you worked out this way."

"Hell," I said, turning away, "it would probably turn their stomachs."

"We're going to fix that, love. In a few weeks, you won't know yourself. Now get your ass into some clothes. I'll wait for you in the hall."

She exited the room with a peculiar look in her eyes. I couldn't decide what it was.

A few minutes later, Samantha led me down past the operations desk, through a long hall and into a large well-equipped gym about the size of a basketball court. Once again, MAG's willingness to spend money became apparent. The gym was outfitted with a full assortment of strength-training equipment, including free weights and Hammer Strength and Cybex machines. It also featured a row of aerobic machines and a padded area to do floor work. The entire room was mirrored on all sides and I acquired a host of unflattering views of my physique from the multitude of reflections. We stopped in the middle of the gym in front of the row of Hammer Strength machines.

"I could spend a session assessing your physical condition, but I already know you're totally out of shape."

"Thanks for that," I said.

"So, we're just going to start kicking your ass right away to get your g-tolerance back up to an acceptable level," she continued as if I hadn't interrupted. "We're going to spend a week on total body conditioning, and then starting next week, we'll do split training and start trying to build some muscle mass on that frame of yours. You'll do weights and Pilates every other day for a week and do interval aerobics and on the days in between. Eventually, we'll get into some yoga."

"Yoga?"

"Don't knock it until you've tried it. It's a lot harder than it looks." She motioned toward the far wall of the gym. "There's your warm-up."

I looked over there and saw something I hadn't noticed when I first entered. Tucked into a corner, concealed mostly in shadow, was a large vehicle tire which looked as if it had come off some sort of heavy equipment, like a road grader or back hoe.

"That's my warm-up? What am I supposed to do, lift it?"

"Nope. Just flip it over, again and again until you get to the far side of the gym. Then flip it back. Piece of cake."

I nodded. "You're the boss. Today, anyway."

She grunted in acknowledgement as I walked over to the tire and rolled it out from the corner it had been resting in. It came from the floor to my shoulders and rolled out to the middle of the floor easily. I tipped it over and it fell with a satisfying thump to the gym floor. Then I nonchalantly squatted next to the tire and tried to pick it up.

It didn't budge.

"You're going to actually have to think about this a little and use your whole body," Samantha said. "Watch me." She walked over and squatted next to the tire. I was envious. She was so flexible she could squat far enough that her ass could almost touch the floor. She placed her hands beneath the tire, lifted her body so that her thighs were parallel to the floor, and leaned into the tire slightly. Then she exploded upward, using her quadriceps. She lifted the tire and allowed it to flip over on its other side. It was poetry in motion. I just stared at her.

"Don't be too impressed," she said. "The tires aren't that heavy. They are bulky, though, and you need to use good technique. Give it a go."

I squatted next to the tire and had difficulty going down far enough to get my thighs close to parallel to the floor, let alone further. I grabbed the bottom of the tire, leaned into it as I saw she had done, and attempted to lift it, using my legs. I raised it about 6 inches and it slipped out of my hands.

"Come on, FNG. You've got to grab that thing like you mean it."

I assumed the position again, got my hands as far under the tire as I could, flexed my forearms hard to tighten my grip, leaned in, and pushed into my quadriceps as I stood. This time the tire came up quickly and I allowed the momentum to carry it over onto its other side.

"Bravo, FNG! Now do it again! Only this time keep it moving."

I lifted the tire again and again, to the far gym wall and back. By the time I returned the tire to its storage place, my heart was racing. I was out of breath and covered in sweat.

Samantha nodded in satisfaction. "Not bad. Now let's get to the real work."

There was a time when I looked pretty darn good with my shirt off, so I'm no stranger to the gym. But I had nothing on Dr. Samantha. She was both scientific and sadistic. We started on the chest press machine and worked our way down the entire row of Hammer Strength machines, then went through the Cybex ones. I can't remember how many sets I did; all I know is that she varied the weight and kept the repetition count between four and twelve. On some we went up and stopped on heavier weights. On others, we started heavy and went down. On still others, we went up and down, in pyramid fashion.

When we were done with the weights, we did Pilates. She demonstrated each exercise first, and then led me through it, ensuring I paused at the right intervals and places to make sure my abdominal muscles got the most stress possible. I had never done Pilates before, and like most men, thought that it was a women's thing. When the exercises were over, I admired anyone who could get through one of these workouts on a regular basis.

"Okay, FNG," Samantha said as we rose from the mat, "you're done with day one and you held up better than I expected. Hit the showers quickly and go to the chow hall for your breakfast. You'll find it in one of the big refrigerators with your name on it."

I nodded briefly, too out of breath to reply and watched her walk out the gym door. When I had caught my wind a few moments later, I followed her.

I walked past the operations desk on the way back to my room to do what fighter pilots instinctively do in a fighter squadron: check the schedule. In this case, the board was a big plasma screen television that displayed a computer-generated schedule for the day's training events.

The flying elements were displayed first and there were two 'gos' of two sorties each. In the AM go, VB and Brinker were slated for a basic fighter maneuvers, or BFM sortie, and in the PM go, Pete and Rug were scheduled for the same. BFM was dogfighting, what the F-16 was made to do. There was nothing like it to keep the 'edge.' I was jealous of them. BFM sorties could vary from highly structured learning situations, like offensive and defensive training, to high-aspect engagements where the two combatants met each other nose to nose and fought it out until the best person won.

The second part of the schedule was for the non-flying elements, and sure enough I saw 'FNG, Igor' listed against 'Physical Training' at 0600. Further down, I saw 'FNG, Blade' listed against 'Transition Academics' at 1100. I looked at the clock on the screen and saw that it was just after 1000.

"Holy shit!" I hurried off to my room to change.

The communal shower thing was no big deal that day. I was the only one in there. The configuration was more private than I had imagined. Each shower had its own stall with the shower area itself and a small dressing area. But the stalls had no doors and if someone took the stall across the way, both parties would be in full view of each other. I hoped that the temperature in the room wouldn't be too cold if I found myself looking across at one of the women in our group.

I finished the shower, dressed, and quickly ate my 'meal' in the mess hall - a protein shake, some peanut butter and bananas, and a cup of surprisingly good coffee. Then I raced to the main briefing room, finding it empty when I arrived.

A table had been set up in front of the stadium seats with a row of books on it that were the 'tools of the trade.' I recognized a thick binder containing the F-16 flight manual. We called it the 'dash one,' short for the technicalese of TO 1-F-16-1.

It was accompanied by its little brother, the 'dash one checklist,' a condensed version of the normal and emergency procedures for use in the cockpit. Other binders rested on the table nearby, including a classified version of the dash one which had all the tech data for the radar, radar warning gear, chaff and flare systems, and electronic counter measures. There was also a set of the dash thirty-four manuals, which contained the general data for weapons delivery as well as the procedures specific to the F-16.

I sat at the table and eagerly began poring over the material, feeling my spirits rise. Ruth came in a few moments later and walked to the dais without looking at me.

"Center screen, on. Lights, dim," she said. Immediately, the center screen illuminated and the room began to get darker. "Stop dim," she said when the light level had lowered enough to suit her. Then she looked at me.

"We'll go through this material as fast as you can absorb it, which should be pretty quickly based on the knowledge level I assessed when I interviewed you. It will be up to you to slow me down." She looked up at the clock on the wall. "I'll talk for about an hour, you'll get a ten-minute break, and then we'll go back into it. We'll go for two sessions, break for lunch, then do five more sessions, and stop for dinner. After dinner, we'll reconvene and do three more sessions before rack time. The faster you get through this stuff, the faster you can strap a jet onto your ass. Are you ready?"

I nodded.

"Academics. Avionics," she said and the first slides for the course came up on the center screen. They were the same slides used by the training squadron at Luke Air Force Base, easily identified because the wing and squadron insignia were still the upper left and right corners of the slides. I knew the slides well because I had been in the training squadron before I retired and had built some of these presentations. Obviously, MAG had found a way to buy them.

Ruth started her briefing and I began to listen and take notes.

TOP SECRET / SPECIAL
COMPARTMENTALIZED INFORMATION
CLASSIFIED BY: US Central Intelligence Agency
DECLASSIFY ON: OADR

From: Special Projects Group [NCS]
Sent: Sunday, 20 September 2009, 0945 EDT (20 September 2009, 1345Z)
To: Director, NCS
Cc: Special Projects Group [NCS]; damrine@cmail.cia.gov; dsmith3@cmail.cia.gov

SUBJECT: Update, Case File: 08-434A (MAG)

(TS) Narrative:

1. (TS) Today, we received the seventh email from Contractor 09-017 (Pearce, Colin M). He completed academic training and begins simulator and flight training over the coming week.

2. (TS) He has received no information on upcoming sorties but he believes there is a schedule driving the pace of his training.

3. (TS) Multiple trace attempts on the emails have been inconclusive. Multiple GPS interrogations have been unanswered.

(TS) CONCLUSION: It is imperative that we ascertain the location of MAG's base of operations prior to the launch of the major strike or we will be unable to prevent it.

(TS) ACTION: Tomorrow at 1000 EDT, we are convening a

meeting of the Special Projects Groups of the DS&T, DI, and DS to brainstorm mechanisms to regain location information on Pearce and MAG's training base. We will present options for Director-level consideration after the upcoming meeting.

(TS) RECOMMENDATION: None. Information only.

TOP SECRET / SPECIAL
COMPARTMENTALIZED INFORMATION
CLASSIFIED BY: US Central Intelligence Agency
DECLASSIFY ON: OADR

CHAPTER TEN

Contract Day Eleven
Monday, 21 September
0900 Hours Local Time
Island Training Base

My first week raced by in a blur of physical training, academics, hurried meals and sleep. Today, as I shed my clothes after my morning workout, I could already see the changes in my body. My stomach was flatter and harder, and my arms and legs were beginning to bulge in the right places. I could move the tire back and forth across the gym not easily, but fluidly, and I was completing my daily regimens with some energy left over. Between the exercise and the drugs, I felt better than I had in years.

The F-16 academics were moving along rapidly. I could drink from the 'fire-hose' of information as quickly as Ruth could spray it. We whizzed through the basic aircraft systems and the classified ones, as well. My mind eagerly recalled all the data about the jet that had been stored away over the years. I felt like I was rebuilding a relationship with a long-lost friend; and today I was ready to take that relationship to the next level with my first simulator ride.

As I stepped out of my room for the shower, my mind touched on another nuance of the situation here that had me puzzled. Ruth and I had spent nearly every waking hour together over the last week and I sensed that she was deliberately keeping a degree of distance between us. I understood and expected that from a commander-subordinate perspective, but there was something more calculated in her behavior. A part of me wondered if she was trying to defuse some kind of growing sexual tension between us. Of course, that could have totally been my imagination. Or even a by-product of the drugs that were coursing through my system.

I pondered this as I shed my robe and turned on the water. And that's when I heard the door open from the girl's hallway and saw Samantha walk in, her strawberry blonde head visible over the partitions. She could have chosen any of the other stalls, but she chose the one directly across from me. She walked into the stall, hung her bag with products on one of the hooks and turned so she was facing me. Then, she shed her robe slowly enough to be seductive but quickly enough that it wasn't an obvious striptease. Her strawberry blonde hair, normally tied up behind her head, was disheveled and fell to her shoulders enticingly. Her skin glistened sensually in the steamy mist.

My jaw dropped open and I discovered that I couldn't close it.

"I'm here to check on you," she said.

Oh my God, was her body fabulous! The proportions were perfect, and although her muscles were definitively cut, she had voluptuous curves in all the right places. Her large breasts jutted forth proudly, with just enough curve against her chest to prove they were real. My eyes traveled down her taut stomach and I could see faint bristles of reddish-blonde hair below. It was obvious that she kept that area completed shaved. I raised my eyes to meet hers, and she smirked playfully, her striking blue eyes dancing.

"I guess you like what you see," she said.

I looked down to find my penis looking back at me with an erection I would have been proud of in my twenties. I couldn't decide whether it was a product of the drugs or the sight of such a spectacular naked specimen of the female gender, and at the moment, I didn't care. I just returned my eyes to her and enjoyed the view.

Then she did the unthinkable. She crossed the aisle and entered my stall.

"I just want to check your muscle tone," she said seriously.

She pushed me under the water flow and got under it with me, grabbing my soap as she did so. She lathered up her hands and scrubbed my body. Replicating the pattern of the initial physical exam she gave me, she felt and kneaded all the muscles in my body as she washed them. She finished with my legs and feet after carefully avoiding the area immediately below my waist.

She stood up in front of me with her arms crossed and a look of professional satisfaction on her beautiful face. "Outstanding," she said at last, "we've made significant progress. I'd estimate that your body fat is down at least five or six percent. A long way to go yet, but a great start."

Her eyes traveled southward on my body again. "Damn nice angle for someone your age," she commented with a sly smile. Then as she turned to go back to her stall, she added, "you do need to get *ahold* of yourself at some point, or it's going to distract you."

Next, as I watched, she turned on her own water, got under it and began to slowly and sensually soap her body, allowing her hands to linger in some strategic places, never taking her eyes off me.

I was completely powerless. All I could do was look intently at her and gape. After a few minutes though, I did follow her advice. She smiled at me across the aisle and played along.

Later, we were both drying off and I was searching desperately for something to say to put the whole event into context.

She saved me the trouble.

"It's my job to continually assess your physical condition," she said matter-of-factly as she donned her robe. "How I choose to perform that assessment is my business." She winked at me. "By the way, if you think this little interlude is going to keep me from kicking your ass tomorrow, you're sadly mistaken."

"Never occurred to me it would," I sighed, slipping into my own robe. I got my arms into the sleeves, and as I began to pull it around me, she put her hands over mine and prevented me from closing it. She put her hands inside my robe and drew my body up against hers quickly. We looked into each other's eyes and the jolt we had felt on the floor of the hangar passed through us once more.

"Wow," she said. Trembling slightly, she released me and stepped back, diverting her eyes away. "I wondered about that."

Then, she gathered her products and towel and walked out of the shower, leaving me standing there. I had a quick flash of déjà vu that took me all the way back to California and Sarah Morton several years ago.

"Holy shit," I said to myself.

Later, I walked into the main briefing room and received a quizzical look from Ruth in the process. I tried my best to stay cool and nonchalant as I sat at the table and promptly rammed one of my knees into one of the table legs. I managed to stifle the string of obscenities which would typically shoot from my mouth and focused my attention on the inscrutable Major Shalev, who by this time had the barest trace of a smile on her face.

"I just spoke to Sammy and she told me that your conditioning training is coming along well and that your muscles are just *popping up* all over."

Raising my hands in admission, I said what I was sure she

expected to hear, "I'm a guy. It happens."

"If it didn't, we'd all be wondering about you," Ruth said, with a note of seriousness in her voice.

Was this some sort of test?

I looked at her intensely. She looked back at me with a satisfied look on her face.

It was a test. And you passed it. What the fuck does that mean?

"Anyway," Ruth continued, looking away suddenly, "in case you've forgotten, today is your first day in the sim."

The pilot part of me kicked in, and I noticed that the projector wasn't turned on, and Ruth didn't have her usual notebook in front of her. I further noticed that the material in front of me on the table was limited to the flight manual checklist and a regulation-issue kneeboard with a few checklist-sized, plasticized pages. These pages were a quick reference in the cockpit for the typical normal procedures: before engine start, engine start, post start, taxi, pre-takeoff, climbout, level-off, descent, before landing, post landing, and shutdown checklists. It was developed because the flight manual checklist was unwieldy for use in the cockpit unless there was an emergency. I examined the pages and grunted my satisfaction.

"Nice hooter," I said.

Ruth smiled. "We try."

The plasticized pages were called a 'hooterized' checklist in the Viper world. It's always been called that. No idea why.

She walked to the table and handed me instrument procedure charts or 'plates' as we call them. I grinned. They were all government-issued plates from Luke Air Force Base, my last assignment.

"I thought you'd be more comfortable starting with something you used to be familiar with," Ruth said. "We'll fly the Luke One Departure, to the Drake VORTAC, level-off at 15,000 feet. Then, we'll do a little area work: steep turns, some aerobatics, and some horn recovery maneuvers. Then we'll go direct to Lenni, the IAF for the Hi-Tacan to Runway 21 right, do a turn in holding, and fly the full penetration and approach. After that, we'll go missed approach and get vectors for the ILS for Runway 21 left and do that to a missed as well. We'll also do some flameout approaches and overhead patterns.

"That's it?" I asked.

"That depends on you," Ruth said calmly, looking right down at me and into my eyes for a change. "Today and tomorrow are devoted to the sim. As soon as you're comfortable and I'm satisfied you're proficient, we're done."

"Done with this phase?"

"No. Done in the simulator," she said. "Our sims are relatively basic, like the instrument sims you trained in at Luke. They've got all the switches and toys, but the motion and visuals are limited. They're good for reinforcing procedures and practicing emergencies, but not for much else. When you're done in the sim, we're going to put you where the rest of your training will take place - in the jet."

A tingle of anticipation shot through me and I stood up eagerly. "Let's get to it!"

I picked up the checklist, knee board, and approach plates, and motioned for her to precede me through the door. She looked at me quizzically.

"Are you just being polite or are you planning to check out my ass?"

She had preceded me through the door several times before today, but it had taken Samantha's debrief of our activities in the shower to break that ice between us.

That's interesting. I played along and snapped my fingers. "Damn it. You got me. And I thought I was being so tactical."

She shook her head and smiled. Then she preceded me out the door and I did indeed check out her ass as she exited the room. It was world class.

We walked past the operations desk, where there were again four sorties scheduled for today. Rug was sitting at the desk, and looked up at us as we walked by.

"Off to the sim already?" he asked. Ruth nodded.

"Cool! You're whipping through the program, FNG! We'll have you named in no time!"

"I hope so," I said.

Ruth looked over at him and caught my eye as she did so. "We'll see," she said.

The simulator room was just past the gym and through a pair of double doors. It was dark when we entered, and Ruth stopped just inside. Then the door closed, and we were enveloped in nearly total darkness. There was the click of a switch, and I heard a generator screech into life somewhere in the depths of the room. Huge lights came on overhead, and the room was bathed in illumination. It turned out that we were on a catwalk about fifteen feet above the main floor, and down below us were two simulators, two F-16 cockpits, each perched on top of its own network of hydraulic legs, hoses, and wires. Each cockpit was surrounded by a small bubble, about fifteen feet in diameter. They were lined up in a row, pointed directly at us, and slightly below us in elevation. In front of them and to our right was a platform that was an extension of the catwalk. I followed Ruth onto the platform, and she turned to her right and sat at a control console.

"On line," she said.

Instantly the control center lit up and I heard the unmistakable sound of several hard drives beginning the boot process for several computers.

"On line, ready," a toneless female voice responded a few moments later.

"Wow," I said. "You obviously don't have Bill Gates running this place; that was entirely too fast."

"Nope," she said, "Cray XT-5; it runs Linux. Much better, much faster."

"Well if you have a Cray to run the sims, why can't they do more for you?"

"The software is too hard to get," she said flatly. "Just getting the stuff to practice transition, instrument, and basic tactical work was a chore. We had to pay a lot of underpaid sim technicians at Luke a lot of money to part with that, and it was nearly all unclassified. We couldn't get any of the more complicated stuff without raising the visibility to unacceptable levels. It doesn't hurt us that much. The physical stress of flying the jet is an important element of the training process, and you just can't get that in a simulator."

"I see."

"Simulator Two, prepare ingress."

I heard the whine of machinery behind me and turned around. The simulator on the right had ejected its cockpit module on a set of rails from the bubble surrounding it. A catwalk had also been raised from the floor, providing a path from the platform to the cockpit module.

Ruth motioned toward the catwalk. "Well, go get reacquainted. Take as much time as you want. When you're strapped in and ready, make sure the battery switch is on and say 'ready for ingress' into the mic, and the cockpit will slide forward into the bubble which contains the visual array. Oh," she said, "hang on a minute." She reached into a storage slot just above the computer console and retrieved a data transfer cartridge labeled 'LUKE TR' and handed it to me. "You'll need this."

I nodded and took the DTC, then walked toward the cockpit, checklist and kneeboard in hand. I knew it was just a simulator, but I had to sit down on the canopy rail for a second and gaze inside. The Viper cockpit looked just the way I remembered it, and the years since my last flight went past in a flicker. I checked the throttle locked into the off detent and inserted the DTC into its slot on the right console. Then I placed my checklist on one of the side panels of the cockpit and prepared to get into the seat. There's only one way to do this correctly and it's an awkward process. I placed my hands on the canopy rails, eased my feet onto the rudder panels and slid into the seat slowly. When my butt found the seat cushion, I settled into the cockpit like I had never left it. Suppressing the lump which had just popped into my throat, I secured the seat belt, strapped the kneeboard on my right knee, put on my headset, and turned on the main battery switch. The cockpit lit up immediately.

"Ready for ingress," I said.

Instantly, the cockpit module began to slide forward, and in just a few seconds, I was inside the visual array. A few more seconds passed before a computerized depiction of the ramp at Luke Air Force Base came up in the displays.

There was a moment of epiphany - a moment when I realized I was returning to what I was always meant to do. Then it was time to go to work.

I tested the fire and overheat lights, then the malfunction and indicator lights, and then moved the Jet Fuel Starter Switch to START2. The JFS is a small turbine engine in the Viper's fuselage. Its only function is to provide starting airflow to the engine. The JFS started as expected and the engine RPM gauge increased. At the appropriate RPM percentage, I engaged the throttle release and moved the throttle out of the off position. The simulator software faithfully reproduced the General Electric engine start sequence and the RPM moved up slowly while the Exhaust Gas Temperature, or EGT, immediately rose. My hands had a mind of their own and they knew what to do. In moments, I had the after start flow and checks completed, including transferring the mission data from the DTC to the aircraft systems. Soon after, I had the sim airborne and was flying the maneuvers and instrument approaches Ruth and I had discussed in the briefing room. With my F-16 switchology coming back rapidly, the rush of returning to the cockpit of the Viper was quickly forgotten as

I made the transition into 'simulator mode.'

Every pilot who has spent a lot of time in commercial aviation has a simulator mode, although they may not call it that. After receiving a type rating in a business jet or commercial airliner, crews must attend recurrent training annually, and this means about a week in the books and in a FAA-certified Level C or Level D simulator. Captains who fly for the airlines or charter companies are in the simulator at least once every six months. As a contractor, I maintained currency in two aircraft on an annual basis, so I trained every six months as well.

So, as I had done so many times before, I became part of the machine I was flying.

##

Apart from a quick break for lunch, Ruth and I stayed in the sim for six hours, and when it was over, we had covered every normal procedure and most of the emergency ones. When we quit for the night and the cockpit slid back on the rails, I exited the simulator and walked back to the platform.

"May I leave this stuff on the console here?" I asked Ruth as I placed the checklist, kneeboard, and DTC on the counter next to the control panel. "I figured we'd just be coming back here tomorrow."

She was just sitting there, staring at me, almost like she was seeing me for the first time.

I looked down at her. "It wasn't that bad, was it?"

She shook her head slowly and looked up at me with an expression on her face that was a cross between disbelief and perplexity. "Not at all," she said finally.

"I'm fortunate," I said, watching her closely as I spoke, "that I was well-taught."

She nodded absently like she had known that all along.

"System shut down," she said in flat voice. The hard drives

and consoles began the shutdown process. She rose from her chair and looked at me expressionlessly. "Good work today, FNG. We'll finish up tomorrow."

She motioned toward the door and I preceded her through it. She killed the power as we exited, then turned to me after the door had shut behind us.

"1000 tomorrow, right here. We'll skip the briefing." She turned and walked toward the operations desk in a businesslike stride.

Rug was sitting at the ops desk as she walked by and I saw him look up at her.

"Grade?" he asked.

She held up four fingers and went by him.

"Four?" he asked incredulously, "he got a four? No one gets a four." Then he looked down the hall at me as I walked in his direction.

"Four, FNG? How'd you muster a four?"

I shrugged and gave him the standard answer that any fighter pilot would give when confronted with the fact that he had been given an impossibly high grade on an evaluated event.

"I give good head," I said.

CHAPTER ELEVEN

Contract Day Twelve
Tuesday, 22 September
0600 Hours Local Time
Island Training Base

True to her word, Samantha kicked my ass in the gym the next day, but it was decidedly different from what I expected.

After the usual tire tossing was over, she led me to the free weight area and stood facing me with her hands on her perfectly-proportioned hips. “This is where it counts. We’ve laid a good foundation with the full body conditioning we’ve done, but it’s time to change gears. Today is strength assessment day. We’re going to determine your one rep max for a few exercises, give you a day off, and then switch your program to a mass and strength gaining one. We’ll be splitting the workouts, doing different body parts on alternate days so we’ll be increasing the frequency and volume of your weight workouts. By the time my month with you is over, you won’t recognize yourself.”

She motioned toward the flat bench. “First things first, FNG. The good old bench press. Give me twenty-five push-ups to warm up.”

I dropped obediently and cranked out a quick twenty-five push-ups. When I rose from the floor, she had an Olympic bar loaded on the bench and one forty-five-pound plate on each side. She stood there resting her elbows on the bar and looked at me with that familiar smirk on her face.

"You remember that conversation you and I had about 'urges' your first day here? After yesterday, I *know* the stuff we're giving you is working. And at some point, you're going to need to deal with the accompanying urges with a woman instead of your right hand. I can make that happen. "But for you to get there, you're going to need to crank out at least one rep with three plates on each side in the bench press, squat, and dead-lift, and do a lat pull with that same amount of weight. That's three hundred fifteen pounds. Personally, I don't think you can get that far in three weeks, but the power of sex is difficult to predict, so we'll see what happens. lie down."

I shrugged and assumed the position on the bench.

"I'll keep loading the plates. I want one, clean rep. Use good breathing technique and good form. Don't cheat the weight up, but do explode to get it to the finishing position. Got it?"

I nodded. "Give it a go."

I lifted the bar off the supports and gave her one clean rep at one hundred thirty-five pounds.

She loaded a twenty-five-pound plate on each side and stepped back again. The bar was at one hundred eighty-five pounds now.

"Do it," she said.

The bar went up and down cleanly again.

"Awesome." She pulled off the twenty-five-pound plates and replaced them with forty-five pound ones. The bar was now at two hundred twenty-five.

"You're on," she said.

I lowered the bar to my chest, pushed it to the top and re-racked it. My pecs and triceps were beginning to talk to me. She put a ten-pound plate on each side. Two hundred forty-five pounds. I lowered the weight again and pushed it back up. I still had something left when I re-racked it, but I could tell we were reaching my limits.

The ten-pound plates came off and the twenty-fives went back on. Two hundred seventy-five pounds. Although I had done more than this in the past, two hundred seventy-five was the most I had ever consistently worked out with. I exhaled forcibly a few times and grasped the bar, making sure each of my index fingers were on top of the small ring of smooth metal on the bar which ensured that my grip was evenly placed. I un-racked the bar and lowered it to my chest.

And it stopped there. I couldn't move it.

Instantly, Samantha's mouth was next to my ear. "You're never going to get any pussy like this, TC," she said in a sensual whisper. "At this rate, it's going to be you and your right hand for the duration."

I don't know whether it was the taunting or raw adrenaline, but suddenly my pecs contracted and the bar began to move up. I closed my eyes and mentally willed it to rise as I pushed with everything I had, blowing the air out of my lungs forcibly.

A few seconds or a few lifetimes later, the bar reached its full travel and I re-racked it.

"Not bad," Samantha said, her businesslike persona back in place. "No question about what motivates you."

The next exercise was the lat pull, and I managed to get two hundred forty pounds down. Samantha nodded her satisfaction.

After that, we did the squat, and after having my technique corrected twice, I could get two hundred ninety-five pounds done there. Squats were the exercise I had been most religious about when I flew the Viper. It was the best single exercise for 'g' tolerance and I had been a 'g-machine.'

"Don't think we'll have much of an issue on that," she said. Finally, we got to the deadlift, an exercise I have always hated. We loaded the bar with 135 pounds and she noticed the obvious look of consternation on my face.

"Your problem is that you're afraid of it," she said. "That's the issue most people have with the deadlift. Doing a deadlift is sort of like breaking a board in a karate class. You have to know you can do it before you try it and mix outstanding technique with overwhelming confidence. Watch me."

She stood behind the bar and exhaled. Then she bent her knees and began to squat while reaching for the bar with her hands. Once her thighs were parallel with the ground and her arms were outside her knees, she straightened her back and focused her eyes straight ahead. Then she inhaled and stood straight up, exhaling as she did so.

I saw the muscles of her legs twitch ever so slightly, just as they had when she had climaxed in the shower yesterday. My mind started to go in a direction it shouldn't have and I reeled it in quickly.

She lowered the weight gracefully and stepped back from the bar. "Your turn."

I walked over and stood behind the bar. Then I squatted and tried to assume a ready position similar to the one she had shown me. In spite of my newfound flexibility, I just couldn't get there.

"Your stiffness here isn't helping us." Samantha squatted next to me and attempted to move my body into a posture that was more mechanically advantageous. She put one hand above my ass and pushed my butt down so my thighs were parallel to the floor while pushing my chest a little so my back remained straight. Then she stood up and went to stand in front of me.

"Look right into my eyes, FNG, and don't take your eyes away from them. Think about pushing your upper body weight into your quads. Now, STAND!"

I did as she instructed me and stood up with the weight. "Wow," I said, "that was easy."

"Well it wasn't a lot of weight, but at least your technique was good. Put it back down and let's try something heavier."

I lowered it and she put twenty-five pound plates on each side.

"Try it again and keep your bloody back straight and your eyes straight ahead."

I assumed the position, made sure my back was straight, and forced the weight into my quadriceps again. The bar came up, not as easily as before, but it came up.

"Good job," Samantha grumbled. "Put it down and let's make it heavier."

I topped out at two hundred twenty-five pounds a few moments later.

"We've got a lot of work to do there, FNG. Help me put these weights up, and then you can hit the shower."

"We're done already?"

"You've done enough, trust me. Your body will start screaming at you in a few minutes. You need to spend about fifteen minutes in the stream room before you hit the shower because if you don't, you'll tighten up like crazy. It's the last door on your left as you walk through the girls' hallway. By the way, no clothes in there; your pores need to breathe and muscles need to be unrestricted."

"Yes, ma'am," I answered as I placed the last plate on the rack.

"Now get out of here so I can get some stuff done."

I went back to my room, stripped off, and put on my robe. Then I made my way down the girls' hallway and found a plain wooden door marked 'Steam room.' I opened it and entered a vestibule area about ten feet square. The transition from the hallway was surprising. Where the hallway had been the standard white drywall, the vestibule was done all in teak, with brass colored hooks mounted at eye level all the way around the three walls of the square to the left of me and a shelving unit loaded with clean towels, next to a bin for the dirty ones. I doffed my robe and hung it on the hook nearest the door, grabbed a clean towel, and went through the opposing door. A wall of steam hit me and it took a moment or two for my eyes to adjust. The room was U-shaped, like most steam rooms I had been in, with tiled walls and teak floorboards. The seating was conventional wooden bleacher style, also in teak, with a lower tier at normal seating height and an upper tier about the height of my chest. Both the lower and upper tiers went all the way around the room, following the U-shape, and both had wood facings extending from the edge of the seat to the next level or floor so nothing could slide underneath. The walls were about twenty feet apart and I couldn't see the back wall yet, but I assumed it was approximately the same distance from the door if not a little farther.

I climbed to the upper level on the left side of the room, spread my towel and lay down on my back, just as the first wave of muscle ache hit me. It started in my lower back and soon spread to my thighs, back, and pecs. I was grateful that Samantha had insisted I come in here. Just as the ache hit me, I could feel the heat fighting it, loosening my muscles, increasing the blood flow, and allowing my body to relax. Involuntarily, I moaned in appreciation as I let my eyes close.

I dozed for a while and dreamt I was back at King Khalid Military City in Saudi Arabia - KKMC to the uninitiated. It was late in the summer of 1990, and I was lying on a cot in a government-issued tent while the government-provided air conditioning fought a losing battle against the 120-degree desert heat outside.

Later, I don't know how much later, I decided to roll onto my stomach. As I did, I lazily opened my eyes. The steam had cleared slightly and I noticed that I was near the end of the U. As my eyes fell to the lower ledge, I realized I wasn't alone.

Ruth was there. She too was lying on her stomach but on the lower level at the end of the U, her head turned away from me. I had no idea when she had entered the room. She could have come in while I was dozing or she could have been there all along.

She had the body of a professional athlete, with sculpted, strong legs and a perfectly-shaped ass. Her back was muscular without being unfeminine and had a definite V-shape to it. She had her arms crossed under her head and I could see the cut of the triceps of her left arm. She was either blessed genetically or she was every bit as maniacal about spending time in the gym as Samantha was. Or maybe it was both.

And then the steam cleared a little more and I saw the scars.

Her back was crisscrossed with streaks of scarlet tissue and it was apparent they had been there a long, long time.

Some of the streaks were about the thickness of a string and hardly visible and others were thicker and angry red. Pits appeared in her flesh here and there along the lines of crimson.

She had been whipped. Savagely. Multiple times. And with an instrument that had something embedded in the cords to dig into her flesh.

Jesus, I thought. *And you have the gall to think you've had it rough, Pearce.*

She turned her head, opened her eyes and caught me staring at her. My mouth must have been agape and I'm sure the expression on my face was not a comforting one because she immediately stood up and wrapped her towel around her. Before I could utter a word, she was gone.

"Brilliant, Pearce," I muttered. "Fucking brilliant."

##

At 1000 hours, I returned to the simulator room and found no one outside the door. Curiously, I opened it and saw that the room was alive with light. I could hear the computer up and running.

I walked down the catwalk to the platform and found

Ruth sitting at the console with her back to me, filling out a grade sheet for yesterday's simulator ride. The format looked remarkably familiar and I could tell it had been copied, nearly field for field, from the grade sheets we used to use at Luke Air Force Base in the F-16 syllabi there. Each mission element had a line with a matrix next to it to grade the event U, for unsafe, and then 0, 1, 2, 3, or 4. Two was satisfactory. Three was above average and four was well above average, a grade that no one ever got. Except me.

This grade sheet showed all 4s, in every mission event and overall, for my first sim ride. I had rendered a perfect performance. I should have felt proud.

"Get in," she said in a flat voice, "I want to get you finished today."

So, in I went. I transitioned to simulator mode once more and performed brilliantly. We started with a little standard instrument and visual pattern work. Then we hit the emergencies hard. We did rejected takeoffs, engine failures after gear retraction, system failures, and flameout landings. She threw everything in the book at me and even attempted to hit me with multiple malfunctions. But the combination of my reawakened knowledge of the jet and my proficiency in simulators made me invincible. And when the cockpit slid back on the rails out of the visual array, I knew that the battle was over.

I exited the cockpit and walked up to her. She didn't look at me.

She was writing a new grade sheet, and this one too had all fours on it.

"How did it happen?" The words popped out of my mouth before I knew what I was saying and I almost clamped my fingers across my lips to keep anything else from leaking out.

"I grew up in a kibbutz on the West Bank of the Jordan," she said flatly, still looking at the grade sheet. "When I was thirteen, we were overrun by a group of Palestinian militants.

I think they were Hamas. I happened to be sunbathing in our backyard at the time in a bikini which, according to Muslim men, made me a slut. They dragged me to the village square, tied me to a post there, and whipped me. My father tried to stop them and he was shot. My mother tried to stop them, and they tied her up and beat her as well. They didn't stop with her until she died from it." She paused for a moment and then added, "You're not the first person to see the scars and be repulsed."

Her words hung in the air for a few seconds.

"I don't know what to say, Major," I said at last. "I can certainly see why you ended up in a uniform."

She nodded. "I'll pass the grade sheet to Rug," she said, still not looking at me. "Check the schedule after it's posted this afternoon. You'll have your first transition ride tomorrow."

I was obviously dismissed.

I turned to go, and then turned back to her. "I'm going to say this and it's not going to sound right because it just won't. I apologize for reacting the way I did... earlier. Samantha gave me orders to hit the steam room, so being there wasn't my idea. When I saw you in there and saw your back, a lot of things went through my head, but repulsion wasn't one of them. It's just that..." I silently cursed my lack of vocabulary. Spending your life flying jets does not build a huge repository of glib and flowery phrases for times like this. "It's rare to see the cost of what someone has sacrificed to become who they are. I happen to think it's impressive." I paused for a moment. "I'm going to find Brianna. I want to see that photo of the guy I replaced. I'll catch up with you later."

I left the simulator room and walked down the hall towards the ops desk. I could see Rug behind the desk, looking over some paperwork in front of him. Brinker and VB were decked out in full flying gear, standing there waiting for a 'step brief,' typically the last few words a squadron supervisor has with a fighter pilot before the pilot steps out the door to fly.

"Weather's great, no ceiling, visibility unlimited, about what you'd expect on an island in the middle of frickin' nowhere. We're on runway 18, all the navaids are up, the telemetry receivers are up, and the wind is right down the runway. Give me a shout before you take the runway and I'll let you know if there's any bogey traffic in the vicinity. Your tail numbers are as posted on the board. Questions?"

VB and Brinker shook their heads simultaneously while they copied their tail numbers on the line-up cards they had on the desk in front of them. Line-up cards are preprinted forms with blanks on them for the flight callsign, check-in, taxi, take-off, and landing times, as well as a host of other mission-related data - especially the engine and take-off data - that you're supposed to check when you take the runway and 'line-up,' hence the name.

VB smiled at me as I approached and Brinker ignored me. Then the two of them went down the hallway past the bar and out the door into the hangar. Rug nodded as I stopped in front of the desk.

"Done in the sim?"

"Yep," I said, "and I'm ready to get some air under my ass."

"Well, it'll be you and me tomorrow for TR-One and possibly TR-Two. We'll take the two jets in the early go because you don't have any PT tomorrow, and depending on how well you do, we might double turn you tomorrow. Plan on an 0800 brief."

"Sounds good to me. What do you need me to get? The TOLD, weather, and NOTAMs?"

Rug shook his head. "No FNG, this isn't the RTU. Just show up. I'll take care of the rest of the stuff."

"Cool." Usually the upgrading pilot in a transition sortie was responsible for getting the Takeoff and Landing Data, or TOLD; the weather briefing; and the Notices to Airmen, or NOTAMs, that affected the field and local area. Rug was letting me off easy.

"Check the board at about 1700 hours. The schedule should be posted by then."

"Roger that," I said.

I left the ops desk and walked down the hallway past the bar and past the door where VB and Brinker had entered the hangar. Then I walked further down and found the admin office. Brianna Blenhem had her back to me and was working diligently on her computer as I approached. I could see Ruth had made it back into her office on the other side of the room.

When I stopped in front of Brianna's desk, she must have seen my reflection in her screen and been surprised, because she jumped slightly and spun around in her chair quickly. As she turned, she looked up at me, then down at my crotch, then back to my face. Her eyes moved so quickly that if I hadn't been staring directly at her face, I would have missed it. She caught me looking at her and blushed slightly. I blushed in return, suddenly and awkwardly, realizing that Samantha had spread the word about our 'interlude' in the shower yesterday.

"Hello, Colonel Pearce. What can I do for you?"

"I'm not FNG to you? Like everyone else?"

She eyed me as if gauging my thoughts on the issue, and then evidently decided she didn't care. "I think the whole nickname thing is a little childish," she said with the slightest touch of defiance.

"Well, I've never been a huge fan it myself."

Now her expression changed to one of suspicion. "You mean you don't like being called TC? I'd think it'd make you feel important or something like that."

I shook my head. "I've always hated the nickname thing. If a nickname follows a pilot throughout his career and people discover it before he gets somewhere, then they make assumptions about him before they ever meet him. And they think they know him before he has a chance to introduce himself. Kind of sucks, huh?"

She looked at me with a slight tinge of red on her cheeks.

I had embarrassed her again.

"Colonel Pearce, listen, I'm—"

"Brianna, I haven't been Colonel anything in about seven years, and if you were about to apologize, don't bother. When you carry the baggage around that I do, you have thick skin."

She nodded at me, grateful that I'd let her off the hook.

"What would you like me to call you?" she asked, obviously relieved she could change the subject.

"Colin would be fine."

"What can I help you with...Colin?"

"Much better. I'm here to see the file of the guy I replaced. Major Shalev said she'd authorized you to show it to me."

Brianna nodded. "I've been keeping it here for you. I expected you to come for it some time ago."

"Sorry about that," I said. "Dr. Samantha and Major Shalev haven't allowed me any spare time before today."

Brianna's face lit up in an impish grin. "I've heard they have been keeping you busy."

"You have no idea. Or maybe you do. Nothing's a secret around here."

"That's the truth," she said as she opened one of her desk drawers, removed a brown multi-section file, and handed it to me. "Here you go."

I reached for it, and as I grasped it, Brianna didn't release it. I looked down at her questioningly, and she looked right back at me. Her eyes flicked to the left quickly and then widened slightly.

She was warning me.

I don't know what I was anticipating, but when I opened the file and stared down at the photograph inside the front cover, I suddenly had a sinking feeling, like the floor beneath me had vanished and I was falling several miles to earth.

It was Burt Magnusson's picture. And the implications of that hit me as I looked at his face staring back at me. I struggled to maintain my composure as I skimmed the paperwork dutifully and attempted to focus on what I was reading. It was his résumé, his statistics, and his flight records. Only the name had been changed.

"Did you know him after all?" Ruth's voice said from behind me. She was trying to sound cordial but there was an underlying edge to her voice that was barely perceptible.

My guts clenched and my blood boiled, instantaneously and simultaneously. This was another fucking test, and it was rudely smacking me in the face with the tragedy of Burt's disappearance. It took every ounce of self-control I possessed to keep my face impassive and my thoughts rational.

How much had he told them about me?

How much did they know?

How in the hell was I supposed to play this?

I turned to Ruth and attempted to keep my voice level and nonchalant. "He looks like a guy I knew once," I said as I slowly closed the file. "But it was a long time ago and the name doesn't match. I guess it isn't who I thought it was." I watched her closely.

She nodded thoughtfully and gave no indication that my words were unexpected or unwelcome. "Too bad," she said. And she returned to her office.

I turned back to Brianna and handed her the file as casually as I could, trying not to allow my hands to shake from the adrenaline racing through my veins. She looked up at me as she took the file and then she did something that was completely unexpected. She whispered to me. So quietly I barely heard her. "You passed," she said.

TOP SECRET / SPECIAL
COMPARTMENTALIZED INFORMATION
CLASSIFIED BY: US Central Intelligence Agency
DECLASSIFY ON: OADR

From: Special Projects Group [NCS]
Sent: Tuesday, 22 September 2009, 0727 EDT (22 September 2009, 1127Z)
To: Director, NCS
Cc: Special Projects Group [NCS]

SUBJECT: Update, Case File: 08-434A (MAG)

(TS) Narrative:

1. (TS) Contractor 09-017 (Pearce, Colin M) completed simulator training today. He begins flight training tomorrow.

2. (TS) Pearce was presented with information indicating MAG probably doesn't know the full extent of his relationship with Informant 08-257 (Magnusson, Burton L., MIA as of late August). As we anticipated, odds are high MAG is not aware Pearce knows of Magnusson's disappearance.

3. (TS) All-source chatter concerning major strike has increased. DI analysts believe sources are being told the strike plan is back on schedule. No word yet on exact dates.

4. (TS) Cross-Directorate Special Projects meeting produced only one viable alternative to flush MAG from hiding and ascertain their position prior to the major strike. That option will be briefed separately and will require approval at the DCIA level to be executed.

(TS) CONCLUSION: Pearce's whereabouts remain unknown but he appears to be operating freely inside of MAG. Once flight training begins, the pressure to get him mission ready inside of MAG will increase. Correspondingly, the pressure for CIA to take action to ascertain MAG's location will also increase.

(TS) ACTION: We are attempting to schedule time on your calendar to present the proposed project briefing. However, due to budgeting meetings and congressional hearings, your schedule is booked through the end of the week.

(TS) RECOMMENDATION: Strongly recommend you clear your calendar for one hour tomorrow AM for project briefing.

TOP SECRET / SPECIAL
COMPARTMENTALIZED INFORMATION
CLASSIFIED BY: US Central Intelligence Agency
DECLASSIFY ON: OADR

CHAPTER TWELVE

Contract Day Thirteen
Wednesday, 23 September
0700 Hours Local Time
Island Training Base

I didn't need the alarm clock to rouse me this morning. I'd spent the night awake as questions careened about inside my head like bumper cars on steroids. I couldn't recall exactly what the questions were. I just remember the words 'fucking idiot' figured prominently in all of them.

I was in so far over my head that I couldn't even *see* the surface of the water above me. I wondered how much longer I would last before I blew my cover or, worse yet, exploded into a fit of rage and tried to kill someone. The bloodlust was racing through me, eager to be fed. Containing it was becoming a full-time job.

I took a quick shower, and after throwing my flightsuit on and running a comb through my hair, I grabbed my 'breakfast' and drugs at the dining hall and was doing my best to be mentally present when Rug began his flight briefing for the first transition ride, TR-1, at 0800.

"Three, two, one hack," he said, starting the briefing with the sacred rite of the time hack, making sure our watches were synced to the second. For military pilots, there is no time window. Eight o'clock is *exactly* eight o'clock, as indicated by the master clocks of the world in Greenwich, England, and Boulder, Colorado, although for today's flight, we were using local 'Island Time.'

Rug looked up from his watch and gazed at me quizzically. "Are we all here, FNG?"

"Uh, yeah, sorry."

"No problem, I just thought I had lost you for a minute."

"Nope," I lied, "I'm good to go."

"All righty then," Rug began. "Welcome to TR-One, your first ride in our syllabus. Like what you've seen so far, it's completely performance-based. When you reach proficiency in a given area, you proceed to the next level. We're hoping that you reach proficiency in each level very quickly, but no pressure." He smiled crookedly at me.

He turned a few pages in the notebook he had in front of him, and then spun it on the table so it was right-side-up from my perspective. The areas in the syllabus were standard. It started with Transition, or TR, which we were doing today. Next was basic fighter maneuvers (BFM), one versus one air-to-air combat, then air combat maneuvering (ACM) or two versus one combat. After that was intercept training, which stresses radar mechanics and intercept geometry. The air-to-air training culminated in air combat training, or ACT, which is about as complex as it gets.

After the air-to-air training was complete, the syllabus went to surface attack (SA) which involved dropping ordnance, usually twenty-five-pound practice bombs, as single ships on a conventional scored range, and we finished with surface attack tactical (SAT), which had us dropping bombs using formation tactics against tactical targets. I could feel the excitement brewing in me and the compartmentalization gears inside my head began clanging doors shut so I could focus on today's flights.

"Okay," Rug began, "before we get into the briefing stuff,

we need to talk to the security issues about our operating location and facility. As you already know, we're on an island, and with the exception of the Boss and Mister Phillips, no one knows exactly where it is. Because you're a target-arm, you'll go through the biases in the inertial nav system and you'll figure out that it's somewhere in the Southern Hemisphere. We're also somewhere temperate because it never really gets cold here. That puts us within about twenty to thirty degrees of the equator. But here's the kicker: for flights around here, we use military grid reference system coordinates for everything and the longitude and latitude displays are inhibited. All the data in the jet will display normally, but the actual grid coordinates you'll see will be meaningless because you won't know either the name or the lat long for the origin coordinates of the grid zone designator."

My eyes suddenly grew wide. "Holy shit!" I said. "That's fucking brilliant."

"It gets better," Rug continued. "Unlike most Block 30s, our jets have GPS units built into them, but they won't work here. There's a GPS jammer on the top of the mountain."

I felt a cold chill creep down my spine. I had taken for granted that Smith and Amrine knew where I was.

Holy shit, I thought. *What if they don't!*

"We also get a downlink of real-time surveillance satellite orbits and locations and we schedule around when those satellites will be overhead. Finally, we have a radar controller who monitors the airspace to ensure no traffic is in the area when we fly."

"Wait a minute," I interrupted, "you have a radar site here? Does he do any GCI stuff for ACT?" GCI is ground controlled intercept.

"Well, he can do that for us, too," Rug said, "but what he mainly does is monitor the acquisition radar and provide aircraft control under instrument conditions. The runway is oriented north-south and is 10,000 feet long, with arresting gear at the approach and departure ends. The arresting cables are always in the retracted position, so you'll have to call for them if you need them. We have an ILS/DME unit installed at each end of the runway for precision approaches. If the ILS goes out, we have pre-programmed RNAV/GPS approaches loaded into the nav system. We also have an aircraft fire truck and a crew on duty in the truck whenever flight operations are in progress. Our working airspace is directly over the island. We'll talk about our conventional range facilities when we reach that portion of the syllabus. Any questions so far?"

I had none.

Rug's briefing was generic and very similar to briefings I had given when I instructed in the F-16 Pilot Requalification Course back at Luke AFB long ago. He covered the 'motherhood' items first: the procedures for checking in on the radio, starting the jets, taxi, take-off, travel to and from the working area, return to the base, pattern work, landing, and taxi back, as well as how we would handle emergencies. Much of this was simplified since the airspace was directly overhead and that there were no controlling agencies to contact.

Then he went into the specifics of the maneuvers we'd perform: basic and advanced handling maneuvers straight out of the TR syllabus. Finally, he talked through the instrument and visual approach procedures.

I sat there and absorbed the briefing, nodding my head when appropriate. I kept my face impassive but my mind was reeling over some of the information he had so casually mentioned. When a company could buy Cray computers to equip its simulators, that should have impressed me enough. But buying an island and building a facility into it with a runway, navigation aids, and radar was beyond impressive. It was scary.

"So," Rug said at last, "that concludes the briefing. Do you have any questions?"

I shook my head. I didn't hear much of what he said, but

considering I used to teach this stuff, I was confident I could perform to his satisfaction.

"Cool. Now to reiterate, here's the deal." He leaned forward across the table. "For the first sortie, we'll make the take-off in MIL power and do a normal climb, straight ahead at 350 knots up to 15,000 feet MSL. Then we'll do the maneuvers. We'll take everything very deliberate and slow. Assuming everything goes well, we'll cut loose on the second sortie."

I nodded. "Sounds good."

"Go get suited up and meet me at the ops desk in ten."

"Roger that."

I went to my bathroom to take care of the preflight ritual that every fighter pilot does, then continued to the life support room. I found the locker with my name on it and opened it, noting it was the standard full-length locker I had seen in the USAF: about my height, a foot wide, and eighteen inches deep.

And there they were: all the accoutrements of the profession I had left so long ago. On the top shelf of the locker was my helmet, with the cloth visor cover in place and the oxygen hose tucked neatly under the chin strap. Hanging inside the locker, below the helmet, was my parachute harness with the life preserver built into it, my anti-g suit, and survival vest.

I don't remember mentally willing it, but my hands reached out for the anti-g suit and began to work by themselves. Although it had been nearly seven years since I had donned this equipment, there was no hesitation in the movements of my hands or awkwardness in my fingers and in a few minutes, all the gear was out of the locker and on my body. I put the helmet into the bag provided and put my checklist and kneeboard into the pockets on the side of the bag. Then, as I turned to walk out the room, I glimpsed myself in the full-length mirror next to the exit.

What I saw there was quite odd. It was the reflection of what I looked like long ago, yet it was the reflection of who I was today. It was me without all the shit I had piled on physically and psychologically over the years.

The guy in the mirror stared back at me. He was cool, confident, and ready to strap on a jet and take it into the heavens. The face was a bit more full and the hair had more gray, but that aside, he could have been the same guy stepping out to do the same thing 10 years ago. I smiled for the first time in a long while. I was ready to go kick some ass.

I walked to the ops desk and met Rug there. Ruth was behind the desk with her back to us, speaking to someone on the phone.

"Okay, roger that," she said, "by the time they're started and ready to taxi, it should be clear. I'll have them call me before taxi just to make sure." She hung up and turned around. "Are you two ready?" she asked.

Rug and I nodded.

"The winds are favoring runway 18. The navaids are all up and operational. The airspace will be free of air traffic in about thirty-five minutes.

There's a twin-engine turboprop aircraft south of us, heading south, and it should be clear by the time you taxi, but call me on Net One before you taxi clear of the awning. The next satellite over-flight will be in..." she looked down at a screen in front of her, "about ninety minutes, so make sure you're on the ground from the first sortie by then."

She looked at both of us to make sure we had understood her. Rug nodded again, and I did the same.

"Okay, your tail numbers are 406 and 805. Both of these jets just came out of a fifty-hour inspection, so make sure your preflight is a good one."

We wrote our tail numbers on our line-up cards, and then walked down the hall and into the hangar. Six of the eight jets were parked in there, some of them sealed up, others in various states of repair. I looked quizzically over at Rug as we walked. He pointed in front of us, anticipating my question.

"You may not remember this from your arrival, but this

hangar is actually built into the side of a mountain, the mountain I mentioned in my briefing. At the entrance is a camouflaged overhang so we can pull the jets out of the main hangar and yet keep them out of sight until we're ready to fly them. You'll see in a minute."

We reached the front of the hangar where the main doors had been left open just wide enough for us to walk through. I came out under what can best be described as a large awning. It was at least one hundred feet above my head and open in three directions. I vaguely remembered it from when I had arrived. I didn't appreciate it then, but I did now. I wasn't an architectural engineer, but I wondered how the weight of it was supported.

After nearly ten days of life indoors, my eyes squinted in the bright sunlight. My nostrils greedily took in the fresh smell of the sea air and my skin enjoyed the sensation of the gentle ocean breeze. The temperature was warm, but not uncomfortable, and it reminded me of the climate on the islands in the Caribbean.

And in front of me were the two jets, canopies open, ladders attached, just waiting for us to take them skyward. I shivered with anticipation.

"See you on the radio," Rug said, veering off to take the jet on the right.

I walked straight ahead and approached the jet on the left. As I walked around the wing, I looked up at the vertical stabilizer reflexively to check that I had the right tail number and saw AF88-406 neatly painted there in dark gray.

Nice, I thought.

By maintaining the original US paint job and numbering scheme, they ensured that a degree of confusion would ensue if the jets were ever seen.

I walked up to the ladder and was met by the crew chief for the jet. He appeared to be in his mid-thirties, blonde, and he had the look of someone who had been doing this job for a while. He saluted me, took my helmet bag, handed me the maintenance log for the airplane, and went up the ladder to stow my stuff in the cockpit.

I opened the maintenance log and found paperwork that looked much like the USAF forms I had used in a previous life. I quickly looked over the status page and checked the logs themselves for any open write-ups. There were none.

I put the book on the ground at the base of the ladder and began my walk-around, using the flashlight which the crew chief had left for that purpose. I looked in the wheel wells, behind each access door, and felt the probes and panels I was supposed to, then returned to the base of the ladder. With an increasing sense of excitement, I handed the chief his flashlight, buckled the leg straps on my parachute harness, and slowly went up the ladder to the cockpit.

As I reached the top of the ladder, I leaned over the edge of the railing to ensure that the safety pins for the ejection seat and canopy were installed. The crew chief had placed my kneeboard and hooterized checklist on the right-side panel, and my helmet bag was neatly rolled up and stowed on the aft portion of the right-side panel, just on top of where the data transfer cartridge loader was installed. He had inserted the DTC for me. Everything was in its place. I assumed the position and slid into the cockpit.

Immediately, the crew chief was up the ladder to help me strap in. First, he snapped the left survival kit strap to the left side strap of my harness while I did the right one. The survival kit was embedded in the seat and would stay with me if I ejected. Next, he inserted my g-suit hose into the jet's fastening as I buckled my seat belt. Finally, he handed me the shoulder fittings for my parachute harness over each shoulder, and I snapped them into place. These fittings attached the parachute, installed in the seat-back, to the harness I was wearing, so the parachute would remain attached to me if I had to eject. He offered me a quick thumbs-up, which I returned. Then he was down the ladder, and a second later, the ladder was removed.

I donned a cloth skull cap, then my helmet, buckling the chin strap and attaching the fitting for the oxygen mask hose to my harness. I looked down on the right-side panel to make sure the oxygen supply was on before I raised the oxygen mask to my face and snapped it into my helmet. I checked the seal on the mask with the oxygen supply in the normal and emergency positions, and then looked over the canopy railing to verify the crew chief was plugged into the jet and ready for engine start. He had his headset on and was just where he should have been, to the left of the nose, crouched down so he could see the JFS doors on the lower section of the fuselage, aft of the main landing gear door. He looked up at me and gave me another thumbs-up.

I switched on the master battery switch and watched the lights in the cockpit illuminate as I became aware of the familiar sound of my own breathing into the mic.

"How do you hear me, chief?" I said into the intercom.

"Loud and clear, sir," the chief responded with a distinct American accent.

"Same here," I replied, "ready to start?"

"Yes sir."

"Hitting start two, chief," I said into the mask, referring to the switch position I was going to use to start the JFS. I hit the switch.

"Door's open, sir." This indicated that the JFS start sequence was proceeding normally, but I would have guessed that anyway because the JFS was already spinning up and generating the usual amount of noise. The sound thrilled me. A few seconds later, the green light on the JFS panel illuminated, indicating that the JFS had reached operating speed. Then the engine itself began to spin up. I watched the engine RPM indicator hunt around a little at the 5 percent mark and slowly wind up past twenty percent. I advanced the throttle to idle and experienced the classic GE engine start, a rapid rise in exhaust gas temperature, followed by a steady RPM rise. A few seconds later the engine stabilized at idle and I lowered the canopy.

This was always a pivotal moment for me as I mentally transitioned from the outside world to the inside one. The canopy reached the rail and moved forward into its locked position. Then I felt my ears pop as the canopy seal inflated and the cockpit pressurized. My womb was sealed around me and epiphany seized me again.

I was home. I was doing what I was born to do.

God, I've missed this, I thought.

I ran the post-starting checks quickly and methodically, finishing the process by pulling the safety pins for the canopy jettison handle and ejection seat, showing them to the crew chief and stowing them in the pocket of my g-suit. Then I had a few seconds before one of the most revered moments in every fighter sortie: check-in time.

I turned on the UHF radio and tuned it to the frequency for the Have Quick portion of the radio to receive a time-of-day signal. Instead of using one UHF frequency for communications and risk having their communications intercepted, MAG used the Have Quick function of the radio. Have Quick, or HQ, is a frequency-hopping feature built into military radios during the Cold War to prevent the Soviets from jamming our radio transmissions during combat. When radios have identical codes programmed into them and get the same time signal, they're synced and will hop across the entire UHF frequency spectrum using the same frequency pattern and timing. But MAG was not using HQ to avoid jamming; they were using it to avoid detection on the UHF spectrum. Damn smart.

The time signal came over the frequency I had tuned.

I selected the appropriate net and switched the radio into 'active' or frequency hopping mode. Then I looked down at my watch and watched the seconds tick off until it read 0930:00.

"Boiler, check," Rug's voice came clearly over the radio with the light clickity-click of the frequency hopping in the background.

"Two," I said.

"Control, Boiler One, flight of two, taxi."

"Cleared taxi, cleared launch, Boiler." Blade's voice was crisp over the radio. "Airspace is clear."

"Boiler One, copy."

I looked over at Rug's jet and his crew chief was disconnecting from the aircraft.

"Cleared to disconnect and pull the chocks, chief," I said into the intercom. "My hands are clear."

"Roger that, sir. Talk to you when you get back."

The background noise in my headset went quiet as the crew chief disconnected his headset from the aircraft. I placed my hands in clear view on the glare shield as he stowed his headset. He looked up at me before he disappeared under the wing to get the chocks in front of the main landing gear. The 'hands clear' thing is a big deal when ground personnel are underneath an aircraft with hydraulically-powered flight controls. If I were to accidentally bump the control stick, the flight controls could deflect and injure or kill someone in close proximity to them.

He reappeared from under the nose and walked out to a place where he was about twenty feet in front of the nose of the jet and offset to the right. Then he looked over at Rug's crew chief, who was in a similar position. Rug's crew chief made the 'run-it-up' sign, waving the index finger of his right hand in a tight circle over his head, obviously mimicking the same symbol which Rug had initiated. The sound level increased, the nozzle on Rug's engine closed, and his jet began to move forward.

He turned left across my nose, and he waved at me as he taxied past. I gave the 'run-it-up' sign to my crew chief, which he enthusiastically returned and motioned me forward. I slowly advanced the throttle and the Viper began to creep forward. I engaged the nosewheel steering and fell in behind Rug's jet, following him down the taxiway.

The first sortie was a little anti-climactic. We flew the standard TR profile right out of the syllabus, like I had flown it in the simulator. Rug stayed in a tight chase position throughout. The jet performed as advertised and there were no surprises.

This sortie also provided my first aerial view of the island where I had spent the last ten days of my life. It was smaller than I expected, probably only about five miles across and roughly circular in shape. A sparkling white beach area occupied the entire western side of the island and had a line of palm trees and other foliage skirting it. This green area backed up into the mountain which dominated the island and went up to a mesa-like top about 3,500 feet above sea level. At the eastern base of the mountain was the north-south runway, tinted a dingy brown color to camouflage its existence to passing aircraft or satellites. At altitude above it, I noticed that the outlines of rocks and boulders had been painted on the runway surface as well to further disguise it. The east side of the island, what little there was, was largely barren, with a few spots of foliage here and there and a lot of plain brown rock or sand.

We landed after a second instrument approach and taxied back under the awning. After a quick refuel and a consultation with Ruth, Rug's instructions told me what I wanted to hear. "Wring it out," he said, "just don't put yourself to sleep in the process."

We started up and taxied out to the runway again, and I took the lead on the runway.

"Let her rip," Rug said on the radio.

"Roger that," I replied.

I ran the throttle up to 90% RPM, gave the engine gauges a

once-over, and released the brakes. Then I pushed the throttle up over the detent and into MAX AB, or full afterburner. Instinctively, I glanced down at my engine gauges to watch the nozzle gauge unwind to about 50 to 85 percent aperture, but the sharp kick I got in the back was confirmation enough. The afterburner had lit.

A clean-configured Viper in a MAX AB takeoff will typically break ground between 1,500 to 2,000 feet after brake release. It's an amazing sensation. The jet accelerates so rapidly it almost seems unsafe. I reached take-off speed in about fifteen seconds and rotated the nose to ten degrees pitch. Since the flaps retract automatically when the gear comes up, I waited a half a second to ensure I was safely airborne and slapped the gear handle up. I checked the red light in the gear handle out at 295 knots, then nosed the jet over a few degrees to let it accelerate.

I peered into the jet's heads-up display, or HUD, as the Viper gained speed. The HUD is fixture on modern fighter aircraft. It displays airspeed, altitude, aircraft attitude, and navigational data on a glass plate that is mounted directly in front of the pilot, forcing him to look through it as he flies the aircraft, hence the term heads-up display. The pilot is able to keep his head *up* while he flies, instead of looking down at flight instruments. While the flight and navigational data display is important, it's the weapons functions that make the HUD so integral to modern fighters. Among the many display modes it provides, the Viper's HUD can show the pilot where his radar and missile seeker heads are looking and also generate the gunsight for the F-16's 20mm Vulcan cannon. In the ground attack mode, the HUD provides the bomb sight for the F-16's weapons delivery modes.

As the green video scale of my HUD airspeed tape hit 450 knots, I smoothly applied back pressure to the control stick and pulled the nose up to about 75 degrees pitch, nearly pure vertical, and pushed slightly to hold it there. Like a thoroughbred that had been kicked in the ribs, the eager Viper shot skyward. Seconds later I rolled the jet onto its back and pulled the nose down to the horizon. Then I rolled 180 degrees back to wings-level.

I was at 20,000 feet and 230 knots.

"It's been way too fucking long," I sighed into my oxygen mask. "Way too fucking long."

I saw a flash of movement in my peripheral vision and Rug popped into the chase position behind me.

"Not bad," he said over the radio. "Now let's see how much Igor's weight training has helped with your g-tolerance. Break left!"

In the time since we had leveled off, I had left the power in MAX AB and accelerated back to about 350 knots. I rolled left to 90 degrees of bank, my wings perpendicular to the horizon, and applied back pressure to the control stick to bring the nose around.

In an airliner or a business jet, when the pilot rolls the aircraft into the typical 30-degree-bank turn, he breaks the lift on the wings into two components or vectors. The vertical component, the part that keeps the airplane flying, remains the larger of the two vectors, but it is the horizontal component of lift that turns the airplane, usually at a rate of about three degrees per second. In a fighter, maneuverability is life, so we can't wait that long for the nose to come around. We roll the airplane, apply back pressure to the control stick, and use the elevators to turn the airplane, making the horizontal component of lift much larger than the vertical one. This is referred to as 'pulling the nose around' in a turn. In the Viper's case, the pilot can 'pull' the nose around as rapidly as twenty-five degrees per second. It is this tighter turn that generates the g-forces experienced by the aircraft and the pilot.

But there is a price to be paid. When lift is increased, drag is increased, and when drag is increased, the thrust must be available to counter the drag. Hence the reason why the Viper is such a turning machine; it has a lot of thrust to counter the increase in drag generated under g.

I did what I had done back at Luke: I blended the back pressure into about six to seven g's and let the nose smoothly track through 180 degrees of turn. The Big-Mouth Block 30 can do that all day long. When I rolled out, I was still at 350 knots and had maintained my altitude. I pulled the throttle out of AB.

I love g-force, by the way. I can't tell you why, but it probably has to do with the fact that it hurts a little. When you fight to stay conscious during several high-g turns, you feel alive while you're doing it and you have a nice little adrenaline rush when it's all over. You also feel a little flushed and breathless.

"Nicely done, FNG," Rug said over my headset, "you didn't make the standard energy-losing turn your first time out. I guess you've done this a few times."

"Once or twice," I said, "a long time ago."

"Comes back, though, doesn't it?"

"Yes, it does."

"Okay, now make that bitch dance."

I took his cue and put the jet though some paces. Several more high-g turns, some in MAX AB, simulating offensive dog-fighting maneuvers, and some in idle thrust, simulating defensive ones. Then I put the jet through all the maneuvers in the Horn Awareness and Recovery Training Series (HARTS) to practice recovering from low airspeed, nose-high situations. I felt like a jockey getting reacquainted with a fiery stallion.

Finally, I flew a simulated flameout approach and touched down perfectly, 1,000 feet down the runway. Rug, still airborne in the chase position, flew by me, pulled up into the closed pattern, and landed a few moments later. As we shut down underneath the awning and climbed out of our jets, my jaw ached from smiling so much.

CHAPTER THIRTEEN

Contract Day Thirteen
Wednesday, 23 September
1400 Hours Local Time
Island Training Base

As the engine spooled down, the ladder appeared over the side rail of the canopy, followed by my crew chief's blonde head shortly after.

"You've got that look," he said, grinning.

"What look is that?" I asked.

"Like you've just been laid."

I laughed. "That about sums it up," I said, "but let me tell you something. As you get older, the whole sex thing becomes overrated. This, however," I patted the rails of the canopy, "never gets old. Never."

"I'll have to take your word for that," he said.

"By the way, what the hell is your name and what I am supposed to call you?"

"The name's Bill, but you can just call me chief. We're not big on names between the O's and E's. Let me get the rest of your stuff."

I took my helmet off and put it in the bag with my kneeboard, checklist, and a few other things. Then I handed it to him and he took it down the ladder. After installing the safety pins for the seat and canopy, I climbed out of the cockpit and did a quick post-flight, admiring the lines on this beautiful machine once again. I patted the side of it, like I would a fine horse, and returned to the base of the ladder to get the maintenance forms.

A few moments later, I headed toward the hangar doors where Rug was waiting for me.

He eyed me respectfully as I approached him.

"If I didn't know better," he said, "I'd swear your last flight was last week, not several years ago."

We walked together through the hangar and found the debriefing area. We were greeted at the desk there by a ravishing female maintenance troop I hadn't seen before and the ever-present Natasha.

"And how did my little pushkins do for you, eh?" she asked.

"Code One here," Rug replied, indicating he had no discrepancies to report.

"And here," I added.

She nodded. "My peepull, they do good work on planes. Of goarse, it is good that US planes are easier to work on than Russian ones."

She looked at me with a half smirk on her face. "Now you are no longer virgin with Natasha's hardware, yes?"

"I hadn't thought about it like that," I said shrugging, "but I guess that's true."

"Good. We have special party for you later."

I nodded. Whatever.

Rug and I exited the debrief office and made our way into operations.

"I don't even want to know what that means," I said to him after the door to the hangar closed behind us.

"It means that she's going to try to fuck you. Again."

"Again," I said, "she never got to it the first time; I kicked her out."

"That's not the story she tells," Rug said, "although none of us pay much attention to her. But I'll tell you something; she's tenacious. She won't give up."

"Great," I said.

We made our way into life support, removed our gear, and then met Ruth at the Ops desk.

"As good on the second as the first?" she asked flatly, looking directly at Rug.

"Better," Rug said.

She nodded. "BFM tomorrow?"

"Absolutely," Rug answered.

"If we double bang tomorrow, I can get him through offense and defense, I think."

Ruth shook her head. "That's tempting, but Sammy will allow only one down day for fitness training and today was it. We'll have to stick to one sortie per day."

Rug nodded. "So be it." He turned to me. "I'd like to debrief this over a beer, but you're not allowed until Sammy says so, so I'll see you in the briefing room in a few minutes."

"Cool," I said and headed off, leaving the two of them talking at the desk.

After the debrief, which lasted about five minutes because Rug couldn't think of anything to critique, I went back to my room. Not hearing any activity in the shower, I stripped off and headed in there. I stood under the stream of hot water for a long time and let my muscles relax. My blood tingled with the thrill of flying the Viper again. I felt like I had been living my life in a weird kind of hibernation since my last flight in the jet. The adrenaline rush from flying the Viper was back, and it was real. It had always been the best drug I had ever experienced and as the water pounded down on me, I realized something I hadn't expected. The sheer fun of flying the airplane, in an odd sort of way, counterbalanced the bloodlust inside me; it almost worked as a type of anesthetic.

"Very interesting," I said to the empty shower.

Then door creaked on the girls' side then, and Brianna came in.

She said 'hello' and was gracious enough to take the next stall over and across the way so that I wouldn't be too tempted to look at her well-proportioned body.

The spell of my solitude broken, I quickly finished my shower, turned off my water, and dried off. Then, I donned the usual terrycloth robe.

"Igor's training is suiting you well," Brianna said as she turned off her shower and stepped into the small dressing area in her stall. I could just see one perfect calf protruding into the aisle between the showers.

"Thanks," I said, "and if I may ask, what do you do to stay in such incredible shape?"

"Martial arts," she said while she toweled herself. "About two hours a day. It's about the only way to keep my sanity. I just finished my workout."

"Remind me never to pick a fight with you," I said. I turned to go. "See you at dinner."

"Wait," she said. She stepped out into the aisle between the showers to hurriedly put her robe on, giving me a quick view of her nude body. She was an eyeful. Her body reminded me of a gymnast's, but with breasts that were much larger than those on the tiny girls you saw flipping around the uneven bars. She knotted the terrycloth tie and walked over to me, looking up into my face.

"I've been given orders," she rolled her eyes, "to come see you later.

I just looked down at her, baffled.

She stood there and shook her head with a half-smile on her face. Her deep, brown eyes sparkled at me. "You're good," she whispered. "You're very good. We've got a lot to talk about tonight. I'll see you about ten or so."

Then she disappeared into the steam before I could

respond.

##

The meal was lively that night and word of my performance had made the rounds. VB looked at me worshipfully, Pete traded barbs with me over rules in the Danish Air Force versus the US Air Force, and Brinker sulked. Brianna caught my eye once or twice and at least one of those times Natasha saw the exchange and was visibly disturbed by it.

The conversation made its way into basic fighter maneuvers, and Rug asked me to explain my theory of the six to seven-g turn versus the nine-g one.

"It's just a question of where you want to spend the energy," I answered. "The Viper will not maintain its energy in an eight to nine-g turn. If I'm on defense, then I might have to spend that energy to drive the attacker's nose off me; but if I'm offensive, I'm not going to spend that energy unless I have to. If I keep about six g's on the jet, with one in reserve, I can maintain a damn good rate of turn and maybe force the guy I'm attacking to make a mistake. If he does, then and only then, do I spend the energy to kill him."

"If you hit his turn circle and pull nine g's, you can put your nose on him right away and kill him; then you don't need to worry about forcing a mistake," Brinker snorted back at me.

"You'd better get it right the first time," I said, "because you won't get a second chance. But opinions are like assholes," I said looking right at him, "everybody has one and everyone else's stinks. The difference here is that you and I can get into a couple of jets and I can prove this one to you."

"And I would kick your arrogant American ass," Brinker said.

"You might," I agreed, "but that doesn't mean I'm wrong about the way the P sub S chart works." P sub S or P_s is the Specific Excess Energy chart which maps airspeed, altitude, turn rates, and radii versus g; it's the dogfight performance chart for the airplane. "Besides," I continued, "I'm an old man who has been out of the cockpit for several years. You should be able to walk all over me."

"I want to be FNG's BFM instructor," Brinker blurted out. Ruth and Rug exchanged a few words and then she stood up.

"I have a better idea. It's time we had another BFM day," she said.

The room went quiet.

"The day after FNG finishes his air-to-air training, we'll surge and run a double elimination tournament among all the pilots with the winner, she paused, "fighting me. This will be a good opportunity to wake all the jets up and to hone our skills."

Brinker grinned at me from across the table.

"What's that expression you Americans use? Bring it!"

I just smiled back at him.

##

I was awake when I heard the light knock on my door later that night. I was dressed in exercise shorts and a T-shirt in expectation of the visit but I threw my robe on over them and went to the door. I eased it open slowly to find Brianna standing in the hallway smiling at me, dressed in a diaphanous robe with a frilly, red chemise underneath it.

I motioned her in as I looked up and down the hall. "I'm hoping I don't have an unwelcome visitor tonight," I said as I closed the door behind her.

She smirked as she walked past me and into the room. "Yeah," she whispered in her Aussie lilt, "I can see why you'd feel that way after the last time."

I shook my head. "Just keep in mind that what she says is her version, not mine."

"No problem." She turned around and looked at me in

disbelief. "What's with all the clothes?" she asked. "How am I supposed to seduce you if you're all dressed?"

I just stood there gaping at her.

"I'm serious," she said quietly, but firmly. "Strip. I'm here on orders. If someone does come to the door, we've got to make this look real."

"Okay," I said, shaking my head as I removed my robe. "I'm totally lost now."

"I'll explain it to you," she whispered, "kill the light and get into bed."

A few moments later, I was in my bed with a beautiful, voluptuous younger woman, and sex was absolutely the last thing on my mind. Okay, so maybe it wasn't the last thing, but it wasn't at the forefront. Yet.

I propped my head up with my right hand and she grabbed one of my pillows, balled it up and hugged it against the upper part of her chest, resting her chin on top.

As my eyes adjusted to the dim illumination from the bathroom nightlight, I could see the bedspread resting about two thirds of the way up her magnificent ass and her entire back was bare. Her long, brunette hair flowed all around her face and stood out against the white of the pillowcase and I could see those deep, brown eyes regarding me in the darkness.

"Amazing how you can be physically naked with someone and yet not have a clue who or what they are, isn't it?" she said quietly.

I nodded and realized that she might not see that in the dimness. "Yes, it is," I said.

"I need to tell you some things," she began, "and I'm not going to be able to tell you how I know them or why I'm telling you."

She must have sensed me tensing across from her.

"You don't have to trust me," she continued. "You can just listen to what I have to say and choose to believe me or not.

I'm on *your* side."

"Fair enough," I said.

"The name on the file was obviously fictitious. The pilot you're replacing was a man named Burt Magnusson, Air Force Academy Class of 1982, F-16 Fighter Weapons School Graduate, and retired US Air Force Lieutenant Colonel. He disappeared several weeks ago."

I looked over at her. Not sure how I should react.

"I know that the two of you were very close." She paused for a moment. "And let me be clear. *They* don't know that. *I* know that."

I felt my defenses dropping. I was fairly adept at spotting liars and my instincts were telling me I could trust this woman.

"What happened to him?" I tried to keep my tone conversational, but the words came out with a degree of urgency I didn't intend.

I saw the gray outline of her petite shoulders shrug. "I don't know exactly. He just disappeared."

"Whaaaaatttt?" I raised my voice involuntarily. She reached out quickly and covered my mouth with her right hand before I uttered another syllable.

"Shhhh. What I can tell you is that it happened while Ron Phillips was here."

I felt my mind go cold, remembering the interplay between Phillips and Ruth at my townhouse.

"So, tell me the story."

"Things were pretty intense around here. We had been contracted for a huge job by someone in the Middle East which was going to provide a much higher fee than usual."

I looked at her quizzically and she must have felt my gaze in the dark.

"I may not know a lot about the pilot stuff, but I do know where a lot of the money goes because I interact with the banks we use. Who do you think makes all the wire transfers?"

I made a mental note to make sure that Smith and Amrine had the opportunity to interrogate this young woman at length when the time came.

"Anyway, Phillips was here because the client kept changing his mind about what 'effect' he or they wanted to achieve. It was driving the pilots crazy because they'd design the attack stuff and then they'd have to start from scratch again. This happened over and over again, for several weeks. Finally, the client made up his mind and we were going to have to get special bombs with which to arm the planes. This time, the pilots had to use a type of attack that none of them had used in a long time, because I remember them talking about it in the bar the night Phillips made that announcement. The next morning, while the mission planning was taking place, Burt went into Ruth's office where Phillips and Ruth were and shut the door behind him. I couldn't hear what they were talking about, but there was a lot of shouting."

"How long were they in there?"

"A long time, I guess. I wasn't there when they finished. Ruth needed me to talk to some of Natasha's people about a personnel issue so I went down to Natasha's office and when I got back, Ruth's office was empty. I never saw Burt again. The next day, Phillips told me that Burt had decided to leave the company and to out-process him."

"Damn," I said. "Damn, damn, damn."

"There's more," she said after a long moment, "if you want to hear it."

I turned my head to look at her.

"Ruth and Burt Magnusson have a history."

I felt like I had been slapped. "But...what...how?" For the life of me, I couldn't form a coherent question.

"They've known each other for over sixteen years," she whispered. "He met her in Israel while he was there on a Black assignment with the Israeli Air Force. The odds are very good that they had an intimate relationship while he was there."

I shook my head against my pillow. "Not Boomer."

She laughed softly and reached out to push my arm in incredulity. "What sort of dream world are you living in? He was away from his wife for over a year and he spent his entire time with the IAF working on their development of the Python 4 missile with an ambitious, single captain named Ruth Shalev. They spent nearly every waking hour together for twelve months. Are you telling me you don't believe they were fucking each other?"

"Not Boomer," I said again. "Anyone else and I wouldn't be saying this, but not Boomer."

"Well anyway, it doesn't matter, because it was Ruth's former association with Magnusson that led to his being hired here."

Again, I had difficulty forming a question and remained silent.

"After Shalev left the Israeli Air Force, she met a dashing older man named Ron Phillips. Later, when they developed the business plan for this operation, they needed a tactical brain behind it. And that..."

"Is where Boomer came in," I finished the sentence for her. "Holy, fucking, shit."

"You got it."

I lay there shaking my head against my pillow and feeling both anger and grief welling up inside me. What I feared was definitely true. I felt my throat swell and tears welled up in my eyes.

Brianna moved over next to me and hugged me tightly.

"Like I said, I know the two of you were close. And I'm really sorry for your loss," she said, her voice tender. "And if it means anything, I thought he was a great guy."

We lay there for a long while in silence as I again mourned the loss of my best friend on earth. I wondered how many more times I was going to have to endure the sorrow and if I would ever truly get over it. I remembered the words my aunt had given me at my mother's funeral so long ago: "The grief never goes away," she had said. "You just learn to live with it."

Eventually, as the emotion subsided, I became increasingly aware of the aroma and softness of Brianna's hair against my cheek and sensation of her skin against mine. I could feel her firm breasts against my chest and her lower body pressed against my leg.

The words of Burt's pastor/mentor in Kansas City popped into my head: "God's biggest joke on man is that he gave man a brain and penis and not enough blood to operate both at the same time."

The drugs racing through me didn't help the situation. Without them, I'd probably be weighing the benefit of a night of sleep versus a night of sex. But with them, it was a different story. A certain part of my body was wide awake.

"What happens now?" I whispered. "Orders or not, you shouldn't have to sleep with somebody you don't want to."

I could feel some tension ease out of her body.

"Thanks," she said. "I kind of wondered about that. I've never really done anything like this. It's not that I don't find you..."

I squeezed her gently. "Brianna, you're very sweet but you don't need to lie to me."

"It's not a lie," she said, her warm breath radiating across my chest. "I've always liked older guys. And you have this whole 'bad boy' vibe thing. It's a total turn on. I've just never jumped into bed with somebody without getting to know them a while first."

'Jumping into bed' had pretty much been the story of my relationship life. Sex was easy if you bypassed all the clumsy relationship stuff. If you kept it purely physical and didn't let that emotional shit get in the way. But I didn't think any of this would help the discussion.

I kissed the top of her head.

"I'm flattered," I said. "But I'm obviously not going to force myself upon you. What do we have to do to sell this without having to actually do anything?"

"I just need to sleep here tonight," she said.

"Not a problem for me," I lied. I had no idea how I was going to get to sleep with a woman like this next to me.

"Good," she said. "Do you mind if I stay like this? I haven't slept with anyone else for a long time. This is nice."

"Not at all," I replied with the most gallant tone I could muster. "I like it too."

She smiled up at me and then shifted her body slightly to get more comfortable. As she did so, her hand lifted from my stomach and came to rest on a portion of my anatomy below my waist.

"Oh, my God!" she exclaimed. "That's incredible!" She rapidly moved her hand to my lower stomach. "I'm sorry," she said. "I didn't mean to do that."

"No problem," I said, laughing back at her. "At my age, you take anything you can get."

Her hand fidgeted restlessly on my stomach for several minutes as we lay there in the darkness. Finally, she turned her head to look up at me. "I know this is really weird, but can I touch you again?" she asked. "I'm sorry, but I just can't believe it. It's like a scientific curiosity thing."

"Sure," I replied. "What the hell."

She lowered her hand and after a few tentative touches, grasped me firmly. "Oh, wow," she said. "This is sooo amazing. I've been with several guys and I've never felt anything like that. You are so hard!"

"I'd love to tell you it's all me," I sighed. "But that shit I drink every morning has a lot to do with it. The damn thing gets hard if the temperature changes a degree. It's ridiculous."

Her hands busied themselves for a few minutes and the 'scientific curiosity' became something else entirely. She tentatively lifted her mouth sometime later, her face begging the unasked question. I answered by lowering my lips to hers and moving my hands to some of the more tender contours of her body. Her lips smiled upon mine and soon her mouth was making other pleasure-related expressions and noises. The sensual tension between us built rapidly and before long, she ended up on top of me. Some moments after that, she moved her hips appropriately, and we were coupled.

Afterward, we collapsed into each other's arms, spent.

"Wow," I said at last, trying to catch my breath, "that was unexpected."

"Yeah," Brianna breathed, her head resting on my chest. "Sorry about that. I didn't mean to take advantage of you."

"You're not hearing any complaints out of me," I said. "That was fantastic!" I gently stroked her shoulder. "I don't know what I did to get the attention. But I'm glad, whatever it was."

"Women have needs too," she said. "Touching you when you were 'like that' sort of brought them all out for me. Anyway," she raised her face and brushed my lips with hers, "now, I have the need to sleep. Is that okay?"

"It was okay before," I answered, "and it's definitely okay now.

Sometime later, there was another knock at the door. I remembered a dream about having mind-blowing sex and woke up to find Brianna still asleep next to me.

I nudged her gently and she stirred and moaned quietly but pleasurably. She lifted her head from my chest and looked at me. I put my finger to my lips and then we heard the knock again.

She shook her head sadly. "That will be Natasha," she said, "checking on me. You need to let her see me in here."

I rose from the bed and went to the door without putting anything on. Brianna arranged the covers so that it was clear, she too, was unclothed. I looked at her, and she nodded.

I opened the door, keeping most of my body behind it. Natasha stared back at me.

"Brianna has been here?" she asked.

"Maybe," I said tiredly. "But if she was, that would be my business, not yours."

"I am to check," Natasha said, sticking her head into the room. She caught sight of Brianna on the bed and nodded and then allowed her gaze to focus on me. Her eyes lingered on my chest and then followed the contours of my body southward. "Igor do good job on you," she said.

Then she inclined her chin toward the bed. "When you get tired of appetizer, you come to me for entrée."

"Have you seen enough?" I said. "I'd like to get back to bed."

Natasha reluctantly nodded and stepped back. I closed the door solidly behind her and locked it loudly. Then I padded back to bed.

I slid under the covers and lay my head on the pillow. Brianna looked at me from her own pillow about a foot away.

"So, do you mind telling me what that was all about?" I asked her.

"Shalev was going to order someone to sleep with you to see if you bought the whole Andy Dickson story," Brianna whispered. "Natasha wanted to do it *really* badly. I convinced Shalev that I'd be the better choice because I was the personnel officer and I knew the facts better."

"How can she do that?" I asked, incredulous. "How can she 'order' the women that work for her to do that?"

"She doesn't have to order most of them. The women here are on a drug scheme that is similar to the men, and they were largely chosen not just for their technical skill but also for their disposition toward 'enjoying themselves.'"

I looked at her closely. "That doesn't sound like you," I said. "How'd you get the job?"

"They needed someone who knew international banking and human resources when their last personnel officer changed her mind about coming here. I just happened to be in the right place at the right time."

"But then why did you volunteer for this?" I asked. "As in tonight."

"You needed to hear the truth," she said. "And I wanted to make sure you got it."

"Why?"

"Because it's my day job," she said.

"Your day job?"

"I'm tired," she said abruptly. "I've told you more than I was supposed to already."

I leaned back against my pillow and stared at the ceiling, feeling not unlike a mushroom. Surrounded by shit and not having the slightest idea what was going on.

"Can I sleep next to you, like before?" Brianna asked softly. "That was really nice."

"Sure," I said. "You're pretty cozy to snuggle up to yourself." I lifted my arm up so she could put her head on my chest. She moved right in and placed her warm body against mine and her hand on my stomach. I put my arm back under the covers and rested my hand on her muscular ass. In a few minutes, the warmth and feel of her skin next to mine reactivated what the drugs inside me made possible. Soon, her hand traveled southward and the festivities began again.

We didn't get much sleep that night, after all.

TOP SECRET / SPECIAL COMPARTMENTALIZED INFORMATION
CLASSIFIED BY: US Central Intelligence Agency
DECLASSIFY ON: OADR

From: Special Projects Group [NCS]
Sent: Thursday, 24 September 2009, 1200 EDT (24 September 2009, 1600Z)
To: Director, NCS
Cc: Special Projects Group [NCS]; damrine@cmail.cia.gov; dsmith3@cmail.cia.gov

SUBJECT: Update, Case File: 08-434A (MAG)

(TS) Narrative:

1. (TS) Contactor 09-017 (Pearce, Colin M.) completed transition training in the F-16 yesterday. He will begin air-to-air training tomorrow. Depending on his proficiency, the air-to-air phase should last six days.

2. (TS) Last night, Pearce spent the evening with MAG's personnel and banking officer, Brianna Blenhem. Blenhem provided information confirming that Informant 08-257 (Magnusson, Burton L.—MIA as of late August) was, in fact, the missing pilot from MAG. Blenhem also provided information indicating she knew about the friendship between Pearce and Magnusson. Additionally, she revealed that MAG's tactical commander, Shalev, Ruth C. (Major, IAF, Retired) and Magnusson had a history together when Magnusson worked a Black assignment with the IAF in 1992. USAF liaison confirmed the assignment. Probability is high that Shalev and Magnusson's acquaintance led to his recruitment to MAG.

3. (TS) Pearce is adamant that Blenhem knew more than she

revealed. She evidently made several references to having to limit what she said to him.

(TS) CONCLUSIONS:

1. (TS) Both Magnusson and Pearce are USAF Fighter Weapons School graduates in the F-16. Analysis suggests that there is a requirement that a USAF FWS graduate be on staff.

2. (TS) It is possible a foreign intelligence agency may have someone on the inside of MAG.

(TS) ACTIONS:

1. (TS) Will research MAG files and sources to determine likelihood of FWS graduate requirement. If requirement exists, it is highly likely it is in place to satisfy the entities or persons backing MAG.

2. (TS) Will query foreign agency liaisons about possible involvement. (Note: will need DCIA approval to reveal file information to foreign entities.)

3. (TS) We are working with executive assistants for the Directors of DI, DS&T and DS to arrange for presentation of the project briefing you approved yesterday. DI special projects team is forming a list of possible targets. We will have the list for your perusal by close of business today.

(TS) RECOMMENDATION: None. Information only.

TOP SECRET / SPECIAL
COMPARTMENTALIZED INFORMATION
CLASSIFIED BY: US Central Intelligence Agency
DECLASSIFY ON: OADR

TOP SECRET / SPECIAL
COMPARTMENTALIZED INFORMATION
CLASSIFIED BY: US Central Intelligence Agency
DECLASSIFY ON: OADR

From: Special Projects Group [NCS]
Sent: Friday, 25 September 2009, 1800 EDT (25 September 2009, 2200Z)
To: Director, NCS
Cc: Special Projects Group [NCS]; damrine@cmail.cia.gov; dsmith3@cmail.cia.gov

SUBJECT: Update, Case File: 08-434A (MAG)

(TS) Narrative:

1. (TS) We received word late yesterday from Contractor 09-017 (Pearce, Colin M.), that MAG's personnel and banking officer, Brianna Blenhem, had been sent to Zurich, Switzerland to perform banking functions for MAG.

2. (TS) At approximately 0100Z this morning, Gulfstream G-550 VP-CFD appeared in radar contact over the People's Republic of China enroute to Zurich. At 1200Z (1400 Local), VP-CFD arrived at Zurich International Airport (LSZH). We dispatched officers from the Zurich field office to intercept Blenhem when practical. As she was enroute to the Credit Suisse main offices at Paradeplatz 8 in Zurich, our officers intercepted her but encountered a team of counter-operatives from MI-6. MI-6 had been following a cash stream out of the UK which they suspected was being used to fund terror. They managed to pull MAG's first choice for banking/personnel and got Blenhem in place instead.

3. (TS) Information gleaned from MI-6:

a. (TS) Blenhem (not her real name - real name kept confidential by MI-6) confirmed that the investors behind MAG required a USAF Fighter Weapons Graduate to plan the attacks in order to assure the effectiveness of the strikes and entice buyers to purchase MAG's services.

b. (TS) Investor cash backing MAG comes from unidentified sources, mainly based in Europe and Russia. Banking support is centered in the United Kingdom and routed through Switzerland. Buyers of MAG's services have come from all over the world. Blenhem debriefed our operatives on the entire contact and payment process for the strikes.

c. (TS) Buyers for the anticipated main strike are mostly based in the Middle East.

d. (TS) Main Strike is on schedule, tentatively planned for early October.

e. (TS) While our field office pursued Blenhem, Gulfstream G-550 VP-CFD departed LSZH enroute to Hong Kong International Airport (VHHH) unmonitored. It never arrived there, apparently diverting to another destination while not in radar contact. We were unable to reacquire the aircraft and track it to its destination.

4. (TS) Per the direction after today's briefing to you and the Directors of DI, DS&T, and DS, we are prepared to present the project briefing to the Director, CIA tomorrow along with the final targetselection.

(TS) CONCLUSIONS: While the information from MI-6 provides additional depth, we are still unaware of MAG's location and the target for the main strike. DCIA authorization for the special project to flush MAG from hiding is our only chance to determine their location and stop the final strike. We do believe the information supplied by MI-6 will enhance the chances of success for the project.

(TS) ACTION: We will add some slides containing the information gained from MI-6 to the briefing.

(TS) RECOMMENDATION: None. Information only.

TOP SECRET / SPECIAL
COMPARTMENTALIZED INFORMATION
CLASSIFIED BY: US Central Intelligence Agency
DECLASSIFY ON: OADR

CHAPTER FOURTEEN

Contract Day Sixteen
Saturday, 24 September
0900 Hours Local Time
Island Training Base

I lay on my back in the steam room, enjoying the solitude. Today's workout was the third one in the new regimen administered by Samantha, who by day was the princess of torture. Each day had focused acutely on specific muscle groups, with weights that were as heavy as I could lift. Not very many repetitions per set, but multiple sets and multiple exercises made up the difference. My muscles were screaming at me.

To add to the toll on my body, the morning workouts had been followed by Basic Fighter Maneuvers flights in the afternoon. BFM was dogfighting and required a great deal of physical exertion just to stay conscious and perform under the constant, punishing g-force. If it hadn't been for the drugs and steam, I was sure my body would have been mush by now.

But despite the punishment, the flying was working its magic on me. As in all the previous times in my life when events or circumstances seemed frustrating and beyond my control, an hour or so 'turning and burning' at nine g's enabled me to keep things in perspective. When I was back in the cockpit of the Viper, it was just me and the machine, and the cares of the earth were left behind. Life was simple, and this simplicity gave me the strength to stay focused on my mission and to keep the anger and lust in check.

But, while life in the air tended to simplify things, life on the ground was getting more complicated...and in a way I least expected.

Samantha had come to my door on Thursday morning to fetch me for my workout, something she hadn't done since my first morning here. Of course, Brianna and I had been fast asleep together after the previous night's frenetic activity and I didn't hear my alarm. Assuming I even set it. The expressions that ran across Samantha's face when she saw Brianna and I together were curious to say the least. There was shock and surprise, but there was also anger and maybe even something deeper. The next thing I knew, Brianna was on her way to Zurich for banking duty and I was getting my ass kicked doubly hard in the gym.

Then there was the constant company over the last several days. With the blessed exception of the shower and steam room, from the time I left my room for the morning workout until the time I returned to it for sleep, there always seemed to be someone around. It was especially tiresome after dinner, when we'd all go to the bar and watch something on TV or sit around and tell flying stories. I longed for the solitude of my room, but the mission came first. I needed to create the illusion of camaraderie and listen in on any conversations where I might acquire some useful information.

There was a constant distraction during these gatherings though; the interplay between Ruth and Samantha where I was concerned. Ruth kept her distance, sitting on the other side of the table or on the other side of the room and rarely engaging in conversation. But her eyes were watchful and appraising. Samantha, in contrast, was by my side as often as she could be. By night, she was Samantha the 'party princess,' joking, laughing and flirting. She'd pay appropriate attention to Rug, but she'd touch me at any opportunity and try to catch my eyes as often as possible. I got the distinct impression she was trying to see something in me.

But it was the glances between Samantha and Ruth that were especially telling. There was some sort of nonverbal communication taking place between them. And I had no idea what it was about.

I cleared my head as the steam circulated around me, grateful again for a few moments' respite from humanity. I've always been a person who required space. When I was in the USAF and we'd go on deployments as a squadron, some of the guys wanted to go out and party together every night. I just couldn't do it. I needed several nights in my room, alone, with a book or a crossword puzzle. That was the most difficult part of the first Gulf War for me; I was around my squadron mates continuously. When the war was over and my turn for leave came up, I took three weeks, found a condo deep in the Colorado Rockies, and shut the world out. It was like heaven.

And then my solitude and equilibrium were both shattered when Ruth walked into the steam room. She nodded as she came through the door naked and walked to the spot where I had last seen her, on the lower tier on the far side of the room. She bent over, spread her towel out on the lower tier bench at the top of the U, and gave me a lingering view of her spectacular ass, with her shaven labia clearly visible below it. Then she turned, arranged herself on the towel, and looked at me.

"I usually try to get this place alone," she said quietly, "but since you've already seen the scars, I didn't think it would be a big deal. Do you mind me barging in on you?"

I was unable to speak and merely shook my head.

She laughed softly and turned to lie on her side with her head propped on her right hand. This was my first opportunity to really see her like this. Where Samantha's body was pumped like a voluptuous weightlifter, Ruth's was more lithe and athletic, like a tennis player. Her chest and shoulders were chiseled, with hints of muscle visible through her skin, and were complimented by her breasts, perfectly sized for her frame. Her nipples were the color of hot chocolate and I nearly licked my lips when the analogy occurred to me. Her abdomen was concave and although her abs were not immediately visible, you could tell they were there, just beneath the skin. Her legs were muscular and strong.

I felt my body stirring below and casually rolled over on my stomach as she watched. She smiled at me, and damn her, she knew exactly what I was doing.

Her olive skin was just starting to glisten with sweat and she was 'nonchalantly' running her left hand up and down her left leg stopping just short of her pubic area.

"You're not uncomfortable being here like this, are you?" she asked me, smiling.

"No," I stammered, as I felt my loins simmering, "I'm just hoping that I don't embarrass myself."

"What's to be embarrassed about?" She laughed softly again and sat there just looking at me. I looked back at her and felt a sudden and strong sexual tension erupt between us, like a surprise spark of static electricity.

"So," she said as she peered at me through the steam, "Talk to me. Tell me something about you that I don't already know."

"Your files seem pretty extensive," I said as I attempted to move my gaze from her. It was no use. My eyes were feasting on her face and her body and they weren't going anywhere. "I'm not sure there's much about me you don't know."

"Tell me more about you. How'd you get into the Air Force Academy? Tell me about your career in the Air Force; and tell me specifically about that business at the end of your career."

"I always wanted to fly jets," I said, grateful for the distraction, "since I was about ten years old. I remember my mom driving us down a highway in Florida that was right next to Patrick Air Force Base and the Thunderbirds flew over our heads in close formation at about two hundred feet. I was hooked from that point forward. It was all I could think about. I worked my ass off to get into the Academy and ended up going to the Academy Prep School for a year before I got in. When I graduated, it was into pilot training and into the cockpit."

Okay, so I spilled my guts to her. I have no idea why. Maybe it was the perceived intimacy of being naked and alone together in the steam. Maybe it was because I thought she might actually understand me. Or maybe I was just hungry for companionship at that moment, which was ironic, especially since I was reveling in the solitude mere moments ago.

Since I was sure she had read all about my F-16 history through MAG's background researchers, and because it gave me a little more distance from Burt Magnusson, I dwelt on my assignments in the A-10. I told her all about flying the A-10 all over Europe during my first assignment in the jet. I went on to explain how I was selected for the A-10 Fighter Weapons School at Nellis Air Force Base, Nevada, and gave her a look inside the ensuing hell of going through that syllabus for four months of my life. Then I told her about my follow-on assignment to England Air Force Base in central Louisiana, where I was checked out in the most difficult mission the A-10 performed, Combat Search and Rescue - a qualification which earned me the greatly respected 'Sandy' call-sign. The Sandy flights began with the pilots in Vietnam who flew the slow, propeller-driven A-1 Skyraiders and kept the North Vietnamese at bay while downed pilots where extracted by helicopter. The 'Sandy' call-sign was carried over into the A-10 community where it did the same mission. It was a badge of honor.

"You were a Sandy?" she asked, interrupting my narrative. "Search and rescue is pretty dangerous stuff. Were you on a Sandy mission when you were shot down during the first Gulf War?"

"Yep." I nodded. "We had a poor Viper guy who was down north of the Iraqi border after dropping bombs on the Republican Guard. He broke his leg when he landed in his parachute and couldn't walk. He was hiding against a burnt-out hulk and the damn Iraqis were just riddling the thing with bullets trying to kill him. We showed up and hosed them down with a little thirty millimeter from the GAU-8 cannon and they lost their appetite for that. But a little later, as the rescue chopper arrived, they showed up with a T-72 tank and started taking pot shots at the place where our guy was hiding and at the chopper. I had just flown over the survivor and given the chopper clearance to land when I saw the damn tank. It just appeared over the top of a dune and the next thing I saw was the explosion when a main gun round impacted near our survivor. Fortunately, the hulk he was hiding behind shielded him from the blast. The next shot landed about halfway between the survivor and the chopper, and it was apparent the tank crew was shifting their attention to the bigger game. I knew I had to do something quickly. I was only about two hundred feet off the deck and about a mile away, and I rolled in, put the gun cross where the turret met the chassis of the thing, and held the trigger down until the tank blew up. I pulled off just in time to miss the explosion, but I didn't see the squad of infantry behind it. Most of whom were dead, I guess. But one of them managed to squeeze off a shoulder-fired missile at me and it blew my right engine off and ignited the fuel lines which led to the right wing. The next thing I knew I was on fire, so I pulled the ejection handles and I was out of there."

"How high were you when you ejected?"

"Two or three hundred feet, not high."

"Did you land okay?"

"If you count landing about half a mile from people I had

just tried to kill 'okay,' then I guess I was. Nothing was broken, but they were on me right after I cut my 'chute away. And they were pissed, let me tell you. The irony is that my getting shot down distracted the Iraqis from what they came there to do: namely shoot down the rescue chopper and keep the Viper guy from being rescued. They wanted to kick my ass so badly they completely forgot about anything else. So, the chopper picked up the Viper guy and got away safely."

"How badly did they hurt you?"

"It's funny," I said. "You're probably one of the few people on earth who could relate to this. They just basically beat the shit out of me. I remember attempting to surrender and being greeted with a rifle butt to the head. Then, other rifle butts followed and I eventually fell. And then came the boots. I remember going nearly unconscious, only to be pulled to my feet and get smacked down again. I think they would have beaten me to death if some officer hadn't shown up and gotten them off me. I vaguely remember him pushing them away, and then I was dragged to a truck so they could transport me to the building where I ended up. And you know what's interesting? That's the only time I was scared."

"Why?" Those deep brown eyes stared at me through the steam with just a touch of curiosity.

"Because in the A-10, we specialized in attacking moving vehicles," I said without looking away. "They had put me on a 'target' for our guys. I don't know whether they were trying to get me killed or not, but the guy at the wheel drove like a maniac to the nearest village."

"And that's the village where you killed all of them?" I nodded again.

"That's the place."

"So, I'm confused. How did all this tie into the business at your last base? And your retirement?"

"Do you really want to hear this? Any respect you have for the American Air Force will be toast when I'm done."

It was her turn to nod.

"Well, I told you that when I killed the three Hispanic gang members, the local paper found out about the Iraq business. I don't know who leaked it to them, but it was all over the papers. The commander of the local OSI detachment decided he needed to launch an investigation for conduct unbecoming an officer where yours truly was concerned."

"For defending yourself?" Blade asked, incredulous.

"Oh, yeah. He felt like it was his duty to persecute, excuse me I meant to say *prosecute,* a disgraceful Geneva Convention violator like me. But someone at a very high level told him to stop the investigation and he did, but not before I had been extensively 'questioned' or interrogated four or five times. Every single time, I didn't say a word, and that just irked the shit out of them, because they had no other evidence other than what they could pull out of me."

"So that's what led to your retirement?"

I shook my head. "Nope. I was set up for something else, something I couldn't have possibly done, and no one in my chain of command stood up to defend me. They just let the OSI run wild and those low-lifes did what they do best. My investigation became a typical OSI witch hunt."

"No way!" she exclaimed.

"Absolutely. I was a liability at that point. I needed to be gone. I'll spare you the rest of the details but it went all the way up to the Secretary of the Air Force level and to this day it still chaps my ass."

"Didn't you fight it?"

"I got to a point where I just didn't care," I said. "I felt like I had been betrayed by the very thing I had served. Especially after seeing Colonels and Generals get away with shit that was much worse than what I was supposed to have done. All I wanted was out. And out was what I got."

She leaned back against the upper tier and exhaled. "What a waste."

I tried to stay focused on our conversation while letting my eyes linger on her glorious, glistening body. "I was glad to get out," I said. "I mean I loved flying the Viper, but if I had stayed in, the bullshit level would have gone up exponentially and I wouldn't have gotten to fly that much. It wouldn't have been worth it."

She looked over at me. "I know what you mean. My own reasons for leaving the Israeli Air Force were a lot about politics."

"You don't seem like the political type," I said. "No offense intended. That's actually a compliment from my perspective."

"Taken as such," she said, smiling at me. "It seems like you and I have a few things in common."

I smiled back, gazing at the woman who had given orders to her subordinates to tantalize me in the shower and satiate me in the bedroom, and who now sat naked before me. Just out of reach.

And in the back of my mind, I latched on to something else. Even though I had recounted the two events in my life that had unleashed my bloodlust, and even though I was talking to a person who undoubtedly had something to do with Burt's disappearance, the bloodlust itself was *not stirring*. While I hoped my adventures in the air were at least partly responsible, I knew that it was largely the sexual tension between us that was having the anesthetizing effect.

A mental warning went off in my head, mimicking the voice reminder system in the F-16. *"Caution, caution,"* it said.

##

A few hours later, Rug and I blasted off for the last ride in the Basic Fighter Maneuver phase of training - the high-aspect BFM ride. The last two rides had placed me in the offensive and defensive roles; and while they had had been demanding, they weren't a true test of my ability. Today's ride would be different. Rug and I would meet nose-to-nose in a neutral position relative to one another and at exactly equal energy states. And then we'd fight it out and the best man would win. I couldn't wait.

Our jets were configured as they had been the last two days. We carried captive Python heat-seeking air-to-air missiles on our left wingtip stations and telemetry pods on our right wingtips. The captive Python was merely a missile seeker head mounted on an empty missile body, but it interacted with the F-16's weapons control system like a real missile did and provided the same aural indication. When a heat-seeking missile 'sees' a heat source, it generates a sound like a growl or a whistle in the pilot's headset. The stronger the sound, the better the heat source. Unlike the AIM-9M Sidewinders I had used in the USAF, which generated a clean whistle when they locked up, the Python growled like a rabid pit bull when it was ready to shoot. The sound made me smile every time I heard it.

It didn't hurt that the Python was a far better missile than the AIM-9M. In the past two days, I had several valid shots against Rug that would have fallen far outside the AIM-9's envelope.

We leveled off at 20,000 feet and assumed line-abreast tactical formation, about two miles apart. Then we executed the 'g-warm-up' turns, 90 degrees in one direction and then 90 degrees in the appropriate opposite direction to put us back into formation. The turns readied our bodies for the high-g loads the engagements would place on us.

As we accelerated to fighting airspeed, I exhaled slowly, rolled my head on my shoulders, and stretched my neck for what lay ahead.

The airspeed tape in the heads-up display in front of me clicked up to 450 knots. It was time.

"Boiler One, split," Rug called over the radio.

We turned away from each other about 45 degrees. Inside

our cockpits, we had our TACAN navigational receivers tuned to each other so the distance between us was displayed without a radar lock. When the distance between us read four miles, Rug called for us to turn in.

I manually slewed my air-to-air radar to the inside of the turn and locked up Rug's jet as I turned towards him. The tone in my headset, generated by my radar warning receiver, told me he had locked me as well.

"One's visual," Rug called, indicating he saw my aircraft.
"Two's visual," I replied.

Fight's on!"

Rug and I pointed just to the right of each other so we didn't collide, and I yanked my throttle back to idle to reduce the size of my exhaust plume and minimize the opportunity for a head-on missile shot. The missile seeker head is automatically caged to the target locked up by the radar, so my Python was looking at Rug's jet. Judging by the anemic tone the missile was generating in my headset, Rug had his power at idle as well. As we approached, I decided to make the first turn and let him decide what kind of fight it would be. The closure between us was about 1,000 knots or just over 1,500 feet per second, and he flashed by me about 500 feet to my left a few seconds later.

Keeping my eyes on him, I turned across his tail in a series of movements and motions that came back to me as if I had last done them yesterday. I unloaded my jet to zero-g to allow a more rapid roll rate and banked to the left enough to aim my vertical stabilizer just below the horizon. This helped me to gauge where my lift vector was pointed and defined the plane of my turn. Then I shoved the throttle into maximum afterburner and applied enough back pressure to the side-stick to get me into about 6 g's. Looking back over my left shoulder a few seconds later, I could see that Rug had done nearly the same thing and we wound up flying in opposite directions, each tracing the circumference of an imaginary circle about six to seven thousand feet in diameter. Because our first turn had turned us in opposite directions, the geometry was called a 'two-circle' fight—a fight that was about discipline, energy, and patience. Just my thing.

We went through a full 360 degrees of turn with neither of us gaining an advantage. He stayed across the circle from me, about 6,000 to 7,000 feet away, with the horizon clearly visible below him, right at my nine o'clock position, on top of my left shoulder. I figured it was about time for Rug to make the standard move to try to force me out of my game plan, and he didn't disappoint. I saw vapor pour from his wingtips and saw his nose begin to track toward me, clearly indicating that he was sacrificing his airspeed for more g and trading his kinetic energy for nose position.

But, the bad thing about fighting a guy in the same airplane is he knows exactly how much energy you're spending when you do something like that. The F-16 doesn't have a V_C or corner velocity, the lowest speed at which maximum g is available. Instead, we have a corner plateau, which is a blessing the engineers gave us when they built the nice clean airframe, equipped it with a digital flight control system and put a big-ass engine inside of it. Our corner plateau is 330 to 440 knots, which means that we can maintain max g anywhere inside that airspeed range and just accept the larger turn radius with the higher speed.

I was baiting Rug. Typically, in a Viper versus Viper two-circle fight, the combatants stay on the low end of the corner plateau, but I had stayed on the higher end and was maintaining about four hundred thirty knots. I kept the jet in MAX AB and did what he expected: I applied back pressure and pulled into nine g's, bringing my nose to his. Once I started to hear the pre-lock tickles from his radar in my headset, I yanked my throttle to idle and kept the turn coming. We wound up nose to nose a few seconds later and passed each other close aboard a few seconds after that.

Then it was time for the surprise. I shoved the throttle into MAX AB and went pure vertical, pulling my nose straight up into the sun. One of the best ways to win a dogfight is to put your jet in a place where your opponent can't go. I had about three hundred knots, and thanks to the momentary readout from the radar lock I had attained before we passed each other, I knew Rug had just less than two hundred. I shot skyward, trading my airspeed advantage for altitude and taking my jet to a place where Rug couldn't follow me. I was also hoping he'd cash in his last energy chips trying to bring the nose of his jet to bear on me and attempt a missile shot while I was going up. Watching him over my shoulder as I climbed, I saw his nose was slowly moving in my direction. I kept going uphill: 1,000 feet above him, 2,000 feet, 3,000 feet. I heard the first tickles of his radar again and slowly pulled the throttle out of AB just in case the Python could sustain a track on my huge afterburner exhaust plume even with the sun behind me.

Then I saw what I had been waiting for. His nose was starting to drop. He had run out of airspeed. I was inverted, 5,000 feet above him with just under 200 knots, thanks to the Viper's thrust-to-weight ratio and my gentle touch on the g.

Now it was my time to cash in. I eased my nose downward. His nose was still above the horizon and angled upward enough that I couldn't take a chance plugging in the afterburner yet, but I really didn't need it. I had potential energy, altitude, on my side now. Rather than aiming my aircraft directly at his, I rolled out briefly and aimed at a place about 4,000 feet above and behind him and flew to that spot until I saw the offensive cues I needed. As he continued to try to keep his nose above the horizon, I reached the place I had been aiming for, rolled back over and began to blend in the g. I visualized the control zone about 3,000 feet behind his jet and reached it about ten seconds later. I pulled my nose into lead and killed him with a simulated gunshot five seconds after that.

"Boiler One, terminate," Rug's voice came over the radio.

"Two terminate," I answered.

"Nicely done, Two. I obviously was trying to get you out of your game plan there, but I was totally unprepared for the vertical move."

He did a quick operations check of our airplanes and determined we had enough gas fuel for another engagement. We got back into line abreast formation, split, and turned toward one another.

"Fight's on."

It wasn't fair. I knew what he was going to do this time and it should have worked for him, especially because as the second guy to turn, he should have gotten behind me. But it just wasn't his day.

We passed abeam one another; right side to right side this time, and dutifully, I turned across his tail. Instead of turning across my tail, though, he decided to go 'one-circle,' turning in the same direction as I did and pulling into the vertical, trying to bleed his energy off and get behind me, *à la* the classic one-circle methodology. I baited him again for just a second or two. I let him get into the vertical first and I allowed myself to slide out in front of him just a little - just ahead of his wing-line.

He took the bait like the first bass of the season. Smelling a quick victory, he started pulling his nose to me more aggressively and cashing in more energy. Meanwhile I was in still in MAX AB with about 400 knots. I pulled into the vertical myself now and visualized his jet as the middle of a large cylinder that I was going to fly around the outside of and performed a 4-g loaded roll around his airplane. Rug's jet stayed in the middle of the 'barrel' and I flew around the outside of the barrel in a flight path that resembled a huge corkscrew, traveling a much longer distance through the air than he did. By the time Rug figured out what was going on, I was behind him and transitioning to guns. He was 'dead' again. The entire engagement had lasted about thirty seconds from the 'fight's on' call.

"Damn," Rug said as we met at the door to the hangar ten minutes later, "it's just not fair that you can be that good and not have flown the jet for years."

"I don't know what to say," I said truthfully. "It's coming back more quickly than I could have ever believed."

"Because you're an artist." Burt's words from long ago rang in my ears.

"You're going to have to show me that loaded roll thing. I've never seen anyone do that successfully, and you did it so fast, that by the time I saw your wings move, it was over."

"A young man by the name of Bill Richards taught me that," I told him, "during my first tour in the Viper. He used it to wax my ass repeatedly until I gained leverage on him and made him tell me the secret."

"Well, this sounds like a good story."

"If you can get a glass or two of single-malt past Samantha's booze boycott, I'll tell you all about it."

"Man," he said looking at me again, "you realize that if I broach this subject, I won't get laid for at least a week. She's quite the hard-ass."

"You have to decide what's important," I said, making a production of looking at the ceiling of the hangar as we walked through, "sex or learning a new trick in the Viper."

For a normal man, this would not have been a problem. For a fighter pilot though, it was a dilemma of the first order. The masculine nature manifests itself in different ways.

We walked back into operations and found Ruth at the ops desk. "There's nothing more I can teach this guy about BFM," Rug said. "He knows more than I do. And how in the hell he can fly the jet so well after being out of it for so long is beyond me. It just isn't fair."

Ruth lifted her gaze from the paperwork she had in front of her and looked first at Rug, then at me. "It seems you're a man of many talents," she said. And for a second, as I gazed into those deep brown eyes of hers, I thought I saw them soften.

"Everyone has to be good at something," I said evenly.

Samantha gave in and I was allowed two glasses of scotch that night. Rug asked her with me present and she looked directly at me and said it would be a reward for my 'performance' thus far. She also got the oddest smirk on her face and told me that I'd owe her for this.

We wound up in the bar after dinner that night. I choose Lagavulin, a well-aged Islay malt, and tried my best to keep my tongue in my mouth as Rug poured it into a nice cut-glass tumbler with a wide mouth. I inhaled the smooth bouquet and was briefly transported to the barren island I had visited a few years ago. Then, I took healthy sip and let the nectar work its way down my throat. The burn felt good and familiar, and soon the glow followed.

"Ahhh," was all I said.

"All right, FNG," Rug said, "I got you your scotch; now tell me the secret behind the roll."

"Wait a minute," Samantha interrupted him, "I want to hear about the leverage you had on the guy who taught it to you. How did you make him tell you?"

I just looked at Rug. "Do you tell her everything?"

Rug looked away for a second. "Pretty much," he said.

"Well you're not going to believe it, anyway," I began as I took another healthy slug of the amber nectar.

Samantha threw her head back to get her bangs out of her eyes and watched me with the oddest expression on her face. "Try us," she said.

"My first tour in the F-16 was at Kunsan Air Base in Korea."

"Ah yes, the Kune," Rug said.

Samantha shot a look at him which told him to shut up but I don't think he noticed.

"As you probably know, Kunsan is a remote tour, so apart from occasional visits, families aren't allowed there. Well, each of the two squadrons there had its own 'party house,' since by that time it wasn't politically correct to get drunk in the officer's club anymore."

Rug nodded sadly. He and I were both about the same age and he remembered the USAF's descent into political correctness all too well, just as I did.

"Were you a Panton or a Juvat?" he asked, referring to the squadron I had been assigned to. The rivalry between the two fighter squadrons at Kunsan, the 35th and the 80th, was legendary.

"A Panton and damn proud of it. Now usually," I continued, "all anyone cared about when they weren't flying was getting drunk, but about halfway through my tour there, something changed."

I had their attention now. All of them: Ruth, Natasha, Samantha, and the pilots. I hoped what I was going to tell them wouldn't disappoint them, but I guessed that original entertainment was hard to come by anyway.

"We discovered that a contingent of young, female, American English teachers lived in the nearby town of Iksan, and we made arrangements to get them clearance to party with us on the base. But the damn Juvats beat us to it, and before we knew it, all the girls were partying at the other squadron's hooch, and we were still looking at the same faces on Friday and Saturday nights. And worse, if we wanted to talk to the girls we had to walk across the green and go into the Juvat's hooch, Bruni's I think it was called, which was demeaning to say the least."

I saw the smirks. They all got it. They understood how fighter pilot pride would be damaged by having to admit that the other guys had something better than we did.

"But then," I said, "somebody decided to put together a band and that changed everything. Bill Richards, the guy who taught me the roll, was a frustrated lead guitarist and he recruited guys to play bass and drums, and even found a particularly talented lieutenant named Brian Brown to play rhythm guitar and sing. And let me tell you, this kid Brian was brilliant. He could have easily been a front man for a real band. He had a voice and he could really play the axe. The band practiced for about a month and then put on its first show in our party house, called Delta House, and brought the place down. The girls came pouring into our hooch, and we owned Friday and Saturday nights. All was right with the world."

I paused and took a sip of scotch. "And?" Samantha asked.

"Well, they had a problem," I continued after I let the scotch do its magic. "The tours of duty at Kunsan are a year in length and the guy who played the drums was due to rotate out one month after the band started playing, and that was going to ruin everything. So, one night, while the band was taking a break, Bill came over to me while I was standing at the bar and asked me to step outside with him. He told me that Hobo, the drummer, was leaving and that they needed a new drummer ASAP. I told him I knew that and that I sure hoped they found one because I was enjoying the eye candy at Delta these days. That's when he looked me in the eye and told me that he had heard that I played drums."

I stopped again and took another drink of scotch. The glass was nearly empty and I was enjoying the glow. I set the glass down on the bar and motioned toward it. Rug looked at Samantha and she nudged him so hard he nearly fell. He filled the glass nearly to the rim.

"Good man," I said as I picked it up.

"Anyway, I don't know how Bill found out that I played drums, because I don't ever remember telling anyone about it, but he did. I argued with him and told him the last time I had played was in college, a long time ago, and I wasn't sure I remembered how. He told me I'd have a month to relearn. I told him I didn't know whether I needed that kind of pressure and he practically pleaded with me. He asked me if there was anything he could do that would convince me. I told him he had to teach me the barrel-roll-attack."

I took a slug of scotch and let it work its way down. "So, he taught me."

Silence followed for a moment and not surprisingly, Samantha broke it. "But what happened with the band?" she asked.

"I went into typical fighter pilot obsession mode," I replied, "and ordered an electronic drum set so I could practice in the dorm without making any noise. It cost me about $2,500, which was a lot of money at that time. They made me a practice tape and even a practice video and I spent every spare moment I had for a month learning the songs and teaching myself how to play again."

I took another pull at the scotch. I could tell that this was something they didn't expect from me. I was having fun.

"The night after Hobo's going-away party, we reopened, and the relief that we could still rock was huge. We had stolen the girls from the Juvats permanently."

"What was the name of the band?" Rug asked, and the grin on his face told me he already knew and was asking for the benefit of the others. The legend of 'the band' at Kunsan was well known in Viper circles.

"Steal Wool," I replied, "and that's spelled s-t-e-A-l. I think it's apparent why that name was appropriate."

Samantha was smiling and Ruth was just shaking her head. Brinker, Pete, and VB had half frowns on their faces like they didn't get any of it.

"I didn't realize you were a charter member of Steal Wool, too," said Rug.

"Well, I wasn't a charter member. I was the second drummer. The lieutenant, whose name I can't remember but whom we called Hobo, was the first. Frankly, he was a lot better than I was, but after a while I was playing with my electronic drums and making up for my lack of talent with technology. Anyway, I was just the drummer when we started to become 'famous.'"

"God, I remember the stories," Rug said. "Some Block 50 guys I flew with went to the Kune for an assignment and then came back into the Block 50 and the stories we heard were amazing!"

"We ruled that place!" I said, full of myself now. "We even took over the O Club at Eielson Air Force Base in Alaska while we there for a Cope Thunder exercise. We were the main act for five weekends in a row."

"Way cool," Rug said. "So, tell me about the roll now."

I took another slug of scotch and began to talk him through it. Ruth and the other pilots listened intently, but it was Samantha who kept attracting my attention. She stood behind Rug and couldn't stop staring at me. Her eyes were shiny in the dim light of the bar, and at one point when Rug was having a sidebar discussion with Brinker, I heard her whisper something to herself.

"And he plays the drums too," she said.

Later that night, I received an unexpected e-mail from Smith and Amrine. Until now, their responses to my communications had been something terse, like 'message received.' But this one was in response to the message I has sent them about Brianna's departure to Zurich and the words were surprising indeed.

"We know about her," it said. "Turns out she's a friend. Hope you two had a chance to talk. Keep at it. Working on a surprise for you."

As soon as I closed the e-mail, it deleted itself.

TOP SECRET / SPECIAL
COMPARTMENTALIZED INFORMATION
CLASSIFIED BY: US Central Intelligence Agency
DECLASSIFY ON: OADR

From: Special Projects Group [NCS]
Sent: Wednesday, 30 September 2009, 1000 EDT (30 September 2009, 1400Z)
To: Director, NCS
Cc: Special Projects Group [NCS]]; damrine@cmail.cia.gov; dsmith3@cmail.cia.gov

SUBJECT: Update, Case File: 08-434A (MAG)

(TS) Narrative:

1. (TS) Contactor 09-017 (Pearce, Colin M.) has one ride remaining in his air-to-air training phase. A major storm system at his location forced a two-day delay in his training. He has been told the storm system will clear this evening and training will resume tomorrow. Meteorological analysis of the Pacific area encompassed by the GMT+12 time conversation zone verifies several severe storm systems, some at Typhoon strength, throughout the Southern Pacific and encompassing thousands of habitable islands. Unfortunately, this information will not enable us to pinpoint MAG/Pearce's location.

2. (TS) MI-6 (via "Brianna Blenhem") has informed us that funds transfers are taking place in preparation for the major strike we were expecting. The funds are being deposited into a numbered escrow account which only disperses when/if the strike is successful. Strike date (inferred by the scheduled final payment schedule) will be 8 or 9 October. No confirmation on target location.

3. (TS) All-source chatter also confirms major strike will occur soon.

4. (TS) In concert with Special Projects Groups from DI, DS&T, and DS, we have researched Director, CIA's proposed alternate project to flush MAG into the open prior to the main strike. DI has produced a suitable target which will accomplish the standing national security objectives. Based on research and further discussions with MI-6 and Brianna Blenhem, we believe the project will provide the desired effect. Furthermore, according to Blenhem, MAG is presently low on cash in their accounts due to the recent purchase of three 'special weapons.' (Probably from stockpile at Ramstein Air Base, Germany—ref: Broken Arrow Report, 08-4/25.)

(TS) CONCLUSIONS:
1. (TS) Based on movement of funds and chatter, we believe there is no doubt the major strike will occur.

2. (TS) MAG's need for cash will increase the probability of success of DCIA's option.

3. (TS) Loss of two days of training for Pearce means the time window to conduct the DCIA option, from contract to execution, is at most, a few days.

(TS) ACTION: Will complete work on DCIA option package so we are prepared to implement immediately on order from DCIA.

(TS) RECOMMENDATION: Press for immediate authorization to execute DCIA option.

TOP SECRET / SPECIAL
COMPARTMENTALIZED INFORMATION
CLASSIFIED BY: US Central Intelligence Agency
DECLASSIFY ON: OADR

CHAPTER FIFTEEN

Contract Day Twenty-One
Thursday, 1 October
0600 Hours Local Time
Island Training Base

As if my body was on remote control, at 0600 my eyes popped open. I was wide awake and alert instantly. Samantha had taken advantage of the two-day operational hiatus forced on us by a passing storm and constructed a regimen of extended exercise, protracted rest, enhanced nutrition and drugs. It culminated superbly. Today, I felt strong, fit, and alert - better than I had in years. My body was one with the universe and it was humming. And best of all, the bloodlust inside me was sleeping soundly.

I was up, dressed, and down the hall to the gym in five minutes flat. Samantha was waiting there for me, in lotus position, in front of one of the mirrored walls. She motioned to the mat beside her and I joined her there.

"I figured that after kicking your ass for eight hours a day for two days, I owed you and your body a bit of a break," she said.

She led me through an extensive series of yoga poses, emphasizing balance and flexibility, although we spent more time in the ones that lent themselves to meditation. I relaxed and enjoyed myself.

"Your energy is very peaceful today," she said when we finally made it to the resting pose, lying side by side on our backs on the mat.

"Ummmm," I murmured pleasurably, with my eyes closed. "I guess I'm feeling peaceful...at least for the moment." It was true. I did feel peaceful. The realization astonished me.

She laughed quietly. "You don't feel this way a lot, do you?" She rolled on to her right side so she was next to me and propped her head up. I turned my head to look up at her and into those impossibly blue eyes.

"You already know the answer to that question. I've pretty much spilled my guts to you over the last few days."

"Well, it seems conversations in the steam room can have that effect," she said, laughing. "There's something about being physically naked with someone that seems to lower the conversational barriers."

I laughed. "True. And if someone had ever told me I could have a platonic discussion with a gorgeous naked woman for hours at a time, I would have told them they were crazy." The lack of sexual tension between us in that environment *had* been amazing. Oh, it had been there all right, just simmering below the surface, but somehow we had silently agreed not to act on it.

"Well, we did need to relax your muscles for a long time after each of the workouts I put you through. And the steam room is one of the few places you can talk around here without *someone* listening in."

She nonchalantly rested her left hand on my chest and smiled down at me. Her touch surprised me and I suddenly felt my heart leap. *What the hell is that about?*

"These last few days have been great," she said. "Addicting, in a way. The thing is, you are so easy to talk to," she said. "Just like..."

"Just like who, Sammy?" I asked gently.

She didn't speak for a moment as she fought an internal battle over what to say. I understood the struggle. Intimacy had always been something I shunned. I truly didn't know whether I was afraid of it or just not capable of it. And looking at Sammy, I sensed her battle was similar to mine.

"Someone very special," she replied, her eyes moistening. A mask of pain and loss ran across her features. She looked at me with an expression I had rarely seen on a woman's face - an expression of trust. "Very special."

I felt a lump forming in my throat. "Well, whoever he or she was, I'm honored you think similarly of me in some small way."

"It was a *he*," she said, absentmindedly stroking my chest. "He died a long time ago."

"Oh, my God, Sammy," I said. "I'm so sorry." Without thinking, I placed my hand over hers.

"He was an RAF Jaguar pilot," she continued, sadly and angrily. "He crashed into the side of some damn mountain in Scotland. We were to be married the following week. He's the only person I ever gave my heart to."

I looked up at her for a long moment. "That giving your heart thing can be dangerous," I said.

She looked down at my chest, averting her eyes. "Is that why you've never given yours?"

Damn. I had never said that over the course of our conversations the last few days, but she had seen it anyway. This was scary. She actually *got* me. *Holy shit.*

I sighed a long sigh. "Yeah," I said at last.

"How many women have you had?" she asked.

"Many," I said. "Enough that I don't remember all their names."

"And you didn't want to give yourself to any of them?"

I shook my head. "I was close with one. Once. But mostly, it's only ever been about sex if for no other reason than the logistics prevented it from being about anything else. But the one time I considered something deeper, the opportunity or invitation wasn't there."

"What does that mean?"

"No one ever asked me for anything else," I said quietly. "And I didn't volunteer."

She nodded. "I've had more men than I can count," she said sadly. "I thought at some point I wouldn't be able to see his face anymore. But it hasn't worked. I still see it every morning and every evening."

"Then you had something incredibly special," I said, stating the obvious. "I'd argue that most people who say they're in love never feel anything like that."

She lowered her head to my chest and my arms went around her. The natural ease of it surprised me.

"Who are you, Colin Pearce?" she whispered wistfully. "Why are you here?"

##

"Welcome to ACT-1 for FNG Pearce, lady and gentlemen."

We were in the main briefing room and Rug was presenting his 'bandit briefing' to our adversaries for the day. It was to be Rug and me, fighting as a two-ship team, against a four-ship formation comprised of Ruth, Brinker, Pete, and VB. Today's ride was the air combat training ride, the culmination of all the air-to-air rides I had thus far. I'd use the radar mechanics and interpretation I practiced on the intercept ride and the two-ship tactics I had practiced on the air combat maneuvering ride along with the one-versus-one combat from the basic fighter maneuvers rides. It was like an air-to-air final exam.

Ruth sat on the aisle seat in the second row of the room with the other members of her formation to her right. I sat across the aisle from her. Rug was behind the podium on the floor below with the projector screen illuminated behind him.

The atmosphere in the room was tense as Rug presented

the 'motherhood' briefing items, the standard litany of things we all needed to understand to run the engagements: what radio calls would start them, what radio calls would stop them, and the training rules we'd abide by as we fought. He also introduced the radar controller who would provide ground-controlled intercept (GCI) instructions. His call sign would be 'Island.'

Rug finished his presentation and then asked the 'bandits,' as the adversaries were known, if they had any questions.

"Just one," Brinker said with the usual sneer. "Blade, is there a bonus for killing FNG?"

I crossed my arms and sighed. If you looked up the word 'predictable' in the dictionary, Brinker's picture would be there. He had played the lone bandit Rug and I had fought in the air combat maneuvering ride I had earlier in the week. He had also led the two-ship bandit element Rug and I had fought on the intercept ride. On both rides, Brinker had done everything he could to force an error on my part and embarrass me. And on both rides, I had soundly kicked his ass.

Ruth looked at me across the aisle in the small auditorium.

"Ten thousand dollars, US," she said with her gaze fixed on me. Her brown eyes were both playful and icy. It was not a good look for her.

"Fight's on, folks," I said, staring evenly back at all four of them.

"Bandits are dismissed," Rug said after a few awkward seconds had passed.

The four of them rose and filed out.

"Hey, Blade," I called before they reached the door, "do I get ten grand for every one of your asses I kick?"

She didn't answer.

"It doesn't matter," I said. "I'd do it for free."

After the door shut, Rug turned to me. "What the fuck was that about?" he asked.

"Just making the game more interesting, I guess."

##

"Island, picture is two groups, range split 10, leaders are bull's-eye 360 at 30; 26,000 head; trailers 16,000 head." The GCI controller was giving us a radar picture from 'God's eye' viewpoint, looking down from above, using a common reference point called the bull's-eye. The closest group to us, the leaders, were 30 miles due north of the bull's-eye, which was the island itself. They were at 26,000 feet and nose-on to us, coming right at us. The trailing group was ten miles behind the leaders at 16,000 feet, also nose-on to us.

It was a spectacularly clear day and we were directly over the island at 22,000 feet, heading out on our track northbound.

The sun glinted off Rug's jet as we rolled out of the turn in line-abreast formation, two miles apart. The water below was deep blue-green except for the turquoise-shaded shallow areas to the west of the island.

I was comfortable in my womb, my oxygen mask clamped on my face, and the Viper's controls in my hands. My fingers rested confidently on the buttons and switches on the stick and throttle and tingled with anticipation of the task before them. I could hear and feel the GE engine below me and its welcome push at my back. We were accelerating through 400 knots and the noise of the wind was just becoming audible over the roar of the engine.

It felt great to be alive.

"Boiler One is targeted leaders, 26,000," came Rug's voice over the radio. "Boiler Two, target trailers."

Rug was taking responsibility for the lead group and assigning me the trail group. I didn't see the trailers in my radar display yet, but I wasn't worried. They were over 40 miles away and there was no chance my radar would paint them at that range.

"Boiler Two, clean trailers," I replied.

We continued down track and our range to the leaders rapidly decreased - at 800 to 1,000 knots of closure, it doesn't take much time. As we approached twenty miles to the leaders, small squares of green video appeared on my radar display about ten miles behind the leaders.

"Boilers offset right," Rug commanded. We both turned to the right to begin the intercept and started to climb rapidly. Rug was doing the right thing. By going to an altitude that kept both groups below us, he eliminated their ability to 'sandwich' us in altitude.

I looked down at my radar again, verifying the position of the contacts by putting my cursor on them and reading the positional and altitude information the radar displayed.

I keyed the mic. "Boiler Two, hits bull's-eye 360, 30; 16,000 head, confirm trailers Island?"

"Island, affirmative, trail group, two contacts now, bull's-eye 360 at 28; 16,000 head."

"Boiler Two, targeted trailers, 16,000." The contacts in my radar had gone steady. I slewed the radar cursor over to the contacts and designated them.

Rug and I leveled off at 32,000 feet and 350 knots, both of us leaving the power in MIL, full throttle without afterburner, to regain some speed. I noted with some satisfaction that we weren't producing contrails, those streams of white vapor jets emit at altitude and which would have been a dead giveaway. I also noted that the sun was high and outside of our flight path, which meant that as we began our final conversion turn at the endgame of the intercept, the opposing jets would have to look into the sun to see us.

We were now about ten miles from the lead group. The track of the radar contacts indicated they were still heading directly for us.

"Boiler One, leaders are aware; bringing them to the nose." Rug pulled his jet to the left to go nose-to-nose with the leaders, and I followed him, falling back to more of a trail position on him. We began to descend.

"Boiler Two, sort group, my nose eight miles, 27,000 head. Island target trailers." Rug had handed off responsibility for the trailers to GCI and now he was putting my radar inside his group. This way, we'd both have maximum situational awareness when we merged with his group.

I broke lock with the rear group and rolled the elevation scan, or EL Strobe, knob to center my radar scan at the lead group's altitude while slewing my cursor over the contacts. The two bogey contacts showed up clearly, side by side, just under two miles apart. I slid my cursors to the western contact and designated him. The entire process took less than five seconds.

"Boiler Two, sorted, western man, 27,000."

"Island is targeted trailers. Now showing trailers flanking west." The trail group had taken a forty-five degree turn toward the west, which meant they were trying to get around to the other side of the upcoming merge. They were trying to trap us, but we had no choice. We had to deal with the groups one by one.

"Boiler One copies. Boilers five miles, heads up."

We were five miles from the merge. I pulled my jet into a slight left turn, moving across Rug's tail and over to his left side, so I wouldn't have to shoot 'through' him when we merged and he made the ID call. I squinted through my heads-up display and canopy to see our adversaries. I could just make out a black dot in the target designator box in the HUD. The TD box gives a visual reference for where the radar was locked. The black dot inside of it was the aircraft onto which my radar was locked. The round circle representing the Python missile's seeker head was superimposed on the TD box. I punched the uncage button on the throttle to allow the seeker head to self-track. But the growl I heard was barely audible. The jet I was locked onto had his or her power in idle. Ordinarily, that would have been an issue but today as the two-ship underdogs, we were equipped with simulated AMRAAMs, the mighty AIM-120 Advanced Medium Range Air-to-Air missile or 'Slammer,' as we used to call it. We weren't actually carrying the missiles, since the F-16's fire control computer could provide all the symbology and logic without the missile being loaded on the aircraft.

I moved my dogfight switch from outboard to inboard, which changed my radar mode and automatically called up the simulated Slammer. The designated launch zone, or DLZ, a thin rectangle of video, oriented vertically, appeared in the lower right side of the HUD. The carat indicating my range to the target was well above the required minimum range. All missiles have a minimum range, by the way. That's the range required for the missile to get clear of the launching aircraft, arm itself, and begin to guide. Because of its speed, the Slammer's min range was quite a bit greater than the Python's, especially with a head-on shot. But that wouldn't be a factor in this engagement. Assuming I was quick enough.

I smiled grimly under the oxygen mask. I'd be quick enough.

I pulled my throttle to idle and looked over at Rug's jet to focus my eyes, and then I shifted them to the area in front of his jet.

"Boiler One, tally one, my nose two miles." Rug saw his bandit.

I raised my visor, squinted and refocused in front of his jet. The pale blue F-16 off his nose zoomed in before my eyes. I placed my right thumb on the pickle button and began to do something we called the 'lobster eye.' Like a lobster with its eyes on independent stalks, I had to try to keep my eyes trained on the jet off my nose and the jet Rug was merging with, at the same time.

Rug's adversary was looming larger in front of him, now only a few thousand feet away. His wingman, my adversary, was several thousand feet further back. Things were about to happen fast.

"Boiler One, ID hostile F-16..." Rug began.

Rug had said the 'h-word.' I pushed the weapons release or 'pickle' button on my control stick while he spoke.

"...bull's-eye 360 for 15; 30,000," he concluded.

The missile time-of-flight indicator had decremented to zero before he finished talking. A real Slammer would have come off the rail in terminal guidance mode and closed the distance to target in less than three seconds.

"Boiler Two, fox three kill, F-16, bull's-eye 360 at 15, straight and level; 30,000."

"Island copies kill," the GCI controller acknowledged. Then a few seconds later he said, "Kill passed," indicating he had passed the kill information to the other aircraft on the bandit radio frequency.

The jet I had shot rocked its wings to acknowledge the kill and made an aggressive right turn up and out of the fight, leaving Rug and me to deal with the remaining bandit.

Meanwhile, Rug had merged left to left with his bandit and the ensuing two-circle fight put Rug in a turn toward me and the bandit in a turn away. The bandit had allowed this to occur, which meant that he didn't know that I had switched sides of the formation pre-merge. I smiled into my oxygen mask. Brinker had made that mistake. I was confident Blade wouldn't have.

"Boiler One, engaged," Rug called.

"Boiler Two, supporting," I said. I slammed the throttle into MAX AB and pulled up into a climbing right turn.

Rug's jet flashed underneath me, about 3,000 feet below, the vapor pouring off his wingtips as he maintained the g in his turn. I looked across the circle and saw his adversary, about 135 degrees through his own turn, vapor pouring off his wingtips as well. As Rug went under me, I rolled to aim my lift vector, represented by my vertical stabilizer, just under his opponent's plane of motion and pulled back on the control stick more forcefully. As my nose came around, I was hoping my move into the vertical would delay the adversary from seeing me. My nose began to track downward and I called up the dogfight mode of the radar.

"Lock, lock," said the luscious female voice in my headset. I smiled. Leave it to the engineers to design a voice warning system for fighter pilots that featured a sexy female voice. These words indicated that my radar had locked onto the target I commanded, Brinker's jet, as it turned below me.

The slammer wouldn't be able to hack the turn in a close fight like this, so I uncaged the Python and was rewarded with a loud, aggressive growl. Brinker was obviously still in full afterburner. I assessed the range and angles quickly and punched the pickle button.

"Python," I said and watched the time-of-flight indicator decrement to zero as I pulled the throttle out of AB, relaxed pressure on the control stick and allowed my jet to 'float' to the outside of the adversary's turn.

"Boiler Two kill, F-16 bull's-eye 360 at 15, left hand turn; 29,000."

"Island copies kill."

I looked to my right and picked up Rug's jet paralleling my flight path, about two miles away.

"Boiler One, egress south," I directed.

Rug rolled out of his turn and I descended to a line abreast position with him on his left side. I didn't need to tell him I was there.

"Boiler One, visual, lead right," he said. Rug had reassumed leadership of the formation.

"Two," I acknowledged.

The first engagement went like clockwork. We had merged with two bandits and 'killed' both in less than one minute. Now it was time to deal with the other two-ship element. Ruth's two-ship.

"Island, Boiler One, picture," Rug commanded.

"Island shows single group, two contracts, bull's-eye 345 at 20; 16,000 head."

Bastards. After we had merged with the lead group, the trailers had offset us to the west. Now they were coming our way. Undoubtedly, just the way they had planned it.

"Island, Boiler One, distance to that group."

"Boiler, group your right four o-clock, 12 miles," the GCI controller said.

We had two choices. We could run from the other group and try to build some distance between us and them before we turned back to fight. Or we could just turn now, get in their faces, and see what happened.

Rug chose the same option I would have.

"Boiler Two, go wedge right." He rolled his jet up on to the right wing and turned hard toward the bandits, instructing me to collapse my formation position. I maneuvered appropriately and got to where he needed me to be.

"Boiler One, targeted group my nose 16,000, head. Boiler Two, sort northern man in that group."

My radar cursor was already over the contacts as Rug's command came over my headset. "Boiler Two, sorted, 16,000."

"Boiler Two, think you can handle a pincer on this one?"

I grinned inside my oxygen mask. I wanted to say, "not only yeah, but fuck yeah," but instead I keyed the mic and answered: "Two, affirmative."

"Boilers, five miles, heads up, action, action."

Rug and I turned away from each other to take the bandits between us, like the claws of a crab opening to pinch its prey. For a second or two, the bandits maintained their track, which would have carried them between us. Then they turned toward me.

"Boiler Two, they're on me," I said into the mic.

"Boiler One," Rug acknowledged.

This was going to work perfectly. Both bandits would

merge with me and Rug would make an unobserved entry from the left and kill both of them.

I peered through the TD box in my HUD and strained to see the jet inside. The gray-blue Viper stood out well against the green water and I picked him out immediately. Then I looked to his right to pick out his formation mate.

Nothing there. The joke was on us. One of the bandits had vanished.

"Boiler Two, tally one only, my nose two miles."

"Boiler One, no joy, radar contact lost, blowing through."

"You son of a bitch!" I yelled into my intercom. I was going to be forced into a one versus one engagement with my bandit and neither Rug nor I knew where the other bandit was. Furthermore, Rug wasn't going to stick around and help me. He was going past the fight, to try to gain some situational awareness, and then he'd pitch back in. I knew the jet I was merging with was the wingman, either VB or Pete. Ruth would be in the jet which had 'vanished.'

And in the meantime, it was going to be me versus two.

I pulled my power to idle and prepared for the merge. My adversary was just off my nose but I couldn't shoot him until I visually 'identified' him. The opposing Viper's shape zoomed into focus before me and at that moment, in my peripheral vision, I saw the 'wing flash' of a jet rolling up on its side, very low and to my right.

It was Ruth. She had descended into the low altitude block and crossed behind her formation-mate, moving from south to north, from his right to his left. She was positioning herself to make an unobserved entry of her own from low to high and 'kill' me as soon as I started turning and burning with my opponent.

There wasn't much time.

With less than a mile to my merge, I rolled to the left and pulled across my opponent's nose as hard as I could, then I rolled back to the right to reduce the distance between us. Now we were going to meet right to right and I had my adversary and Ruth on the same side of my jet.

"Now, go two-circle with me, pal. Just go to two-circle."

I was doing the 'lobster-eye' thing again, keeping track of Ruth as she tried to sneak around low and to the right, and watching the guy I was merging with.

My opponent's jet flashed by me on the right. "Boiler Two, ID hostile, F-16," I announced.

I was already into my turn, with MAX AB selected and my lift vector below my adversary's plane of motion. I pulled into about six g's and waited to see what he was going to do.

I could barely see the side of Ruth's airplane below and to the right of my nose, about three miles away. Because of the direction she was flying, she was going to have to wait for me to pass her, inside of her orbit, before she could make an entry. I kept my turn going so she wouldn't be able to tell that I saw her.

"C'mon, pal, make your move," I muttered as I mentally willed my opponent to turn across my tail.

A second later he did.

"Thank you!" I said. That gave me about thirty seconds before his nose would be anywhere near me as he executed his turn. I rolled my jet inverted and pulled the nose down for a second or two. Then I unloaded the g and pushed on the control stick to straighten my flight path. Blade's jet was now right off my nose, its blue-gray paint scheme clearly discernible above the waves below.

I was into the 'Dogfight' radar mode, and I put the boresight cross in my HUD right on her jet, and then pushed the target management switch on the control stick forward.

"Lock, lock."

The DLZ for the Python came up on the lower right side of my HUD as I uncaged it. I was in range.

"GRRRRRRRR."

"Let me save you for the close-in fight," I said into my

intercom as I went inboard with the dogfight switch and called up the AMRAAM. The DLZ for the Slammer came up and I was in range for that as well, so I let her have it. Then I got back into my turn against my own adversary.

"Boiler Two, Fox Three kill, F-16 below the fight, bull's-eye 355 at 15, 6000, right hand turn. Boiler Two engaged with remaining bandit there."

I still had a handful to deal with. By rolling out to nail Blade, I had allowed the guy I was fighting to make some angles and gain some vertical turning room above me. As I got my lift vector back up and applied the g to resume my turn, I could see that he was well aft of my wing-line and was approaching an offensive position in a slight descent himself. Ordinarily, going low to high in a situation like this would have resulted in a bad energy situation for me, but I had a plan. I gasped in a few extra breaths of air and got deep into my anti-g straining maneuver. Then I pulled on the stick as hard as I could to bring my nose around to the bandit.

I'd rather be lucky than good. Because I had straightened my flight path to go after the other jet, I had built some additional range between my adversary and me. He should have immediately noticed that fact and taken advantage of it by increasing his own g, pulling his jet more toward my six o'clock when I wasn't turning, but he didn't see it. His lack of vision was about to kill him.

As I pulled my nose to him, he noticed the maneuver and pulled his nose to me. I yanked my throttle to idle and we merged about two seconds later, passing right to right. I started into a right turn and waited. He turned left across my tail.

"Perfect!" I yelled into my intercom.

I unloaded the controls, rolled left to reverse my turn and pulled into the vertical, just tapping the AB as I did so.

We were now in a one-circle fight. He was on the opposite side of the circle, in front of my wing line.

But because I had come low to high, I was much slower. In fact, I was just over 200 knots and I was guessing that he was well above 350, and he continued to move out in front of me due to his higher speed. I began to roll my jet until I was nearly inverted, just applying enough back pressure to keep my nose to paralleling his. I was about 2,000 feet above him, about half a mile offset to his right.

I could feel his hesitation. He didn't know what to do. If he came up to me, he'd be in a geometry he hadn't seen before. If he stayed down, he'd be 'dead' soon and he knew it. He did what he had been taught to do. He put his lift vector on me, kept his AB cooking, and pulled up into me for all he was worth.

I rolled around him and took advantage of his faster speed and my slower one, as well as my longer flight path, to spit him right out in front of me. Then the gunsight was on him and 'bullets' went through his canopy.

It was a work of art, if I do say so myself.

"Boiler Two, tracking kill, F-16, right hand turn, bull's-eye 360 at 15; 12,000."

"Island copies kill. Island shows picture clean."

"You're goddamn right it's clean," I said into my oxygen mask.

I turned back toward the island and the holding point from which Rug and I had started this engagement. The standard procedure when flight mates are separated is to proceed to a rendezvous point.

"Boiler Two is enroute to the CAP point, in the 10 to 14 block."

"Boiler One will be in the 20 to 24 block."

I nodded to myself. "I'll see you back there, Rug." Then I keyed the mic.

"Island, Boiler Two."

"Boiler Two, Island, go."

"Island, tell Blade One that Boiler Two says she owes me

forty grand. Also tell her that if she has any other surprises cooked up, I hope they're a little more original than the last one."

##

If the tension in the air at the preflight briefing could have been sliced with a knife, the tension in the debrief would have taken a chainsaw. Everyone was so tightly wound I thought I'd hear a loud 'snap' and find body parts splayed around the room. Rug debriefed the mission in his usual, thorough manner and did his best not to dwell on the fact that in every engagement we had not only beaten the bandits, but they had never even been able to take any shots. Ruth was completely silent during the entire proceeding. She stared straight ahead at Rug and ignored the telemetry animation and gun camera footage for the shots taken. Finally, when Rug finished and asked for final comments, she nodded.

She rose from her seat and made her way down the few stairs to the floor in front of the chairs. I watched her walk by. Her hair was in a tight ponytail behind her head and there was a small sweat stain on her flightsuit between her shoulder blades. She turned around when she reached the middle of the floor.

"Tomorrow will be the BFM day," she said without hesitation. "We'll start with a mass briefing at 0700 and keep flying until we're done." Her eyes swept over all of us without stopping on a single face. "It will be double elimination - that is, you'll need to be killed twice to be removed from the tournament. It will be guns only, no missiles. The winner among you," she turned and fixed her gaze directly on my face, "will fight me. Any questions?"

There were none.

"Rug will present the mass briefing tomorrow and I'll maintain the ladder. Get some sleep tonight guys. You're going to need it."

Then, she left the room.

I had the shower all alone later. I laid on the tile floor, with my legs up one side of the stall and my head rested on the other side; and then I let the stream of water fall on me while I closed my eyes and retreated inside my head for a few brief minutes.

I didn't know whether it was the drugs or the fitness program or just the high I got from kicking multiple asses in air combat, but I felt extraordinary. All my former instincts and abilities were alive and raging. I was my old self again. And a part of me didn't want any of it to end.

But someone else did.

The attack came as I was rising from the floor of the shower, right when I was most vulnerable and had the least leverage. With all my training and experience, I should have been more alert. But at that moment, I was lost inside myself and oblivious to the world around me.

My lack of focus nearly killed me.

I felt a sharp impact, like a light kidney punch, against the skin of my lower back, near the right side of my abdomen. Instinctively, I leapt further into the shower and spun around, trying to get the maximum distance from my attacker. I raised my fists in self-defense.

No one was there.

I heard the slap of footsteps on the shower floor. Rage seized me and I jumped out into the aisle in time to see a figure in dark clothes exit into the guys' hallway.

"Son of a bitch!" I spat into the air.

Only then did I look down at my right side. The brown wooden handle of a dining hall steak knife looked oddly out of place against my skin. There was a small circle of red blood around the haft where it touched me. I felt the front of my body where the knife's point would be and was rewarded by tinge of sensitivity just under the skin. There was no real pain yet. But it would come when the adrenaline rush subsided. I didn't have much time.

I retrieved my robe, draped it loosely around me and headed for the door. The hall was empty. I could hear some laughter from the bar and padded down the carpet, turned the corner and walked in. My eyes saw Ruth and Natasha standing against the counter and then the agony set in with alternating sensations of searing, white hot pain and deep muscular throbbing, like intense muscle cramps.

"Holy shit," I breathed. I leaned against the side of the entry way and motioned to the two women as I fought through the torment.

"Pearce? What are you doing here?" Ruth asked. I pointed awkwardly at my right side.

"Sammy," I said through gritted teeth. "I need Sammy. I've been stabbed."

I watched Ruth's face carefully as the words registered. A rapid and complex series of emotions ran across her features, the most vivid of which was raw panic.

She doesn't know anything about this. The thought comforted me for some reason.

Ruth and Natasha put their drinks on the bar and were at my side in an instant.

"Goddamn, this hurts," I said involuntarily. "I think I'd rather be shot." I looked down at my right side and saw a widening red stain seeping through the white terrycloth.

In moments, I was in one of the clinic's examination rooms and I was unceremoniously stripped of my robe and pushed down onto a table, face down.

"Jesus!" I heard Sammy's voice say. "What happened?"

"Someone stabbed him," Ruth answered, "while he was in the shower, apparently."

I felt the swab of an alcohol pad and then the prick of a needle.

"This will help with the pain, Colin." Sammy said. "We've

got to get that thing out of you."

The drug acted quickly. The pain seemed to dissipate. Or at least it went to a part of my brain where I didn't care about it any longer. I had a mental image of a big furry monster being forced backward into a closet and the door being shut, imprisoning him.

"He's got to be able to fly tomorrow, Sammy," I heard Ruth's voice say. "We can't get behind schedule."

"Well we're lucky," Sammy replied. "Whoever stabbed him didn't get anything vital. Just muscle and flesh. I'll have him patched up in no time. Now if the wound had been about five inches to the left, we'd be looking at a perforated kidney. That would be a whole different story."

Sometime later, I awoke back in my bed. Sammy was seated next to me, with her hip against mine and her hands resting on a clipboard in her lap. Her hair was down and she was wearing a white lab coat with a stethoscope around her neck. As my eyes regained their visual acuity, it became apparent she didn't have a damn thing on under the coat.

"Do you see all your patients dressed like this?" I asked.

She smiled and shook her head in amazement. "You're something," she said. "Someone tries to kill you and you're making jokes. When I got the call about you I was just getting into bed. I grabbed a coat and ran down to the clinic. Would you have preferred that I had taken my time and gotten properly dressed before I attended to you?"

I shook my head. "Sorry. I'm grateful, believe me. But there's just something about a gorgeous blonde naked under a white coat. I've probably seen too many porn movies."

"I won't argue with you there," she said sardonically. "So, what happened?"

I described the attack to her in detail. There wasn't much to convey. But she studiously took notes and asked me a few questions to ensure her account of the event was complete.

"So, how bad am I hurt?" I asked at last.

"Well, considering the knife wasn't very big and didn't hit anything vital, not very."

"You mean it wasn't some long, serrated, pig-sticker? I must be a wuss. That hurt like crazy."

She nodded. "Stab wounds are the worst. Your body goes into shock right away, which is why you don't feel the pain immediately. But then when it comes, the whole intrusion thing sends your pain receptors into overdrive. Believe it or not, superficial wounds hurt more than deeper ones, so you should be glad it hurt as much as it did. By the way, good job on not trying to pull it out of you. That would have made things a lot worse."

I closed my eyes. "I have a little experience with this sort of thing. So how did I get back here?"

"Ruth and I walked you down. We didn't want you to spend the night in the clinic. It would attract too much attention. It would also let whoever stabbed you know he or she was successful."

"Well, whoever it was knows they stabbed me."

"Yes, but they don't know you're relatively unhurt. That's the important thing."

"I guess."

She reached down and put her hand on my upper chest. The movement was tender and familiar. I felt my heart leap in my chest. Again.

You're an idiot, I told myself.

"You're going to need to fly tomorrow. Ordinarily, I'd keep you on bed rest and observation for at least a few days with something like this. But evidently we don't have time for that. Ruth has some of sort of schedule she has to stick to."

I grinned at her.

"I suspect there will be additional drugs involved?"

She laughed and nodded. "Oh yes, quite the cocktail. We'll get you through this."

"That's great," I said, my eyes suddenly felt heavy. "So

what happens now?"

"I have to monitor your condition all night. So I'll be staying here with you."

"Goddamn it, this just isn't fair," I said sleepily.

"What isn't fair?" she asked playfully.

"You're in my bed and I can't do a damn thing about it."

She leaned down and kissed my lips lightly. "There will be other times," she said.

TOP SECRET / SPECIAL
COMPARTMENTALIZED INFORMATION
CLASSIFIED BY: US Central Intelligence Agency
DECLASSIFY ON: OADR

From: Special Projects Group [NCS]
Sent: Thursday, 1 October 2009, 0700 EDT (1 October 2009, 1100Z)
To: Director, NCS
Cc: Special Projects Group [NCS]; damrine@cmail.cia.gov; dsmith3@cmail.cia.gov

SUBJECT: Update, Case File: 08-434A (MAG)

(TS) Narrative:

1. (TS) Contactor 09-017 (Pearce, Colin M.) has completed air-to-air training. There is a basic fighter maneuvers (1 v 1 dogfight) competition scheduled for tomorrow. Pearce believes it's as much about exercising all the jets in preparation for something else as it is about the training aspects. He has heard no discussion about the major strike. We also learned that he was attacked last night. Based on the reactions of MAG's leadership, we are assuming they were not involved. Apparently, someone else inside of MAG doesn't want the main strike to succeed. We will keep you updated.

2. (TS) We learned late last night that the Director, CIA has approved the operations order for execution, including the target we identified.

(TS) CONCLUSIONS: None.

(TS) ACTIONS: Will begin work to execute the DCIA

operations order immediately.

(TS) RECOMMENDATION: None. Information only.

TOP SECRET / SPECIAL
COMPARTMENTALIZED INFORMATION
CLASSIFIED BY: US Central Intelligence Agency
DECLASSIFY ON: OADR

CHAPTER SIXTEEN

Contract Day Twenty-Two
Friday, 2 October
0700 Hours Local Time
Island Training Base

The mass briefing began at 0700 as advertised. Rug went through the 'motherhood' and outlined the flow for the day. Each ride would consist of two offensive/defensive engagements with the pilots swapping roles, and one high-aspect engagement. The pilot who won two out of the three engagements was the victor. Thanks to the double elimination rule, everyone would fly at least twice as we worked our way to the top of the ladder. And the final winner would meet Ruth and fight her.

I felt surprisingly good. Sammy had provided me with yet another dose of drugs that morning, and the knife injury seemed like ancient history. I couldn't even feel it.

I calmly watched the tension build around me. There wasn't a doubt in my mind that I could take every one of these guys. Brinker and Rug would take longer than VB and Pete to kill, but Ruth was the only question mark. And I was itching to get at it.

"First round," Rug concluded, "Brinker and VB to east and Pete and FNG to the west. Good hunting, gentlemen."

We suited up and walked out to our aircraft.

Today, the hangar's main doors were completely open and sunlight flooded into the cavernous facility. I had only seen it in near darkness or with the overhead lights illuminated, and the sight of it bathed in natural light was awe-inspiring, especially considering it was all chiseled out of solid rock.

The vast floor was unusually empty because all eight of the unit's Vipers were aligned, wingtip-to-wingtip, under the awning outside the doors. The sun was still slightly low in the eastern sky and it gleamed off the jets' aluminum skins and Plexiglas canopies. The jets themselves had been wiped down completely and looked nearly spit-polished. They were parked with their noses pointed out to the taxiway and they reminded me of stock cars lined up and waiting for the green flag.

"This is as big of a deal for the maintenance folks as it is for us," Rug had told me when I was at the Operations Desk, receiving my 'step brief' earlier. "Unless we're supporting projects, we don't get all of the jets out very often and don't turn them quickly ever. This sort of thing lets us wring the jets out and find out if there are any discrepancies lurking in any of them."

"Sounds like a surge," I had answered. Surges were flown in USAF units every few months and were basically about replicating the sortie rates flown in combat.

"Exactly," Rug said.

My jet was parked on the far-right side of the line-up. I walked up to it and began the preflight inspection. As I was strapping in a few minutes later, I noticed Brinker getting into the jet next to mine. Before he put his helmet on, he tied a bright red scarf around his neck and looked over at me.

"This is so you'll know who's gunning you," he said.

"Thanks," I answered, "it'll give me a better target to aim at."

He flipped me off and began to lower his canopy.

Moments later we were all airborne and headed to our areas. I was paired with 'Pete' Petersen. We met in the area, did some g-warm-up turns, and then got right into it. I let him have his choice and he said he'd like to start on offense.

It didn't help him.

He started behind me, executed the initial entry into my turn circle well and kept good pressure on me for nearly 270 degrees of turn after that. But then he made the standard 'young guy' error. He started to see the offensive picture he wanted and got greedy. He pulled his nose way in front of mine to take the gunshot without having his closure under control. I put my lift vector on him and applied back pressure on the stick to generate all the g I could muster. I could have stayed with that tactic and forced him to pull up, but I began a slow roll around him to see what would happen. If he had stayed with his original plan at that point, it might have worked out for him, but he rolled with me and we ended up in a maneuver called a 'rolling scissors,' in which both aircraft continually roll around each other as each pilot tries to gain an advantage.

Having been in several of these things, I knew where this maneuver would end, but Pete didn't. I merely stopped rolling when I was directly beneath him. This forced him to stop rolling above me and we were now in a 'high-low' stack. Then, it became a waiting game. Because he was the high man and I was directly below him, every time he wanted to see me, he had to roll up on one wing, causing him to dump lift and sink down toward me. When he fell to within a few hundred feet above me, I pulled my nose up to him and zipped him with simulated 20mm.

I was offensive for the second engagement and it didn't take as long as the first.

We landed and got out of our jets while the ground crews serviced them. Pete and I met just inside the hangar to quickly debrief. He was understandably upset about the ease with which I had defeated him.

"It's all about the energy, Pete," I told him.

As we discussed the specifics of some of the maneuvers,

Brinker and VB taxied in and shut down. They climbed out of their cockpits and walked over to us. Brinker's body language told me everything I needed to know about who had won that contest.

"One down and you to go," the Dutchman said as he walked up.

I shrugged and looked at him the way I'd eye a bug crawling across the floor.

"Hey guys," Rug walked across the hangar floor to us, helmet bag in hand. "It's Brinker and Pete, and VB and me on the next go. FNG, this is a bye round for you."

"Cool," I said.

"You won't think so later," he said with a smirk on his face. "Go into the main briefing room. You can watch the fights on ACMI."

"Sounds good."

I strolled across the hangar floor and made my way to the dining hall to get a cup of coffee. Things were quiet inside the facility today as nearly all the maintenance personnel were outside working on the jets. I briefly considered making my way down to the clinic to look in on Samantha, but I decided against it. As calm as it was, I knew that nothing went unnoticed, and I didn't want to get her in any sort of trouble.

I walked back to operations. Ruth was seated at the ops desk with a phone in her ear and did not look up as I walked by and into the main briefing room.

"How are we going to fit it in?" I heard her ask. There was a pause as the caller spoke to her.

"Well I know we need the funds, but do you think it's wise when we're so close to the big project?"

Another pause. I slowed my step slightly so I could hear the rest of the conversation.

"It's tight, but it's possible, I guess. I'll check with Natasha to ensure we have the munitions and I'll call the freighter liaison as well."

I couldn't slow my step much further or it'd be obvious; but it didn't seem to matter as I heard her hang the phone up a second later.

Wow, I thought, *I wonder what all that was about?*

As Rug had promised, the ACMI was called up. ACMI stood for air combat maneuvering instrumentation. It was a telemetry system which beamed signals down from the maneuvering aircraft to a computer system. When the engagements were over, the maneuvering was recreated using computer animation and it gave a meticulously accurate view of the fight, complete with airspeed, altitude, g-loading, and weapons parameters. It could even be tilted during playback to show a 'God's eye view' perspective, an angled perspective, or the perspective from the cockpit of each of the combatants.

I sank into one of the comfortable stadium seats and waited for the show to unfold. Rug and VB were the first two to blast off, followed by Pete and Brinker a few minutes later. Both contests went to three engagements with Rug and Brinker victorious, as I expected. Pete and VB were done, but I was glad to see that Pete had lasted longer against Brinker than he had against me.

I walked to the door of the briefing room, stuck my head out, and looked over at Ruth. "Well, Pete and VB are done. Who's next?"

She looked down at something on the desk in front of her. "Brinker and Rug," she said.

"And your prediction is?"

She looked up at me and her features grew thoughtful. "It will be close, but Brinker will beat Rug," she said.

"Why?"

"Brinker is more aggressive and innovative than Rug," she said. "Having said that, if I was flying a project tomorrow and had to choose between the two, I'd take Rug because I could completely count on him to perform as instructed. Brinker, not so much." She shrugged. "They both have their valuable traits."

"Interesting."

"How are you feeling?" she asked.

"Completely good to go."

She smiled and nodded at me. There was a hunger in her eyes that I couldn't quite define.

I went back into the room and waited for them to take off. A few moments later, Pete and VB walked in dejectedly and plodded to seats in the row above me.

"That didn't take long," VB said.

"Hey," I said, "both of you made it to the third engagement, so you did something right."

"Only because my offensive engagement was a tie," VB said. "He totally spit me out when I went in for guns."

Then we heard the initial radio calls as Rug and Brinker checked into their area and we trained our eyes on the ACMI screen to watch the fight.

It was a good match.

Rug won his offensive engagement but Brinker made him work for it. Brinker won his offensive engagement with a little less effort.

Then they were into high-aspect. They split, turned in, hit the merge, and went two-circle. At first the turns were mirror images of each other, but soon Brinker was gaining ground.

ACMI displays can generate a history behind each of the cartoon airplanes the computer uses to represent the real ones. The history for this display depicted the last thirty seconds of elapsed time with a dotted line behind each computer-generated jet. I pointed to the 'God's eye view' display. Brinker was clearly further around his circle than Rug was around his.

"What's he doing?" VB asked. "I can't even tell the difference." "Look at their flight parameters," I said, pointing to readouts next to their call-signs on the adjacent screen. "Brinker is flying his jet like a machine. He's gaining because he's managing his energy more judiciously."

It was true. Rug was all over the place. His airspeed varied between 300 and 380 knots and his g-loading wandered between 4.5 and 7. Brinker, on the other hand, was rock-solid and kept his airspeed at 340 to 350, and his g between 6 and 7.

"Holy shit," Pete commented.

"Now the real question will be how he uses the advantage he's gaining and how Rug reacts," I said.

About 360 degrees of turn later, Brinker had made enough angles on Rug that he transitioned to offense and Rug had no choice but to transition to defense. It took a while after that, but Brinker eventually shot him.

I found the engagement highly illuminating. For all his talk, Brinker had played a very strong energy management game plan. I had to wonder whether that was really his philosophy or whether it was for my benefit. But his performance underlined one of the classic BFM tenets: you fight what you see. It didn't matter what he did in here. What mattered was what he did out there.

"Good match," I said, rising. "Well, I guess I'm on. See you guys later."

"Good luck, TC," said VB, "er, I mean, FNG." I smiled at them. "See ya," I said.

I walked through the door and out past the ops desk. Ruth looked up at me.

"Which one do you want first?" she asked. "Assuming you defeat both of them, the second guy will only be a single elimination; but, he'll just have to live with that."

"I'll take Rug first. I want Brinker rested and arrogant so I can kick his ass so thoroughly he'll feel like he's been beaten twice."

She nodded. "Brinker will try to take a head-on gunshot during the first turn when he's offensive. It's his favorite 'secret' trick. Don't let him spook you."

"And to what do I owe this piece of intelligence?' I asked, more than a little skeptical.

"I don't want him to beat you."

"It'd be naïve of me to suppose that's because of any recent events. Let me guess. It's because you want that pleasure all to yourself."

She nodded with a mischievous smile on her face. "Now you're getting the picture," she said, her eyes radiating a glow that was unabashedly sensual. "You need to be spanked."

"Really?"

"Oh, yes," she said with a playful edge in her voice, "you've been a very bad boy."

"You know sometimes the 'spanker' becomes the 'spankee.'"

"That won't happen this time," she said confidently. "You're not a rule-breaker."

"I might surprise you."

"We'll see."

What could I say to that? I went back out to my jet and Rug and I blasted off a few moments later.

I had to hand it to him. He fought well and even tried to use a few of my own tricks against me. But Ruth was right about him. In the end, it came down to me showing him stuff he hadn't seen before and using his hesitation reacting to it against him. I could have killed him in two engagements, but I let it go to three. I liked Rug and I didn't want to embarrass him.

He shook my hand later while we waited for the ground crew to refuel my jet. "I expected to lose," he said, "but that vertical game plan in the high-aspect set-up was awe-inspiring. I hope you didn't waste your best stuff on me."

"I got a million of 'em," I said. Then I leaned over to him and whispered. "The flight between Brinker and me won't get to the high-aspect engagement."

Rug looked at me with his eyebrows raised.

"Trust me," I said. "He wants me way too badly."

Rug smiled and turned to leave. "Have fun!" he said.

Brinker and I met in the airspace twenty-five minutes

later.

"You would like offense or defense first?" Brinker asked me over the radio.

"Your choice," I answered.

"Very well," he said. "I will humble your offense first, and then kill you when you are on defense."

That's kind of how this will work out, I thought. *Only backwards.*

We set up for my offensive engagement. Brinker was in a slow right hand turn and I was about two miles behind him, closing to the 'fight's on' position at a mile and a half.

Usually, when an offensive/defensive engagement begins, the offender flies to where the defender was at the start of the engagement to enter the defender's turn circle. The defender goes into his best 'break turn' to foil a potential missile shot and prepare for his follow on defense. The fights tend to be fairly 'flat' because the F-16 can sustain so much energy under g that if one combatant uses the vertical dimension, he gives his opponent extra room to turn.

At the 'fight's on' call, I did something I knew he had never seen. Instead of 'stepping up' or climbing slightly, as I flew toward the turn circle entry point, I descended about 2,000 feet. Usually, the defender orients the plane of his break turn in relation to the offender and the horizon. By descending as I drove to the entry point, I took the horizon away from Brinker as a reference. He had no alternative but to increase his angle of bank and reorient his lift vector on or under my plane of motion. If he didn't, he'd allow me too much vertical turning room below him.

In my cockpit, I watched him coming down to me and nodded. *Perfect.* He was through about 135 degrees of turn and descending when I made my entry turn. I unloaded the aircraft, rolled my left vector to just above his plane of motion and pulled into about seven g's. It worked just as I expected. He came downhill, gaining energy, a position in which the defender *never* finds himself. I blasted through the horizon at 420 knots in MAX AB, pulled back to max stick deflection, and got nine g's from the jet and one from gravity. This generated a very tight, very quick 180 degree turn inside his turn and placed me just inside his flight path and about 4,000 feet behind him. I pushed the TMS button forward on the control stick.

"Lock, lock," said the female voice in my headset.

The PGU-12 20mm round has a lethal range of up 6,000 feet in the air-to-air environment, and I knew that Brinker never thought he'd see himself on the receiving end of a gunshot like this. I pulled my nose further inside of his turn, placed my gunsight slightly above and in front of his canopy, and held the trigger down.

He rolled his aircraft and aggressively pulled into the vertical in a 'jink' maneuver to avoid the simulated bullets.

But the bullets were already on the way and aimed exactly where he was going.

As he got into his jink, the scoring circle, which shows where the bullets will be one time-of-flight later, tracked neatly across his canopy. I laughed into my oxygen mask. The red scarf was clearly visible through the circle.

I made the kill call and Brinker's shock was obvious.

"We will have to review the film on that one," he said after a few seconds had passed.

"You're welcome to do so," I said. "The BATR circle looks great on a red background."

Then we went into my defense with Brinker behind me. This time, Brinker did what Blade predicted he'd do. At the 'fight's on' call, instead of flying to where I was, he pulled his nose directly in front of mine to attempt a near head-on gunshot. But the geometry of this maneuver requires that the defender stay in his turn so the offender can keep his lead angle constant and aim his bullets one time-of-flight in front of the defender's jet. It also assumes that the defender will play along with the standard defensive game plan. I intended to do neither.

As I began my 9-g break turn and saw him pulling his jet into lead for the gunshot, I increased my bank angle and oriented my lift vector well under his plane of motion. Someone who was fighting with their brain and not their ego would have abandoned the gunshot at that point and thanked the gods that the stupid defender was giving up a ton of vertical turning room above his plane of motion. But that wasn't Brinker. At least not today. He stayed with the gunshot, and to do so he had to keep *forward* pressure on the control stick to keep pushing his nose down. Pushing on the stick puts the aircraft into a near zero g state and because zero lift is required at zero g, lift-induced drag goes to zero as well.

And the jet accelerates like a son-of-a-bitch.

So, I had my left vector oriented downhill and Brinker was coming downhill to get me and accelerating like crazy.

I leveled off at 5,500 feet, 500 feet above the 'floor' of the airspace and watched Brinker flash by me on his way down.

"Brinker One, check altitude," I said calmly into the mic.

"Brinker One is four thousand, five hun...Goddamn it! Knock-it-off, knock-it-off."

I had 'scraped' Brinker off against the simulated ground, otherwise known as the floor of the area, and 'killed' him.

Our match was over.

Ruth was waiting for me as I climbed out my jet. "Looks like it's you and me," she said.

"Apparently," I said.

"That was a dirty trick you played on poor Brinker," she said with a smirk on her face.

"He killed himself."

About that time, Brinker walked up to us. His face was nearly as red as his scarf.

"Blade, we must review the gunshot FNG took on the first engagement. I don't think it's good. And a floor kill should not be a valid way to settle the match, especially in my case with single-elimination."

She kept her eyes on me and didn't even look at him. "I watched the ACMI review, Brinker. He cut you and your airplane in half with the gunshot. And the floor kill is valid. We briefed it that way. Remember?"

There was silence.

"Do you need to pee or anything?" Ruth asked me.

I shook my head.

"Are you perfectly rested and ready?" She asked, raising an eyebrow. We both knew what she was talking about.

I nodded.

"We'll take the two jets on the left side. We'll blast whenever you're ready."

We were airborne twenty minutes later. I rejoined to close formation and flew on her wing into the airspace. We split up and got our g-warm-up turns. When that was done, I heard her voice over the radio.

"What do you say that we dispense with the offensive-defensive shit and get right into the high-aspect? I have a feeling that's where this will end up anyway."

"Sounds good," I said.

"Blades, split," she said.

We split and let the range build between us. When our navigational gear indicated we had five miles between us, she called for the turn in.

"Blade visual," she said.

"F-N-G visual," I replied, enunciating each letter clearly

"Fight's on."

At that point, a line from one of the Matrix movies popped into my head: "You never truly know someone until you fight them." I was about to discover who Ruth/Blade truly was.

We merged, left to left, about fifteen seconds later.

I turned across her tail and she turned across mine and the fight was joined. I settled my left vector to put her about a 'fist's width' above the horizon, held the g at about 6 or so, and waited to see what kind of picture would develop.

She didn't disappoint. She stabilized across the circle from me and we stayed like that for several 360 degree turns, burning gas at 34,000 pounds per hour in a jet which only held about 7,200 pounds. Finally, she got impatient and decided to make something happen. I watched her nose rotate in my direction and knew what was coming. I got further into the straining maneuver and laid into the g to pull my nose to hers. We were about 2,000 feet from each another when we rolled out and we passed abeam a few seconds later, left to left, about 1,000 feet apart.

I knew what was coming. She was waiting for me to turn so that she could pull her 'phone booth shit.' Remembering my engagement with Brinker, I checked my ego and pulled across her tail. She immediately turned to the same side I had and the inevitable one-circle fight ensued.

We both ended up turning west from different directions, me from the north, she from the south. I looked across the circle at her. Her jet was about 3,000 feet away and just above the horizon. The ocean spread out below us like a green blanket. I could see the entire top of her airplane and the sunlight clearly illuminated the inside of her cockpit. Her visored face watched me, and she waited for the next move.

I rolled out slightly and pulled into the vertical, trying to force her ahead of me over the ground. Without a second's hesitation, she came up with me, first matching my climb angle, then exceeding it, to force me ahead of her. Before long, we were both climbing, at about 60 degrees nose high, in full afterburner.

I rolled into her gently and applied a little back pressure on the stick, trying to get my nose to her, but the stall-prevention algorithms in the Viper's flight control computer (FLCC) wouldn't allow me to have much nose authority.

She rolled into me and moved closer while she increased

her climb angle even more.

I matched her climb angle and we continued to slow as our altitude increased. The Viper began to feel a little sluggish in my hands and I deliberately released the stick with all but two fingers, trying to not over-control the airplane. My airspeed was somewhere below 100 knots.

We were now in a classic flat scissors.

I would turn in to her, trying to get behind her, she would turn in to me, denying me the turn and we would swap sides. Then the process would repeat itself. Our flight paths resembled a series of superimposed S's through the air. We were stuck in the worst possible environment for the Viper. Low speed, high angle of attack. The FLCC, or 'HAL' as we used to call it, would not allow us additional control authority because of the risk of putting the jet out of control.

Then the impossible happened.

As I was watching her jet, abeam her and five hundred feet away, co-airspeed, and going uphill at ninety knots, her nose suddenly began to move rapidly toward me. Before I could react, she ran her nose, and with it, her gunsight, through me from nose to tail. She dove out of the fight as she made the kill call.

I was shocked. And 'dead.'

Rug was right. She was a knife fighter. I sat mute in my cockpit until we landed and shut down. Other than our crew chiefs, there was no one on the ramp when we got out of our jets. As we walked into the hangar to debrief maintenance, she had a huge grin on her face.

"You'll want to see the film, I'm sure," she said.

"That's fine," I said. "I just don't understand how you were able to make the jet do that. It's one thing to get beaten and know why you lost. It's another to not have a clue."

She winked at me. "Maybe if you're *good* later on, I might tell you."

"I'll do my best," I said, having no idea what she was

talking about."

Blade entered the main briefing room to thunderous applause by the four other pilots, maintenance, and support personnel. She raised her hands in acknowledgement and I bowed in her direction in as gentlemanly a fashion as I could.

"It was a good fight," she said when the noise had subsided. "FNG Pearce flew a good jet."

We looked at the footage of her shot both on ACMI and her HUD tape and sure enough, it was valid. The scoring circle zipped my jet from nose to tail. She was professional enough to run it twice, without being asked, and I conceded the fight to her.

"Good kill," I said, obligingly. But something nagged me about it. My brain was telling me it didn't make sense.

"Party time, folks!" Blade said. "Let's get the beach set up!" The room exploded in cheers.

It turned out that the beach area I had seen flying above the island was accessible through double doors in the dining hall. After asking Rug for directions and guidance on the appropriate attire, I returned to my room. I downed the container of fluid Sammy had left on my dresser, changed my clothes, and went out there.

The doors opened out to one of the most immaculate white-sand beaches I had ever seen. It was about a mile side to side and three hundred yards deep, with graceful palms growing up and down the length of it, some in clumps, others singly. There was a tiki-bar and a grill about halfway to the water, beneath one of the larger groups of palm trees. Beyond the tiki-bar, near the water, was a beach-volleyball net, and beyond the beach lay the turquoise sea. The entire complement of the unit's personnel was out here. Some were sitting around the bar; others were playing volleyball, swimming, or lying in the sun.

We could have been on Maui.

I took a seat at one of the few empty chairs at the bar. Rug was behind it, carrying on about three conversations at once, serving drinks and minding the grill. He looked like he was totally in his element and he smiled when he saw me.

"I told you she was a knife fighter," he said.

I held both my hands up in acknowledgement. "You were right. I should have listened."

"You're not the first to think you could beat her," he said, "and you won't be the last. What can I get you?"

"Well, I'm not sure. I'd love to have a beer, but I'm not sure what my training status is."

"You're cleared. I asked Sammy about it earlier."

I looked around and didn't see her. "So where is she?" I asked, trying to sound nonchalant.

"Sleeping," he said, shaking his head. "Evidently she was up late last night working on something. It's too bad. We don't get to have beach parties very often and she loves them."

I felt a tinge of both guilt and regret. "That's too bad," I said. "I guess I'll take you up on a beer, then."

"Coming right up!" he said enthusiastically.

He served me about a pint of beer in a large, clear, plastic cup. I lifted the cup to my lips and drank down a long, satisfying draught. "It shouldn't taste that good," I said when I took the glass away. "It just shouldn't taste that good."

Rug nodded at me, smiling. "I know what you mean. Now what do you want to eat? We have the standard hamburgers, hot dogs, or boneless chicken breasts, and sides of chips, baked beans, and coleslaw."

"How about a double hamburger with cheese and some baked beans, sir?"

"My pleasure."

The food was delicious, and after I ate, I complimented Rug on his cooking expertise. Then I got a refill on the beer and made my way to a palm close to the beach. I sat down as carefully as I could so I wouldn't spill my beer and leaned up against the tree, planning to just watch the world go by for a while.

I looked over to the beach volleyball pit and saw Brinker and Pete playing VB and Natasha. From the look of it, the teams were evenly matched. Natasha had a black bikini on and I realized this was the first time I had seen her body. I found myself surprised at how toned and athletic-looking she was, and then chided myself for thinking that. Other than once or twice in the bar, the only other place I had seen her was in maintenance debrief, and she had always been fully clothed. Obviously, a stereotype had formed in my mind.

"Mind if I join you?"

I looked up to my right and Ruth was standing there, in very short coral-colored 'boy-shorts.' She also wore a white tank top through which a bra matching the shorts was clearly visible. Her hair was loose and flowed down to her shoulders. She looked good enough to eat.

"I was just thinking that I had never seen Natasha without her clothes on," I said.

"Well, be careful. You might see more of that than you want to," Ruth said.

Sure enough, the volleyball game ended, and Natasha and VB turned down Brinker's earnest invitation for another game. Then the two of them walked closer to the water's edge and stripped out of everything they were wearing.

"Hmm," I said. "It would seem that trimming certain areas of one's body is not so much in vogue in Mother Russia."

"At least not the part of if that she comes from," Ruth said, grinning. "Uh oh."

"Uh oh, what?"

"Mister Brinker would like you and me to play him and Pete in Volleyball? Are you up for it?"

"Sure," I said as I rose and finished my beer. "It's not my strong suit, but I'm up for a little fun." I didn't tell her that between the drugs, the alcohol, and the adrenaline rush from the dogfighting, I was fit to be tied. I needed the release of energy and I needed it badly.

"Oh, it's not about fun for Mister Brinker."

"I guess I should have known that

Ruth and I walked over the 'court' and the game began shortly thereafter. Pete and I possessed a basic knowledge of the game and the athletic talent to hit the ball, but neither of us knew any special moves or tricks. Brinker and Ruth, on the other hand, knew the game. The two of them would duel at the net, Brinker with his gym shorts, blonde hair, and muscles, versus Ruth, who was substantially shorter but lithe, quick, and muscular in her own right.

Eventually, Brinker and Pete won after the two-point lead had been exchanged several times.

"I'm done," I said. "I just want to relax a little. It's been a hard day." I turned to walk away.

"I am not surprised you would give up on more competition, loser," Brinker said to my back. And then he bounced the volleyball off the back of my head. Hard.

I took a deep breath, picked the ball up, and walked over to Brinker. I handed it to him and looked him directly in the eyes. "You played a good game, Brinker. Let's just leave it at that."

I turned to walk away and the ball hit me on the back of the head. Again.

I don't know what happened inside me just then. It was like something snapped. The bloodlust went from fully dormant to explosively awake in a fraction of a second. I whirled and rushed him, bending over at the waist like a pulling guard on the offensive line. He had his fists up, naively thinking I was going to fight him fairly, but he was living in a dream world. I hit him at a full sprint, grabbed both of his legs behind the knees, and lifted him off his feet, silently thanking Sammy for the strength she had created in me. I released him as he fell and managed to stay on my feet. He hit the sand heavily, flat on his back, and emitted a surprised 'oof' sound. His gray eyes flashed and he attempted to regain his footing. And that's when I planted my right heel squarely into his groin. He immediately went into the fetal position and groaned loudly.

"Don't start a fight you can't finish, Brinker," I said, and turned to walk back to the bar, desperately trying to clear my head and put the lust back into its place.

Jesus, I thought to myself. *So much for keeping things under control.* But I could feel the blood singing in my veins and a touch of the euphoria I remembered from long ago. A maniacal grin was etching itself into my features.

Shit.

Ruth caught up with me a moment later. "That was pretty brutal," she said. Her eyes were glowing sensually.

I forced a level tone into my voice. "I live my life by some pretty simple rules and one of them is: don't fuck with me or people I care about and I won't fuck with you." I motioned over my shoulder with my right thumb. "Brinker broke that rule."

"I see." She gently took my arm and guided me down to the end of the beach. The touch of her skin upon mine ignited a powerful fire inside me. I remembered this as well. After my rescue in Iraq, the fire had found refuge with a willowy, raven-haired nurse in USAF hospital in Jeddah, Saudi Arabia. And after the gang thing in Phoenix, there had been the extra touch from highly attractive, blonde detective from the local police department. My 'interview' had continued for several hours.

I knew what was coming. And I welcomed it.

"Come this way," Ruth said. "I've got something to show you."

We walked to what appeared to be the edge of the beach coastline on the south side where the rocky terrain from the mountain went out to the sea. But there was a small niche in the rock and without saying anything more, Ruth took my hand and led me into the niche and through a small passageway in the rocks, barely wide enough for us to walk in single file.

And we came out into another, smaller beach, bounded on the other side by a natural rock wall. It was about a hundred yards long by about fifty yards deep and was shaded on one side by a few palm trees.

"This is my retreat," she said. "Care for a swim?"

She led me to the shaded area up against the base of the mountain. Underneath the palms were a small wooden table, a few chairs, and a futon on a low wooden frame.

"I don't think I can," I replied, motioning to my wound.

"Sammy said it's okay," Ruth said, eyeing me while shedding her clothes unselfconsciously. "She actually said the saltwater would be good for it. And I've got some stuff here to bandage you back up. It's up to you."

Ruth left her clothes on the table and then slowly waded into the water until it was up to her chin, without looking back at me.

I paused for a moment, watching her glorious body disappear into the sea. I was out of my clothes in seconds.

There was no skin shock on my body when I waded in a few moments later. The water temperature had to be near 90 degrees Fahrenheit. I dived underwater and opened my eyes, surprised to see how clear the water was. Without a mask or goggles, I could easily see well off into the distance over the white sands. I could even see Ruth's tanned legs and splendid ass.

I surfaced about ten feet away from her.

"Wow," I said, "I needed this. This feels great." I looked around. "Doesn't anyone else come here?"

"They're forbidden to," she answered, turning to face me. "Like I told you. This is my retreat."

"I see," I said, nodding. "It's good to be the queen."

She giggled. "Yes. Sometimes it is."

She stroked over to me and encircled my waist with her legs like it was the most natural thing in the world. Then she interlaced her fingers behind my neck. My arms reflexively went around her waist. Her skin felt electric upon mine.

She looked at me and cocked her head. "You were surprisingly good today," she said.

I raised my eyebrows. "Surprisingly?"

"I've been following your progress, and you've done really well; but honestly, I was starting the think a lot of the stuff Rug was saying about you was hype. That's why I started trying to ramp things up against you toward the end of the air-to-air phase. I needed to see what you were made of. Today you proved it. You were brilliant. Even with your injury."

"I wasn't brilliant enough," I told her. "You kicked my ass."

She wriggled closer to me and I could feel her erect nipples against my chest. "Maybe I'll tell you how I beat you later," she said. "After you've earned it."

I needed no further enticement.

##

"Okay," I said a while later, as we lay on the futon catching our breath, "how did you do it?"

She laughed. A throaty, carefree laugh. "I cheated," she said. "That's all you need to know." She looked over at me challengingly. "So are you ready for round two?"

I looked back at her, the fire still cracking inside of me. "I'm just getting started," I said.

TOP SECRET / SPECIAL
COMPARTMENTALIZED INFORMATION
CLASSIFIED BY: US Central Intelligence Agency
DECLASSIFY ON: OADR

From: Special Projects Group [NCS]
Sent: Friday, 2 October 2009, 0645 EDT (2 October 2009, 1045Z)
To: Director, NCS
Cc: Special Projects Group [NCS]; damrine@cmail.cia.gov; dsmith3@cmail.cia.gov

SUBJECT: Update, Case File: 08-434A (MAG)

(TS) Narrative:

1. (TS) Contactor 09-017 (Pearce, Colin M.) completed the BFM (dogfighting) tournament yesterday, defeating every pilot on staff except for the unit's commander, Ruth Shalev (Major, IAF, retired). He begins air-to-surface training tomorrow.

2. (TS) Pearce heard Shalev on the phone asking about 'fitting something in' and being concerned about something that will get them funds but is also so close to the 'big project.' She went on to say she was going to check on the munitions supply and contact a 'freighter liaison.'

3. (TS) Initial contacts for DCIA-approved Operations Order 09-548, now code-named 'Persian Light,' have been successful. We'll have final word on acceptance within the next few hours.

(TS) CONCLUSIONS: None.

(TS) ACTIONS: We have plans in place for monitoring and tracking should Operation Persian Light be fully executed. Foreign offices have been provided warning orders.

(TS) RECOMMENDATION: None. Information only.

TOP SECRET / SPECIAL
COMPARTMENTALIZED INFORMATION
CLASSIFIED BY: US Central Intelligence Agency
DECLASSIFY ON: OADR

CHAPTER SEVENTEEN

Contract Day Twenty-Three
Saturday, 3 October
0600 Hours Local Time
Island Training Base

After a sound night of sleep, I was up at the usual time. I downed the ration of drugs Sammy had left for me and headed to the gym, presuming she and I were still on the same schedule. I sifted through my thoughts as I walked. A part of me wanted to feel guilty about the activities of the previous evening, but another part of me wanted to embrace the necessity of it. And between those two thoughts, I found myself wondering if this, too, had been some sort of test.

God, how fucked up is this?

I opened the metal doors to find the gym empty and the lights.

Well, there's only one other place she could be.

I walked down the hallway to the clinic. I found her there, sitting behind a desk in her office, fully and professionally attired, and working through some paperwork on her desk. She heard me coming and looked up. I saw a sad smile form on her lips.

"What, no workout?" I asked.

She shook her head. "Not today," she replied. "Because of

your wound and...other things."

"Sorry to hear that," I said. "I like starting my mornings with you."

"Let's have a look at your wound," she said hurriedly, rising from her desk. "I'm thinking you need to be re-bandaged."

She led me into one of the examination rooms and motioned for me to raise my shirt and turn around. I did as I was commanded.

"Who did this?" she asked with an impatient tone.

"Ruth," I said sheepishly. "The old one came off after we went swimming yesterday afternoon."

"Swimming?" Sammy asked incredulously. She spun me around. "Swimming, like in the ocean?"

I nodded dumbly.

"Are you really that stupid?" she asked. "You had a recently stitched puncture and laceration and you went swimming in the ocean?"

I nodded again. "Ruth told me you knew all about it. She said you said the saltwater would be good for it."

A long and colorful stream of obscenities shot out of Sammy's mouth. Her English accent took the edge off them but even after spending a good portion of my life around flight crews, I found myself slightly shocked.

"Let me guess," she added, "she finished up with the old fuck on the futon routine."

I discovered that I couldn't make my mouth work. I felt like a kid who had been caught with his hand in the cookie jar just before dinner time.

"Do you have any idea what intense physical activity like that could have done to your stitches? Or to the fucking hole that is inside your body?"

Uh oh.

"So how many times did she make you do her?"

I held up some fingers.

"Jesus!" Her face was reddening with anger. "Did you do

anything else yesterday I should know about besides fucking Ruth three times and pull nine-g's on multiple occasions?"

"Well, there was this volleyball game..."

She actually smacked my face then. The force of the blow practically knocked me down. I blinked in surprise, shook my head to clear it, and returned my gaze to her. She was trembling in anger and her eyes were shiny.

"Do you have any idea how much damage you could have done? How much blood you could have lost? It's enough that the stupid bitch needs you to keep flying but between that and fucking your brains out and then there's the fucking volleyball. I've heard fucking everything..." Her voice cracked. Just enough that we both knew what had happened. "Strip," she said, regaining her composure. "I've got some work to do. Aren't you flying surface attack today?"

I nodded.

"Good, that will keep the g's down. What are you waiting for? Strip!"

##

"Welcome to surface attack," Rug said later with a note of glee in his voice. "All that air-to-air shit may be fun, but it's moving mud with iron that gets the job done." He looked at me across the table. "Are you ready for this?"

I nodded enthusiastically. My mind was as sharp and clear as the finest pharmaceuticals could make it but I needed thrust at my back and air under my ass right now to push everything back into its proper place. Nothing was a better drug than that.

"More than you know," I said.

"Let's get started!" Rug opened his briefing book and began to call up his first slide on the screen in front of me.

Suddenly, the door opened and Ruth walked in. Rug and I looked at each other.

"We have an issue," she began before she reached the table. "We've been given a pop-up project to service. And it needs to be done day after tomorrow." She stopped at the edge of the table and looked down at me. Her eyes were different today. There was a degree of respect in them and a degree of expectation. "You're going to get one air-to-ground ride," she said. "You need to make it a good one."

I looked up at her and nodded. "Count on it," I replied.

"Rug, make it so."

"Wilco, boss."

Then she left and there was silence for a moment after the door shut.

"Alllllll righty then!" Rug said. "I guess this will be for all the marbles. Let me get through the 'motherhood' here and we'll get into the bombing."

I had wondered where MAG did its conventional bombing practice, and today I got the answer. On the eastern side of the island, where the terrain was more rocky and barren, a circular area about 150 feet in diameter had been cleared of rocks and local flora. In the center of the circle was a brightly-painted red boulder about the size of a full-size pick-up truck. I expressed my dismay at not having seen it before.

"They paint it red only for bombing rides and they use a water-based paint," he said. "When the ride is over, they spray water on it until the paint goes away and it resumes its natural color."

"Brilliant," I said, shaking my head in amazement. "Just brilliant."

For bomb-scoring purposes, two high-definition video cameras were mounted on higher rocks a few hundred yards west of the circle. The practice bombs we'd be using today housed a spotting charge, and when they impacted, the charge would provide a large puff of white smoke. The cameras would triangulate on the smoke and the bomb's position would be plotted in relationship to the target. The 'error,' or distance between where the bomb landed and the target itself, was expressed in a score of meters and clock position from the target to the impact. For example, if the bomb landed 30 meters short of the target, the score would be '30 at 6'; if it landed 15 meters to the right, the score would be '15 at 3.' A 'bull' was self-explanatory.

"We'll be carrying 12 BDU-33s today in two SUU-20 pods," Rug said.

Practice bombs were nearly always carried in SUU-20s or on TERs, triple ejector racks. The SUUs were about ten feet long, nineteen inches wide and 12 inches thick. Roughly an oval, the underside of the SUU was open and held mounting points for six of the 25-pound bombs.

"For today's events, we'll just keep it simple and stick to our bread and butter events," Rug said. "Most of the projects we have flown use low-altitude bombing attacks; but today we'll warm up with a high-altitude attack, just to get you back into the swing of things. We'll do three 45-degree high-altitude release bombs from the conventional pattern, three 20-degree low-angle low-drag pop-ups, three 10-degree low-angle high-drag pop-ups, and finish with three dive-toss passes. I assume you've done all these before?"

"Yep," I nodded, "but it's obviously been a while."

"Well, hopefully this will come back to you as quickly as everything else has."

"We'll see."

Rug went into his bombing basics briefing and I listened intently. It never hurts to review the fundamentals.

An unguided bomb is unpowered and ballistic, so it only has the velocity and trajectory imparted by the aircraft releasing it. That velocity and trajectory gives the bomb a range: the distance it travels laterally as it falls to the ground. In the days before computing bombsights, the pilot of the attacking aircraft had to fly a specific point in space where he met a set of aerodynamic conditions defined by his airspeed, altitude above the ground, and dive angle. These conditions imparted a specific range to the bomb. To get him to a place where he met those conditions at the proper range from the target, he relied on a bombsight to measure that range for him. But the bombsight only had one setting for each set of conditions, so that meant the pilot had to arrive at those conditions with the bombsight superimposed on the target. I had dropped hundreds of bombs from the A-10 this way, before it was upgraded with a computing sight, and the techniques we'd used weren't that much different from those used in the Second World War.

But luckily, in the Viper, we had help. The Viper had three computer-assisted bombing modes and the one we'd be relying on mostly today was CCIP, continuously computed impact point. The ballistic profiles of all munitions the jet could carry were loaded into the jet's fire control computer or FCC. As we rolled in to bomb a target, we called up the CCIP mode and the FCC displayed a line of video in the HUD that represented the path along the ground where the bomb would fall - logically called the bomb fall line, or BFL. At the end of the BFL was a small circle with a dot in the center of it. The dot was the 'pipper' and it represented the CCIP, the point at which the bomb would impact. We called it the 'death dot.' On each bombing pass, we rolled in and placed the BFL on the target. Then as we descended in the dive, the CCIP 'pipper' would track across the ground. When it touched the target, we pressed the weapon's release or 'pickle' button, and the bomb we dropped would hit what we aimed at.

It sounds like an expensive video game, and to an extent it was. But even though the computer did a lot of the work for us, we still had to get the aircraft close to that particular point in space, because the delivery conditions were based on some hard numbers, such as the amount of altitude required to recover from the dive, the amount of time the bomb had to fall before it armed, or the minimum height to stay out of the fragmentation pattern of your bombs or those of a flight-mate. So, unlike most video games, there were real consequences if we didn't hit the numbers.

Rug finished his briefing and we got suited up, step briefed, and headed out to our jets. Our F-16s were configured for air-to-ground. Each had two external fuel tanks installed on the weapons pylons closest to the fuselage, stations four and six as looking from left to right behind the airplane. On stations three and seven, the two pylons outside the fuel tanks, were two of the SUU-20 pods.

I performed my pre-flight inspection and had repeated flashes of déjà vu as I gently shook each of the twelve small, blue BDUs in the two pods and made sure all the appropriate connections and safety pins were secure.

Rug and I started our jets, ran our post-start checklist, and then called for arming.

We displayed our hands in plain view while arming teams went underneath the wings and pulled all the bomb safety pins from the BDUs. When they came out from under the wings, the team leaders gave us a 'thumbs up' and Rug checked us in on the radio.

"Control, Boiler One, taxi."

"Boiler One," Ruth's voice came over the radio, "cleared taxi, cleared takeoff. Use runway 36 with a right turn out. Right pattern for range work. Contact me this frequency for range clearance."

"Boiler One," Rug acknowledged.

We took off to the north ten minutes later with twenty second spacing. Rug left his power in mid-AB and I joined to a loose formation as we climbed to 25,000 feet, the pattern altitude for 45-degree high-altitude release bombs. It took us a few minutes to get up there, and we did a full orbit around the island in AB as we ascended.

It was another brilliant, blue day, and I again had time to look outside my cockpit as I climbed. My thoughts drifted for just a second as I gazed at the brown and green island surrounded by the crystal waters of the ocean below. Today we were practicing the unit's primary mission: blowing shit up. It wasn't as if I hadn't known that before, but the reality of climbing out with ordnance bolted to my jet brought it in to a clearer focus.

Damn, I mused. *D-Day isn't too far away now.*

Rug and I leveled off, left the power up and accelerated as we flew around the bombing pattern once to get oriented to the ground references. The bomb circle stood out plainly and I wondered why I hadn't seen it before.

We turned on to the base leg, with me on the outside of the turn and about 100 feet off Rug's left wing. I looked through his airplane down to the target, trying to get a feel about where the 'base leg' position would be for my first 'hot' pass.

Rug started his turn to final. I followed him and called up the air-to-ground mode on the up-front controller. All the appropriate symbology came up in my heads-up display in front of me and in my right multi-function display of the lower right instrument panel.

"Boiler flight in, high and dry," Rug called.

"Boilers cleared on," Ruth's voice said over the radio. Evidently, she'd be playing range-control officer from the ops desk or main briefing room or wherever she was.

"Boilers green 'em up," Rug commanded.

I reached down on the lower left console and selected the 'ARM' position of the silver MASTER ARM toggle switch. The green 'READY' light illuminated. Today was the real deal. When I pushed the pickle button, stuff would be coming off the jet. I grinned under my oxygen mask.

"Boilers, standard bet?" Rug asked over the radio.

"Two, affirmative," I said.

Betting on bomb scores has been a tradition since pilots have been dropping things from airplanes. Typically, the bet is a quarter a bomb, a quarter per event, and a dollar for lowest overall average error with the winner taking all: enough to make it interesting, but not enough to hurt those who lost.

We passed over the bomb circle on the run-in heading, Rug waved and turned sharply away from me, the vapor pouring off his wings as he pulled some g in his turn. I counted seven seconds and followed him, easing into the g as I turned crosswind so I would maintain my airspeed.

We dropped three high 45s and then descended to the 2,000 foot downwind altitude for the 20-degree 'pop-up' pattern. The pop-up delivery started with a run-in to the target at low altitude, similar to the way we'd do it for real. For today's purposes, we'd extend the downwind leg well past the target until we were looking back at the target behind our right shoulders. Then, we'd make a descending turn to the target and level off at 500 feet. At a predetermined distance from the target, we'd 'action,' or turn away from, the target, 30 to 45 degrees. We'd hold this heading for a few seconds, and then execute an aggressive climb at an angle greater than the planned dive angle for the attack. When we reached our 'pull-down' altitude, we'd roll the jets nearly inverted and apply g to stop the climb, and pull the nose to the target. From that point on, it looked like a normal bombing pass.

I watched Rug begin his descending turn to his base leg in front of me. "Boiler One, base for 20s. Boilers ops check."

I checked my fuel level and engine instruments and watched Rug's aircraft as he leveled off at 500 feet above the surface of the ocean. I could see his gray jet zipping across the green waves below and to the right of me. He'd be 'popping' any second now. I was approaching the descent point for the base turn.

"Boiler One, up," Rug called. His jet shot skyward and climbed rapidly.

I rolled my jet past 90 degrees of bank, which killed my lift and allowed my nose to fall. Then I went to MIL power, 100 percent power without afterburner, and began to pull the nose around for 135 degrees of turn

"Boiler One, in," Rug said. I could see his jet about two miles in front of me now, gray-blue planform, the entire top of his aircraft, against the terrific tropical blue sky, nearly upside down as he pulled his nose down to the target.

"Cleared hot One," Ruth said.

"Boiler Two, base," I said a few seconds later.

I leveled off at 500 feet on the radar altimeter and let the jet accelerate to 500 knots while I centered the flight path marker on the CCRP steering line. CCRP stands for Continuously Computed Release Point and enables the jet to release ordnance 'blind' against a target for which coordinates have been entered into the navigational system. In this case, I was using it as steering and distance reference to the target.

I watched the distance readout in the HUD decrease and when I saw the number I was looking for, I plugged the power back into MIL, and turned 45 degrees away from my original heading. Then I rolled out. I had two seconds to hold down.

"One thousand one, one thousand two," I counted. Then I keyed the mic. "Boiler Two, up."

I smoothly pulled the nose up to 30 degrees nose high and checked the throttle in MIL. The jet zoomed into the azure tropical sky, leaving the water far below. The altimeter increased rapidly and as it approached my 'pull down' altitude of 2,800 feet, I rolled the jet on to its back and began blending the g to bring the nose down to the target. It was clearly marked by a nice, white puff of smoke from Rug's bomb.

"Boiler Two, in," I called.

"Cleared hot, Two," said Ruth. "Bull, One."

"One," Rug acknowledged.

I called up CCIP by pushing the nosewheel steering button on the side of the control stick, but I wasn't watching the HUD where the data was projected, just now. I was looking through the top of my canopy at the target and doing the mental math to put my jet on the right wire to it. The nose came down smoothly, with about three to four g's of back pressure on the stick and as the nose descended through the horizon, I made sure the airspeed was above 400 knots and pulled the throttle out of MIL and toward the mid-range. Then, I looked into the HUD.

While I was still inverted, I pulled the bomb fall line to the target and then rolled out to wings-level. I applied a little back pressure to place the target at the right place on the BFL. Once the placement was assured, I pushed forward slightly to keep my dive angle constant. I was now on final.

My dive angle was good, I was right on 20 degrees, and my airspeed was slowly passing 440 knots on its way to 450. The familiar rush of adrenaline coursed through me as I went 'down the chute.' I flexed my thumb quickly and then watched as the 'pipper' tracked neatly up the BFL to the target. When the green dot hit the base of the red rock, I punched the pickle button and held it until I felt the mild 'thump' of the bomb being ejected from the SUU-30. Then, I began the recovery.

Five g's in one second until the nose was 20 degrees above the horizon, then relax the back pressure, but allow the nose to continue up to thirty degrees. Getting the recovery right was important. Typically, low-drag bombs delivered at low-altitude explode directly under the jet releasing them. This recovery maneuver generated altitude separation from the detonation and kept the pilot from getting blown out of the sky by the bomb he had just dropped.

The entire process, from the 'action' until I had completed my recovery maneuver, took about twenty seconds.

I threw my head over my right shoulder to see how I had done and was rewarded with a puff of white smoke wafting up from the red rock.

"Bull Two," Ruth's voice announced.

"Two," I acknowledged, smiling under the oxygen mask. I had not lost my touch.

We did two more passes each in this event. I had two more

bulls and Rug had a bull and a five-meter bomb.

We switched to 10 degree low-angle high-drag deliveries and dropped three bombs each in that event. I was in my element. Dropping conventional bombs on the practice range had always been my favorite thing to do when I was in the USAF. It was like target shooting with a jet. It used all my concentration and all my talents and required me to think outside myself to get into the groove; that place where I could get the jet to the right point in space and push the button at the right time. Discovering that I still possessed these skills, so many years later, was more professionally satisfying than anything I had done in my civilian aviation career.

As we set up for the Dive Toss passes, I realized that Rug was ahead of me in the bet as it currently stood. He won 45s, I won 20s, and we had tied in 10s, but I had a 7-meter bomb and that was the largest error so far. If I didn't do well in Dive Toss, I'd owe some quarters for the overall average error in the debrief.

Dive Toss, or DTOS, was a stand-off visual loft. The goal was to release the bomb between a mile and a mile and half from the target and then turn away to remain at least a half-mile from it. The mechanics of the pattern were very similar to a pop-up delivery, but executed further away from the target to build in the necessary range. The pop-up only had to be high enough to get line-of-sight to the target. Once the pilot saw the target, he slewed the DTOS aiming reference, a small box with a dot in the center, to the target and designated it. This told the jet's fire control computer where the target was on the ground. Then the pilot applied g and lifted the nose. The bomb came off the airplane when the FCC told it to and flew an arced trajectory which took it right to the designation point on the ground. With BDUs, Dive Toss was reasonably accurate. With heavy bombs, like 500 or 2,000 pounders, it would drive nails.

"Boiler One, up and in," Rug called as he made his first

dive toss.

"Cleared hot, One," Blade replied.

"Boiler Two, base," I said a moment later.

I leveled off at 500 feet, inbound to my action point and watched Rug roll in and fly 'down the chute.' After a few seconds on final, he released and began his escape maneuver. Then it was my turn. I lifted the nose up to about 15 degrees.

"Boiler Two, up and in," I called.

"Cleared hot Two," Ruth replied. "Twenty at 12, One."

I called up the DTOS weapons delivery mode and slewed the box just below the flight path marker as I rolled in. Then I pulled the nose of the jet just long of the target and continued to slew as I pulled the throttle back to midrange. Using as delicate a touch as I could, I positioned the DTOS box so the dot was at the base of the rock. Then I designated with the target management switch on the stick and moved my thumb to the pickle button. I applied gentle back pressure to the stick and ensured that the flight path marker was exactly on the steering line as the nose came up. Then I felt the kick from below and I saw the flight path marker flash which indicated the bomb was away.

The recovery here did not require specific g-loading or timing. Instead, I merely applied g to break the descent rate and rolled into a hard right turn to stay outside of a half mile from the rock. Then I turned back to the left and paralleled the attack heading, still maintaining my spacing, and watched the rock for the bomb impact.

Because of the arced trajectory, it took the bomb a few more seconds to get to the target. But it bounced off the front face of the rock when it did.

I smiled as I climbed to downwind.

"Bull, Two."

"Dick," Rug said over our intra-flight radio.

I just laughed.

We landed after two more Dive Toss passes in which both

of us had bull's-eyes, but the maximum CEA or circular error average was now his. I had beaten him but it had been a good fight. I'd probably tell him to keep his money.

But I didn't get the chance.

When we walked back into the main briefing room, nearly everyone else in the unit was there. Two seats in the front row were unoccupied, ostensibly reserved for us.

Ruth motioned us into the room. "You can debrief later," she said. "For now, we need to talk about this new project."

We entered the room and took our seats.

"Ladies and gentlemen," Ruth began, as she dimmed the lights and called up two of the video screens in front of us. "Welcome to the preliminary mission briefing for project 09-04. The target is an oil terminal located on the Iranian coast in the Persian Gulf."

She called up two slides simultaneously, one on each screen. The slide on the left showed a map of the Persian Gulf area with a triangle, the standard map symbol for a target, placed on the Iranian coast just north of the Strait of Hormuz. The slide on the right was obviously satellite imagery of the target in question. It was taken from high altitude but the detail was striking. I wondered who they had paid to get that sort of imagery or whether it was provided by the client. The photo showed two piers about half a mile offshore and a mile apart. Just onshore were twenty large storage tanks arranged in four rows of five tanks each. Other assorted buildings and support structures lined the compound, but the tanks and the docks were obviously the points of interest.

"Our client has asked for no specific DMPIs," she said.

That surprised me. DMPIs were designated munitions points of impact, the exact spots where the bombs needed to hit. That was unusual.

"Instead this is a," she paused for a second, "a 'chaos-style' attack which is just intended to generate as much confusion and destruction as possible. Due to the response time of

Iranian air defense, we need to get four aircraft on and off target in less than one minute."

She shut off the screens.

"Our contractual obligation for this project requires us only to get at least four 2,000-pound-class munitions on target with high-order detonation."

The tension level in the air immediately lessened. I didn't even notice it until just then. Apparently, this was an 'easy' project.

"We'll begin mission planning tomorrow at 1000. The transports will arrive tomorrow night for loading. We'll launch before dawn day after tomorrow and service the project later that day." She looked around the room. "Are there any questions?"

Everyone was silent.

"There will be a naming ceremony for FNG Pearce in the bar at 1800. Everyone is welcome to attend. If there are no questions, you are dismissed."

The room emptied and Rug and I rose to leave. Ruth walked over to us and looked at Rug with an expectant expression on her face.

"How'd he do, Rug?" she asked. "You're the best bomber in the group. You should know."

Rug looked down at his shoes for second and then raised his eyes to hers.

"He did okay," he mumbled.

"Okay?" Ruth asked with incredulity. "Just okay?"

There was a pause.

"He took," Rug acted like he was having trouble getting the words out. "He took my fucking money, goddamn it!"

CHAPTER EIGHTEEN

Contract Day Twenty-Three
Saturday, 3 October
1800 Hours Local Time
Island Training Base

Nicknames, handles, personal call-signs have been a tradition in fighter aviation since its inception. Where there is tradition, there is ritual. Where there is ritual, there is ceremony. I had seen the full gamut of these in my USAF career, from a few drinks at the officer's club on a Friday night after work, to downing a yard of beer or a few shots of tequila while fellow pilots formed a circle around you and chanted, to 'sweep parties' at Kunsan Air Base in Korea where entire bars downtown were devoted to the naming ceremonies. I walked into the bar that night wondering where tonight's festivities would fall on the scale.

I could hear Burt Magnusson's words from his e-mail to Smith ringing in my ears: "*They've tried to make it like a normal fighter squadron here but instead it's like a whole different world. There are parts that make sense and other parts that don't any make sense at all.*" So far, Boomer's words had been right on the money.

The place was packed with the unit's personnel. I wanted to believe it had something to do with my naming ceremony, but I was sure it had a lot more to do with the smorgasbord of hors d'oeuvres and plentiful alcohol.

I had no sooner set foot inside the room when Rug's voice boomed at me from behind the bar. "There he is!"

A cheer went up from the crowd, and Sammy, who had apparently had a role in the process, shimmied out to meet me in a flightsuit that could have been painted on her fabulous body. I thought about resisting for a moment but before I could, she took my arm and led me to the end of the bar nearest the center of the room.

She leaned her head toward me and whispered as we walked. "Relax and enjoy this," she said. "It's all for you."

"I'll do my best," I said, trying to concentrate on her words as I took in all the activity around me. Crowds had always made me uncomfortable and I've never liked being the center of attention. I could feel my palms getting clammy. When we reached the end of the bar, we stopped and she pointed at a wooden box, about eighteen inches high, sitting on the floor.

"You need to stand on that," she said.

I did as I was told.

"Let the naming begin!" Rug bellowed. Another cheer went up from the crowd.

"Fucking New Guy Pearce," Rug yelled above the din of the bar, "what is your most hated form of that evil in liquid form, alcohol?"

I paused for a second, wondering how much Rug knew about me from other sources. As far as I knew, I had never told him the thing I hated to drink above all others.

"And I warn you, Mr. FNG," he continued loudly, "I have some intelligence on what that form is and it will be used against you if you do not speak the truth. You will be required to drink five penalty shots if you lie to this august gathering."

Rug was in rare form. I looked over at him and he smiled at me broadly. I could tell he was already about two sheets to the wind.

"Tequila," I said loudly. "I fucking hate that stuff."

Rug nodded. "That is what I have been told." He motioned toward the back of the room. "Ladies, bring forth the swill!"

The crowd parted and two women, whom I presumed worked in maintenance, came forward carrying a tray between them. They were both dressed in the skimpiest of bikinis imaginable and a chorus of wolf whistles from both guys and girls followed them as they made their way to the bar. They could have walked off the cover of the Sports Illustrated Swimsuit issue. One was raven-haired with expressive, deep blue eyes and elegant high cheek bones. The other was a redhead with hazel eyes, and sensual, pouty lips. The tray had a liter bottle of Tequila on it, with several shot glasses, a large shaker of salt, and a bowl of lime slices. The brand was Patron, but it didn't matter. All that stuff tasted like rotgut to me. But at this point, I probably would have consumed the fluid they use to deice airplanes if it could have helped me to get a buzz on quickly.

"These gracious ladies have volunteered to be your tequila caddies," Rug said. "And for each nickname presented which you refuse, you shall be required to drink a body shot from one of them."

Now the rules of tonight's 'game' became clear. And make no mistake, there is always a 'game' at naming ceremonies. I had to hold my liquor well enough to make it through all the 'bad names' to get to the one I wanted.

The two girls made it to the bar and placed the tray on the end of it. Then, the redhead jumped up on the bar, ass first, and lay down dutifully.

I looked over at Sammy and our eyes met. She was smiling radiantly at me. I couldn't help smiling back.

"Now," Rug continued, "I have before me a list of possible names for you, FNG, and for each one, you must decide yea or nay. If you decide nay, you must drink. If you decide yea, we, the crowd will vote and you may still have to drink. At any rate, there will be at least five drinks before you are named.

"Ladies and Gentlemen," Rug intoned, sweeping his hand before him in an inclusive gesture, "are you ready?"

The crowd roared in response and Rug nodded in satisfaction. "Indeed, you are," he said. Then he paused for effect. "FNG Pearce, are you ready?"

"I am," I said.

Rug raised his hand to his ear. "I'm sorry, FNG Pearce, I thought I heard a fly go by my ear, I asked you if you were ready."

I grinned back at him. "Sir, yes, sir!" I exclaimed loudly.

He grinned smugly and nodded again. "We shall require one penalty shot from you for your weak answer." He motioned toward my end of the bar. "Ladies?"

While Rug had been speaking, the shot glasses on the tray had been filled with tequila. I dismounted from the box and walked the few steps to the bar. The raven-haired beauty smiled at me and placed one of the lime slices into the redhead's mouth with the rind between her teeth and the fruit portion facing out. The redhead made a production of assuring that the lime was seated in her full, luscious lips. Then the raven-haired girl sensuously bent over and licked a patch of skin along the curve of the upper part of the redhead's right breast. While the area was still wet with her saliva, she sprinkled a healthy portion of salt on the area and motioned that I should partake.

Boy, oh boy, I thought. *This was going to be a long evening*. I hated tequila, but I loved body shots. I sincerely hoped one would offset the other.

I bent over the redhead and licked the salt from her breast. The black-haired girl handed me a shot glass and I pounded the tequila, the taste of it tying my stomach into the usual knots. Without thinking about it too much, I leaned over to bite the slice of lime out of the redhead's mouth. As my lips touched hers, she grabbed my head with her hands and held my mouth on hers as I bit the meat of the lime from the rind. Then, without releasing my head, she turned her head sideways, spit the rind out and returned her lips to mine, this time burying her tongue in my mouth. I was too stunned by how rapidly everything happened to move. I enjoyed the kiss for a few seconds, then gently lifted my head while she still held on. She used that opportunity to move my head to her left breast and forced my mouth down to the cloth of her bikini top. As my lips touched the flimsy material, I could feel the peak of her nipple right below it. The crowd hooted with glee.

I obediently sucked through the cloth for a moment, then gently removed the redhead's hands from my head and rose from her. As I looked down at her young face, I wondered if I was old enough to be her father.

I remounted the box, faced Rug, and performed a mock bow. "Sir," I yelled, "I stand ready for the first name on the list."

Rug played his role well. He nodded gravely and stroked his chin while he consulted a sheet of paper before him. "The first name we will present has its genesis in the fact that you have been spending an inordinate amount of time in a room with a lot of equipment with a person named Igor."

A chant rose from the crowd. "Igor, Igor, Igor..."

Sammy played her part to the hilt. She jumped up on a chair and did a slow pirouette while the crowd continued to chant her name.

"And the name which we derive from this series of events is..." The crowd went silent.

"...Dr. Frank-en-sch-tein!" He deliberately dragged out the 'sch' portion of his pronunciation.

"Frank-en-stein, Frank-en-stein, Frank-en-stein," chanted the crowd.

Rug allowed the chant to continue a minute or two before he raised his arms. "Silence!" He commanded. And then he gestured to me. "FNG Pearce, what be your answer to this nickname? Be it yea or be it nay?"

"Yea or nay, yea or nay, yea or nay," went the crowd.

I paused to allow the noise to die down a little, "I vote NAY!"

The crowd approved of my decision with a roar. Obviously, the party couldn't end this soon.

"Then, you must drink!" Rug cried above the roar. "You must drink a penalty shot!"

I descended from the box to find that the black-haired girl had replaced the redhead on the bar and I repeated the body shot process. The black-haired girl tried to entice me with a deeper kiss than the one the redhead attempted, but I understood the game now, and I participated enthusiastically. I lifted my mouth from her lips and managed to dodge her attempt to move my head to her breasts. She gave me a look of mock disappointment. I gazed down at her lineless face and couldn't believe that I was nearly fifty and making out with a woman who was probably half my age. There would have been a time when I would have beaten my chest and drawn attention to that fact but, to my surprise, I was finding that there was only one set of lips that I wanted to kiss, and they weren't currently available.

I shook my head as I climbed back on the box and wondered if my newfound conscience would survive another three shots or more of tequila.

"Sir," I announced, reeling a bit as the tequila began to do its damage, "I stand ready for the second name."

"Very well!" Rug said and he bent over his list again. "The second name we will present has its derivation in an incident which occurred in the officer showers a few weeks ago, in which you demonstrated your ability to shoot, as it were."

"Woooooooo," went the crowd.

"In fact," Rug continued "eyewitness accounts indicated you didn't just shoot, you blasted!"

I bowed my head, remembering my encounter in the

shower with Samantha. *Oh, my God.*

"And since you were performing a certain act at the time, the name we derive is master...blaster."

The crowd loved it. "Master Blaster, Master Blaster," the voices went.

I couldn't help smiling. It was pretty damn funny. Nothing was fucking sacred.

"FNG Pearce, what is your decision? Yea or nay?"

"Master Blaster, Master Blaster," continued the crowd.

Instead of trying to overcome the noise, I held my arm straight out with my thumb extended, parallel to the floor and I let the chant continue. I shook my thumb back and forth to create the impression that I was indecisive.

"Master Blaster, Master Blaster," the crowd went on.

Then I rotated my wrist and pointed the thumb down.

The crowd had mixed emotions about this decision. A series of boos came from one side of the room and cheers came from the other side.

"Drink!" Rug commanded.

I descended from the box to find that the redhead was back on the bar, and lo and behold, the top of her bikini had disappeared.

"Amazing," I said as I positioned myself for the shot, "weren't you dressed when I came in?"

She smiled at me as the raven-haired girl put the lime slice in her mouth. Then, the redhead pushed her breasts together as the other girl placed the shot glass between them. Finally, the black-haired girl licked the redhead's inner thigh, very close to her crotch, and sprinkled salt on it.

I stole a quick glance at Sammy to see how she was taking all this in. She nodded at me but then looked away.

I licked the salt off the redhead's thigh and let my tongue run closer to her crotch, which made the crowd go nuts. Then I placed my mouth around the shot glass and lifted my head, letting the raunchy stuff pour down my throat without using my hands on the glass. I spit the glass out and lowered my mouth to the redhead's and I kissed her for at least a good minute. When it was over, her eyes were shining and her pupils were dilated. Her lips were parted and she was slightly breathless.

I ascended to the box again with the roar of the crowd in my ears. I was winning them over.

"FNG, are you ready for the next name?" Rug bellowed across the room.

"Sir, yes sir!" I yelled.

Rug consulted his list once again. "The next name comes from an incident which occurred in your room after your first two transition rides..."

I hung my head again. I knew where this was going and it *so* wasn't good.

"And you had a certain visitor from our staff who is unfortunately not here to defend herself..."

"Woooooooo," went the crowd.

"And during this visit certain activities of a carnal nature took place..."

"Oh nooooooooo," continued the crowd.

"And since this young lady comes from the land 'down under,' the name we derive is delta uniform foxtrot or DUF!" It was pronounced duff. He shouted it out explosively.

I shook my head from side to side. I knew exactly what it stood for.

"DUF of course being an acronym for Down Under Fucker!"

"Duff! Duff! Duff!" the crowd picked up the chant immediately and enthusiastically. "Duff! Duff! Duff!"

"What say you, FNG, to this most prestigious nickname?"

My mind was transported to the numerous parties like this I had attended in the past. For just a second, I wanted to believe in this feeling of camaraderie emanating from the room and from the crowd.

"Duff! Duff! Duff!" said the crowd.

I extended my arm with my thumb parallel to the floor and shook it back and forth. Then I started to turn it slightly toward the ceiling and the chanting grew louder. Suddenly, I rotated my wrist and pointed my thumb down.

The crowd didn't like that. The 'boos' were much louder than the cheers this time.

"Drink ye!" Rug bellowed.

I descended from the bar to find the black-haired girl on the bar again, sans bikini top of course.

The redhead, still topless herself and completely unselfconscious about it, placed the lime in the other girl's mouth and the shot glass between her breasts.

I licked the salt, drank the shot and finished her with a kiss that left her as breathless as the redhead had been. After that, I slowly climbed back on top of the box to await the next name, swaying slightly from the tequila as I did so. "Proceed, good sir!" I called out to Rug. "I'm just getting warmed up!"

Cheers flew through the room.

"Very well, FNG. We seem to be nearing the end of the list. There are two more names here."

"Boooooooooooooo," said the crowd. No one wanted things to end this soon.

"The next to the last name has its roots in the fact that you are a man of rather advanced years playing in what is a young person's game, both in the air and, shall we say, in other various places around our fine establishment..."

"Oooooooooooooooooooooooooooooo," went the crowd.

"While your prowess in the air at your age may be understandable, your prowess elsewhere, and the associated requirements from your...equipment, bespeak of a degree of artificial, nay, shall I even say, drug-produced enhancement!"

I just smiled and shook my head again. At first, I didn't understand where he was going with this one and now it was becoming clear.

"Indeed, our leader, the ravishing Major Blade, has confirmed your ability to produce and sustain a certain condition from your...equipment. So the name we propose is COLONEL VIPER!"

"Viper," I yelled, "that's almost cool. Why Viper?"

"Easy," Rug answered without missing a beat, "VIPER stands for Viagra Induced Penile Erection Record because you have set a new record here for the number of times an old guy has achieved that state! And indeed, what is produced is a veritable trouser snake anyway."

After the crowd got over its initial laughter, the chant began. "Vi—per! Vi—per! Vi—per!

"What say you, FNG? Will you accept Viper? You must confess, it has a certain ring to it and it's not even a cock ring!"

I just stood there grinning stupidly. I should have been ashamed, but I wasn't. Guys have been named much dumber things for much dumber acts.

"Vi—per! Vi—per! Vi—per!"

I again extended my arm and again shook my thumb in the neutral position. I started to make it point skyward and I let it get about forty-five degrees above neutral before I pointed it down.

"Boooooooooooooooooooooo," the crowd really didn't like that decision.

"Aren't you hard to please, Mister FNG? You must drink two shots for refusing that name. It was truly a work of art."

I descended from the box to find both girls sitting on the bar. Both had the slice of lime in their mouths and the prefilled shot glasses at their sides. In what was clearly a pre-coordinated routine, they licked the middle and index fingers of one hand, rubbed the skin just above their bikini bottoms with those fingers and sprinkled salt on it with their other hands. After that, they reclined on the bar, placed the shot glasses between their breasts and awaited me.

The crowd went nearly into frenzy. I bent my head to lick

the salt from the redhead and found her legs wrapped around my head as I did so. I gently slid upward while she kept her legs wrapped around me, licked the salt, did the shot glass, spit it on to the floor, and proceeded to the lime. She was ready for the kiss this time and wrapped her legs and arms around me completely. I repeated the process on the black-haired girl while the crowd roared its approval.

Then I slowly and unsteadily made my way back to the top of the box. The tequila, six shots of it by now, on a nearly empty stomach, was having its way with me. I could barely keep my balance and I found I was having trouble focusing my eyes.

"Master Rug," I called out, "you may proceed to the next name and if I am required to drink any more shots off these fine ladies," I motioned down to them, "I must request private surroundings."

"That can be arranged, sir!" Rug said. "Now," he continued, "we come to the last name on the list and it is unknown to most people here. It finds its past in the first Gulf War and the escape of a Sandy A-10 pilot from his Iraqi captors. It was legend throughout the American Air Force and was spoken of only with the highest reverence. It is the name of a man who stole the knife from one of his captors and used it to kill not one, but several of them before escaping into the night."

The crowd was dead silent as Rug shouted out the story. He told it the way he had heard it. I guess I never had known that there was something of an urban legend about this incident which had followed me throughout the Air Force. Like every good 'war story,' this one was half-truth and half-invention, but he told it well and he had the crowd's rapt attention. I enjoyed the story nearly as much as the assembly did and the blood raced through my veins in rhythm with his words. I had the ethereal sense of the bloodlust inside of me as an independent presence, swimming like a shark, happily and unhurriedly, just beneath my skin, watching for the opportunity to jump up, open its jaws, and feed on the nearest thing it found.

If I hadn't been so inebriated I would have been terrified.

"And this incident, this legend, produced a name that has lived on, un-imitated for nearly twenty years."

Holy shit, I thought. *Has it really been that long?*

"And that name," Rug continued, "is none other than Tango Charlie, or TC. TC for THROAT CUTTER!"

He bellowed the last two words like the ring announcer at a wrestling match and the crowd went completely mad. Shouts, cheers, clapping and pounding of feet on the floor followed. And of course, the chant erupted.

"Tee—cee! Tee—cee! Tee—cee!"

I looked down and even the two girls on the bar were clapping and chanting. I then looked around the room and had the oddest sense that the people present were looking to me for something more than entertainment. There was an undercurrent of something else. I just had no idea what it was.

I glanced down at Sammy. Her eyes, shiny with moisture, were fixed on me and I saw something in them that struck a chord inside me, despite the effects of the tequila. Then I shifted my gaze to find Ruth. She was standing to Rug's right, in the corner of the room, looking at me appraisingly, and smiling at me with an unabashed lustful gleam in her eyes.

The crowd's chanting was growing louder and more impatient.

I extended both of my arms this time, with the thumbs pointed toward each other and waited another few seconds as the crowd continued to chant.

Then I rotated my wrists and pointed the thumbs at the ceiling. The ensuing roar was nearly deafening.

"We have a name!" Rug shouted. "We have a name! From this point forward, FNG Pearce shall be known as TC. So let it be written, so let it be done!"

"Tee-cee! Tee-cee!" the crowd continued.

I bowed politely to the crowd and held my hands up to them, palms out, accepting their acknowledgement. Then I decided to get off the damn box I was standing on before I fell off.

The moment my feet hit the floor, I was engulfed by the crowd. I received slaps on the back, handshakes, hugs from some of the female members of the unit and warm words from everyone. Then as the congratulating and welcoming subsided, the two 'tequila girls' appeared beside me. As their arms went around my waist, I found that I was having trouble making my legs perform the act of walking. Then the room started to slowly rotate around me in a blurry kaleidoscope of color.

"Are you okay, TC?" one of the girls asked me.

I couldn't move my mouth to respond. In fact, I couldn't even breathe. The rotation of the room switched from horizontal to vertical and suddenly, I could see the wooden floor of the bar rushing up to meet me.

The last thing I remembered was the warm sensation of blood pouring out of my nose and the fetid smell of the floor.

CHAPTER NINETEEN

Contract Day Twenty-Four
Sunday, 4 October
1100 Hours Local Time
Island Training Base

I was underwater. I could see the prismatic effect of the sunlight reflecting off the surface far above me and appreciated how beautiful it was.

Because I knew it was the last thing I'd ever see.

My lungs were burning and they felt as if they would blow themselves apart any second. How had it come to this? I've lived my whole life with a phobia about drowning, even though I grew up on Florida's Space Coast and had the Atlantic Ocean in my backyard for my entire childhood. I loved to swim, but not too far from shore and never underwater for long. I had long feared my last breath on earth would consist of water, not air.

And now here I was and it was all about to come true. Life's a bitch.

"Colin, open your eyes. I know you can hear me. Open your eyes."

What the fuck? My eyes are open! How can I hear you if I'm underwater?

"Colin, listen to me. Open your eyes. You have to fight this.

You need to open your eyes." It was a woman's voice.

What are you doing down here?

"Colin, open your eyes. Listen to the sound of my voice. You're safe now. Open your eyes."

I felt a warm sensation on my forehead, like someone was touching me there. I also felt pressure around my fingers and realized someone was holding my hand. I was dreaming. But it was more than just dreaming. I was down a lot further than that.

"If this doesn't work soon, you're going to have to force him out of it," another female voice said.

"I know," the first voice said. "But that will really fuck him up if I do that."

"Can't be helped. We need him to plan the strike. I wish I could find the mother fucker who was pulling this shit. I'd tie him to the wing of a Viper, take him up to 20,000 feet, and drop him."

"Colin, it's Sammy. Focus on my voice. Open your eyes."

I tried to obey the voice and but it was tough. My eyelids were glued shut. I had heard of situations like this. About people in comas who could hear other people talking to them and about them, but were unable to climb the ladder into consciousness. Trapped forever inside their brains. The panic that gripped me at that point put my phobia about drowning to shame. I imagined myself in the gym, with Sammy, doing a dead lift. Getting my legs into position...bending my knees... grasping the barbell...straightening my back...one...two... three...LIFT!

My eyes popped open. The harshness of the artificial light overhead ripped into my eyeballs and threw the pain switch inside my head. Then my stomach woke up and I had the distinct feeling there was a porcupine running around inside it.

"Ooooooohhhhh," came out of my mouth like a long sigh.

"Jesus, Colin! You scared the shit out of us!" Sammy yelled.

I turned my head and saw Sammy and Ruth standing side-by-side.

"What happened?" I asked groggily.

"You were poisoned," Sammy said. "You've been out for about fourteen hours."

My mind was swimming its way back to the here and now. It was slow going.

"Let me guess," I mumbled. "The tequila, right? I knew there was a reason I hated that shit. Nothing good ever happens when I drink that stuff," I rambled on. "Nothing good at all."

"You're lucky to be alive," Ruth chimed in. "Sammy recognized your condition, and we got you here ASAP and pumped your stomach. Fortunately, she had something to counteract the barbiturates."

"So why didn't I wake up?" I asked. I was finding that if I focused on their mouths when they spoke, it made my brain work. I could feel the cobwebs starting to clear, gradually.

Sammy shrugged. "Alcohol and barbiturates are an unpredictable combination. We got the drugs out of you and some sodium succinate into you quickly enough that you didn't go into cardiac arrest but you just didn't snap out of it. I decided to see if you would sleep it off. But after twelve hours you weren't stirring. We've been trying to wake you up for about the last two hours."

I looked up at them. Their two visages were contrasting studies in juxtaposition. Ruth's face was concerned, but detached. I was a thing to her. A capability. An asset. Sammy's face showed something else entirely. Apprehension, a little guilt, but most of all, relief. And beneath all of that, maybe even something deeper.

"What would you have done if I didn't wake up?" I asked, getting more alert by the second.

Sammy looked away for a moment. "You don't want to know," she said. She returned her gaze to me. "Can you sit up?"

"Let's find out."

I raised my upper body and swung my legs onto the floor, pulling the covers off me and exposing my nakedness. I didn't care.

Then I tried to stand up. My stomach suddenly felt like it had turned sideways inside my body and my brain lurched within my skull.

I sank back against the examination table.

"Whoa, cowboy. Give your body a chance to catch up," Sammy said.

Ruth stood back a few feet, crossed her arms and shook her head. "This is really starting to piss me off," she said. "Whoever this person is, they're determined. The knife thing may have been spur of the moment, but this was planned." She looked at me intently. "You need to be careful. We can't do the strikes without you. We need you to plan them and obviously we need you to fly them. From now on, I want you to stay out of the steam room, and try to only use the main shower during normal hours. Even better, call Sammy or me to stand guard for you."

I nodded at her weakly.

"Get him cleaned up and drugged up. I need him in the mission planning room in forty-five minutes." She looked me up and down, tilted her head and smiled sardonically. "Sammy's done really well with you. It's too bad about last night. I had something extra special planned for us." She tapped her watch and looked at Sammy. "Remember, forty-five minutes."

Sammy was looking at my face. I saw her roll her eyes. "Forty-five minutes, boss," she replied.

Ruth walked out.

"We need to get you into the shower," Sammy said. "I have a private one here in the clinic."

I smiled at her. "Are you going to scrub me again?"

She touched the side of my face tenderly. "You are something," she said, looking into my eyes. Then she quickly looked away. "No," she said. "I need to get to your room and get you some clothes and also mix you up yet another cocktail of drugs to get you through the day."

She led me to a small room down the hall that featured a sink, toilet, and shower all in a single tiled room with a common drain. She reached in and turned on the water, adjusted the temperature, and pushed me under it.

"I'll be back in a few," she said.

I stood there for several minutes and let the water stream over me. The sensation of the warm shower was heavenly, and I felt like my skin was reawakening. I shampooed my hair and endured the spikes of pain that came every time I touched my scalp. As I finished, Sammy came through the door with a towel, some clothes, my bag of toiletries, and a pair of hypodermic needles.

She handed me the towel and I dried off as she watched. Then, before I could get dressed, she turned me around, wiped a cheek of my ass with an alcohol swab, and gave me two quick injections. While she was back there, she changed the bandage on the knife wound.

When she was done, I shaved, combed my hair, and donned my clothes, all as she stood there. Oddly enough, it didn't feel weird at all.

"You'll make someone a good wife one day," I said absentmindedly as I turned back to her. Her eyes glistened and she nodded.

"Maybe," she said. "Come with me."

She led me to her office and offered me what looked like a protein shake in a plastic container. I took it from her and sat down in one of her chairs. Then I lifted the container to my lips. I felt my stomach heave when the first drop hit my tongue.

"I'm not sure I can do this," I said, lowering the container.

"You have to," she said. "It will suck getting it down, but once it's there, it will calm your stomach quickly. Between that and the two shots I gave you, you'll feel better in a hurry."

I nodded at her. With as much fortitude as I could muster, I willed my churning guts into submission and downed the stuff.

"They're doing the mission planning for the project tomorrow," she said as I drank. "They need you for the attack stuff. There's some sort of rule about it."

"I'm not sure I'm in good enough shape to be useful," I said.

But even as a spoke, I could feel my body recovering. It was as if the physical and mental pieces of me were snapping back into place. In just a few minutes, my stomach was much more settled. Then the pain in my head disappeared.

"I've learned not to ask what you give me anymore. But this was amazing."

She shrugged. "The injections were analgesics, vitamins, and a mild stimulant. The shake had something in it for your stomach and enough protein and carbs to get you through the day so you don't have to eat lunch. I know you won't want to."

"Better living through chemistry," I said, handing the container back to her. I stood up, and found that once again, after all I had been through, I felt completely normal. "This is amazing shit."

Sammy raised her eyebrows at me. "It will wear off this evening and you need to let it do that. Try to eat a normal dinner, but stay away from the alcohol afterward. And for God's sake, please just try to be careful."

"I'll do my best."

She reached out and took one of my hands, in a movement that seemed both reluctant and involuntary at the same time. She looked up at me.

"Colin? How important is all this to you?"

"How important is all...what?" I asked.

"This stuff. This job. Doing what it is that you do here." I shrugged.

"It's a job," I said. "Just another contract job. It's the way I live my life. This one has cooler airplanes, more danger and better pay; but at the end of the day, it's just a job. Although, I can truthfully say it's the first job I've had outside the military where someone tried to kill me. That's new."

She nodded and looked down. "Is that all it is? Just a job?"

I thought about that for a moment. We both knew there was more going on here than that. I just didn't know how to verbalize it in a way that wasn't awkward. Then, something occurred to me.

"A few years ago," I began, "I did a contract job for the flight department of a men's magazine headquartered in L.A. I spent three weeks or so there, almost fell head over heels for the chief pilot, and it could have changed my life forever. So while that was just a job, it had an effect on me that went a lot further."

"So, what are you saying?" She still wouldn't look at me.

What was I trying say? My mind went back to the three weeks with Sarah Morton. Although there was electricity between us, she had never communicated that she had wanted anything more than the physical relationship we had enjoyed together. But there had been moments, timeless moments when I had thought I could sense something more. Moments that felt like the present one.

I reached down and put my hand under Sammy's chin and raised it so that our eyes met.

"I guess I'm saying that this feels the same to me." I lowered my lips to hers and kissed her.

Eventually, I made it to the mission planning room. As I walked in, a heated discussion was underway at the table in the center of the room.

"Nice of you to join us, TC!" said Rug when he saw me.

I saw Ruth's head turn toward me and her eyes caught

mine. I looked right at her as I replied, "Well, I told you that I hated Tequila, Rug. Now you can see why. It hates me right back."

"So it seems," he said. "Are you feeling okay now?"

I nodded confidently. I glanced at Ruth. She nodded imperceptibly with the hint of a smile of gratitude on her face.

"Would you care to join our discussion group, TC?" Rug asked. "We seem to be having a little trouble deciding what we want to do here."

I walked up to the edge of the table and reviewed the materials they had laying there. A large scale 1:500,000 rectangular map dominated the table. It encompassed the Iranian coast where the target area was, all of the UAE, and a good portion of northern Oman. Next to that was a 1:50,000 scale map which included the target area itself in much greater detail. Finally, there were a series of target photos which provided visual features in the target area.

"So refresh my memory," I said. "What are our objectives, other than the chaos thing?"

Pete had the answer. "Four 2,000-pound class weapons on target with high order detonation."

"Well, that's easy," I said. "We go in there with a four ship formation carrying two Mark-84s each." Mark-84s were the USAF's standard 2,000-pound high-explosive bomb.

"That's the decision of the quorum," Rug said. "Fusing?"

"If the goal is chaos and not real damage, I'd go with an airburst." I looked over at Rug. "Do you have FMU-113 fuses?" The FMU-113 was a radar proximity fuse which could be mounted on the front of the Mark-84. The typical detonation height above ground was about 15 feet.

He nodded. "We have all the USAF stuff, fuses, bombs, et cetera. It reduces issues with the stores management system on the jets."

"But," Brinker interrupted impatiently, "if we use the FMU-113 we have to release all the bombs low drag. We can't mix attacks."

He was right about that. The FMU-113 was only compatible with the low-drag mode of any weapon, not the high-drag one.

"I know a way we can put all four jets on and off simultaneously." I had their attention now. I pointed at the target photos lying on the table. "This target arrangement, with the tanks in the back and the docks out front, spaced as they are, favors a four-ship simultaneous attack. Rather than run in as a four-ship box, with one element behind the other, we run in with the element leaders line abreast about two miles apart and their wingmen in wedge formation on them. At the appropriate action point for a normal 20-degree low-drag, the elements action away from each other. The leaders will pop to 20-degree low-angle low-drag deliveries on the dock areas on their respective sides, and the wingmen action with their element leaders and perform Dive Toss deliveries on the tanks. The wingmen will have to do a loaded loft from about three miles away and recover quickly to stay out of their leader's frag; but if the northern guys action left, roll in right, and come off right, and the southern guys action right, roll in left, and come off right, we'll get four guys on and off target in about thirty seconds and wind up in a great position for us to regain mutual support."

"Why not have the leaders do the dive toss on the tanks and the wingmen do the 20-degree attack on the docks?" Rug asked thoughtfully.

"It makes the attack geometry too unpredictable, and would make the wingmen have to work way too hard to hit their parameters and maintain their positions. Granted, if accuracy was the goal here, this attack wouldn't work. But for the stated objective, basically getting at least four bombs out there, it does the trick."

Silence ensued. All of them, Rug, Brinker, Pete, VB, and Ruth, stood around the table, staring at me. It became apparent that they had been arguing over weapons, attack parameters, and geometry all morning.

"Well," Rug said, as he cleared his throat, "I guess it's good we have a weapons school guy." He looked at me. "If you were in charge of planning this thing," he continued, "how would you plan the ingress?"

"Do you have a threat plot?" I asked him. A threat plot was a wartime tool that depicted air-defense system coverage. When we trained to fight the war at low altitude, during the Cold War, the threat plots even provided radar coverage maps, showing where concealment from enemy radar could be found by flying at low altitude.

"Sort of," Rug said. He unfolded a chart which showed the locations of all the air traffic control and military early-warning radars in the region. Sure enough, it had the light magenta coloring over the terrain to show where radars could see a low-flying aircraft and no coloring where they could not.

"I'm not even going to ask you where you got this," I said.

Rug motioned in the direction of the simulator room. "It's all loaded in the CRAY," he said. "It knows where all the radars are as well as their capabilities. It just spits this stuff out, along with maps, satellite imagery, et cetera."

I looked at the map carefully. The terminal itself was near Bandar Abbas and served the refinery that was nearby. Staying out of Iran's airspace until the last minute dictated that the final segment of the flight would be over water with nothing to hide behind for about fifty miles. Anything we could use to minimize detection until then would help us.

"Let me ask the important question," I said while looking at the map. "Where are we going to fly from?

Rug pointed at a circle drawn on the 1:500,000 map in the country of Oman, seemingly in the middle of nowhere. "From here," he said. "There just happens to be a runway here that no one knows about. Ten thousand feet long by one hundred fifty feet wide. We'll launch and recover from there."

I nodded. "In that case," I said, tracing the route with my

fingers on the map as I spoke, "I'd plan the ingress initially through the mountains here in northern Oman. Then I'd stay in the mountains and split the border between Oman and the UAE, dash across the strait, hit the target, then egress out the mouth of the Gulf, and only turn back in to Oman to land after we were well out over the Arabian Sea."

"Why go so far over the water?" Brinker asked with his usual sneer. "It costs us much more time and fuel."

"Tactical deception," I answered. "We want the last anyone sees of us to be our asses headed out over the water. The odds of our attracting some company on the egress are high. We don't need to drag any unwelcome guests back to our recovery site."

I looked down at the Omani coast as it turned south past Muscat. "It's possible we could turn this corner earlier," I said. "It just depends on how pissed the locals are at us."

Silence fell again. I could almost hear their brains churning. They all wanted to find fault with the plan but none of them could.

After several moments, Rug cleared his throat. "Well, it looks good to me," he said. "Boss?"

Ruth nodded with a satisfied look on her face. "I like it," she said.

"Okay, guys," Rug said, "you know what to do. Pete, you'll draw the ingress maps. VB, I want you on the computer to get us the weapons delivery numbers. Brinker, I want you to put the line-up cards together and load the data transfer cartridges. TC, you and I will draw the attack maps. Then, when we're finished, we'll all put the attack folders together. I'll have the dining hall bring some food in for lunch. Let's hit it, gentlemen. We're burning daylight."

We split to our tasks and worked throughout the day. After I worked with VB to get the correct weapons delivery parameters out of the computer, we selected an 'Initial Point' for the target run. The Initial Point, or IP, was the last navigational checkpoint prior to the target. There were three islands in the Gulf off the coast where Bandar Abbas was located. We chose the eastern end of the small island farthest out in the gulf as our IP. It gave us about a twenty nautical mile run to the target, two minutes at our typical attack speed of 540 knots.

Given the numbers and the Initial Point, Rug and I set to work drawing the attack maps. Attack maps provide a 'God's eye view' of the attack geometry, drawn to scale. The maps used are normally 1:50,000 scale maps, the same maps the Army uses in ground operations. The scale is large enough that actual houses and buildings appear on them in true proportion.

"Amazing," Rug said, as we looked down at the map sometime later. "It looks like you said it would. It's like you knew that was going to happen."

"Imagine that," I said, smiling at him.

Around the room, VB, Brinker, and Pete were finishing their parts of the process. Rug and I returned to our maps and began inking over the penciled lines we had drawn. We also wrote the parameters for the deliveries on the maps, next to the appropriate sections of the attack diagrams so the pilot would only have to look at one piece of paper as he was conducting his attack.

Periodically, Ruth would come into the room and check on us. She wouldn't say anything; she'd just stop at each work station and watch for a few minutes, then move on.

Finally, just before dinner time, in fact, we were done with our individual tasks. We took the attack map to the color copier, reduced it in size, and made eight copies: four for the guys chosen to fly the mission, two for the pilots in the spare jets, and two extras. Next, we made copies of the ingress maps which showed how we'd get from the launch point to the target. We added a large-scale map of the entire area, a few satellite photos of the target area, and the line-up cards Brinker had made. The materials were divided into eight individual packets and placed inside folders to keep everything together. Next to each package was a data transfer cartridge to load all the mission information into the airplane.

As we finished the last packet, Ruth entered the room to inspect the final products. After looking closely at an example packet, she nodded her approval. "This will do, gentlemen." She lifted her head. "Whose turn is it to lead?"

I saw Brinker lift his head up and felt my gut tighten.

"Okay Brinker, you're number one."

She nodded at me. "TC will be number two since he needs a baptism by fire and this mission is relatively generic." She looked over at Rug and Pete. "You two will be three and four. VB and I will be the spares. Any questions?"

There were none.

"Get to bed early tonight, gentlemen. We'll do the formal mission briefing before departure tomorrow morning at 0500 hours. It's about a sixteen and a half hour flight to launch site, and you'll get some rest on the transports, but you know how that is."

We all filed out of the mission planning room and made our way down to the dining hall. The menu that night included baked ham and potatoes au gratin, both of which I found surprisingly tasty in light of my earlier stomach problems. I followed Sammy's instructions and ate ravenously, following the main course with a helping of first-rate chocolate mousse.

"Okay, Rug," I said, as I tried to get the last glob of chocolate mousse out of the dish. "So, tomorrow there is a briefing and transport planes will carry us to the launch point. Care to explain how any of this will work?"

"If I tried to explain it to you," he said, finishing some apple pie himself, "it would create more questions than it will answer."

I started to talk and he raised his hand.

"Trust me on this one. Tomorrow, get up at about 0400

and spend some time in the hangar before the mass briefing. That, the briefing, and what happens afterward will more than answer your questions." He must have seen the look on my face. "I'm not trying to keep anything from you. It's just too hard to explain."

I looked around the table and saw VB, Pete, and Brinker all nodding. Ruth wasn't with us.

"You won't believe it," VB said. "I didn't."

I tried to go back to my room. I even made it to my door. But then the scotch craving hit me.

I weighed Sammy's instructions briefly, mumbled a quick apology to no one in particular, and went back down the hall to the bar.

The room was unoccupied and dark. I turned on a single light and found a bottle of Dalwhinnie single-malt scotch near the front of the liquor cabinet. I poured myself a healthy shot of the stuff.

The bar was sparking clean and I would have never guessed that there had been well over a hundred people in here last night if I hadn't known it. No odor of alcohol lingered, nor was there a trace aroma of food, sweat, or any of the bodily fluids emitted when people drink too much. I repressed the urge to smell the floor.

I went into the corner of the room opposite the door, took a seat, kicked my legs up on a nearby table and slowly sipped the scotch, letting it do its wondrous work. I've heard drinking alone is dangerous and I think that's bullshit. Many of the most contemplative moments of my life have been while I've been sitting by myself in some corner of the world, sipping a glass of nice single-malt.

I examined how I felt about bombing an oil complex in Iran. I knew that Iran was a rogue nation these days and that its president belonged in a mental institution; but a lot of innocent people would die tomorrow, many of them at my hands. I searched inside myself to see if I could detect any regret or conscience or hesitation about what I needed to do. But there was nothing at all. I didn't know if it was ambivalence or a lack of energy.

I took another sip and lifted the glass in front of my face to stare at the stuff as it warmed its way down my throat. It was probably wrong to love a form of alcohol the way I loved single-malt. It was one of the few things in my life I could always count on. It tasted deep and complicated, it hurt a little to drink, and it freed my mind from itself in a way that let me relax. Every single time.

"Doctor's orders?" Ruth's voice came at me through the open door.

I waited a few seconds before answering. "Actually, quite the opposite. Sammy told me to stay away from the stuff tonight. I hope she doesn't find out. She kicked my ass the last time I disobeyed her instructions."

"She's been asleep since lunch. She was up all night with you." I nodded.

"Good thing, I guess."

Ruth walked up to my table. She wasn't dressed in the normal businesslike flightsuit. Instead, she wore tight cotton shorts and a thin t-shirt. Ordinarily, my eyes would have searched the clothes for telltale signs of what she was or wasn't wearing under them. But I didn't have the will or the energy tonight.

"I had a deadbolt installed on the inside of the door of your room. Lock it when you go to sleep tonight. Use the shower in the clinic tomorrow morning before the briefing. I don't want anything else to happen to you. We're on a tight time schedule."

I nodded my acknowledgement.

"What are you thinking?" she asked softly, as she settled herself opposite me. The light hit her upper body as she sat. I could just see the dark outline of her nipples underneath the thin cotton shirt. Apparently I wasn't too tired to be perceptive.

Great.

I lifted the glass of scotch and peered into its amber depths to distract myself. "I was just wondering if I liked scotch too much."

"You might," she answered, taking the glass out of my hands and downing a healthy slug of it herself, "but who cares?"

I looked across at her. Her olive skin was glowing, even in the dimly lit bar, and her eyes sparkled at me. "Nice coincidence," I said, returning my gaze to the glass as she handed it back to me, "that's exactly the same conclusion I came to."

"You did well today," she said, leaning back in her chair. Her voice was soft and mellifluous in the semi-darkness. "Even in spite of all that's happened to you. I don't know what we would have done if you weren't in there."

"One of your other guys would have figured something out," I replied softly. "What I came up with wasn't rocket science."

"It was the right mixture of complexity and simplicity for this particular project. If Rug had planned it, all four jets would have done exactly the same thing from the same attack axis, and if Brinker had planned it, it would have been some sort of double-back flip with a triple gainer and it would have confused everyone."

I grunted in response. "Glad to be of service, ma'am. That's what you're paying me for."

I could see her nod in the dimness.

"Well, I just wanted you to know it's appreciated." She paused strategically, as if deciding what or how to say what was to follow. "*I* also appreciate the...other...services you've provided."

I smiled reflexively but suddenly found I felt more than a little disgusted with myself. The interlude on the beach with her had been memorable, but it had been fueled by the need to quench the fire, not by desire. To my surprise, I found I regretted it.

"It all comes with the package," I said. "No extra charge." The words tasted sour in my mouth.

Several moments passed. I took another sip of the Dalwhinnie and let it crawl down my throat. She took the glass from me again and had a sip of her own, looking me in the eyes as she did so. I found myself trying to characterize the energy that was passing between us.

I felt like a chess master who was enjoying some quiet camaraderie with his soon-to-be opponent. There was a mutual admiration and mutual understanding, mutual respect and mutual wariness. Yet under it all, there was a sensual attraction accompanied by a mutual knowledge that in the end, it wouldn't matter.

We sat there in silence in the darkness and drank the glass of scotch together. It was the first of three that night.

TOP SECRET / SPECIAL
COMPARTMENTALIZED INFORMATION
CLASSIFIED BY: US Central Intelligence Agency
DECLASSIFY ON: OADR

From: Special Projects Group [NCS]
Sent: Sunday, 4 October 2009, 0600 EDT (2 October 2009, 1000Z)
To: Director, NCS
Cc: Special Projects Group [NCS]; damrine@cmail.cia.gov; dsmith3@cmail.cia.gov

SUBJECT: Update, Case File: 08-434A (MAG)

(TS) Narrative:

1. (TS) Contactor 09-017 (Pearce, Colin M.) has completed training. He participated in mission planning earlier today for a strike on the Iranian Oil Complex at Bandar Abbas. He relayed all details of the strike to include the airfield MAG will launch from, route of flight, and attack details. He was also attacked again. The leadership of MAG is apparently ignorant of the attempts on his life, which indicates additional elements inside of MAG that may not want the final strike to succeed.

2. (TS) Our Funds transfers have been completed and contracts have been signed to implement DCIA Operations Order 09-548, 'Persian Light.'

(TS) CONCLUSION:

1. (TS) MAG will be forced out in the open by this strike. We will be able to track their arrival at the launching airfield, their flight, and the attack itself. While we certainly can track them

back to their origin after the attack, we have an opportunity to capture the entire working portion of the unit when they deploy.

a. (TS) Advantage: High probability of preventing the main strike we've been anticipating.

b. (TS) Disadvantage: High probability we will not learn the location of the island training base without extensive interrogation.

c. (TS) Disadvantage: Will require extensive liaison with the government of Oman and possibly the government of the UAE, and classified information about MAG would have to be disclosed in the process.

2. (TS) We might also be able to engage and destroy the attacking force when they come off target.

a. (TS) Advantage: Probability of preventing the main strike better than fifty percent.

b. (TS) Disadvantage: Only four of MAG's eight jets will be destroyed.

c. (TS) Disadvantage: High probability we will not learn the location of the island training base.

d. (TS) Disadvantage: International visibility on an engagement like this will be extensive.

e. (TS) Disadvantage: Contractor 09-017 will probably die in the engagement.

(TS) ACTIONS: We alerted US and Royal Navy ships in the

region to be prepared to track and/or engage MAG as the strike is conducted.

(TS) RECOMMENDATION: Do not engage or detain MAG as they conduct the strike. Track them back to their point of origin and engage them there.

TOP SECRET / SPECIAL
COMPARTMENTALIZED INFORMATION
CLASSIFIED BY: US Central Intelligence Agency
DECLASSIFY ON: OADR

CHAPTER TWENTY

Contract Day Twenty-Five
Monday, 5 October
0335 Hours Local Time
Island Training Base

The vibration of my BlackBerry awakened me from a sound sleep the next morning. I had sent an e-mail to Smith and Amrine before retiring with as much detail about the mission as I could remember; hoping some of that information would enable them to determine the location of the island. The conversations between us thus far didn't give me a lot of confidence that the CIA knew where I was.

I padded to my desk in the darkness and took the BlackBerry out of the pencil drawer. Sure enough, there was a new e-mail from Phil Collins. I clicked open the e-mail and found a two-line reply.

"We know about the upcoming festivities. Be ready."

It deleted itself about ten seconds after I had read it.

"What the fuck does that mean?" I said to the empty room.

I looked over at the digital clock on the nightstand next to my bed. It read 3:35 a.m. I had slept about six hours. I grabbed my shower stuff and headed down to the shower in the clinic. I had a date in the hangar.

I walked through the double metal doors a few minutes

before 0400. The hangar floor teemed with human activity, all of it highly organized and focused on getting the Vipers configured and loaded in the transport aircraft. It was one thing to have heard about this. It was another to see it.

The outer hangar doors were completely open to the air and parked in front of them, on the ramp and under the awning, were three Boeing 747 air-freighters. All had nose cones on hinges, which were swung up and out of the way so the fully-loaded F-16s could be rolled into the cargo bay. As I walked across the hangar floor in wonderment, I watched as a fully-loaded Viper, with external tanks, 2,000-pound bombs, and two Python missiles already mounted on it, was pushed up one of the 747's cargo ramps by an electric aircraft tug, the same sort of tug I had seen at executive terminals all over the world. The outer three feet of the Viper's wing was hinged and folded back on top of a wedge-like cushion of some sort that was strapped to the outer portion of the rigid section of the wing. I was dumbfounded. I had never seen an F-16 configured with a folding wing modification, and after flying these aircraft for several weeks, I had not even noticed the hinge point in the wings at all. The craftsmanship involved must have been spectacular. Then I remembered the briefing Smith and Amrine gave me and I recalled the time difference from when the jets were originally stolen and the first air-strike. Adapting the jets like this had taken considerable time.

As the loaded Viper was pushed to the top of the cargo ramp, I could see beyond it and made out another Viper in the back end of the 747's cargo bay. All the other transports were completely loaded. Each 747 carried two Vipers.

We'd land somewhere and the Vipers would be rolled out, the wings would be bolted into position, and we'd fly away to do the mission. When we returned, we'd shut down, have the wings unbolted, and the 747s would take off again.

I was flabbergasted at the precision of the choreography. "Impressive, isn't it?" Ruth said from close by.

With all the noise around me, I never heard her walk up. "I've never seen anything like it," I said.

"We load the freighters with two pilots, two jets, and their associated launch and recovery crew. We have the mission brief before we depart so everyone knows the game plan and we only need to get two of the three freighters to the launch site to complete the project."

"Good thinking," I mumbled.

"I was looking for you," she said. "I wanted to tell you something, in person and alone before the main briefing. I guess I could have told you last night. I just didn't want to spoil...the moment or...whatever."

I turned to her.

"I'm counting on you to keep an eye on Brinker today."

"Isn't that Rug's job as number three?"

"Rug won't stand up to Brinker. You're the only one who has ever stood up to him. That's why I put you in his element."

I nodded. "So, I guess as a spare, the odds are you won't fly."

"No," she said with a dejected shrug, "not unless Rug or Brinker has a maintenance issue. I don't lead anymore. I know too much. If I were shot down and captured, eventually I'd talk. Everybody does. I flew on the first few projects, before anyone knew anything about us. But not now. I'll start engines with you guys, but that's usually about as far as I go unless we need more than a four-ship."

I nodded dumbly.

"Shall we?" she asked, indicating that we should head back into the building. "We have a briefing to attend."

We walked back toward the rear of the hangar together.

"There is probably...something else we need to discuss," she said, looking over at me. She sounded almost reluctant. "I need to make sure you're not one of those types that gets business confused with...other stuff. Do you know what I'm talking about?"

I nodded back at her and a passage from one of the old Matt Helm spy novels ran thought my head. Matt, a US government assassin, was in bed with Vadya, a Russian agent. And she was saying something like, “Darling, you can’t believe this really means anything? You know this doesn’t make the slightest difference?”

“You can keep those two areas separate, can’t you?” Ruth asked. It was like she was reading the same book.

I eyed her, remembering that Matt Helm ends up shooting Vadya later in the same book. *That* was an interesting thought.

“Well, around here,” I said, conversationally, “it’s hard to see the line between the two sometimes. And my understanding is that’s the way *you* want it.”

She cocked her head in acknowledgement. “To a degree, that’s true. But even so, it’s still all about the mission. It *must* be about the mission. You get that, right?”

“Oh yes,” I said quietly. “If there’s one thing that comes across loud and clear, it’s that. *Everything* is about the mission.”

She nudged me playfully. “Well, you don’t have to sound quite so glum about it.”

We reached the double doors which led into operations. As I reached for the door handle, Ruth stepped in front of me and put her back against the doors.

“There’s one more thing we need to discuss,” she said, looking up at me.

“I’m listening.”

“I want you to stay away from Sammy,” she said firmly. “Your workout program has come far enough that you don’t need her to train you anymore.”

“You’re the boss,” I replied, trying not to show the disappointment. “Can I ask why?”

She peered at my face, trying to gauge the reason for the question and then just decided to answer. “Because you’re getting under her skin and it’s fucking her up,” she said. “From the pictures I've seen of him, you could be her dead fiancé's brother. She's been carrying a torch for him for twenty years. Longer than she and I have known each other. I thought she was over him, but ever since she started spending time around you, she's been getting all emotional and stupid. I can't have that. Not now. There's too much at stake."

The soldier in me understood that. But a deeper part of me was stinging. It was a sensation that was new to me, like feeling the pain from nerve endings I didn't know I had.

I nodded. "Understood," I said.

We went through the metal doors and I decided to show some good will. "I'm going to grab a cup of coffee before the briefing. Can I get you one?"

"That'd be nice," she said, her eyes suddenly sparkling at me. "Cream and sugar, please."

"Coming right up," I replied. "I'll see you in the main briefing room."

##

"Five, four, three, two, one, hack," Ruth said, "0500 hours local time. Welcome to the mass mission briefing for project 09-04. I'm going to brief the transport, set-up, and recovery portions of the mission. Natasha will brief the jet off-load and re-load. After that, we'll split for the separate transport and fighter briefings."

Ruth flashed to the first slide, which featured a series of times and associated events.

"Transport take-off time is 0630, Island Time. Transit time will be approximately 16.5 hours which includes a fuel stop for all aircraft. All three transports will take separate routes to be in place at the launch site by 2300 hours Island Time. Flight plans and detailed route instructions are in the transport crews' mission folders. Mission launch will take place at 2335 Island Time. Depending on threats and conditions, the mission should last between one and one point five hours. Recovery will occur between 0035 and 0105 Island time. Loading will follow immediately and we'll expect to have the last transport wheels up at 0135 Island Time. Transport three will already have departed when the recovery begins. Transports one and two will take off separately, stop for fuel at their appropriate locations, and make their way back here. The wind forecast indicates that the flight time on the eastbound return will be about fifteen hours. We expect to have all transports back on station by 1700 Island time tomorrow afternoon. Questions on the timeline?"

There were none. She nodded and continued, changing slides as she did so. A 1:500,000 scale map came up which showed the general location of the airfield, marked with a circle someone had drawn on the map. I noticed with some curiosity that the airfield was not printed on the map itself. That meant that none of the official government agencies which cooperated to produce cartographic products knew it existed.

"The launch site is OO47, oscar oscar four seven, an auxiliary field for the Omani military located about 20 miles south of Al Qabil. The ICAO identifier, oscar oscar four seven, is classified and does not appear in any standard navigational database." She changed slides again and an airfield diagram came up which showed a nice long runway with the usual parallel taxiway and large ramp area off to one side. "The runway is oriented 03-21 and is 10,000 feet long by 150 feet wide. It is served by ILS approaches on both runways and a VOR/DME. The frequencies and instrument approaches have been provided in the mission packages for all pilots." The 03-21 orientation of the runway meant that the concrete ran north northeast to south southwest.

"Are the approaches certified?" one of the transport pilots asked. He had a distinct Brooklyn accent.

Ruth nodded.

"Fuel?" he asked. She nodded again. "Three trucks will be provided with operators."

"Cover story?" another transport pilot asked with an Arabic accent.

Ruth smiled. "You're going to love this one. The Sultan of Brunei's nephew wants to pick up his new Arabian horses at an isolated location and have a riding party."

I looked at the transport pilot's face. He smiled back. "That works," he said. "They'll buy that."

Ruth nodded. "They should. We've spent a lot of money putting the pieces in place, especially since this is happening at the last minute."

She looked around. "Any other questions?" There were none. "Natasha?"

The Russian maintenance officer took the floor, pulling her black hair behind her ears as she did so. She called up two slides, side by side on the two screens. The slide on the left showed a timeline, similar to the one Ruth had displayed, while the other showed a diagram of the front end of one of the 747s.

"Upon arrival and transport engine shutdown, the clock begins," she began in her thick Russian accent, "like it always has. I show you slides and timeline for one transport, but process will be the same for all three."

She clicked a slide on the side with the diagram and the next picture came up. It showed the cargo jet with its nose door open. "By arrival plus five minutes, area will be secured and cargo doors will be open on all transports and all interior securing mechanisms released."

The next slide showed the door open and the first Viper being pulled down the ramp by an electric aircraft tug, similar to the one I had seen in the hangar. "By arrival plus 10, first aircraft will be off-loaded."

Another slide appeared, this one showing the second Viper being pulled down the ramp while the wings on the first were lowered and bolted into place. "By arrival plus 15, second aircraft will be off-loaded and the first aircraft will be readied for flight."

The next slide came up. Both Vipers on the ground in front of the cargo jet with their wings in the normal configuration. "By arrival plus 20, both jets off-loaded and ready for flight."

A new slide showed the two jets with pilots in the cockpits and the canopies closed. "Arrival plus 25, fighter engine start."

Another slide took its place, this one with personnel under the wings of the aircraft, obviously pulling arming pins and wires. "Arrival plus 30, arming."

A final slide in this series went up, showing the aircraft taxiing. "Arrival plus 35, taxi and takeoff."

She paused for a second and then continued. "All six jets will start and arm. Once we get four airborne, the remaining two will be pinned, shut down, and reloaded into their transport. That transport will be refueled and will return to the base here. This covers the launch sequence. What are your questions?"

Silence throughout the room.

She called up the next slide which showed two Vipers parked in front of the 747 again. "Upon recovery and shutdown of the aircraft, the wings will be stowed by shutdown plus five minutes."

Another slide came into view, this one showing the first Viper being pulled into the cargo hold. "First aircraft will be on board by shutdown plus 10 and," the next slide emerged, showing the second Viper under tow into the transport, "second aircraft will be on board by shutdown plus 15."

The last slide came up and the nose door of the transport was closed again. "Finally, by shutdown plus 20, fighters will be stowed and lashed down for transport. Any questions?"

I had several, but none that I would ask aloud.

Ruth stood and took the floor again. "Ladies and gentlemen, that concludes the combined briefing. Fighter pilots will brief here, transport pilots can have briefing rooms one and two."

Everyone but Ruth, Brinker, Rug, Pete, VB, and I filed out of the room. Brinker followed the last person to the door and shut it. Then he returned to the floor and started his own briefing.

He started by covering crew variations depending on which transports made it to the launch area and which airplanes were serviceable after engine start. As Natasha had mentioned earlier, we'd all get in the jets and start engines, but assuming the originally-designated four jets made it into the air, Ruth and VB would shut down and their jets would be stowed. If a wingman's jet broke or wouldn't start, VB would take his place. If an element leader's jet broke, Ruth would take his place.

Then Brinker went over the formation we'd fly on the ingress, which would be a standard 'box' formation: one element line abreast in front, the second element line abreast about two to three miles back. We went over radar search responsibilities, targeting plans and sorting plans. Then, he briefly discussed the air-to-air game plan, what we would do if we encountered any other aircraft along the route. The overall mentality was the same as what Rug had discussed with me several rides ago: do our best to get by other aircraft and not attract attention, but if the other aircraft showed awareness, we had to get to them, engage them, and proceed on our way as quickly as possible.

After the air-to-air portion, he discussed the route we'd fly, when we'd transition to the attack formation we needed, and how we'd conduct the attack. Next, he briefed how we'd deal with surface-to-air threats, expected to be light today, nothing more than small arms and automatic weapons and maybe a shoulder-fired missile or two. Other than any threat-related radio calls, the mission would be conducted radio silent, as nearly all missions like this were. He finished his presentation and asked for questions.

"Get your gear, your drug packs, and board your

transports," he concluded. "TC and I will be in transport one, Rug and Pete in transport two, and the boss and VB in transport three. Good hunting, everyone."

We all rose from our chairs and did the things we needed to do before departure. I went to my room, took care of some personal business, and then made my way to the life support room. I packed my helmet, anti-g suit, and parachute harness in my helmet bag; then grabbed my survival vest and moved towards the door.

Just in time for Sammy to come through it. We both stood there awkwardly for a moment, eyeing each other.

"As your doctor," she began, "I just wanted to make sure you were physically and psychologically ready for this mission."

"I appreciate that. As it turns out, I feel fine."

She nodded. "That's good. So, no ill effects from the drug regimen or your injuries or anything else..." Her voice trailed off.

"None that I can think of," I said, silently cursing my inability to say something more loaded with meaning.

"Good!" she responded pertly. "Well," she turned to go, "good luck on your mission. By the way," she turned back to me, "there's always a beach party after the completion of a project. Maybe I'll see you there."

I looked away from her. "I don't think so, Sammy."

"Well, you don't have to see me of course, I just thought..."

I sighed. "I'm not allowed to see you. Ruth told me to stay away from you. She said I was 'messing you up.'"

She just stood there and looked at me, her piercing blue eyes peering out from the strawberry blonde bangs. Oddly, rather than a disappointed expression on her face, there was a hopeful one.

"So just how do you feel about that?" she asked quietly, raising an eyebrow.

"Truthfully, it pisses me off a little."

"A little?" she asked, putting her hand on her hips. "Just a little?"

I smiled at her. I couldn't help it. "Okay, it pisses me off a lot."

She was in my arms a second later and her lips found mine a second after that. Our bodies slammed into the metal lockers behind me, but it didn't matter. After several moments, our lips parted and her head dropped to my chest. She was clinging to me so tightly I felt as if our bodies were bonded to each other.

"Fuck her," Sammy said into my shoulder, with cheerful vehemence. "That bitch thinks she can run my life. Fuck her!"

"No thanks," I said seriously. "I have that t-shirt and I don't want another one."

Sammy laughed and squeezed me. "Listen," she said. "After the projects, Ruth has a ton of paperwork to deal with. She never makes it to the post-strike party. I'll meet you on the beach in her little retreat area."

"I thought no one was allowed there but her."

Sammy smirked at me. "She's a little impressed with her authority sometimes. Everybody goes there from time to time. When they want to be...alone."

"I'll be there."

"Okay. Now kiss me."

We lost ourselves in one another for a few more moments. When the kiss ended, she looked at me sternly. "Please don't get yourself killed or anything stupid like that."

She gave me another quick squeeze and was gone through the door before I could respond.

##

Our 747 roared off the Island's runway about fifteen minutes later, followed by the two others. As we turned in to the dark sky to the west, with the sun just breaking the horizon to the east, I realized why the timing for the transports' arrival, loading, and departure had to be so precise. The unit didn't want a satellite or aircraft passing overhead and seeing three 747s launch off a seemingly-deserted island in the middle of the ocean.

There was an air traffic control issue here as well. About the only place where a heavy jet could just 'appear' at high-altitude without being noticed was in the middle of the ocean, out of land-based radar coverage. I guessed false flight plans had to be on file somewhere, or the first controlling agency the transport pilots checked in with would get suspicious. Maybe the timing of the launch also had to do with a shift change at the applicable controlling agency. More likely, there was payoff money circulated to get the controllers to look the other way.

I pondered these thoughts as I surveyed my temporary accommodation on the airplane. The passenger area on the 747's upper deck behind the cockpit was sumptuous. There were thirty fully reclining seats with independent video and audio players and privacy partitions. It was almost like each seat had its own room, very similar to ultra-high end first class seats on some of the Middle Eastern airlines I had flown.

The galley, between the passenger area and the cockpit, was laid out for self-service. All the food and drinks were behind glass refrigerator doors and there were both a microwave and conventional oven available to heat the selected food. The food selection was extensive and encompassed everything from sandwiches to three-course meals.

I decided to have a look in the cargo bay. I rose from my seat and walked to the ladder to descend to the lower deck. The 'flight attendant' stopped me. He was a large, muscular man, seated in the crew seat next to the galley. I remembered seeing him directing the loading of the Vipers earlier and assumed he served double duty as a loadmaster.

"And where do you think you're going?" he asked harshly.

I looked into his eyes. “I’m going to get my ass into one of those jets in about fifteen hours; and when I do, I’m not going to have a lot of time to preflight it. I’m going to do that now.” I didn’t give him a chance to respond and brushed past him to the ladder. A few moments later, I was on the cargo deck.

I had never been inside a 747 freighter before and I was impressed by what I saw. The inside of a USAF C-5 cargo plane was cavernous; high as well as wide. This cargo area was smaller but more efficiently arranged, given the constraints of the 747’s hull. The F-16s and associated equipment took up a lot of space on the deck, but did not fill it. I wondered whether the cargo area had been specially modified to accept the jets. The two Vipers themselves were securely lashed to the deck, with their wheels chocked and heavy straps running from the nose and main landing gear assemblies to tie-down points on the edge of the deck. In front of the first Viper, nearest the nose cargo door, the electric tug which would pull the jet out was already in place. Typically, electric tugs have a small metal deck, which slides under the jet’s nose wheel and a securing strap which lashes the jet to the tug. This system eliminates the need for a tow bar or other special apparatus to move the aircraft. This tug’s metal deck was still underneath the nose wheel of the lead Viper, exactly where it had been when the tug pushed the Viper onboard. I could just picture the nose cargo door opening, the ramp deploying and this jet down that ramp a few minutes after.

God, do these guys have their shit together, I thought.

I pre-flighted both jets as carefully and thoroughly as I could. I was especially attentive to the configuration of the arming wires on the Mark-84 bombs.

Eventually, I climbed the ladder back to the upper deck. I had given some thought earlier to going up to the cockpit and talking to the transport pilots but the ‘NO ADMITTANCE’ sign stenciled on the cockpit door killed that idea. Besides, I got the feeling the troll guarding the door might not like it. I made my way back to my seat and settled in, nice and cozy. The passenger area was comfortably dark, lit only by a few streams of partial sunlight coming through the shades that had been drawn over the windows shortly after takeoff.

Well, nothing to do now but relax, I thought. I used the buttons to recline my seat and raise the leg rests to the horizontal position. Then, I put a pillow under my head and a blanket over my chest. I was asleep in seconds.

##

We flew for about eight or nine hours and then landed briefly for refueling. I don't know exactly where that was. I knew it was hot and I knew there was a lot of water around so it was a coastal city or an island. I stuck my head into the cockpit while the refueling was underway and the troll was below for a few minutes. I asked a few innocuous questions, more so I could look out the windscreen than to learn anything. The transport pilots were courteous but businesslike, and I was informed that 747 freighters have about half to two-thirds of the range of their passenger-carrying brethren, which explained why the fuel stops were necessary. I excused myself few minutes later. We were starting engines about thirty minutes after shutdown and I was startled that it all happened so fast. I had made refueling stops all over the world in the G-IV and the Falcon 900EX, which held a lot less gas than this thing, and they had taken longer than this.

##

We flew for about another seven hours. Most of the people in the cabin, Brinker and I included, had something to eat and made a trip or two to the lavatory. At the seven-hour point, the lights were turned on in the passenger area and the pilot's voice came over the intercom.

"One hour to landing," was all he said.

The activity in the cabin noticeably increased. The maintenance personnel talked among themselves and from the snippets of conversation I could overhear, I could tell they were going through the off-loading sequence and the associated events. Then, I felt the 747's engines reducing thrust and the jet began to descend. Not long after, the speed brakes and flaps were deployed. Finally, I felt the landing gear come down, and about five minutes later, we touched down.

The usual increase in heart rate and sweaty palms hit me then. This was about to get real.

As we taxied in, the personnel in the cabin began to rise and I noticed that they split into two clearly-defined groups. The larger group was composed of people I had seen earlier, discussing the off-loading sequence and the other group was smaller, quieter and much more solemn-looking. I figured out who they were about the time Brinker came over to my seat.

"We wait here in the passenger area until the security crew has deplaned and deployed and the jets are off-loaded," he said.

I nodded. It was starting to make sense. I was wondering what they did to ensure that no intruders messed up the operation on the ground once it began. As I watched the security detail load, charge, and strap weapons to their bodies, I had my answer.

The jet stopped and the security detail scurried down the ladder, closely followed by the maintenance personnel. Then the engines wound down and I heard the cargo door open.

Instinctively, I switched the function on my watch to stopwatch and I started the timer.

I could hear the low whine of the electric tug's motor immediately after the hydraulic system finished extending the cargo ramp. It was less than three minutes after shutdown. They were ahead of schedule.

The tug came back into the cargo deck again less than five

minutes later. They were really ahead of schedule.

"Outside, gentlemen," came a voice over the intercom.

Brinker and I descended the ramp at about shutdown plus thirteen minutes on my stopwatch and we walked out under a brilliant, blue Arabian sky. There, arrayed before us, the six Vipers stood ready, with wings bolted into place and canopies open. They bristled with the wing-mounted missiles and bombs, eager for flight. I just shook my head in awe.

"I can't fucking believe this," I said, involuntarily.

"I know what you mean," Brinker replied in a rare moment of candor, "I've done this several times now and I still don't believe it." Then he looked over at me and smiled. "Let's mount up," he said.

We were in our jets a few moments later. Within two minutes, all the jets were started and the canopies were down. We did our post starting checks. Then our hands all came up, and in unison, six arming crews went under the wings and pulled the safety pins for the bombs, the missiles and the 20mm cannon. Then they came out and, God help me, they stood at attention and saluted us, all at once. We saluted back and the check-in came.

"Breaker check," came Brinker's voice with the Have Quick radio's 'clickity-click' in the background.

"Two," I said.

"Three," Rug chimed in.

"Four," came Pete's voice.

"Five," Ruth's steady voice intoned.

"Six," VB concluded.

"Breaker, any alibis?" Brinker was asking if any of us had an equipment or ordnance malfunction which would prevent us from accomplishing the mission.

"Two, negative."

"Three, negative."

"Four, negative."

"Five, negative."

"Six, negative."

"Breaker Five and Six, you are cleared off," Brinker said. "Two, Three and Four, on me."

Brinker's jet was on the end closest to the parallel taxiway and next to mine. He circled his fingers in the 'run-it-up' signal and his crew chief echoed the sign. Then he taxied out and I followed him, with Rug and Pete behind me.

We taxied out to the end of the runway staggered in standard fighter fashion, with one main gear on the centerline of the taxiway and without talking to anyone. I could only assume that this had all been appropriately coordinated. In short order, we made it to the approach end of our chosen runway, Runway 03, oriented on a heading of 030 degrees. Without asking permission, Brinker led us out on to the runway and we lined up in echelon formation, with Brinker on the far left side of the runway, and the rest of us in flight order, two, three and four, next to him and back just enough to look up the preceding guy's wingline.

Brinker looked over and gave me the 'run-it-up' sign and I passed it on to Rug, who passed it on to Pete. Then I pushed the throttle forward to 90% rpm and watched the engine respond. I carefully surveyed my engine instruments and noted that the fuel flow, nozzle gauge, exhaust gas temperature, oil pressure, and temperature indicators all looked normal. Then I looked over my right shoulder at Rug, who was looking over his right shoulder at Pete. Rug turned his head and nodded at me. I turned my head and nodded at Brinker. Brinker nodded back at me, and instantly, his jet sprang forward, and I hit the timer hand on the Viper's internal clock. I watched Brinker's nozzle close as he rolled away from us, indicating that he had gone to MIL power. A second later it opened widely, accompanied by the long, orange flame of the AB.

The clock reached twenty seconds and it was my turn. I released my brakes and my jet leapt forward, impatient for flight. I advanced the throttle to MIL and watched the nozzle gauge swing closed, and then I pushed the throttle over the detent and all the way forward into MAX AB. The nozzle gauge swung open just as I felt the familiar kick in the middle of my back as the GE engine went to full power at 28,000 pounds of thrust.

I checked my acceleration rate at the 1,000 foot marker and I was well past the minimum check speed of 100 knots. Then I swept my eyes across the engine instruments to make sure everything was normal. My airspeed was approaching 165 knots.

"Good engine," I said and smoothly applied back pressure to the side-stick controller. The sleek jet with its fearsome ordnance lifted off, and I slapped the gear handle up.

I could see Brinker begin his easy right turn in front of me, his blue-gray jet silhouetted against the brown mountains in the background. I rolled, pulled, and aimed my jet inside his turn to gain my formation position.

Déjà vu smacked me in the face at that moment as the all too familiar mixture of excitement and dread bubbled up inside me. The feeling of going into combat – a feeling I hadn't experienced in nearly nineteen years.

Jesus, I thought. *I forgot how much I fucking love this.*

CHAPTER TWENTY-ONE

Contract Day Twenty-Five
Monday, 5 October
2335 Hours Island Time
500 Feet AGL and 480 Knots
Over Northeastern Oman

We rejoined to four ship 'box' formation a few moments later and flew across the expanse of flatlands that lay between us and the mountains. Brinker and I were in line abreast formation 12,000 feet apart. Rug and Pete were in the same formation about two to three miles behind us. We stayed at 500 feet above the dry desert floor, avoiding any small settlements or towns as we made for the higher terrain. We didn't expect to be identified as intruders by any of the Bedouin locals, but it never hurt to be cautious.

There's nothing like flying 500 knots at 500 feet or lower. The ground seems to rush under the nose of the aircraft and flash by the canopy. The sense of speed is unlike anything else anywhere. In my USAF career, between A-10s and F-16s, I had had spent thousands of hours at 500 feet AGL—above ground level. I was delighted to discover my eyes still knew the picture.

The mountains loomed before us and Brinker led us into the heart of them, flying between some of the smaller peaks as he did so. The mountains were as brown and desolate as the flatlands we just flew over, although they were obviously craggy and more rugged. They were only a few thousand feet high, but they hid us as well as taller mountains would have. I stayed attentive at the controls of my jet as we got into the rocky terrain and began our turn to the north, dropping low down in the valleys to elude any curious radar sites looking our way. Our radar warning receivers (RWRs) were set to pick up the slightest radar 'tickle,' and mine, at least, had been silent. We also watched the radar closely. So far, the contacts we detected appeared to be crossing traffic, so we didn't even discuss them on the radio.

I looked down at my route map and checked our progress. We were flying up the east side of the Arabian Peninsula. Although we were presently well into Oman, we'd pass over a portion of the United Arab Emirates and I knew that Air Force was highly capable. The good news was the UAE Air Force also flew F-16s, and there was a strong chance we'd appear as native aircraft if we were spotted.

We had about two hundred miles to go to the target - about twenty-five minutes at 480 knots groundspeed. I kept busy with some last-minute target area study and monitoring the radar contacts which showed up in my area of search responsibility. Dubai was about forty miles west of the centerline of our route, and one of the arrival routes into its busy airport was directly above and in front of us. I watched each contact closely for any telltale sign of awareness.

We crossed into the UAE a few minutes later and the arriving traffic into Dubai disappeared off my radar screen as it was now directly above us. The radar still 'painted' a fair amount of air traffic in the airspace over the Gulf, now about fifty miles in front of us, but it was all at high altitude and traversing the normal air routes.

As I thought about crossing the Gulf, something popped into my head. Brinker had not briefed how we'd respond if we encountered a US Navy Carrier Strike Group during our ingress or egress. The Persian Gulf usually has at least one US Navy Carrier Strike Group patrolling it, and I sincerely hoped the current group was nowhere near the mouth of the Gulf today.

Ten minutes to the target. We were eighty miles away and just crossing back into the part of Oman called the Musandam Peninsula, on the tip of the Arabian Peninsula. The terrain was still mountainous and rugged. I stayed abeam Brinker's jet and avoided the rocks as I continued to watch the green, monochromatic squares of video dance back and forth across my radar.

Blue water appeared before us and we descended into a fiord that would lead us out to the Gulf. Brinker had instructed us to go down to one hundred feet once we were over the open water, so I prepared myself for that. The task prioritization scheme changes dramatically at very low altitudes. Five hundred feet is a fairly benign environment. The pilot has to pay attention, but he can still perform cockpit chores, look at his maps, and program avionics, as long as he doesn't stay 'heads-down' for more than a second or two. At one hundred feet, all the pilot has time to do is look out the front and fly the airplane. I adjusted my attack map so it was easily visible on the clipboard strapped to my right knee.

The water at the edge of the fiord went underneath us and I ran my 'FENCE' check. I turned the MASTER ARM switch on and was rewarded with a green light on the weapons panel. I currently had the air-to-air mode called up, so if I hit the pickle button, I'd shoot an air-to-air missile. When I went to the air-to-ground mode, the bombing symbology would appear and the bombs would be ready to drop as well. I also armed my chaff and flare countermeasure dispensing system and ensured that the correct program was loaded. The lights on that panel blinked back at me. The jet was ready for combat. I hoped I was as prepared as it was.

Brinker descended closer to the water, and I followed him down. We were starting to see small boats here and there as we streaked across the fiord. Some were fishing boats and others were small pleasure craft. I saw the occupants of a sleek speedboat wave at us as we passed about half a mile away from them. I guessed that today probably wasn't the first time they had seen a low-flying fighter aircraft.

The mouth of the fiord came up before us as the terrain on either side of it sloped to the sea, and suddenly we were out over the Persian Gulf, surrounded by blue water.

The target was fifty miles away. A little more than six minutes to go.

The sea before us was like a superhighway for ships. Tankers, freighters, warships, and the occasional passenger liner were arrayed in rows on their way in and out of one of the busiest sea passages in the world. Brinker and I descended to one hundred feet, and the whitecaps outside my canopy looked close enough for me to reach out and touch. A huge red and brown supertanker loomed in front of us, and Brinker climbed slightly so his jet would clear the tanker's superstructure. I could see the gray outline of some sort of warship in front of my jet about five miles away. Suddenly, my radar warning receiver came to life and I heard the intermittent buzz associated with a search radar in my headset. An 'S' appeared on the RWR display a second later. A search radar was annoying, but not life threatening. Now if they turned on a target-tracking radar for a surface-to-air missile system, that would be a different story. I turned toward Brinker's jet slightly and changed my course so that I wouldn't overfly the ship. I hoped that when they saw I wasn't pointed at them, they'd get the message I wasn't hostile. My move must have worked because no additional radars came on line, and I flew right off the stern of the vessel a few moments later with no shots fired. I did see a crowd of faces looking up at me, though, and there were some people pointing at my jet. I couldn't tell the nationality of the warship, although I knew it wasn't US. I wondered how visible the US markings on our jets were as we zipped by at 100 feet and 500 knots.

Thirty-five miles to the target. A little over four minutes to go. The Initial Point, or IP, would be our next navigational fix. Brinker clicked his mic button twice, and then turned toward me to take up a heading that was perpendicular to our course to the IP. I collapsed to a wedge formation on him. We maintained that heading until we heard two more clicks on the radio frequency, indicating that Rug's element was approaching its position for the final attack formation. Brinker turned back toward the IP and I flew to the place I needed to be, about one mile away from him and about forty-five degrees back from line abreast. I looked beyond Brinker's airplane and I could see Rug and Pete, in a formation that mirrored ours, about three miles away.

A few more ships passed between Brinker's airplane and Rug's. I couldn't imagine that four F-16s flying at low altitude across the Persian Gulf towards Iran would go unnoticed or unreported for too much longer. There were just too many ships and too many observers now. My radar, with forty-mile range selected, was now painting the airspace over the target and just beyond it. I could see a few contacts at 25,000 feet about seven miles on the other side of the target. These got my attention. They weren't aware of us, but they also weren't established on a known route. It looked suspiciously like a combat air patrol, or CAP, holding point - a point where air-to-air fighters loitered until they were vectored to intercept incoming intruders.

I keyed my mic. "Breaker Two, single group, multiple contacts, bull's-eye 360 seven; 25,000, marshalling." The bull's-eye for today was the target itself.

"Breaker Three, same," Rug said.

"Breaker Three, target that group," Brinker commanded.

"Breaker Three, targeted, 25,000."

When a possible air-to-air threat is identified near the target at this point during the ingress, the flight leader has to make a choice. He has to decide whether he'll abort the target run, use his entire four-ship to engage the potential threat, break the formation up and have one element attack and the other engage the threat, or blow off the threat and continue as planned. I could almost hear the cogs in Brinker's brain turning.

"Breaker Two, One. What's your assessment of the group?"

I was shocked, Brinker was asking my opinion. Publicly even.

I centered my elevation scan on the group and engaged a radar mode called Track-While-Scan, or TWS. TWS automatically replaces the raw video data of the contacts in its scan area with symbology which shows the contacts' movement and direction. It has its limitations; but in a situation like this, it comes in handy.

I bugged one of the contacts, looked at him for a second, and then used the target management switch to jump the bug to the three remaining contacts in the group, one by one. Their orbit wasn't oriented in our direction.

"Breaker One, Two. They're definitely marshaling, but I don't think they're pointed at us. I don't think they're capping. I think they're doing something else."

"Breaker One copies. Breakers, continue." Brinker had made his decision. We were going for it.

Our island IP appeared before us. I could also just make out the coastline of the much larger island to the northwest of us. My heart rate was increasing. The show was about to begin.

Brinker's jet started to slowly move away from me and I knew that he was accelerating to the briefed attack speed of 540 knots. I pushed my throttle up to keep pace with him.

The jet began to gyrate slightly, the way it characteristically did when carrying Mark-84 bombs at a speed that was approaching the transonic regime. The east end of the island passed below us in a blur about twenty seconds later. A mosaic of green land, hills, buildings, cars, trucks, boats, ships, and people went by my canopy. The island was part of Iran, and I had no doubt our presence would be discovered now. The only question was how swiftly the reaction on the ground would come.

I took a last look at the group of radar contacts we identified before and verified that their status hadn't changed. They were still in their orbit, and if anything, moving away from the target area. I called up the air-to-ground mode and watched the mileage to the target decrease. The action point was 3.5 miles from the target. We'd be there in about a minute. Already, I was seeing several tanker ships sitting at anchor, out into the Gulf and away from the terminal at Bandar Abbas. I wasn't consciously counting them, but I knew they were into double digits.

"I sure as shit hope their insurance is paid up," I said into my intercom.

The radar warning receiver came alive and generated 'S' symbols in front of us. I heard the associated buzzes in my headset. At one hundred feet above the ground, the curvature of the earth will hide an incoming aircraft from ground-mounted radar at ranges greater than eighteen nautical miles. Inside eighteen miles, if there is no obstacle between the radar and the jet, the radar sees all. They knew we were here.

I switched my radar to the air-to-air mode for a few seconds to see if the group beyond the bull's-eye had been tasked to intercept us. They were now about thirty miles beyond the target, but they were all line abreast and headed our way. At this point, they wouldn't catch us, but it meant that we'd undoubtedly have a welcoming committee on the ground.

"Breakers continue," I said into my mic, "group beyond bull's-eyes has committed on us. Group thirty north of bull at 25,000."

No one responded. They all knew what it meant.

Brinker rolled his jet to the right as he began his action. I banked with him and applied a little back pressure to parallel his course as I called the air-to-ground mode back up. A few seconds later his jet started climbing rapidly as he began his pop-up. I climbed with him.

Almost instantly, my radar warning receiver started whining at me with the high-pitched, multiple beeps of a high-frequency, fast-updating radar - the kind that guides missiles and anti-aircraft artillery. On the shoreline beyond the terminal, muzzle flashes became visible, and I thought I saw the corkscrew smoke trail of a shoulder-launched surface-to-air missile.

Brinker rolled in on his terminal and dispensed a burst of chaff and flares. The sunlight from the west reflected off the foil chaff, and it looked like small strips of silver fire were following his airplane. The flares were bright bursts of light in the sky. We had clearly identified ourselves as hostile aircraft to the people on the ground. I rolled in with Brinker, punching out a chaff and flare program of my own, and selecting the Dive Toss mode as I did so.

A huge supertanker was docked alongside of the terminal and I could see several streams of people running up and down the mooring area. The reality of the number of people we were about to kill suddenly hit me. This wasn't war and these people had done nothing to deserve the destruction that was about to rain down upon them, except maybe piss off someone who had a lot of money.

"You poor bastards," I said.

While the chaff and flares illuminated the sky around me and the bullets sliced through the air in search of my jet, I slewed the Dive Toss box to the middle of the right side of the array of storage tanks, designated, held the pickle button down, and began my pull-up. In front of me, I could see Brinker recovering from his dive. My flight path marker blinked just as I felt the heavy single thump of both 2,000 pound bombs leaving my jet. Then I was into my recovery and rolling my jet up to stay inside Brinker's turn as he came off target. I kept the g on my aircraft and banked slightly past ninety degrees to get a downward vector on my jet. The waters reached up to meet me and I rolled to wings-level with the g still applied and broke my descent rate. I was about two hundred feet above the waves.

I had no sooner re-attained my line-abreast position with Brinker and was easing back out to two miles separation when a series of terrific explosions ripped through the two oil terminals and the storage area. Huge bursts of light flashed in sequence, clearly visible pieces of metal went flying skyward and heavy black smoke billowed into the air. The low pitched 'whump' sound of the explosions was so loud that I could hear it in my jet with a helmet on my ears and the air noise of five hundred knots airspeed outside my canopy.

I looked over my shoulder and was relieved to see Rug's element about two miles behind Brinker. Rug and Pete had made it off target too.

Our egress route took us right out of the mouth of the Persian Gulf. We streaked along the water at five hundred feet - high enough that we wouldn't run into any ships and low enough that we were still under the detection range of most radars in the area. Also, if any airborne radar were looking down on us at this point, it would have to sift through the clutter of all the other aircraft flying back and forth in the area. We passed the Makran coast of Iran on the left side of the formation and I was relieved to see the wide expanse of the Indian Ocean before us.

Then I heard the radar tone in my headset. It was sharp, distinct, and sounded like a synthesized version of the music from a bad science fiction movie. I knew it well. It was the tone generated by the APG-73 radar mounted in a US Navy F/A-18.

"Fuck!" I screamed into my intercom. I looked at my RWR

scope. A triangular symbol, which we called a 'wingform,' illuminated at twelve o'clock on the display. I looked at my radar and noted that the airspace above 15,000 feet was clear of any traffic headed our way. I was about to key my mic and inform the formation that I was 'spiked'—that is painted by air-to-air radar—when I heard Brinker's voice.

"Breaker One, single group, two contacts, my nose, 25 miles, 10,000, head."

We had found the carrier strike group. I knew how this worked. The guys coming our way were their long-range patrols.

"Breaker Three, One. Notch right and go direct to the recovery point. Cleared off."

It wasn't what I would have done, but I saw the utility in the plan. Brinker and I would occupy the Navy while Rug and Pete made it back to launch point and got their jets stowed. By making a sudden hard turn perpendicular to the incoming fighters, Rug and Pete's jets would fall into the Doppler 'notch,' and temporarily vanish from the F-18's radar. Modern air-to-air radars rely on Doppler shift, movement toward or away from them, to maintain contact with incoming targets. When Rug and Pete turned perpendicular to the F-18's radar, their relative movement toward the radar would be reduced to nothing and they would disappear into the ground clutter.

"Breaker One, offset left."

Brinker began his offset turn to run a standard intercept against the incoming fighters and I collapsed my position to stay with him.

"Breaker Two, sort group my nose, 15 miles, 10,000, head."

I rolled my elevation knob down and found the two jets immediately. Unlike the Viper, the F/A-18 is a very 'dirty' airplane radar-wise. I bugged the jet on my side.

"Breaker Two, sorted western."

"Breakers, jettison tanks."

A few seconds later, Brinker's external tanks left his

airplane and mine followed. If we were going to 'turn and burn' with Hornets, we didn't need the extra drag of two 370-gallon tanks.

It was possible that the F-18s were only on a routine patrol and decided to just put their radars on us to see who we were. It was also possible that they might have let us continue on our way. But now we had put our radars on them, and if their radar warning gear was anything like ours, and the truth was, it was probably better, they'd know that we were looking back at them. My radar told me that they were accelerating, descending, and coming our way.

Brinker abandoned the offset and turned in to me, driving my position forward on him. We were nearly line abreast again and headed directly for the F-18s. I had no idea what his plan would be when we hit the merge. I knew the F-18s would not do anything before they visually identified us; and the fact that our jets had US markings would undoubtedly confuse them and buy us some time. But beyond that, I didn't know what Brinker would do. Would he rock his wings, and then gently turn away, trying to get the Hornet pilots to believe we were just out on a routine flight?

At five miles from the merge, Brinker keyed his mic and called for the pincer.

I turned away and tried to get as far from him as I could without losing sight of his jet. I watched him begin a climb to meet the F-18s as they came down to us and noted, with some satisfaction, that both Hornets were headed for Brinker, which meant that they either didn't see me or wanted to increase their odds against one bandit. I also noted that my RWR display was clear and that my headset was quiet.

We were three miles from the merge when Brinker fired the missile.

I watched, dumbstruck, as a trail of white smoke left his wing and headed straight toward the F-18 on his side. The poor Hornet driver never had a chance. I'm sure he didn't expect to be shot at and he had come to the merge to look, not necessarily to fight. The Python detonated just as it passed the canopy of the lead Hornet and blew the aircraft in half with an accompanying fireball.

Holy fucking shit!

The other Hornet, who had been just aft of line abreast with his leader and about a mile displaced to my side, was now turning toward Brinker to engage him, and I was sure that if the pilot in that jet hadn't been ready to fight before, he was definitely ready now.

I shoved my throttle in to MAX AB and pulled up sharply so I could get above the fight and see what I could do to help. A US Navy pilot had just died. I could taste the bile rising in my throat.

Brinker and the other Hornet merged. Brinker turned across the Hornet's tail, and he made an aggressive move into the vertical. The Hornet pilot was ready for that, and he turned to the same side as Brinker did and went one circle with him, also going vertical.

Not good. This will be a scissors in no time.

The Hornet is exceptionably maneuverable at low airspeed and high angle of attack, unlike the Viper. For a Viper to get into the 'phone booth' with a Hornet was suicide. Brinker, being Brinker, probably didn't consider that.

I didn't have much time.

The two jets were climbing, passing through my altitude of about 5,000 feet, leaving the surface of the ocean below them and trying to get their noses into a position of advantage as they turned toward each other. It was an odd sort of ballet to watch from my perspective. Both jets were in full AB and the flames coming out from the tail cones were clearly visible. The smoothly-contoured gray-blue Viper was dancing with the more angular Hornet, the two of them creating a series of overlapping S's in the sky.

I rolled my jet on to its back and applied some g to stop my climb and then I aimed my nose directly at them. I estimated that they were going uphill at about 120 knots, and I was hoping they'd get far enough above me for the plan I had in mind to work. I kept the throttle in MAX AB and accelerated to over 500 knots. I had about three miles to close before I'd be in place.

As the scissors progressed, I could see the Hornet pilot steadily gaining nose position. Brinker was fighting hard, but with each S the two jets transcribed, the Hornet's nose was getting further around the circle than the Viper's. This was going to be close. The Hornet would be in position to shoot in another thirty seconds or so.

I didn't want to alert the Hornet pilot by locking him with the radar just yet, so I visually estimated the distance remaining to them, added the differences in our energy states, counted to five, and yanked my throttle to idle while deploying my speed brakes.

My climb slowed rapidly as they continued back and forth across my nose. With 2,000 feet to go, I lined up behind the Hornet as he passed over Brinker's jet, heading to the outside of the circle. I put my radar into dogfight mode and locked the Hornet up.

The DLZ for the Python came up and I had the minimum range I needed, but I didn't uncage it. I didn't want to kill this guy.

The Hornet pilot's radar warning gear alerted him to my presence. He turned hard into me, undoubtedly trying to get sight of my jet and fight me. But by that time, my gunsight had settled in and I was five hundred feet behind him. I didn't want to risk igniting any of his internal fuel tanks, so I put the pipper just behind the tail of his aircraft and then tracked it forward a few feet, hoping to disable his elevator and rudder. He began to turn into me, and I tapped the trigger, firing the shortest burst of twenty millimeter bullets I could manage. I watched the bullets blow off pieces of his elevator slab and tail. Then, a few of them struck the afterburner section of his engines, just under the vertical stabilizer, and a fire erupted. The nose of his jet abruptly dropped as he lost pitch control and then started rolling to the left. He had lost control of his aircraft. I pulled up and to the left, circling his airplane as it plunged to the sea in a tight turn.

"Punch out, Goddamn it!" I yelled into my intercom. "Punch out!"

I was rewarded with the sight of his canopy departing the crippled airplane a few moments later, closely followed by the bright flash of the ejection seat as it propelled him clear of the wreckage. The seat separated away a few seconds after that and he was under a beautiful brown parachute. His Hornet continued seaward in its 'death spiral' and hit the sea, generating a huge splash and geyser of water upon impact.

I breathed a long sigh of relief into my oxygen mask.

Then, I saw Brinker.

He had deployed his landing gear and flaps to keep his airspeed low and was making a slow turn to bring his nose to bear on the descending pilot under the parachute. He was going to use his cannon to kill him.

The bloodlust seized me. I rolled toward Brinker and pulled for all I was worth. The radar went into dogfight mode and his jet was locked up three seconds later. I uncaged the Python to let the big dog eat. I keyed the mic and a voice came out of me that I didn't recognize.

"You pull that trigger, motherfucker, and I'll blow your Dutch ass out of the sky, right here, right now!"

Brinker hesitated a moment as he flew toward the pilot. Then, he retracted his gear and accelerated, climbing and turning back toward the recovery point as he did so.

My senses were alive with adrenaline. I was breathing heavily and actually trembling with anticipation. The MASTER ARM switch was still engaged and the Python was still growling eagerly in my headset. I could have so easily killed him and made up a cover story about it. My right thumb hovered over the pickle button, caressing it. I could visualize the missile leaving the launch rail and detonating on his jet in a satisfying fireball, and watching the pieces of him and his airplane descending to the blue waters of the Gulf below.

Now! The lust screamed at me. *Kill him now!*

But I didn't press the button. Because a more sinister, more calculating thought came to me. *If you kill him now, you'll only get one. If you wait until later, you'll get them all.*

I smiled grimly under my oxygen mask, re-caged the Python, turned the MASTER ARM switch off, and rejoined to a line abreast formation with him soon after.

It took thirty minutes to fly back to the launch point. With the fuel we had remaining and the fact that we had to return at low altitude, we didn't have much choice about the routing. We went present position direct to OO47 at five hundred feet, coasting in between the cities of Muscat and Subar. Fortunately, the flight back was uneventful. Brinker sent me to trail when we were about five miles from the airfield, and we landed, one behind the other, a few minutes later.

Our 747 was the only other aircraft on the field. The ground crew was waiting for us and I was prepared for the same synchronized performance I had seen on the launch.

I wasn't disappointed. They marshaled us in and shut us down, side by side. I had no sooner raised my canopy when the tug was attached to the front of my airplane and two sets of people with ladders and tools were attaching the bolting points for the wings to fold them up.

I made it down the ladder as the first wing was unbolted and the second one followed shortly thereafter. Then the tug was moving and my jet was being backed up the ramp into the 747, with the muscular loadmaster/flight attendant guiding the tug's driver as the Viper was pushed into the cargo bay.

I climbed the ladder to the passenger compartment and got out of my flight gear, neatly packing it all in my helmet bag and placing it next to my seat. Brinker ascended the ladder a few minutes later and I could hear his jet being tugged into the 747's cargo area through the ladder opening. Apart from the transport pilots, who were busy in the cockpit, he and I were the only two people up there.

The lust wasn't going to go completely unfed.

I waited for him get into the passenger area and take his gear off. Then, I slowly rose from my seat and walked over to him, staring into his eyes as I did so. I could tell he wanted to look away from me, but he just couldn't do it.

"What do you have to say for yourself?" I asked him.

He just looked back at me without speaking, his face slowly assuming its typical defiant expression. As he looked into my eyes, I stepped forward rapidly and kneed him in the balls with as much force as I could muster. He bent over and moaned in shock and surprise. I grabbed his helmet bag off the floor and hefted it. Like me, he had packed it with his helmet, g-suit, and parachute harness. It probably weighed about twenty pounds and had lots of nice, hard metal things inside it, just under the thin layer of Nomex cloth. I took the bag in both of my hands, cocked my body, and shifted my weight to my rear foot. Then I swung for the fences, using Brinker's bag as my bat and his head as my ball. The blow lifted him off his feet and spun him around. As he turned, he smacked his head against one of the hard metal cabinets at the entrance to the galley. His legs buckled then and he collapsed to the floor and lay motionless.

"What was that?" said a voice from the cockpit.

"Nothing," I answered. "My friend just slipped. He'll be fine."

"Okay," said the voice.

I dragged Brinker to his seat and put him in it. Then, I reclined it, put the partitions up, and threw a blanket over him.

TOP SECRET / SPECIAL
COMPARTMENTALIZED INFORMATION
CLASSIFIED BY: US Central Intelligence Agency
DECLASSIFY ON: OADR

From: Special Projects Group [NCS]
Sent: Monday, 5 October 2009, 1000 EDT (5 October 2009, 1400Z)
To: Director, NCS
Cc: Special Projects Group [NCS]; damrine@cmail.cia.gov; dsmith3@cmail.cia.gov

SUBJECT: Update, Case File: 08-434A (MAG)

(TS) Narrative:

1. (TS) DCIA Operations Order 09-548, code-named 'Persian Light' was successfully executed today. Four F-16's from MAG were on and off target at approximately 1620 target area local time (1220Z).

2. (TS) DI assesses the docks at Bandar Abbas at 40% destroyed. The oil storage area is assessed at 55% destroyed and is still burning. DI believes the terminal will be unable to be used for its primary function of exporting oil to and receiving weapons from North Korea for at least six months.

3. (TS) Communication intercepts indicate that Iranians believe the attacking aircraft were from the UAE.

4. (TS) On egress, two MAG aircraft engaged two F-18Es from the Nimitz Carrier Strike Group at approximately 1628 local time (1228Z). The two F-18s were destroyed. One pilot was picked up by a nearby merchant ship. The other pilot remains

missing in action. This engagement occurred in spite of the stand down order issued to the Commander of the Nimitz Strike Group, Admiral James L. Bennett, Jr. Admiral Bennett has been subsequently relieved of command.

5. (TS) Tracking assets attained contact with all MAG 747 freighters as they launched. At this hour, we continue to track them as they fly eastbound.

(TS) CONCLUSION: None.

(TS) ACTIONS: (TS) We have notified US Special Operations Command (USSOCOM) to stage forces for an invasion of the island base once we have confirmed its location. USSOCOM has estimated it will take 48 hours to get forces briefed and in position.

(TS) RECOMMENDATION: None. Information only.

TOP SECRET / SPECIAL
COMPARTMENTALIZED INFORMATION
CLASSIFIED BY: US Central Intelligence Agency
DECLASSIFY ON: OADR

TOP SECRET / SPECIAL COMPARTMENTALIZED INFORMATION
CLASSIFIED BY: US Central Intelligence Agency
DECLASSIFY ON: OADR

From: Special Projects Group [NCS]
Sent: Tuesday, 6 October 2009, 1145 EDT (1 October 2009, 0345Z)
To: Director, NCS
Cc: Special Projects Group [NCS]; damrine@cmail.cia.gov; dsmith3@cmail.cia.gov

SUBJECT: Update, Case File: 08-434A (MAG)

(TS) Narrative:

1. (TS) Between 0245 and 0315Z, surveillance contact was lost on the three 747 transports carrying the MAG aircraft, approximately thirty minutes after they flew over New Caledonia in the southwestern Pacific Ocean. The aircraft were out of air traffic control radar contact and were being intermittently tracked by US Navy ships, Royal Navy ships, and satellites when they disappeared.

2. (TS) An analysis of the aircraft range, radar, and satellite coverage, limits their area of landing to somewhere west of New Caledonia, east of the Cook Islands, and south of both Fiji and American Samoa.

(TS) CONCLUSION: Will not be able to neutralize MAG's Island Base until we have a more precise location.

(TS) ACTIONS:

1. (TS) We are moving US Navy Aegis cruisers into the area mentioned above to attempt to locate MAG's freighters when they launch for the main strike in the next few days.

2. (TS) Special Forces are still deploying into position. We expect them to be on station within 36 hours.

(TS) RECOMMENDATION: None. Information only.

TOP SECRET / SPECIAL COMPARTMENTALIZED INFORMATION
CLASSIFIED BY: US Central Intelligence Agency
DECLASSIFY ON: OADR

CHAPTER TWENTY-TWO

Contract Day Twenty-Six
Tuesday, 6 October
1655 Hours Local Time
Island Training Base

I was the last guy to climb down the ladder from the passenger area when we returned to the Island. Brinker had been among the first people off the 747 after the cargo ramp opened and I was sure he was stirring up trouble for me somewhere. I didn't care at that point. All I wanted was a shower and some sleep in a real bed. And maybe a drink or five.

I dropped my life support equipment off and made for my room. I got through the door, stripped off the flightsuit, boots, undershirt, and shorts, and went into my bathroom to grab my shower stuff. There, attached to the mirror, I found a note from Sammy.

"Don't forget the beach party outside. XOXO, S."

"Goddamn it," I said to the empty room. I really did not want to be around people right now. I did want to see Sammy though. I just had no idea what kind of company I'd be. "Shit!" I said resignedly. I donned my robe and made my way out into the hallway.

Alone in the clinic shower room a few moments later, I stood gratefully under the water with my eyes closed for a long time, trying to clear the images of the mission from my head. I could still see the streams of people running up and down the terminal dock when Brinker was rolling in on his bomb pass, and I could feel the explosions which ensued. Then there was the broken F-18 hitting the water. It was like streaming video on an endless loop, repeating over and over. But with each repetition, my imagination added additional details which hadn't been there before. Like body parts flying out of the explosions or the F-18 pilot's young children crying by his grave site.

This had never happened to me before. In the first Gulf War, the feeling I had after a successful strike was almost one of euphoria. I was glad to be alive, sure, but I was also pleased and proud to have accomplished something that mattered. Something good. There was no second-guessing and no visualizing of what I had done. And, I slept soundly at night.

But today was different. We laid 16,000 pounds of bombs on a nearly helpless target and killed God knows how many people.

For what purpose? Money?

I leaned up against the wall of the shower and let the water cascade down upon me. There were a few things I had done in my life that still haunted me, years and years later. I had just added another one to the list.

Later, I dressed, left my room, and walked down the hallway. I made the left turn at the operations desk and headed for the dining hall. The lights were only on at about half-intensity and they made the sheetrock walls look even more institutional than usual.

As I neared the administrative area, I could see that there were lights on inside and I wondered who would be working while the party was going on.

I should have known.

Ruth stuck her head around the corner as I approached. She had obviously been waiting for me.

"Can you come into my office, TC?" she asked. Her tone was flat.

"Sure."

I followed her through the vacant administrative area and into her office.

"Shut the door behind you," she said as we approached the doorway.

I walked in, pulling the door closed behind me, and was unsurprised to see Brinker sitting on the sofa cross from her desk. Poor Brinker. He was sporting a nasty-looking shiner on his left eye and there was a bandage on the back of his head - probably where it hit the cabinet in the 747's galley. I elected to remain standing.

"Brinker tells me you assaulted him after your mission. Is that correct?"

I nodded.

"Would you mind telling me who the fuck you think you are, assaulting one of *my* pilots?"

I stood there with my arms crossed and stared back at her evenly. Her face was impassive and I couldn't tell if she was serious or if this was a show for Brinker's benefit.

"He broke the 'don't fuck with me' rule. He took us to the merge with two US Navy Hornets with no plan other than to shoot first and ask questions later. He shot the lead F-18 in the face pre-merge and anchored us in a two versus one engagement for nearly two minutes inside a carrier strike group's scramble range. Did he tell you I saved his life?"

Ruth looked down at Brinker, then back to me, and shook her head.

"Genius here allowed a Hornet to go one-circle with him and immediately ended up in a flat scissors. Everyone knows you don't get a Viper in the phone booth with a Hornet and survive, let alone win."

Ruth cocked her head a little at that. "Well, actually," she said musingly, "there are ways."

I just looked at her. "Ways to beat a Hornet when you're slow speed, high AOA, and on the limiter?"

"Well, you have to cheat a little," she went on.

Something tugged at the back of my mind just then, but I ignored it and continued my tirade. "Well regardless, Brinker was about two turns from getting himself gunned before I shot down the Hornet he was jousting with."

"Brinker, is that true?"

The blonde Dutchman nodded reluctantly. "But that doesn't change the fact that he assaulted me."

I walked over to him.

"Brinker, do you remember the last time you fucked with me? On the beach?"

He looked up at me and nodded again, his face a mask of hate.

"That was relatively minor compared to this. This time you almost got me fucking killed because you were arrogant and stupid. Consider the bruise on your face and bump on your head a cheap lesson. You're a lucky man."

"And why is that?" he snarled.

"You're lucky I didn't kill you."

I didn't wait for a retort or even a dismissal. I just walked out of there.

The party was in full swing when I hit the sand a few moments later. Calypso music floated in the air and Rug was again playing master of ceremonies, running both the grill and the bar and obviously enjoying himself. Steaks were on the grill this afternoon and I could smell the aroma of barbequing beef.

I found that I wasn't hungry.

I stopped at the bar long enough to get two large plastic glasses full of beer. Rug and the other boys tried to engage me in some conversation, but I begged off and made my way toward the niche in the rocks which led to Ruth's retreat.

I was on the small lagoon's beach a few minutes later and

I padded across the sand to the area under the trees. I set my beer glasses down on one of the tables and plopped onto the futon to relax. The cushion slid off the side of the low wooden frame as my body made contact, so I rose and lifted the cushion to realign it. As I was tucking it back into the frame, I saw the dark shadow of a long metal box of some kind, just below the surface of the sand beneath the frame. I made a mental note to investigate it later, when I actually cared what it might be.

I sat down on the futon and sipped my beer, feeling the warm tropical breeze blow over my skin. I stared across the sand at the waves and out to the horizon, trying to lose the images that kept haunting my brain by focusing on the rising and falling surf and the warmth the cold beer brought to my brain.

I don't know how long I sat there, staring at the ocean, before I saw Sammy come through the rocks. Her strawberry-blonde hair sparkled in the sun as she jogged up the beach in tight red shorts and a matching tank top. From the movement and the highly defined contours visible through the fabric, I guessed there was nothing under either garment. I felt my spirits lift a little.

She threw herself into my arms and kissed me urgently for an incredibly long time. Then she placed her head on my shoulder and held me to her as tightly as she could manage.

"I heard about the thing with Brinker," she said between breaths. "I'm just so glad you're ok."

We held each other for a while and listened to the sound of the gently-lapping waves. It should have been relaxing and peaceful, but I couldn't get rid of the shit that was careening about inside my head.

"How do these guys deal with this?" I asked, looking off in the distance and trying to rein in my thoughts.

"First of all," she began, "you need to know that everyone goes through this after their first few missions. It's a normal reaction."

"I thought I'd be able to deal with it better," I said. "God knows I've dropped enough bombs and killed enough people in my life. But this is different. It's a lot different."

I felt her nod against me. "Well to answer your question, VB, Pete, and Rug tend to drink a lot afterwards. Brinker tries to fuck as many different women as he can in a single night; and Ruth...I don't know what she does, besides fill out paperwork."

"Everyone has their own coping mechanisms, I guess."

"Yes. And slowly, over time, they get more used to it."

I shook my head. "I don't want to get used to it."

She squeezed me gently. "I know that about you. It's one of the reasons I...it's one of the reasons I'm here."

When we made it back to the main beach, the party had largely subsided. Rug was still behind the bar, serving drinks. Citronella candles had been lit to ward off the mosquitoes, and the light which they cast on their surroundings provided an intimate glow to the area.

Sammy escorted me to a stool and I sat. She patted me tenderly on the shoulder and sat next to me.

"How is he?" Rug asked her.

"Fucked up," she said softly.

Rug nodded. "The sad fact is it gets easier," he said to no one in particular. "I don't know what that says about us or who we are, but it's true."

I closed my eyes. "Great," I whispered.

"Here's what you need," Rug said, shoving a tumbler full of caramel-colored liquid under my nose. "Something to take your mind off things."

I couldn't help myself. It was scotch, and normally I would have stopped and sniffed it and made a ceremony of it, but instead, I swallowed half the tumbler in one gulp, almost without tasting it.

"Easy there, cowboy," Rug kidded. "That's Macallan 18

you're knocking back."

I looked around the bar. Sure enough, it was just Pete, VB, Rug, Sammy, and me.

VB looked over at me. I could tell by the sway of his head and the gleam in his eye that he'd had more than a little to drink.

"What happened with the F-18s?" he asked.

I cradled the glass of scotch in my hands on the bar and looked into its golden depths. "Brinker took us to the merge without a plan," I said softly, "and I had to clean up the mess."

I repeated the story to best of my recollection. When I finished speaking there was silence for a few moments.

Then Pete spoke. "We heard about what you did to Brinker after the mission. Would you have really killed him?" he asked, with just a little hesitation in his voice.

"You don't want to know the answer to that," I said. I raised the glass to my lips and drained the last drops from it. "I need to hit the rack, guys. I'll see you tomorrow."

I rose from my stool and headed for the door back into the mountain. Sammy appeared at my side a few seconds later.

"Sammy," I whispered to her, "you can't do this. I don't care if she kicks my ass, but I don't want to see yours get kicked in the process."

"I'm still the unit flight doctor," she said defiantly. "And if I think the mental health of one of our pilots might be affected by our operations, I'm going to look into it." She smiled at me. "Now shut the fuck up."

We walked back to my room and entered it together. There, on my bed, I found my second note of the day.

"Steam room at 2000 hours?" It was written in Ruth's distinctive scrawl.

"That's actually funny," I said as I crumpled the note and tossed it into the waste can. "She just told me not to go in there."

"She's not going to like this," Sammy said quietly.

I looked at her and smiled tiredly. “She’ll have to get over it. I fucked her once because I had to. I’m not going to do it again.”

Sammy eyed me with a half-smile on her face. “Have I actually heard a fighter pilot turn down a hot piece of ass?” she asked.

“You have,” I said. “Mark it on the calendar.” I began to disrobe. “I’d apologize for taking my clothes off in front of you, but after the last few days, I’m not sure what the point in that would be. I will apologize for not being terribly social. Between all the drugs and the excitement of last forty-eight to seventy-two hours, I’m too exhausted. “

I pulled the covers back, got into bed and shut my eyes for a few blessed seconds. A few seconds later, I felt Sammy sit down on the bed next to me. When I opened my eyes, I saw her looking at me with a look somewhere between clinical concern and personal affection on her face. I opened my mouth to speak again, but she her fingers on my lips.

“No offense taken. You do need to get some more rest,” she said. “Your body is still recovering. There will be other times.”

I wanted to tell her there actually wouldn’t be other times. I wanted to tell her that the end was coming and there would be no guarantees for anything, let alone more time for the two of us. But instead, I pulled her down to me and wrapped my arms around her.

And then I slept.

CHAPTER TWENTY-THREE

Contract Day Twenty-Seven
Wednesday, 7 October
0800 Hours Local Time
Island Training Base

I don't know how long I would have slept if there hadn't been a knock on my door. I opened my eyes and lay in my bed, staring at the ceiling. *I guess my damn internal clock took the day off.*

The knock sounded again, more insistent this time.

"Coming," I said in a groggy voice. I threw my legs over the side of the bed reluctantly, gradually rose to my feet, donned my robe, and stumbled to the door.

I opened the door to find Ruth standing there, eyeing me curiously. "When I didn't see you at breakfast," she said, "I decided to check on you. Tough night?"

I shook my head. "Not really. Guess I was just tired. I don't sleep well on airplanes."

"Sammy told me that you were having some trouble dealing with the last project. Do you want to talk about it?"

"I'm not sure there's much to talk about. I guess I just need to get used to it."

"Well if it matters, the rest of them haven't been as 'crowded' as that one was. Usually they're out in the middle of nowhere with minimal personnel, or they're pseudo-military targets with battle-hardened troops guarding them. We're usually very meticulous about avoiding collateral damage or casualties."

I nodded. "That's good to know."

"Can I come in?" she asked.

"Sure." I stepped out of the way and let her enter.

"Would you mind closing the door?"

I eased it shut and then leaned against it. "What's on your mind?" I asked.

She crossed her arms and looked at me. "How much time did you and Sammy spend together yesterday?"

I raised my hands, palms out towards her in a placating gesture as I ran through things I could tell her. I settled on a version of the truth, hoping it meshed with whatever Sammy had told her. "Nothing happened between us, Ruth. She said it was her job as the unit flight doctor to talk to me about the psychological blowback from the strike. We talked for a little while on the beach and then for a while back here. There wasn't any sex or anything like that."

Ruth sniffed the air a few times. "Well, you're not lying about the sex. If there'd been any fucking in this room I'd be able to smell it."

"Satisfied?"

She nodded slowly, still looking at me. "You know she's totally nuts about you. It's sort of sickening."

I didn't know how to reply to that so I kept my mouth shut and tried to keep my face impassive.

"When she was talking about debriefing you on the strike, she kept getting this shit-eating grin on her face." Ruth paused and looked at me intently. "So, have you fucked her yet?"

I let the question hang in the air for a moment or two. "No," I said at last. "If it matters, I haven't fucked her at all."

"There was a time when she and I would go through men like blackjack dealers through a deck of cards. She'd fuck them for a while and pass them to me or vice versa. Sometimes, we'd share them together. I enjoyed those times."

A mental image of a Sammy, Ruth, and me in a threesome went through my head and I frowned reflexively.

"Does that bother you?"

I looked at her. "Ruth, I'm the last person in the world to preach morality where this kind of stuff is concerned. If what you were doing made the two of you happy, then more power to you."

"Well, she doesn't do that kind of thing anymore. In fact, she barely has sex with Rug these days."

My mouth dropped open. "What? Do you have some sort of spreadsheet where you're tracking this stuff?"

"Keeping things 'balanced' around here is a big deal," she replied. "I've gone to some great lengths to ensure that there are 'outlets' for people to utilize so they can stay focused. When something happens that affects that balance, I get concerned. Very concerned."

"Because it affects the mission."

She nodded. "Exactly. Now today, at 1100 hours, we're going to be starting the planning process for the biggest project we've ever done. After that, we're going to fly it. And I need everybody to have their eyes on the ball. Sammy needs to fuck Rug tonight, more for him than for her. And I'm planning to send either Sheila or Sheena from the naming ceremony, or maybe even both of them, to see you. You need to let all of this happen and go with it."

I looked at her evenly. "Ruth, what happens behind closed doors with Sammy and Rug is their business, not mine. But I don't need any sort of release to keep my head in the game. If you send either or both of those girls my way, I'm going to send them right back. A good meal and a good night's sleep are all I need."

"Fair enough," she said, nodding. She headed toward the door of my room. I backed away to allow her to open it. "Main briefing room at 1100. See you there."

I shut the door behind her, shaking my head in wonderment.

I risked a shower in the normal place, grabbed some lunch, and made it to the main briefing room in plenty of time for the 1100 briefing. I found a seat in the first row of stadium chairs and plopped into it. Brinker wandered in next, still bandaged and whimpering. He sat without looking at me. The rest of the pilots filed in a few moments later, followed by the appropriate maintenance and support personnel. Shortly thereafter, Ron Phillips and Ruth walked in. I was surprised to see Phillips and wondered if he had just arrived. Every blonde hair was in place and his Armani suit hung elegantly on his fit frame. He looked at me and nodded in recognition as he took the floor. I nodded back.

"Good afternoon ladies and gentlemen and welcome to the preliminary mission briefing for project number 09-05," Phillips began. "You'll notice there are no slides of the target area or the geographic area behind me. The location is sensitive, so we're going to keep it restricted to those who are required to know it."

People were whispering to one another and there was a low undertone of conversation. Apparently, this was a new twist on the usual process.

Phillips ignored them. "Before I get into more of the details of this mission, I wanted to thank everyone for the work you put into this last, late-notice project. We met the client's objectives perfectly and he provided a bonus for us, which will be passed on to all of you."

A murmur of contentment passed through the room and transitioned into a spontaneous round of applause.

Phillips smiled and raised his hands. "You're the ones who made it happen," he said. Then, as the applause died, he continued. "Now on to our new project, since we're on the subject of bonuses. As you know, this project has been delayed for some time due to," he paused to choose his words, "regrettable circumstances."

That's putting it fucking mildly, Ron, I thought.

"Also, as you know, the client for this project changed his mind several times about his desired objective. As we prepared for the final planning about six weeks ago, we were informed the client wanted us to provide a tactical nuclear strike."

The room was instantly quiet.

Interesting, I thought. *No one else knew about this. How had Burt found out?* But the answers were clicking into place. Ruth told him. She had tried to recruit him to help plan it and had even enlisted Phillips to assist. But Burt, being Burt, had a line he wouldn't cross. He had resisted and had been killed for it. The scene that Brianna had described in Ruth's office now made sense.

"We've been provided one DMPI which we are to hit with at least one 300 kiloton B-61 Mod 7 weapon," Phillips continued. "Our contractual obligation requires us to get at least one weapon on target with full order detonation in the ground burst mode." He paused for effect. "Because of the extreme nature of this project, each of you will be paid a bonus of one million dollars upon successful conclusion of the strike."

Cheers erupted throughout the room, along with handshakes and slaps on the back.

All I could do was sit there in stunned silence.

##

We met in the mission planning room afterward to begin the process. Rug, Pete, VB, Brinker, and I stood around the large, rectangular planning table in the center of the room as Ruth and Phillips walked in. Phillips carried a large cardboard, cylindrical tube. He stopped at the edge of the table and looked at me reflectively.

"You didn't seem too excited about the extra bonus, Mr.

Pearce."

I regarded him coolly. "Maybe I'm overestimating, but I value my ass a little more than one million bucks," I said.

"Are you saying the bonus payment isn't sufficient? The terms of your contract..."

I interrupted him. "This isn't about money. I'm worried about getting my ass blown off. Nuke deliveries are tricky and I need to see the target and devise some tactics so I can be sure we can survive this drop and live to spend the money you're promising."

Phillips barely nodded but looked at me appraisingly. "Fair enough," he said. He opened the tube and emptied a series of maps onto the table. "We'll be using these maps."

I rifled through them and found the usual 1:500,000 scale maps for the route, as well as the target area 1:50,000 scale ones. But these maps had been sanitized. There were towns and cities on the map but no names accompanying them. No rivers, mountains or natural landmarks were labeled; and most importantly, there were no latitude and longitude lines. Everything was in military grid reference system coordinates. We had enough data to plan the mission, assuming someone loaded the latitude and longitude of the grid zone designator, but we had no idea of the location involved.

I looked at Phillips quizzically. "So is this a special capability of the Cray in next room?"

"No," he said. "These maps were created for this project. We made the decision to keep the target location a secret to avoid...issues."

I felt my guts tighten. "Well, this is a new twist," I said. "Can you tell us where and what the target is on the map and where we can find the launch point?"

Ruth stepped forward. She unrolled one of the 1:500,000 maps and grabbed a plotter and pen from one of the organizers that held these implements in the center of the table. She looked intently at the lower right corner of the 1:500,000 map and traced a few roads until she found the spot she was looking for. Then, she laid the plastic plotter on that spot, and using the plotter's template as a guide, she drew a perfect circle around the spot.

"This is the launch point. It's an 8,500-foot runway oriented north south, 17-35." Then she located a large freeway-looking road on the left side of the map and found an intersection on it with a smaller road, which occurred in a mountain pass. She followed the smaller road with her fingers to the west as it went up into the mountains and found a small city there. She put the plotter over the city and used the triangle-shaped cut-out to draw the target symbol. "This is the target. It's a conference center in this small town located in this mountain valley. The town is a ski resort and is barely occupied this time of year so the loss of life should be minimal. Also, the mountains around the target should reduce the collateral damage from a ground burst nuclear detonation."

"If you don't count the radiation contamination which will make the area uninhabitable for a hundred years or so," I commented dryly.

Ruth eyed me and pulled one of the 1:50,000 maps in front of her. She located the target area and drew the requisite triangle on it. I walked around the table to stand next to her and look at the terrain from her perspective. And then the déjà vu hit me. I *knew* this place. I had been here. I just couldn't remember exactly where it was.

"Okay, this is making me feel a little better," I said, fighting to steady my voice as I leaned forward to survey the target area. I traced an imaginary path from the high desert area to the north of the target to the target itself. "We can attack from the north and loft the weapons at max range. The mountains are higher south of the target than north of it, so the terrain won't block the trajectory of the bombs. But those northern mountains will partially protect us from the blast as we egress."

Ruth looked at me and nodded. "That's good," she said. "Since you and I will be the ones in the two jets doing the lofting."

I looked back at her. "We should look at a shooter-cover thing. Two jets expending, two jets flying cover to make sure the shooters get to where they're going."

She nodded again. "Sounds good. Keep going."

"That means that the attack formation we need to employ is similar to the last project. One and Three, the aircraft expending, will attack line abreast, with about two to three miles separation; and the cover ships, the wingmen, will fly a wedge formation on them throughout."

"Makes sense to me," she said. "We won't have any threat reactions to worry about on this project, so we'll fly that same formation throughout the ingress and egress. "I want those wingmen close to keep," she looked right at me, "eyes on us." She looked around the table. "Gentlemen, do you have any input?"

Silence and shrugging.

"Very well," Ruth said. "I'll fly as number one and TC will fly as number three." Rug started to say something and Ruth cut him off. "I know he's not a flight leader, Rug. But for this mission, putting him in that position gives us more...options."

Rug nodded his acknowledgement.

"VB will be number two and Brinker will be number four." She looked at me. "See if you can restrain yourself from beating him up this time."

I started to say something in protest but quickly thought better of it. "I'll do my best," I said.

"Rug, you and Pete will be air spares. You'll launch with us and perform CAP duty over the launch zone until we've released weapons. That way if there are issues...you'll be available to assist." Ruth looked around the table again. "Questions, gentlemen?"

No one spoke.

"You guys will draw the maps, build the folders, and start the line-up cards, but I'll load the Data Transfer Cartridges and fill in the nav coordinates on the cards."

That meant that she'd be the only one who had any clue where this place was. She held the key. She leaned back and looked at Rug.

"Okay," Rug said. "Tasks. TC and I will work the target area map. Brinker, I want you and VB to draw the route maps. And Pete, you can work on the line-up cards and mission packets." He looked over at me. "Do you want to run the loft numbers on the computer?"

"You bet your ass I do."

"Cool. Okay guys, let's do it."

"Ron and I will be in my office if you need anything," Ruth said. "I'll have lunch and dinner sent in. The transports are still here and we'll need to launch a little later for this strike, so we'll brief tomorrow at 1000. That should give all of you plenty of time to get some rest."

She and Phillips walked out and I watched them go. As they reached the door to the room, Phillips paused to let Ruth go first and casually placed his hand on her waist to guide her through. A little bell went off in my head just then.

"Well, I guess before you run the loft numbers, you'll need to pick an IP," Rug said.

I nodded. "Absolutely," I replied as I turned back to the map, "absolutely."

I found where Ruth had drawn the target. "Here," I said. "The way this road valley runs east-west through the target, then goes out to the north, combined with this smaller mountain range to the east, allows us to run in from the east, northeast." I found a prominent dry riverbed on the map about twenty miles east of the target. I ran my finger down it until I saw a large road bridge. "And here we go. We'll use this road bridge. It should stand out, even at five hundred feet."

Rug looked at it and nodded. "I like it," he said.

"Hey, Brinker," I called to the Dutchman. "Can you see this?"

Brinker craned his neck over the table to see where I was pointing on the target area map. I pulled a 1:500,000 map next to it and tried to find the IP on the larger map. It stood out clearly there, too. I pointed at the IP.

"Rug and I were thinking of using this as the IP. What do you think?"

Brinker's professional mode was in place again. He walked to my side of the table and looked at both maps. After a few minutes, he nodded. "Looks good. I can run the route from the launch point, north of these mountains, then west to the IP. It will keep us well hidden from this much larger city to the south."

"Sounds good to me," I said. "Rug?"

"Yep," he said, "let's make it so."

Rug and I returned to the target map and extracted the data I needed to run the numbers for the maximum-range loft delivery, the way nukes are typically delivered by fighter aircraft. The run-in is made at low altitude and high speed, following the CCRP steering line to a target location which is loaded into the Viper's navigation system. At the pull-up range, a cue appears in the heads-up display, and the pilot pushes the pickle button down, applies back pressure, and lifts the nose of the aircraft up under g, keeping the flight path marker centered on the steering line. At the appropriate place in space, the fire control computer releases the bomb, and it flies an arced trajectory to the target. Most nuclear weapons have a parachute built into them, which deploys as the weapon passes the apogee of its trajectory and begins its downward journey. The parachute slows the descent of the weapon to allow the delivering aircraft more time to escape the blast. Typically, the weapon leaves the jet between four and five miles from the target. Then, the delivering aircraft has to make a 180 degree turn at max g and full AB to get as far from the target as possible. I practiced this delivery a few times during my initial training and again at Fighter Weapons School. But, that was a long time ago. I couldn't believe I was planning it for real. The conversation I had with Smith in the Applebee's in Wilmington floated through my head.

God, was that really just a few weeks ago?

The numbers came out of the computer quickly and I returned to the target area map a few minutes later to begin drawing the attack. As I got the plotter and pencil onto the map, I noticed a peculiar pattern of lines imprinted on the map, lines that ran the entire length of the mountain valley where the target was, extending northwest and southeast of the target through the mountains. I consulted the map's legend to see what the lines corresponded to. Nothing was there. As I looked at the lines and stroked my chin, the déjà vu feeling hit me again - stronger this time.

"Damn," I said.

After the mission planning tasks were completed and we were dismissed, I hit the gym. I needed to work off the angst building inside of me. I warmed up quickly with the tire, and then hit the bench and pull-up bar, alternating bench presses and pull-ups, ten sets, until I couldn't do any more of either. After that I did dead lifts and dumbbell shoulder presses using the same methodology, and finished with triceps pushdowns and bicep curls. I worked myself until my muscles were screaming at me. When I was finished, against Ruth's wishes, I headed for the steam room to let them relax.

It was late and no one was roaming the halls. I entered the vestibule for the steam room and saw, to my surprise, there were two towels and robes already hanging there. That was disappointing. I didn't want to deal with people tonight.

Oh, well. Sounded like a good idea.

I turned to leave but then I heard Ruth's voice - in the throes of orgasm.

I'll be damned.

I stepped lightly over to the door and put my ear on the crack between the door and the frame.

"God, I've missed you," I heard her say. "No one can do that to me, no one."

"That's good to hear, my love," Phillips said. "We've been apart too long."

I heard her kiss him. "That's true and you know how I am. I can't do without for long."

"By now, I would have expected you to have hooked up with Mr. Pearce, just for recreation." Phillips was trying to sound nonchalant, but it wasn't convincing.

"He does nothing for me. I fed him to Brianna and I tried giving him to some of the girls in maintenance, but he wasn't interested."

"It's of no consequence," Phillips intoned. "Soon this will be over, and you and I will be together forever, wealthy beyond our wildest dreams. But what's more important, the deaths of your parents will be avenged. What could be more perfect?"

"You're right, of course," she said, but there was just a hint of something else in her voice.

Phillips didn't pick up on it as he continued his narrative. "In about thirty hours, the peace negotiations will be abruptly and violently ended by our strike, and the blame placed squarely on Iran and Hezbollah," he continued. "Your countrymen will retaliate with a nuclear strike on Iran and an invasion of both Lebanon and the West Bank. When the dust settles, no one will trifle with your country again, and after the investors are paid off, the three of us will be about a billion dollars richer. Our years of work will finally come to fruition."

Three of us?

If my jaw hadn't been connected with bones and skin, it would have been on my chest.

"Now that the investors are satisfied that a US Air Force weapons school graduate planned the strike, when do we have to get rid of him?" Ruth asked.

"You sound like you'll regret dispensing with our American friend," Phillips said with a slight edge to his voice.

"He's been an excellent resource, nothing more," she said, quickly.

"We can't have any loose ends after the strike, my love. That was a condition of the contract. If it's any consolation, he won't die any sooner than any of the others. We'll have some independent mechanics deal with the island, and the transports will have an encounter with the American Air Force on their way out of the country. Meanwhile, you will be safe with me on one of the G-550s, sipping champagne on the way to our villa in the Caymans."

American Air Force?

Suddenly all the map images came into focus. We were bombing the southern California resort town of Wrightwood. Just off the Cajon Pass between San Bernardino and Hesperia, California. But that wasn't the worst part. This was about a lot more than stopping peace talks. This was about killing as many people as possible in the process. Wrightwood lay directly over the San Andreas Fault, represented by the hashed lines on the map. A ground burst nuclear weapon there could initiate an earthquake that would be catastrophic for all southern California. The number of potential casualties could easily be into the millions. My throat went completely dry.

Oh my God.

"What are you doing here?" Sammy's surprised voice rang out as she entered the vestibule. Then she added: "I've been looking for you everywhere!"

The voices in the steam room went silent.

Shit!

I shot across the room, grabbed her and whisked her out of there. I looked up and down the hallway for a moment and suddenly had a crazy idea. I hurriedly led her to my room and shut the door behind us. I eyed the deadbolt briefly and elected to leave it unlocked.

"Strip," I told her as I hurriedly removed my clothes.

She wanted to question me but the look on my face changed her mind. She was out of her clothes in a flash.

"It's time for your Academy award," I said. "This is about life and death. I know this isn't how you probably imagined it, but we need to pretend we've been fucking each other's brains out for the like the last half hour or so."

Her eyes were wide.

I pulled the covers down the bed and lay on my back, motioning for her to straddle me. She complied as I heard the faint sounds of footsteps in the hall.

"You need to be convincing but careful," I whispered. "If they look too closely they'll see we're not...connected...and that will make them more suspicious than if we weren't doing anything at all."

She nodded and lowered herself to me, wrapping the covers around her waist. The footsteps came closer.

"Action!" I whispered.

She began moving earnestly back and forth on top of me with her eyes closed and her back arched. The ensuing moaning could have rivaled Meg Ryan's simulated orgasm in *When Harry Met Sally*.

Behind her, I could see the door opening slightly. I squinted and leaned back into the pillows, trying to watch the door without making it obvious. The hallway was dark and the room was dim, but it was easy to discern the shapes of two heads looking around the door, one after the other. I pushed my body up against Sammy's, trying to 'sell' the act even more. In an odd moment of detachment, I suddenly realized why Hollywood actors claimed that real sex was the last thing on their minds when they filmed scenes like this. Sammy, in all her naked glory, was resting upon me, and the two parts of our bodies where the action took place were rubbing against each other, but all that mattered was how it looked to the observers on the other side of the door.

Finally, a few moments later, the door shut quietly and I listened for the footsteps to go down the hall. They were gone. I exhaled in relief and put my hands on Sammy's hips to signal her that she could stop her movement. She did so, but slowly and almost reluctantly.

"So," she whispered back, "you want to tell me what that was all about?"

"Ruth and Phillips were in the steam room together. I overheard something I wasn't supposed to. Then you came in and there's a chance they heard your voice. I didn't want them to know that either of us was there. I'm not sure if we fooled them, but we sure put some doubt in their minds."

"So do you think they got a good show?" she asked, smirking.

I nodded. "I do. Just like watching fake porn on Cinemax." Then I exhaled loudly and shook my head. "We're both going to be on Ruth's shit list. I think the only reason she's not giving us grief already is because her boy, Ron, is in town. They were doing each other in the steam room right before you came in."

"Not a surprise. She's been using him in all sorts of ways for a long time. They're quite the team."

"Well they're into some pretty diabolical shit here," I said. "The strike is in Southern California and the target is directly on the San Andreas Fault. I'm not a seismologist, but I bet several kilotons detonating on the surface there could initiate a big-ass earthquake."

Sammy gasped. "Oh, my God!" she exclaimed softly. "Millions of people could be killed!"

I nodded. "That is part of the plan, evidently. They've been building up to this for a long time and they're expecting to make a boatload of money. And," I looked at her, "they're planning on eliminating *everyone* when it's over."

Sammy opened her mouth in mute protest.

"One thing I've learned is that you can never predict the reactions of people when money is involved. Especially if there's a lot of money involved. Sammy, you're going to be a loose end. Like all of us. They're planning on having the American Air Force shoot down the 747s, and they have a mercenary team standing by to deal with the Island after the transports leave. They've got the whole thing planned out."

She sat there atop me in stunned silence, the false sensuality of a few moments ago all but forgotten.

"What are we going to do?" she asked at last.

"Someone has to stop them," I said grimly.

Several minutes passed while neither of us moved. But there's something about a close brush with death or impending doom that releases inhibitions. After she had digested my words, Samantha looked down at me for a few moments, while I looked up at her. We became aware of each other almost at the same time. I could feel myself stiffening as I looked up at her firm, round breasts rising and falling as she breathed. Her mouth parted as she regarded me, and a warm wetness began to emanate from her loins. Suddenly, all the sensual electricity that had been hovering in the air for weeks arced between our bodies, and I was engorged and throbbing against her sex. She smiled at me and leaned forward slightly, placing her hands on my chest and positioning herself better. Then, as she looked into my eyes, she slid down and enveloped me.

The act of physical copulation is fascinating in its subtlety. While the mechanics of it are basically the same, the results can be radically different, all depending on the partner. Until I had met Sarah Morton, years ago, sex had been about cold satisfaction and the fulfillment of physical need, nothing more. But as Sarah and I explored each other, we crossed an invisible line and suddenly it became about something far beyond physical. It could have even gone further, but as the path was revealed to us, it seemed that we both became wary and stopped the journey. And while I couldn't speak for Sarah, in the years since our time together, even when the sex was fun, there was something missing.

Until tonight.

My night with Brianna had been light and fun. The tryst on the beach with Ruth was lust-driven and coldly satisfying. But both of those interludes faded into the background as I lost myself in Samantha, she lost herself in me, and any boundaries between us vanished.

I don't know how long we spent joined together, but time seemed to lose meaning. The experience was intensely serene: no frantic thrusting, no limbs flailing, and no frenzied changes in positions. Instead, our bodies moved through the night as one, smoothly and gracefully, interspersed with moments during which we simply kissed or looked at one another while we remained coupled. We reached the pre-orgasm plateau and stayed there for a long while, feeling the powerful delight of the physical sensations and reveling in the total closeness we had created.

Then we jumped off the plateau together. The movements changed from smooth to deliberate and then from deliberate to forceful.

"Oh, my sweet, sweet Colin," were the words she whispered when her time came. And then her femininity clenched around me powerfully, again and again.

I was already there, pouring myself into her. My mouth was open but I couldn't utter a sound.

I became aware of a constriction around my arm sometime later. I don't know how I felt it. I should have been sound asleep. Maybe I was in one of the lighter phases of the sleep cycle, where the slightest stimulus would bring me back to consciousness.

I opened my eyes to find Sammy fully clothed and sitting next to me on the bed, lightly tapping the inside of my left arm below the tourniquet she had tied around my bicep.

She wasn't looking at my face; she was minding her work,

watching the inside of my elbow, waiting for a vein to appear. The usual latex medical gloves were on her hands and she had a large hypodermic syringe with a red liquid inside it.

The pieces came together in my mind like footage of an exploding object shown in reverse. Who could create a knife wound that didn't do any real damage? Who could poison someone so that they were nearly at the point of death but not quite?

The answer was obvious. A doctor. The only doctor on the island.

I felt the cool wetness of the alcohol swab as she sterilized the inside of my elbow. She had found a vein.

I guess there are those who might have been stunned by seeing the person they had just had sex with in the act of trying to kill them. They might have become contemplative or empathetic as they watched the act progress. They might have even tried to reason with their killer. But these are the same people who don't believe in capital punishment and who believe that people are all 'inherently good' or other such nonsense.

I wasn't one of those people. It took my brain a nanosecond to process what I saw, because I realized that I expected it. Even though I had wanted to *believe*, I had always expected it.

"What was the plan this time?" I asked, without mentally willing myself to do so. I found it was hard to speak with my jaw clenched in anger. "Take me to the edge of death again or kick me over the side?"

She jumped when I spoke, but recovered her composure quickly and moved the needle into position.

There wasn't time to be gentle or tactful, or to ask why. So I slapped her as hard as I could on her left ear, cupping my hand as I hit her. The blow totally stunned her and allowed me to get both of my hands onto her. I quickly spun her around and pulled her on top of me, face up, and peeled the syringe from her gloved fingers. Then as she recovered and began to struggle, I shoved the needle into her neck and thumbed the plunger home.

"No!" she pleaded. "No, you don't understand. You don't under..."

"You broke the rule, Sammy," I said icily. "You broke the fucking rule."

The drugs were astoundingly potent. Her struggling became ineffectual, then weak, then it ceased completely, all in less than a minute. Within moments, her body relaxed and her breathing became deep and even.

TOP SECRET / SPECIAL
COMPARTMENTALIZED INFORMATION
CLASSIFIED BY: US Central Intelligence Agency
DECLASSIFY ON: OADR

From: Special Projects Group [NCS]
Sent: Wednesday, 7 October 2009, 1200 EDT (1 October 2009, 1600Z)
To: Director, NCS
Cc: Special Projects Group [NCS]; damrine@cmail.cia.gov; dsmith3@cmail.cia.gov

SUBJECT: Update, Case File: 08-434A (MAG)

(TS) Narrative:

1. (TS) No further contact from Contractor 09-017 (Pearce, Colin M.).

2. (TS) Surface surveillance platforms are in place to monitor MAG transport launch. JRO has tasked satellites to monitor southern Pacific Ocean.

3. (TS) All-source chatter about the strike has gone quiet, as chatter typically does immediately preceding a major even.

(TS) CONCLUSIONS: To meet their predicted schedule, MAG will have to launch aircraft in the next 24 hours.

(TS) ACTIONS: We will be ready to initiate tracking and destination prediction for the major strike. We will keep you updated.

(TS) RECOMMENDATION: None. Information only.

TOP SECRET / SPECIAL
COMPARTMENTALIZED INFORMATION
CLASSIFIED BY: US Central Intelligence Agency
DECLASSIFY ON: OADR

CHAPTER TWENTY-FOUR

Contract Day Twenty-Eight
Thursday, 8 October
1000 Hours Local Time
Island Training Base

I sat in the main briefing room in my own little daze, nursing a cup of coffee, while the troops filed in for the pre-strike briefing. Dealing with Sammy's unconscious body hadn't been easy, especially since the complex was starting to awaken when she had made her attempt on me. But I managed to get her back to the clinic unseen and put her into one of the patient beds there. Then, I draped her thoroughly with blankets, pulled the isolation curtain around her, ensured all the lights in the place were off, and locked every door I could with the keys I found in her pocket. She was still breathing evenly when I left her, and I hoped my efforts would be enough for the next few hours.

On my way back to my room, I had a brief attack of guilt. Maybe I had rushed to judgment and reacted too harshly. Then, as I was cleaning up, I found the other syringe on the floor next to my bed: the one that was undoubtedly meant to finish the job the first hypodermic had started. I had my view of the world reinforced yet again, and the rage inside of me was bristling.

Ruth and Phillips walked into the room and Ruth took her place at the podium. As she looked at those assembled, her eye caught mine and she nodded at me. I noticed no trace of surprise or discomfort. She had expected me to be here. I nodded back.

What the fuck were you up to, Sammy?

"Three, two, one, hack." Ruth's began. "Welcome to the mass mission briefing for Project 08-05. Due to the highly-sensitive nature of the geographic location for this project, we'll be doing the briefing in a non-standard format," she said. "I'll give a sanitized version of the transport, set-up, and recovery portion of the briefing. Natasha will brief the jet off-load and re-load normally, then the transport and fighter pilots will go to the separate smaller briefing rooms, Mr. Phillips will brief the transport pilots, and I'll brief the fighter pilots. Any questions so far?"

The assembled personnel were silent.

"Transport take-off will be in three hours, at 1300 Island Time. We're risking a daylight transport launch for this project because the strike window is very narrow. Transport arrival at the launch point will occur at 0100 Island time. Mission launch will occur at 0135 Island Time. Threat conditions in this target area are non-existent. We expect the mission to last between .8 and 1.3 hours. Recovery will occur between 0225 and 0305 Island time. Loading will follow immediately and we'll expect to have the last transport wheels up no later than 0320 Island Time. For today's project, jets five and six will launch and act as airborne spare aircraft for the mission. They will not land until jets one and three have released ordnance with successful detonation. Once jets five and six land, they will be loaded, and transport three will launch. Upon recovery of jets one through four, transports one and two will depart. All transports will make fuel stops on their way back and we expect to have the all transports back on station by 1530 Island time tomorrow afternoon. Questions on the timeline?"

There were none.

"The details of the launch airfield will be covered in the separate transport and fighter briefings. I'll now turn the floor over to Natasha Rasletin to brief the off-load and on-load."

Natasha stepped onto the floor and gave the same briefing that she had rendered the last time we did this, but I paid rapt attention anyway. I was still amazed at the precision with which all this occurred.

When Natasha finished, Ruth dismissed the maintenance personnel and the transport pilots filed into one of the smaller briefing rooms while Ruth, Brinker, Pete, Rug, VB, and I went into the other. We sat at a rectangular table as Ruth began to go over the mission details.

"I've been doing some thinking about the lineup," she said, "and I've decided to make some changes. I'll still lead with VB as number two.

But now Brinker will fly as number three with Pete as number four. Rug and TC will be the airborne spares, five and six respectively. Any questions or problems with that?"

We all shook our heads. Brinker flashed me a triumphant sneer and I shrugged. I honestly didn't care where I was in the formation, but if it was up to me to keep Ruth and Brinker from dropping the nukes, it'd be damn difficult to catch them if I was orbiting the field.

Ruth transitioned to a discussion of the route, air-to-air game plan, and the attack. As she described the route, I made the mental correlations to where all of this was taking place. I was positive the launch airfield was Jacqueline Cochran Regional Airport, in the same valley as Palm Springs, California, and just north of the Salton Sea, a landmark which had been conveniently left off the maps. Our route would take us north, past Twenty-Nine Palms, then west through the Lucerne Valley. The initial point for the attack run was a road bridge coming out of the town of Hesperia, south of Victorville and Apple Valley, in the High Desert of Southern

California. The run-in would take the attacking four-ship across Interstate 15 and toward the ski resort of Wrightwood, a pretty little mountain town where I had spent several enjoyable nights with an enthusiastic blonde enlisted woman back in the mid-1980s. Of course, that was before the USAF started sending people to prison for having consensual sex.

A thousand years ago.

Ruth finished her briefing and dismissed us. I was mildly surprised I wasn't detained for a lecture about the time Sammy and I had spent together, but then Ruth couldn't lecture without revealing how she knew about it. And that would be awkward.

As we disbursed, I recalled the e-mail I had sent to Smith and Amrine after my errand this morning. It contained everything I could remember about the strike. I hoped it would be enough for them to do what had to be done.

"It looks like it'll be you and me together on the transport, TC," Rug said, bringing me back into the here and now as we walked from the briefing room. "Feel like a little Texas hold 'em?"

I eyed him. "Maybe. What are the stakes?"

"Fifty-dollar buy-in and once you're in, you stay in for the whole flight out and back."

"Is this a supplemental income source for you, Rug?"

The heads of the other pilots, even Brinker, turned toward us and nodded.

"He's a shark!" VB said. "He lures you in and then he takes your money. Every time!"

"He's taken money from all of us," Pete chimed in. "Even you, Brinker?" I asked.

The Dutchman nodded in an uncharacteristically humble fashion. "Yes," he said. "Coming back two projects ago. He cleaned me out."

"So I guess it's my turn, eh? Okay Rug. What the hell. It'll pass the time."

Rug smiled at me brightly.

And I looked back at him and hoped I wouldn't have to kill him.

I spent the next hour or so in the hangar watching the maintenance troops and freighter personnel finish loading the F-16s. In each 747, the Vipers flying the cover role had already been loaded. The tug vehicles were now backing the remaining Vipers into the 747s - the ones with the real payload. The sleek, black, B61 nuclear bombs looked ominous mounted on the centerline stations of the airplanes, like the fingers of the Grim Reaper, poised to crook themselves at the next victims selected to cross over into the land of death.

I shook the image away.

There was a bright side, though. Apparently, MAG was so eager for this mission to succeed that they had also equipped all the jets with two AIM-120 AMRAAMs in addition to the standard two Pythons. The deadly, radar-guided missiles were attached to wingtip stations on each Viper, and they reminded me of the exposed talons on a bird of prey. I felt my pulse quicken. With two Pythons and two 'Slammers,' I might stand a chance of stopping these guys.

Of course, there was a downside. It also gave them more shit to shoot back at me.

I went down to the clinic to ensure that Sammy was still in her place. She was. Then, as I walked past the orderly room, I saw the door to Ruth's office closed and could just make out the blare of a speaker phone inside. I quickly looked both ways up and down the hallway and slipped into the room. I got as close to Ruth's door as I could and strained my ears to listen.

"...can't postpone. The funds have been transferred and all the necessary agencies have been contracted. It must go as scheduled." The tinny sound of the speakerphone made me strain to hear the words.

"But it's possible we've been compromised," Phillips' voice said.

"Again?" the voice asked. "Didn't you deal with this once before?"

"Yes," Phillips said. "But..."

"And didn't you choose someone better this time?" I could hear the sneer in the British-accented voice of the caller. "That's what you guaranteed."

"Well, we thought so, but..."

"What evidence do you have?"

"Well, nothing. It's just a hunch."

"The investors aren't going to sacrifice a billion dollars on a hunch. Take the appropriate measures and make the strike happen."

"Well, we already have, to some extent. We've relegated him to a back-up position with no weapons."

I could feel my cheeks flush. *They knew.*

"Good. Hopefully the three of you can pull this off with no cock-ups. I don't need to tell you what this means."

I heard some voices echoing in the hallway and ducked between the desk Brianna had been using and the credenza behind it. As I huddled there, I noticed one of the doors to the credenza was partially open and I saw something inside I never expected - stacks of cash. I silently slid the door open a little further and pulled one of the stacks out. It was 100 one-hundred-dollar bills—ten thousand American dollars. The stack was bound in a paper bank wrapper and was a little over half an inch thick. There were hundreds of the stacks inside the credenza. All I could think of was that it must have been traveling money for Ruth or Phillips or even Brianna. Suddenly an idea popped into my head. I pulled an empty plastic trash bag from the nearby wastebasket and started piling stacks of the bills into it. I got thirty of the stacks into the bag before it started looking suspicious, and it didn't even make a dent in the supply in the credenza.

The voices in the hallway had subsided, so I exited the room quickly and walked the few steps back into operations.

I made my way into the life support shop, stuffed the plastic bag down into my helmet bag, and packed my other gear on top of it. The extra bulk of the plastic sack barely showed.

Holy shit, I thought to myself again. *They knew.* That's why I was being relegated to the least important flight position, the cover jet in the spare flight. The one jet whose failure meant nothing to the success of the mission. So why wouldn't they just break the jet once we got to the launching airfield? The answer came to me immediately. *They need it to look normal. At least until the transports were shot down.*

But I was willing to bet they wouldn't stop there. They'd want to do something else to ensure my jet couldn't stop them. I was sure of it. In fact, I was counting on it.

Two hours and thirty minutes later, we were at 35,000 feet in the passenger area of the transport and the Texas hold 'em game was well underway. There were about ten of us playing and Rug obviously knew the game better than any of us. He lost very little, and when he won, he typically won big. I didn't know how to win consistently, but I did know how to not lose a lot. So, I folded often, raised rarely, and only bluffed once or twice. My conservative tactics gained me ridicule from my fellow players, but over time, they allowed me to spot the potential target I was looking for. At the three-hour point, I was hopeful. By the five-hour point, I was certain. We took a break at the six-hour point, while the jets were descending to make their fuel stop and I decided to make my move.

"Hey, John," I said to the guy I was focusing on, "you're a munitions troop, right?"

He nodded glumly. He had lost five thousand dollars so far in the flight and it was obvious that even with the money MAG was paying him, it was too much for him to lose. John was a lanky, black-haired man who had probably never made it past the rank of technical sergeant in the USAF. One of those guys who knew his job well but couldn't play the political games required for the promotions to Master, Senior Master, and

Chief Master Sergeant. He spoke slowly, with a slight southern drawl. But behind the brown eyes, a keen mind was at work. A mind I hoped to take advantage of.

"Before we do the fuel stop, can you show me something on the jets?" I asked. "It's been a while since I've seen a real AMRAAM and I've forgotten how it's mounted."

Rug didn't even look up from his winnings as I spoke. He was well into the counting phase.

John and I descended to the cargo hold and he showed me the finer points of mounting the AMRAAM on the F-16. Then I made my pitch. I watched him do the math in his head and it didn't take him long to add the numbers. Before the game started on the next leg, he got his tools out and we went to work.

TOP SECRET / SPECIAL
COMPARTMENTALIZED INFORMATION
CLASSIFIED BY: US Central Intelligence Agency
DECLASSIFY ON: OADR

From: Special Projects Group [NCS]
Sent: Wednesday, 8 October 2009, 2200 EDT (9 October 2009, 0200Z)
To: Director, NCS
Cc: Special Projects Group [NCS]; damrine@cmail.cia.gov; dsmith3@cmail.cia.gov

SUBJECT: Update, Case File: 08-434A (MAG)

(TS) Narrative:

1. (TS) Three 747 freighters launched from an island 250 miles due south of Fiji at approximately 0100Z time, 9 October 2009. They assumed a flight plan previously filed and falsely updated with the controlling agency. Their current flight plan schedules them for a refueling stop in Hawaii before proceeding to their next destination.

2. (TS) No further contact from Contractor 09-017 (Pearce, Colin M.).

(TS) CONCLUSIONS:

1. (TS) Given Hawaii as a refueling point, the range of the freighters leads us to believe the target area is in the continental United States.

2. (TS) We have been specifically instructed not to take action against the freighters or their cargo until we have 'undeniable

and overwhelming proof' that the aircraft represent a 'grave and immediate threat' to the United States. (Quotes from US Attorney General memo concerning this file.)

(TS) ACTIONS: We will continue tracking and predicting destinations and potential targets.

(TS) RECOMMENDATIONS:

1. Contact CINC NORAD and request air defense assets in the western United States be placed on alert.

2. Exercise Executive Order 08-537 allowing for air defense assets to be placed OPCON to DCIA.

TOP SECRET / SPECIAL
COMPARTMENTALIZED INFORMATION
CLASSIFIED BY: US Central Intelligence Agency
DECLASSIFY ON: OADR

CHAPTER TWENTY-FIVE

Contract Day Twenty-Eight
Thursday, 8 October
0600 Hours Local Time
Jacqueline Cochran Regional Airport (KTRM)
Thermal, California, USA

The 747's landing gear thumped down and the security folks began making their preparations to disembark. They were more heavily armed this time than the last. I saw grenades clipped to their web gear and a few of them were toting crew-served heavy machine guns instead of just the normal handheld ones.

Then it hit me. This wasn't like the last project, where they just had to provide security. They were going to have to take this airport over and hold it for nearly two hours. I wondered how they were going to make that happen without attracting a huge amount of visibility from the local people and authorities, but I imagined if this part of the operation were as thoroughly honed as the rest of it, there wouldn't be any issues.

We touched down lightly and the 747's engines went into reverse thrust. The big jet taxied to the end of the runway and turned off to the left. The security personnel scurried down the ladder to the cargo deck, presumably to be in place when the doors opened. Then the big jet's engines shut down and I could hear the hydraulic pumps kick in to open the nose cargo door. Suddenly, I heard shouting and a burst of automatic weapons fire. Maybe the locals weren't going quietly.

"Clear!" one of the security people yelled up the ladder a few moments later.

The maintenance folks began to descend the ladder, and Rug and I donned our flying gear. John, the munitions guy, paused at the top of the ladder and looked at me. I waved to him, took the plastic trash bag out of my helmet bag and placed it on my seat. He nodded back at me and headed down the ladder.

Rug eyed me as he zipped up his anti-g suit. "Are you ready to do this?" he asked.

"As ready as I'm going to be," I replied, watching him carefully as I spoke. "Besides, odds are you and I won't do anything but orbit the field and wait for word from the others. And you can think of how much money you can win on the return trip."

His eyes didn't grow distant and he didn't look away. Instead, he smiled brilliantly. "You're right!" he said enthusiastically. "And maybe you can even play like you have a pair this time."

I kept the smile glued on my face and nodded. "We'll see."

I could hear the tug moving the Vipers out of the cargo hold and onto the ramp and the shouted orders of one of the maintenance troops as the jets were readied.

"They're ready for you outside," one of the transport pilots announced over the intercom a few minutes later.

I motioned toward the ladder. "Age before beauty."

Rug smirked at me and began his descent. I followed him down.

The combination of artificial humidity and salt air hit me the moment my feet landed on the cargo deck. We were in Thermal, California, located about twenty miles southeast of

Palm Springs and about seven miles north of the Salton Sea, the second largest salt lake in the US. The entire southeast end of the Palm Springs valley has been artificially irrigated and produces the abrasive stink of humid air in an environment that is normally arid. Add that to the salt air wafting in from the Salton Sea and it's a unique atmosphere. I began perspiring immediately.

"Let's move it, TC," Rug was already on his way down the cargo ramp.

The ramp area here was much smaller than the airfield in Oman. Our jet was the only freighter at this end of the field, parked on a rectangle of concrete barely large enough to hold it, just west of the north end of the north-south runway. I could see the tails of the other two 747s parked on another ramp south and west of us. From the proximity of the jets and the buildings, I could tell there wasn't much room there either.

I scrambled up the ladder into my cockpit, looking around as surreptitiously as I could for any sign the CIA had arrived to stop the festivities at hand. The airfield looked like a ghost town. No aircraft were taxiing, taking off, or working the landing pattern. No one else was here.

Goddamn it. Maybe they'll arrive after we got airborne.

Rug and I got our jets started, closed the canopies, and ran our post-start checklist. Then we motioned the ground personnel under our aircraft to arm us. The arming crew came back out from under our jets and saluted. John looked at me and gave me a thumbs-up. I nodded at him. Rug looked over at me through the tinted Plexiglas of his canopy and I nodded at him. Then, he applied power and turned south on the taxiway paralleling the runway. I followed him.

Ruth, VB, Brinker, and Pete were taxiing out from their ramp on a taxiway that intersected ours. Rug waited until all four jets had pulled out, and then he and I fell into trail behind them. I gazed back over my right shoulder as we taxied. Security guys were all over the airfield, positioned evenly on the tarmac, forming a human line between the jets and the buildings. They were also in place at entrances, roads, and other buildings. They seemed to have everything under control. At least for the moment.

We approached the end of the runway and did our final pre-takeoff checks. The runway was too narrow for us to line up on it, so each of us was going to take off as rapidly as we could take the runway and do so. Ruth turned her jet on to the concrete surface, lit her afterburner, and roared down the runway as VB taxied into position behind her. Brinker took off, then Pete, then Rug. I was the last to go.

I mechanically pushed the throttle to MIL power, watched the gauges stabilize, and then shoved the throttle into MAX AB. I felt the familiar kick in the center of my back and watched the nozzle gauge rotate to the open position. As the Viper accelerated eagerly down the runway, I could clearly see the ruts in the runway made by the 747s' landing gear. Fortunately for us, the Viper's main landing gear was close together and we could take off between the ruts; but when the 747s departed, they were going to feel it. Eventually, someone was going to have to pay to have the runway resurfaced, and that was going to cost a bundle.

My jet lifted off and I slapped the gear handle up. And then the waves of pre-combat emotion hit me. Excitement and dread were there in equal measures, but there also a deep sense of anxiety, something I hadn't experienced before. This flight was different than any other I had ever made. This time, the success or failure of the whole thing was on me. I was going to be the one who had to stop this business. And if I didn't, thousands, possibly millions, of people would die. I momentarily longed for a return to my former, solitary life flying business jets and doing a job no one cared about. It was an empty life, but also an easy one.

I followed Rug's jet into a climbing orbit over the airfield and did a little mental arithmetic. The route Ruth and the boys were flying was shaped like the letter L, laying on its side and upside down. The short leg ran due north from the airfield here, then they would turn west down the long leg. That gave me the opportunity to cut them off. But I didn't have much time to catch them.

I keyed the mic on our intraflight VHF radio. "Blade five, six. Let's go Winchester. I have something funny to tell you." Winchester meant frequency 30.30, a bit of trivia only an American pilot would know.

"Blade five copies," Rug's voice sounded downright amiable on the radio. "Blade five push Winchester."

I switched the frequency dial on my radio and waited for Rug to check me in.

"Blade five check," he said.

"Six," I replied.

"What's on your mind, six?" he asked.

I was about a mile behind Rug's jet and I had the boresight cross on my heads-up display superimposed on his airplane. I pushed the target management switch forward on the control stick and the radar locked him up.

"Lock, lock," said the voice in my headset.

I uncaged the Python on station 2 and waited, hoping that the deal I made had paid off.

"GRRRRRRRRRRRRRRRRRRRRRRRR," the missile sounded like an angry pit bull.

I smiled grimly. *Best 300,000 dollars of someone else's money I ever spent.* I moved the silver MASTER ARM switch to ARM and was rewarded with green READY lights.

"Checking your weapons, six?" Rug said over the radio conversationally. "That's a good idea. But don't be surprised if they don't work. Blade One said she wanted them all deactivated for some reason. I don't know why."

"But yours work, right?" I asked.

"Well, yes," he said. "One of us had to have something to shoot."

"Then that would be me, Rug," I said ominously. "I paid off one of the munitions guys. My jet has the missiles that were on yours. My ammo drum is full because you guys always keep them that way and my gun pin is pulled. And right now, the Python on my number two station is looking right down your ass and wants to eat."

I could almost see the question marks over his canopy during the ensuing silence.

"Don't even think about it Rug," I cautioned him. "I've kicked your ass every time we've fought and right now you're carrying a seven-hundred pound weight under your belly that you damn well know you can't jettison to fight me."

"What exactly do you want, TC?"

We were in a lazy right turn and the nose of his airplane was just coming through east.

"Roll out of your turn with your nose on the body of water to the south, which just so happens to be the Salton Sea. We're in southern California and your fellow idiots are about to lay nukes on a target that lies over the San Andreas Fault."

He did as he was commanded.

"Now start a ten-degree dive and aim the jet toward the middle of it."

"What the hell?"

"I'm letting you live, Rug. That's all you need to know. The other four aren't going to get the same treatment. Now do it before I lose my patience. I don't have a lot of time."

He lowered the nose on his aircraft and it began to descend.

"So now what?" he asked sarcastically. "I bail out or ride it in and hope for the best?"

"Pull the ejection handle, Rug. Pull the handle and live. You assholes killed my best friend, Burt Magnusson, and the only reason you're still alive is because you're the one pilot who actually has shown a little humanity. Now pull the fucking handle or die. Your choice."

Another pause. I could almost hear the cogs in his brain

turning. But Rug was smart, and he realized he didn't have any other options. He also knew that TC had not hesitated in the past when it came to killing people that pissed him off. Maybe that would convince him.

"Alpha Mike Foxtrot," Rug intoned in the radio. There was a bright flash of light and the canopy separated from his jet, followed a millisecond later by the seat traveling up the rails.

"Alpha Mike Foxtrot," I replied automatically.

Adios Mother-Fucker.

I re-caged the Python, pushed the throttle into MAX AB, and pulled my nose around to the northwest, hoping like hell I had time to catch the rest of the flight before I saw two mushroom clouds over the high desert of California.

Almost instantly, I feel the adrenaline surge inside me as the lust came alive. My muscles tightened and my eyes grew wide. I could feel the maniacal grin spreading upon my lips.

It was feeding time.

TOP SECRET / SPECIAL
COMPARTMENTALIZED INFORMATION
CLASSIFIED BY: US Central Intelligence Agency
DECLASSIFY ON: OADR

From: Special Projects Group [NCS]
Sent: Thursday, 8 October 2009, 0940 EDT (8 October 2009, 1340Z)
To: Director, NCS
Cc: Special Projects Group [NCS]; damrine@cmail.cia.gov; dsmith3@cmail.cia.gov

SUBJECT: Update, Case File: 08-434A (MAG)

(TS) Narrative:

1. (TS) MAG's Three 747 freighters touched down at Jacqueline Cochran Regional Airport, California, (KTRM) at 0603 Pacific Daylight Time. Their original flight plan had them filed into Palm Springs International Airport, California (KPSP). They diverted with twenty minutes to landing, catching our containment teams off guard. We are repositioning.

2. (TS) Radar indicated six fighter-sized aircraft launched from KTRM at 0631 PDT. Four disappeared from radar coverage as they headed north from KTRM at 0635 and two briefly orbited over KTRM. One aircraft impacted the Salton Sea at 0639 for unknown reasons and the other is currently flying towards Victorville, CA at medium altitude and extremely high speed.

3. (TS) NORAD has scrambled two F-16s from the 144th Fighter Wing at March Air Force Base to intercept.

4. (TS) We have established a field command post at Edwards Air Force Base, California, and will monitor the situation from that location.

(TS) CONCLUSIONS: None. Information only.

(TS) ACTIONS: We will continue to keep you informed.
(TS) RECOMMENDATION: None. Information only.

TOP SECRET / SPECIAL
COMPARTMENTALIZED INFORMATION
CLASSIFIED BY: US Central Intelligence Agency
DECLASSIFY ON: OADR

CHAPTER TWENTY-SIX

Contract Day Twenty-Eight
Thursday, 8 October
0642 Hours Local Time
15,000 Feet MSL and Mach One Plus
Over the High Desert of Southern California

There was just no way I was going to get there in time.

I was at 15,000 feet and had my throttle parked in MAX AB. The airspeed had topped out at about 730 knots, well over the speed of sound, and the jet was vibrating all over the place. It had never been designed for this sort of velocity at this altitude. I knew my sonic boom was breaking glass all over the place beneath me, but it couldn't be helped. If these bombs went off, the broken glass was going to be the least of anyone's worries.

To make matters worse, the corridor of airspace I was tearing across was a major artery between Phoenix, Palm Springs, and the LA Basin, so I had to keep my air-to-air radar focused in front of me so I wouldn't hit anyone. Which took it away from the more critical task of looking for Ruth and the gang.

A flash of green as the San Bernardino National Forest went underneath me and I could see the blue jewel of Big Bear Lake, nestled into the verdant mountain background off my nose. They were about to get a loud surprise. Big Bear had its own airport as I recalled, so I rolled the elevation of the radar down a little to see if there was any air traffic in front of me that might make for a potential collision. Nothing there.

I looked up from the radar tube in time to see a Southwest Airlines 737 appear just above me and to the right, so I pushed over on the stick slightly to clear him. Then I set the scan pattern of the radar to look into the valley just north of the mountain range where Big Bear was and peered into the tube to see any telltale crossing movement from right to left.

At first, there was nothing, just the occasional video square generated by a small plane or two. But, then I saw something: four dark green squares of video in perfect attack formation, moving at high speed from right to left, about twenty miles in front of me. I put my radar cursor on each one of them to check their altitude. They were at about 500 feet above the ground. I knew this airspace reasonably well. There were no high-speed military training routes in this area. There was nothing else out here that would be going that low and that fast.

It was them.

I switched my radar over to the track-while-scan (TWS) mode to get a better look at their formation and to see which ones were the leaders with the nukes, Ruth and Brinker, and which were the wingmen, VB and Pete. The two Slammers aboard my jet had Ruth and Brinker's names on them. But my current side look-angle on them, from about their eight o'clock position, made it too difficult to see who was who, and even with my cutoff angle and superior speed, I'd never catch them before they reached the loft point.

Damn.

The ingress route had been programmed into my avionics, so I could see the Initial Point for the attack run off my nose. The four jets were almost there. The loft point was only about two miles inside it. I didn't have much time. The four F-16s passed over the Initial Point and across my nose about fifteen miles away. I banked to the left and pulled my nose in front of them to try to close the distance between us a little more. I glanced down into the radar display again. The TWS display was beautiful. It showed the four contacts, with their altitudes, airspeeds, and headings, but it depicted them all line abreast. I still couldn't tell who the leaders were and who the wingmen were. I realized that I was just going to have to shoot at the two inside aircraft, hoping that the two wingmen were on the outside of the formation like they were supposed to be.

I used the target management switch on the control stick to step the designation bug over the contact second from the bottom of my display. The radar settled and I glanced up in the HUD to check the designated launch zone display for the AMRAAM on my left wing. I was well within range. I placed my thumb on the pickle button to fire it.

Then suddenly the contact's altitude began to increase rapidly.

Shit! They were into the loft maneuver. The AMRAAM was an incredibly fast missile but it would never get to them before they released the weapons.

"Fuck!" I screamed in helplessness into my intercom. "Fuck! Fuck! Fuck!"

The contacts continued their climb and now it was painfully easy to see who the leaders were as the wingmen weren't climbing nearly as rapidly or as high. I felt a cold clamp in the pit of my stomach. Scads of people were about to die and it was my fault. I didn't know whether I even had the heart to engage these bozos as they egressed. What would be the point?

And then I saw something extraordinary.

"Son of a bitch," I said in amazement as I looked down in the tube. The four TWS contacts in my display had turned into six contacts. And four were turning back to the east, while two were still headed west, at much slower speeds.

The radar was tracking the bombs! They were flying their loft trajectory toward the target and were slowing down as they climbed and the radar was showing it all.

"Holy shit!" I exclaimed.

A thousand thoughts went through my head, and I cursed my inattentiveness during the B61 class in Fighter Weapons School so long ago. I didn't know when the damn thing armed. I knew it wouldn't detonate until impact in the ground burst setting, but I had no idea when it armed or what would happen when it was hit by fifty pounds of warhead traveling at nearly Mach 5.

Fortunately, my thumb wasn't listening to my brain. It reflexively stepped the designation bug onto the northernmost contact and pushed the pickle button.

WHOOOOOOOOOOOOSHHHHHHHHHHHHH! The first AMRAAM roared off the rail.

I stepped the bug to the southern contact and pressed the pickle button again.

WHOOOOOOOOOOOOSHHHHHHHHHHHHHH! The second AMRAAM was on its way. I could almost feel my ears ringing. Even from inside the canopy with 700 plus knots of air noise going by, the sounds of the twin missile launches had been nearly deafening.

I watched the time-of-flight indicators in my heads-up display count down. The AMRAAM gets its initial target information from the launching aircraft, but at some point in its flight it goes into active terminal homing and doesn't need the radar support from the jet that fired it. Both missiles were in terminal guidance mode now and were seconds from impact. I should have averted my eyes in case the missiles detonated the nuclear warheads on impact, but I didn't. I just watched dumbly as the AMRAAMs raced to their targets.

And then I saw a small orange fireball to the north. A second later, I saw one to the south. I looked down into my radar. Both contacts representing the bombs had vanished.

I exhaled loudly in my cockpit and didn't realize I'd been holding my breath.

Hopefully the radiation damage wouldn't be significant. But I did remember from my classes that the cores of the weapons were very stable. They had to be to sustain the g forces they were subjected to.

I pulled my throttle out of afterburner and made a slow turn back toward the west, orienting my radar down and changing the mode to range-while-search (RWS). There was still a lot of work to do here. The four F-16s showed up easily once again. They were just rolling out on their east-bound track and were almost directly under me. I didn't know if they were waiting for the nuclear blast behind them or had seen the two explosions in the sky a few seconds ago. What I did know was, that for the moment, they didn't see me.

I could feel the grin stretching my lips and the adrenaline singing through my veins. I rolled my jet inverted and looked through the top of my canopy down at the brown desert below. The four gray shapes of the Vipers appeared readily, their four-ship formation back intact after the attack. They were streaking across the terrain, heading back for the launching airfield. I knew their eyes would be scanning the sky around them, looking for potential threats, but the one place they wouldn't be looking was directly above them.

I gently began to pull my nose down to them. I had a plan, but I didn't know how far I'd get with it. The two nearer ones would be the first victims. I was hoping I could get lucky with a few surprise gunshots and then engage the other two with the Pythons. But once we all got 'turning and burning,' I knew the plan would change.

I rolled out slightly aft and high above the two jets on the north side of the formation and dove down upon them, jettisoning my external tanks as I descended. They were about a mile apart, just as they should have been, with the wingman behind and outside of his leader. I called up the dogfight mode of the radar and placed the boresight cross on the wingman's airplane and paused as I waited for the distance between us to close. I didn't want to alert him too early with a radar lock. I looked across the formation at the other two jets, about three miles away, and hoped they were spending more time looking forward than looking back. Typically, in a formation like this one, it was the pilots on the opposite side who detected attacks on their flight mates. That was the reason the formation was designed the way it was - to maximize visual lookout.

I was about six thousand feet away from the wingman when my luck ran out and all hell broke loose.

The two jets below me went into tight break turns to the left, a clear indication that I had been spotted. I locked the wingman's jet with my radar as he went into his turn and let the level 5 gunsight settle for a second. The pipper appeared on the center of his fuselage and I pulled the trigger at a range of 3,800 feet. The bullets closed the gap between our jets in just over a second and holes materialized in the top of his fuselage.

There was a bright flash and then a fireball appeared, with the cockpit of the jet protruding from the front of it. I didn't wait to see if there was a parachute. I banked up and pulled my nose to the right and down, toward the far side of the formation and the jets that had the best chance of engaging me. The flight leader of the wingman I had just destroyed would be out of the fight for a good thirty to forty-five seconds as he or she completed the turn. In the meantime, I had my hands full with the jets across the way.

I pulled aft on the target management switch and selected the 10 x 60 dogfight mode of the air-to-air radar which looks sixty degrees up from the nose. Since my nose was oriented toward the lead jet on the other side, the radar found him or her quickly.

"Lock, lock," went the luscious female voice in my headset.

I uncaged the Python and got a roaring tone in my

headset. I checked the ranges and let the missile fly. I heard the WHOOOSH sound of the missile leaving the rail. There was an arcing smoke trail, and then I saw the fireball as it detonated next to the other airplane an instant later.

"Jesus, what a missile!" I exclaimed into my intercom. "The AIM-9 would have never been able to fucking do that!"

Pieces of the jet tumbled to the earth as I continued my turn to engage the wingman on the far side. He had stopped his turn as his flight leader exploded and now seemed to be puzzled as to what to do next. He was flying in a left bank, at one g, his nose barely tracking across the horizon. I didn't have the time to be nice or to query him about his intentions. Instead, I locked his jet up, called up the gun, and settled the pipper on the canopy of his aircraft. Then, I pulled the trigger.

The Plexiglas was coated in red instantly and a fire broke out just behind the cockpit. I rolled wings-level and pulled into the vertical just as the crippled jet banked to the left and plunged to the desert floor below. I looked back over my shoulder and saw the explosion of the impact in my peripheral vision just as I tried to gain sight of the one remaining aircraft.

My radar warning gear was strangely silent and I briefly wondered if Ruth would have run instead of staying to fight. Then I quickly dismissed the idea. She knew by now that her plan had been completely foiled, and that in spite of her efforts, I was the reason. There was no way that would go unanswered.

I pulled the nose of my jet back to the left, toward the north, still climbing. My head was on a swivel as I searched for her jet. She didn't have me locked up with the radar, which meant she couldn't shoot me with an AMRAAM and probably wouldn't use the gun. She could still lock me up with the Python without locking me with the radar, but she'd have to have her nose pointed at me, and that would mean she had to be on the inside of the turn.

Unless.

There was only one trajectory she could have attained that would have put her in that position in the amount of time she had to get there.

I pushed forward on the control stick, unloaded my jet to zero g, rolled abruptly to the right and down, applied maximum g, and yanked the throttle to idle. Then I smacked the countermeasures dispensing switch.

The Python flew past, so close to me that I could discern where the body of the missile stopped and the flame from the engine began. It detonated somewhere behind and under my aircraft and I felt the bump from the explosion. I scanned my engine instruments and hydraulic gauges rapidly. There were no telltale indications it had done any damage.

Holy shit!

Then I saw Ruth's jet, high and on the inside of my right turn, about 2,000 feet back. She was inverted, looking through the top of her canopy at me, but her nose was high and pointed outside of the arc of my turn.

Her greed had fucked her. She had continued her break turn through north and then through west and arced the fight as I killed the two other jets. Then, when I began my turn back to the north, she had seen her opportunity. But instead of taking a nice conservative shot a mile or so behind me and maybe following it up with a second missile, she had closed the distance between us, presumably to finish me off with a gunshot if the Python didn't do the trick. She had wanted to see me die.

I looked up at her and assessed our positions and energy states. "It's time you and me got into the phone booth again, Ruthie," I said into the intercom. "And only one of us is coming out alive."

I pushed the throttle into MAX AB and unloaded the aircraft. It was a dangerous gamble but I was counting on her greed to win out over common sense or even good tactics. I looked back at her nose. Without a radar lock, she couldn't fire a missile at me without pointing at me. Now that the element of surprise was gone, I didn't think she'd be shy about using the radar. But I also thought she'd want to kill me more 'personally.'

And that would be her undoing.

Her nose began to track back toward me and down back to the inside of my turn circle.

Which was what I was expecting. I kept the power in MAX AB, rolled my jet so that my vertical stabilizer was aimed right at her airplane, and pulled back on the stick for all I was worth.

In a second, I had taken away all the turning room she had thought she was going to have. She rolled out of her turn rapidly and pulled her nose up and behind me, attempting to stay in an offensive position by staying behind my wingline.

"Perfect," I said to myself.

I kept the back pressure on the stick and stomped on the left rudder. It was like my jet pivoted in space. It both yawed and rolled to the left rapidly and in a mere few seconds, my fuselage was aligned with hers and we were heading in the same direction, looking at each another, about 2,000 feet apart.

We were in a flat scissors. It was textbook.

I keyed my UHF radio. "Look familiar?" I asked.

She answered by pulling her nose up just as she should have and I responded by doing the same. Then she pulled into me, I pulled into her, and we went by one another and transcribed our first 'S' in the sky. Then it happened again. We were now in full afterburner with our noses nearly vertical.

And I was waiting for her to do what she had done before.

She didn't disappoint. The 'aerodynamically impossible' happened once again, and her nose suddenly began turning toward me impossibly fast. I heard the audio of her radar in my headset.

Two can play that game, sweetheart.

She was cheating, again. But this time, I knew what she was doing. On the left forward console in the Viper's cockpit, there's a switch labeled MPO, manual pitch override. The purpose of the switch is to allow the pilot to override the flight control computer and exceed the pitch limiters on the jet in emergency conditions only. Apparently, though, Ruth liked to use it to give herself a little slow-speed control authority. Like when she had beaten me in the BFM tournament.

But I had her number today.

I dispensed countermeasures, chaff, and flares, and yanked my throttle to idle as I flicked my own MPO switch and increased my nose track toward her. I watched a stream of white smoke emanate from her left wing as she fired her remaining Python at what had to be its absolute minimum range. The smoke trail came straight towards me, but there was no way the missile had time to arm with the limited distance between us. It flew harmlessly past me towards the flares I had dispensed. My nose continued around, and I met her nose-to-nose at about 1000 feet range, just long enough for me to squeeze my trigger and see a few 20mm rounds rip through her left wing and elevator. I saw smoke stream from the left side of her jet as she attempted to shoot at me as well, but I was moving too quickly.

We both dove out of the fight, heading downward, but I had expected this scenario and she had not.

I shoved the throttle back into MAX AB, rolled wings-level, and pulled back on the control stick, arresting my descent rate as she continued downward on my right side. Then I stepped on the right rudder and the Viper made a slow, sluggish roll to the right. And when it was completed, I was above and behind her jet, 3,000 feet back. I pushed forward on the target management switch.

"Lock, lock," went the soothing female voice in my headset.

Ruth was turning now, below and in front of me, trapped in a nearly horizontal plane by her limited energy state. I could see her head moving frantically in the cockpit to keep sight of me. I pulled my jet out of AB and allowed the distance between us to close slightly. My right index finger tensed on the trigger. Death was calling for Ruth Shalev. And I wanted her to see it coming.

Two thousand feet behind her now, nearly there.

Then her voice came over the radio. "Why are you trying to kill me, Colin? What have I ever done to you?"

"Burt Magnusson." The voice came from me but I didn't recognize it.

I was 1,000 feet behind her now and just above her jet. I centered the pipper on her canopy.

"It wasn't even my idea," she protested, "we were on the beach and he just wouldn't..." And she went into an aggressive vertical jink at that exact moment. I was suddenly looking at nearly the entire top of her airplane, and I had a severe closure problem. She had completely suckered me.

"Fuck!" I spat into my oxygen mask.

I pulled my nose up to keep the pipper in place on her canopy, but she was rolling now. She stopped the roll when she was nearly inverted and pulled her nose earthward to get out of the plane of my gunshot and to bring me in even closer.

I was inside a 500 feet range.

I could clearly see the texture of the skin of the airplane now. In another few seconds, we'd be neutral.

Not fucking today.

I rolled with her and wound up inverted, just like she was, with my nose pointed just underneath the right wing of her airplane and about 300 feet away. There was no time to sweeten the shot, no time to wait for the computerized gunsight to catch up. I depressed the trigger and held it as I gently pulled and pushed on my control stick, bringing my nose back and forth, above and below her right wing, as the M-61A1 twenty millimeter Vulcan cannon in my jet spat out 100 high-explosive incendiary bullets per second.

A few seconds later my gun emptied and went silent.

For a moment, I thought I all my bullets had missed her jet. But then as I rolled slightly and turned away from her, I was rewarded with the sight of a good portion of her right wing separating from her airplane. It broke off cleanly, just outside the external tank pylon, and tumbled away. There was no fire at all. Her jet then began a roll to the right, since the left wing was still generating lift and had nothing to counter it on the right. The roll rate increased rapidly as her jet nosed over and plunged to the ground.

"I hope you drown in a sea of your own puke," I said.

"Bingo, Bingo." The luscious female voice of the warning system was telling me I was low on gas. Then I heard the sound of something much more ominous. It was the sound of an F-16 radar painting my jet.

"What the fuck?" I said.

I switched my radio over to the UHF emergency frequency or 'Guard' as we call it and keyed the mic.

"Attention aircraft over the Lucerne Valley, my callsign is TC, Tango Charlie, I'm in the remaining F-16 over the valley. I'm a government contractor. Do not fire. All hostile aircraft have been eliminated."

There was a pause as someone, somewhere, digested this information.

"Tango Charlie, this is Darkstar on Guard. Push 347.8." I was stunned. Darkstar was an AWACs callsign, the Airborne Warning and Control System, an airborne radar center which typically controlled fighter aircraft in a theater of operations.

Were they waiting for us?

"Tango Charlie is pushing 347.8"

I changed the frequency on the UHF radio. "Darkstar, Tango Charlie on 347.8"

"Tango Charlie, Darkstar, squawk mode three 7711."

I entered the code in the upfront control and commanded the Viper's radar transponder to respond to interrogation. It had been shut off for the strike.

"Tango Charlie, Darkstar, radar contact, 55 miles southeast of Edwards Air Force Base. Snap to heading 345."

I began a turn to the northwest and looked down at my fuel gauge and got yet another shock. The amount of fuel programmed into the system to provide the 'bingo' warning was 1000 pounds. A lot less than it should have been. Someone had messed with the data load for my jet and I had never even checked it.

Great.

"Darkstar, Tango Charlie, I don't know if my fuel state will allow me to reach Edwards. Can you give me coordinates for the airfield?"

The controller read me the longitude and latitude for Edwards and I punched the numbers in to my navigational system. The airfield was 50 miles away now. Not good

"Darkstar, Tango Charlie is declaring an emergency, I need an unrestricted climb to flight level 400 and all traffic cleared between me and Edwards."

"Tango Charlie, Darkstar will contact LA center. Proceed as required."

I advanced the power to MIL, 100% percent thrust without afterburner, and lifted the nose up. I needed to get as much altitude as I could before I ran out of fuel and my engine flamed out. I kept the airspeed at 350 and climbed, trying to do a little mental math in the process. The jet was light and the temperature must not have been too oppressive. I was climbing at about 5,000 feet per minute and burning about 9,000 pounds per hour. I had a few minutes before I ran out of gas. I shook my head as the desert floor receded underneath me and I climbed into the clear, blue desert sky. I hoped it would be enough.

As I was climbing through 10,000 feet, I could see the vast whiteness of the Muroc Dry Lake Bed in the distance. Edwards lay on the far side of the lake but the lake bed itself was suitable for landings, as numerous space shuttle missions had shown.

I heard the F-16 radar sound in my headset again and saw a pair of large shadows pass over my canopy.

Uh oh.

At that moment two F-16s smoothly moved up on either side of me. The tail insignia showed they belonged to the California Air National Guard. I leaned my head back against the headrest and watched as those beautiful jets stopped in position, their canopies about ten feet away from each of my wingtips. They didn't look like they had hostile intent. If I had to guess, I'd say they looked like they were here to escort me.

They really were ready for us.

"Tango Charlie, Bear one, how do you hear?" the voice came over the UHF radio. It didn't sound like that of a younger pilot but one that was more mature, like mine.

"Bear One, Tango Charlie, loud and clear."

"Nice work out there today but you didn't leave anything for us."

I smiled tiredly under my oxygen mask. "If I had known you guys were coming, you could have had it all."

"What's your gameplan? FO landing at Edwards?" FO meant flameout landing.

I nodded at him. "I've got about five hundred pounds of fuel left."

"Can't you eject if you don't make it?"

I thought about that for a second. MAG had done just about everything to fuck with my airplane. Disarming the ejection seat was well within the realm of possibility.

"I'm not one hundred percent sure it will work."

I saw him nod.

I was passing through about 20,000 feet when something else occurred to me.

"Shit!" I said into my oxygen mask. "Darkstar, Tango Charlie. You have three broken arrows in this area."

The pregnant pause wasn't reassuring. Then a different voice, one I recognized, came on the air.

"Tango Charlie, this is Juliet Alpha and Delta Sierra, do you copy? John Amrine and Dave Smith. It was Amrine's voice.

"Tango Charlie affirmative."

"Is one of them in the Salton Sea?"

"Affirmative," I replied.

"Okay roger, we have a containment team enroute. Where are the other two?"

I paused. They weren't going to like this.

"Somewhere between Hesperia and Wrightwood. I destroyed them with AMRAAMs after they separated from the attacking aircraft."

"Copy that," Amrine's voice sounded unruffled. "We saw where that wreckage came down and we have containment teams enroute there also. We'll alert them."

I nodded. So they were on it. I allowed my mind to drift for a second as I considered how much chaos had been visited upon this area today.

How in the hell were they going to spin this?

The engine flamed out just as I reached 30,000 feet. According to my navigation systems, we were 28 miles from the airport.

"Engine just flamed out," I said over the radio. I heard the whine of the Emergency Power Unit, or EPU, as it kicked on and instantly attained working rpm thanks to its volatile hydrazine fuel. The EPU provided the jet with electrical and hydraulic power when the engine stopped working. But it only carried enough fuel to last for about twenty minutes, and that was about how long it was going to take me to get down.

"If it's not one fucking thing, it's another," I said to myself.

My gut was telling me I could make it. I just hoped the hydrazine in the EPU held out. As my airspeed decreased and my angle-of-attack increased, I found the AOA setting I was looking for and adjusted my descent rate to maintain it.

"Okay, guys," I said into the mic, "here we go. I'll be using the southern runway."

"It will be 22 left," replied my escort. "It's 15,000 feet long by 300 feet wide. We'll be going to a chase position."

"Roger that," I said. "If you haven't already, please tell the folks at the airport I'll be stopping straight ahead on the runway. You might also tell them that my EPU has been activated." Once the EPU was activated, the hydrazine fuel required HAZMAT procedures when I landed.

"Already done," said the flight leader.

The two ANG F-16s climbed above me and disappeared from view.

I was alone again. Story of my life.

So now it was just a question of energy versus distance and making sure I got the jet to the end of the runway with enough airspeed left over to break the descent rate. I could see the airfield easily now on the far side of the dry lake bed and the two parallel runways stood out clearly against the brown desert floor. I was still heading about 345 and the runway heading was 220 or so. I'd have a 125-degree turn to align with the runway. That would be too much at the endgame. I turned to the right slightly and aimed my jet about two miles east of the runway complex to build some additional turning room.

I passed through 20,000 feet with about fifteen miles to the field. Given that the airport was 2,300 feet in elevation, I was right on profile. The normal FO landing profile called for flying the entire descent with the landing gear extended, but my 'energy voice' had two words for that: "not yet." I listened.

Ten thousand feet at six miles. Almost eight thousand feet above the ground. My energy state vis-à-vis the runway was getting higher. It was time to lower the gear. I looked at the hydraulic pressure gauge and hoped I had sufficient utility pressure to do that without using the alternate extension mechanism. I placed the handle in the down position and was rewarded with three, steady green lights shortly thereafter. Life was good.

Five thousand feet on the altimeter at three miles. I switched over to the tower frequency of 318.1 and began a slow left turn to line up with the runway heading, 220 degrees.

"Edwards tower, Tango Charlie Emergency, turning final for 22 left."

"Tango Charlie Emergency, Edwards tower," the controller responded. "Check wheels down. Cleared to land, Runway 22 left. Emergency vehicles are standing by."

"Tango Charlie is gear down," I said, smiling. The 'gear down call' was a fixture in USAF aviation. It had been years since I'd said it on the radio. "Tower, Tango Charlie has a live air-to-air missile on station eight on the right wing."

"Tower copies. We'll scramble munitions personnel."

I aligned with the runway passing about 3,000 feet on the altimeter, 700 feet above the ground with about a mile to go. I drove the jet down, pointing it at the end of the overrun, the concrete which extends beyond the usable surface of the runway, and held it there. Five hundred feet to go. I began to apply a little backpressure to pull the nose up. The EPU flamed out suddenly as the end of the runway went beneath me and the time to be gentle with the jet was over. I pushed on the stick slightly and touched down with all three wheels, at just over 200 knots. I had about two and a half miles to stop, which sounds like a lot, but with 18,000 pounds going over 200 knots and limited braking available, it's not much. I thumbed the speed brakes open and hoped there was enough hydraulic pressure left to extend them. Then I began to gently apply the pedal brakes. The brakes on the F-16 aren't great when they work perfectly, and now I only had residual hydraulic pressure and the nitrogen pressure in the brake accumulators. The jet began to slow.

The 10,000-foot-remaining marker went by and I thanked my stars that I had landed on one of the longer runways in the southwest. I was at 150 knots.

Then the pedals went to the floor. It was time for the emergency brakes. I dutifully lifted my feet off the pedals, activated the emergency brakes, and slowly reapplied pedal pressure. The jet continued to slow. But not fast enough.

"Edwards tower, Tango Charlie, cable, cable, cable."

All USAF fighter bases have arresting cables built into their runways to stop jets aborting takeoffs at high speed or landing without brakes, like I was.

The 5,000-foot-remaining marker went by and I was indicating one hundred knots. The emergency brakes weren't working so well.

"Tango Charlie, Edwards Tower, Cable is in the raised position."

I clicked the mic twice in reply and hit the switch to lower my arresting hook.

Three thousand feet remaining and I was at 70 knots and the pedals were fully depressed. The jet just wasn't stopping quickly enough. I swallowed hard. This wasn't how I had envisioned all this ending.

Then I felt the hook catch the cable and the Viper rapidly slowed to a stop. After a moment or two of straining against the tension of the cable, it rolled backward several feet.

I exhaled slowly and put my head back against the headrest. "Well, that's about all the fucking excitement I can stand for one day," I said to no one in particular.

The emergency vehicles rolled up then, red lights flashing and diesel horns blaring: three large fire trucks in the typical Day-Glo green color, with the foam guns mounted on top of the cabins; a boxy-looking red and silver ambulance; and a red pick-up truck which was probably the fire chief. The moment the vehicles stopped rolling, ground personnel poured out of them, dressed in HAZMAT suits, standard practice when the hydrazine-powered emergency power unit had fired on an F-16. I nodded to myself. Some of the ground personnel worked their way around to the right side of my jet and gave me the signal which asked if they could put the safety pin in the EPU. I nodded to them.

They approached my airplane, put the EPU pin in, then backed away and gave me a thumbs-up. A few others came out from under my jet and gave me signs indicating that my landing gear and the Python on Station 8 had been pinned. I was getting ready to turn the battery power off when the last radio call came.

"Tango Charlie, Bear One. You all set?"

"I'm good. Thanks for your help, guys."

"Bears, push two five seven six, see ya." And they were gone.

One of the ground crew brought an F-16 ladder to my jet. I raised the canopy and shut down the electrical power. The ladder appeared on the rail before the canopy was all the way up. I pinned the ejection seat, disconnected myself, and climbed out of the cockpit.

At the bottom of the ladder, I took my helmet off. Then I bent over slightly, unclipped the leg straps from my parachute harness and stowed them. As I stood up, I noticed for the first time that a platoon of serious-looking men dressed in black tactical garb with automatic weapons had cordoned the jet off.

A black suburban with heavily-tinted windows pulled up and a serious-looking man in black got out of the front passenger door, opened the door for the second row of seats, and motioned me inside. I collected my helmet and other gear, and walked to the vehicle.

It all felt so surreal. After weeks on the Island, in that 'whole different world,' not having any idea whether I'd live through the experience, and then undergoing the most intense combat of my life, I was suddenly back safely in the US and it was all over. It was just so damn hard to process.

As I got to the big SUV, I stopped for a second and turned to look at the Viper I was leaving behind, the jet that had saved my life. The gray-blue aircraft and its shiny canopy sparkled in the sun. The fighter looked fearsome but forlorn.

"Good bye, baby," I whispered. "I'm gonna miss you."

I got into the Suburban and let the guy outside shut the door. The vehicle had a beige leather interior and still had that 'new car' smell. It also had an impressive array of gadgetry in the front and an equally impressive weapons rack in the back.

I looked to my left and found CIA Operations Officer Dave Smith seated next to me. He had an impatient expression on his face.

"Are you done, Pearce?" he asked. "We actually have some more work to do here."

CHAPTER TWENTY-SEVEN

Contract Day Twenty-Eight
Thursday, 8 October
0800 Hours Local Time
Edwards Air Force Base (KEDW)
Edwards, California, USA

The big SUV tore across the taxiways and runways at the airfield and into a hangar on the north side of the ramp. The hangar doors were open just wide enough to accommodate the width of our vehicle and after we drove through, I watched the hangar darken as the doors closed behind us. Smith was out of his door before the driver put the SUV into park.

"This way," he said.

I left the vehicle and followed him. He was walking swiftly across the hangar to a door on the far side, his shoes clicking on the highly-polished concrete floor.

"We have an ops center upstairs," he explained as we walked. "We knew they were going to strike in southern California somewhere, we just didn't know where."

"So, you didn't get my last e-mail," I said.

"No, we didn't. We got every other one you sent, but not that one for some reason."

"I was surprised you got any of them. I was never in a place where the BlackBerry would have been able to get a satellite signal."

"That little device has its own bag of tricks. If there are any WiFi networks around, it has a worm program that digs a tunnel and builds a discrete, secure channel inside. Usually, the owners of the network never know about it. Either MAG discovered it or had their network powered down when you sent the last message."

"They were preparing to leave the Island and never come back," I said thoughtfully. It's totally possible they powered down." I looked at him. "Did you ever get a position signal on me?"

Smith hung his head a little.

"No. We lost you after the G-550 that picked you up refueled at Anchorage. They had a ghost G-550 that assumed the original jet's flight plan, and the original one pretty much vanished into thin air. They did something similar with the transports. It's revealed some rather wide gaps in the security of the international air traffic control system that we're going to have to examine, that's for sure."

"So how did you know we'd be attacking here?"

"We tracked you from the Island," he said.

"What?"

"We had surveillance ships and satellite coverage of the approximate area where the Island was in the Southwest Pacific. When we got three solid radar hits departing at the same time, we tracked them. After they stopped for gas in Honolulu, they took off for Palm Springs. We couldn't take them in Honolulu because the attorney general demanded we have 'undeniable and overwhelming proof' that these guys were a threat before we acted. We had to wait until they got someplace and launched the jets. We figured we'd have to take them at Palm Springs. When they pushed to Jacqueline Cochran, it was a bit of a surprise, but we managed to get our forces in place and take the airfield about an hour and fifteen minutes after you landed."

"But how did you even get close enough to know where to look for the Island? I mean, from the time differences and all, you can narrow it down a little, but there's a lot of ocean out there."

Smith looked at me.

"You know the strike you flew on the oil terminal in Iran?"

I nodded, just as my throat went dry.

"We played client and ordered it. Brianna Blenhem helped us with that, by the way. Thanks for alerting us to her arrival at Zurich. She's actually a British agent, and she played her role as the banking contact throughout all of this."

"Holy shit," I mumbled.

"We ordered the strike," he continued, "so we could follow you back to the Island. As it turned out, though, we could only locate the general vicinity of the Island, not the actual place. The transports pulled the old switcheroo on us again and lost us a few hundred miles out from landing."

"All those people," I said softly. "We killed all those people."

Smith slapped me on the back. "You did a good thing. MAG actually did a good thing. That entire oil terminal exists to support the arms trade between Iran and North Korea. Anyone working there was in the wrong job at the wrong place. That airstrike made the world a safer place, trust me."

That helped a little, but not much. "What about the F-18 pilots?"

Smith looked over at me. "We lost one of them. But that's not your fault. The admiral in command of the strike force was given a direct order not to engage you guys. But he thought he knew better than we did so he launched a patrol flight anyway."

"Hampered by the normal rules of engagement, I'm sure," I said morosely, looking at the pavement.

Smith nodded. "Yeah, this admiral's name is Bennett. I've got some friends in the NCIS. No one knows how the guy got promoted to flag rank. Evidently, he's a complete idiot."

I was shaking my head. "Well, he directly caused the death of one of his subordinates. I hope he feels better about himself," I said.

"After we reported his antics to the Chief of Naval Operations, Bennett was relieved of command. He'll be spending the rest of his career in some sort of harmless administrative position until he can retire."

We went through a door into a stairwell. I walked up a set of government-issue metal stairs to the hangar's second floor and waited at the top of them for Smith to lead me to where we needed to go. He jogged past me, opened the door to the hallway, and led me down to a set of double metal doors. He knocked twice.

Yet another businesslike man in black opened the door, looked Smith and me over carefully, and let us in. Smith stepped through and I followed him.

The room was a hive of activity. A large conference table dominated the center with maps and satellite photos spread all over it, and people sitting and standing around it, some talking among themselves while others were on phones. Some of the men and women were in USAF uniforms. I saw at least one colonel, but most were civilians. People also sat at tables against the walls, speaking on phones and radios, or typing into computers. The activity produced a loud din in the room.

All the commotion ceased completely when I stepped through the doors. Everyone stopped what they were doing and stared at me.

Smith didn't waste the opportunity. "Ladies and gentleman, our primary contractor for this case, Contractor 09-017, Colin Pearce."

There were appraising and appreciative looks throughout the room. I could see Amrine at the far side of the table eyeing me with a half-smile on his face. Then the smile vanished and he cocked his head. He had a headset on, barely visible underneath all the blonde hair. He looked at me and motioned me to him while he frantically looked through the maps and photos on the table.

"Okay, stand by," he said into the microphone.

I approached the table and the people there cleared the way for me.

"We have several containment teams in the field dealing with the aircraft wreckage and recovering the nukes," Amrine began, "but something more pressing has come up." He paused for a moment as trying to choose his words carefully, and then apparently decided not to bother. "I need to know if you can visually confirm that you killed the four pilots you engaged. We know one bailed out just north of the Salton Sea. We have him in custody."

I thought for a second and started to nod, and then I remembered the end of the dogfight with Ruth clearly. "I can confirm three," I said. "I can't confirm that I killed Major Shalev. I crippled her jet to the point that she'd have to bail out of it, but it didn't explode, and I didn't have time to watch what happened because I was being intercepted by the guard F-16s and didn't want them to shoot me."

Amrine frowned and nodded. "We thought as much. We found the wreckage of one F-16 just east of Hesperia with the ejection seat missing. As we expanded the search, we found the seat and the parachute." He looked at me. "She got away."

"Son of a bitch," I said, shaking my head. I felt empty inside. Like I'd been cheated. Then something occurred to me. "Did you get Phillips and the G-550?"

"What are you talking about?" Amrine interrupted.

"I overheard the two of them talking in the steam...Well it's not important where I heard it, but I heard Phillips say he was going to pick her up at KTRM in the G-550."

"Well shit, that explains it." Smith said, looking at Amrine. "We were monitoring the frequencies for SO-CAL approach control and we heard a Gulfstream check in and then change its destination from Palm Springs to Hesperia. Obviously, it wasn't using VP-CFD as a callsign, or we would have paid more attention to it."

"By that time, we were already transitioning from Palms Springs to Jacqueline Cochran, so we didn't think much of it," Amrine continued. "We knew there was something weird about it, but it didn't seem to fit."

"How long is the runway at Hesperia?" I asked.

A woman from across the room overheard the question and answered. She must have had an airport database open on her computer.

"Just under 4,000 feet," she said, "and 50 feet wide."

I looked at Smith and Amrine. "That's doable in a G-550. I wouldn't want to do it in a G Four, but the G-550 has a slower approach speed."

"Okay people," Amrine raised his voice, "I need police reports. Abandoned vehicles, hitchhikers in flightsuits, whatever."

I looked down at the map. "Where'd you find the parachute?"

Amrine put his finger on the western mouth of the Lucerne valley, just south of the main road, Highway 18. "Here," he said. "Goddamn it. She caught a car and rode it to Hesperia airport."

Smith looked at Amrine. "She obviously had a cell phone with her and she called the sat phone on the jet," he said.

"Cell phone to sat phone call originating in this area in the last two hours. Get on it, people," Amrine ordered.

"Got it," said a man in another corner of the room a few minutes later. "Zero seven fifteen this morning, cell phone to sat phone. The tower that took the call was," he walked over to the table with a piece of paper in his hand and pointed to a place on the map about two miles west of where Ruth's parachute was found, "here."

"Get on the horn to the CHP," Amrine said, raising his voice again, "and tell them to get a couple of units over to Hesperia airport ASAP. We're looking for an abandoned vehicle and we need to interview anyone who saw the Gulfstream land and saw the person who got on it."

"I'm on it," said a man at the table as he punched a phone on the table and started talking.

"She got away," I said, shaking my head. "She got away. I don't fucking believe it."

"Call the FAA," said Smith to a woman seated at the other end of table. "I want to find where that Gulfstream went."

"They would have departed VFR," I said to Smith.

"What?" Smith said.

"They would have departed VFR, without a flight plan on file, and they'll fly VFR without talking to radar agencies, to someplace where they can land, get fuel, then depart under an IFR flight plan without attracting attention. I wouldn't be a bit surprised if they didn't have magnetic panels with different aircraft registration numbers onboard either."

Smith looked at me appraisingly, but I could see the disappointment on his face.

"You won't find him," I said. "If I were flying that jet, you wouldn't find me."

"Shit," Smith said and walked away shaking his head.

"The CHP is on site at Hesperia," said the man at the phone a few minutes later. "They found an abandoned Dodge pickup truck in the parking lot."

"How do they know that's the right truck?" Amrine asked.

"There's a dead, white male in his early sixties in the bed of the truck. He's been shot once in the forehead with a nine millimeter or something of that size."

"What a ruthless little bitch," I said.

"And a woman boarded the G Five," he continued, looking at me, "wearing a military-style flightsuit. She had dark hair."

Amrine exhaled loudly.

A radio crackled into life in the corner of room. "Control,

this is charlie echo six, how do you read?"

Amrine pushed a button on the panel his headset was plugged into. "Charlie echo six, control, five by five."

"Island is cleared. We intercepted the inbound hit team and engaged them before they could do any damage to the facility or the people there. It was a good thing we got there when we did. The unit didn't leave too many people behind, and those left weren't eager for a fight. We've got the transport choppers inbound, and we'll scavenge what we can before we blow the place."

"Any casualties?" Amrine asked.

"Negative," the voice said.

"Ask him if they took any medical personnel or patients into custody," I said to Amrine, who repeated the question over the radio.

"Negative again," replied the voice after a few moments consultation. "The clinic area was completely empty. One of the beds looked like it had been recently used, but that was about it."

She wasn't there. And that bothered the shit out me. It meant I had missed something.

Whose side are you on, Sammy?

The answer occurred to me a few moments later and shocked the shit of me. "I'll be damned," I said to no one in particular.

"What are you thinking?" Smith said, eyeing me.

"About what an idiot I've been," I replied looking back at him.

##

A few hours later, the level of activity had wound down and most of the personnel had departed. I had observed the entire process, duly impressed by the efficiency of the apparatus Amrine and Smith had assembled.

"So what now?" I asked them as they were tidying up their paperwork.

"The operations part of this thing is wrapping up," Amrine said, looking up from the stack of paper in front of him. "So now we need to debrief you while everything is still fresh in your mind. We've kept the people behind from the different directorates in the agency who participated in the case."

"Directorates?" I asked. "The CIA has directorates? Like a corporation?"

Smith nodded. "There are essentially four, the Directorate of Intelligence, they do most of the analysis work; the Directorate of Science and Technology who handle the 'gadgets' and associated tech stuff..."

"It's where all the geeks work," Amrine whispered with a conspiratorial smile.

Smith was shaking his head. "Some of my best friends are geeks," he said. "Anyway, there is also the Directorate of Support, which does exactly what the name implies and then finally there's the Directorate where John and I work: the National Clandestine Service."

"Wow," I said. "Impressive. So you guys are the real deal. You're professional spies."

"More like counterspies and counter-covert ops; or, in this case, counter-*overt* ops."

"I see."

I could see two digital video cameras being set up, one on each side of the table and pointed at a vacant chair at one end of it. An attractive young lady with red hair and wearing the standard black attire sat at the other end of the table with two notebook computers in front of her and a headset on. She looked over and smiled at me. I smiled back. Then she looked over at Smith and Amrine.

"Ready," she said.

"Colin," Amrine said. "If you'd be so kind as to take the seat of honor at the head of the table, we'll start knocking this out."

"Sure." I took a bottle of water from the case of them on a side table, walked over to the chair, and sat down.

"Interview one, Contractor 09-017, Mr. Colin Pearce," Smith began, reading from a clipboard in front of him. "Mr. Pearce is the principal contractor for case file 08-434A, mike alpha golf. Wednesday, October seventh, 2009, 1100 hours, off-site location, Edwards Air Force Base, California. Operations Officer in Charge, John Amrine. Assistant Operations Officer in Charge, David Smith."

Smith stopped reading from the clipboard and looked at me. "Mr. Pearce, tell us, in your own words, everything that you experienced or encountered from the time you were picked up by Fieldstone's G-550, approximately four weeks ago, until you left your aircraft on the runway at Edwards Air Force Base this morning. I encourage you to leave absolutely nothing out. The smallest nuance, even the slightest perception, may have crucial significance to the national security of the United States."

I took a healthy slug of water from the bottle in my hand and began to speak.

CHAPTER TWENTY-EIGHT

Contract Day Thirty
Saturday, 10 October
1200 Hours Local Time
Edwards Air Force Base (KEDW)
Edwards, California, USA

I talked to them for two full days and part of a third. We broke for meals and bathroom stops, and I even got a shower in there somewhere. They did allow me about five hours of sleep but the process was, as I understood it, to get as much information out of me as quickly as possible.

Questioners came and went. Some were civilian, some were military. I'd be asked to retell the same story several times to different listeners and sometimes additional details would emerge. It was a grueling process, almost like an interrogation.

Early on the third day, my things from the Island were returned to me. I put my navy-blue Brooks Brothers suit back on with a fresh shirt and pretended I was a normal human being. The questions stopped later the same day. Everyone around the table had either a notebook computer or several pads of paper in front of them and they were all consulting their notes.

Finally, Amrine lifted his eyes from his notes and looked

at Smith. "Are we done here?" he asked.

"I think so," said Smith. "Anyone else have any questions for Mr. Pearce?" No one answered and he nodded. "Then we're done." He looked at me. "Do you have anything else to add?"

I was shaking my head. "No, I just wish we'd found Burt's body," I said. "I feel like there won't be any closure for his wife."

Smith was shaking his head, too. "It's a damn shame," he said. "I guess we'll never know what really happened to him."

Amrine raised his head from the paperwork in front of him and looked at me. "You know that Shalev and Phillips are still out there," he said.

I nodded.

"Do you have any issues with the mechanism we've discussed for reeling them in?"

"Not at all," I said. "I'm glad to still be in the game." He nodded back at me.

"If there are no other questions," Smith said, "we'll put our report together. Colin, there are two gentlemen in a Citation Ten downstairs who will take you back to Wilmington."

I rose from the table. "Sounds good."

Amrine walked up to me and shook my hand. "Damn good work, Colin," he said. "This country owes you a debt of gratitude, and so do we."

I smiled at him tiredly. "You're paying me well," I replied. "There's something to be said for that."

The other people at the table shook my hand as well, and the cute young redhead who was responsible for the recording might have held my hand about half a second too long. I smiled genuinely but tiredly at her, and then grabbed my bags to get out the door.

"Let me give you a hand with one of those," Smith said. He took my roller bag and led me back down the stairs that we had ascended a few days ago, and then we walked out into the hangar. Our feet clattered across the highly polished concrete floor as we walked to the waiting jet. We didn't speak for a few moments.

"I have a question for you," I said as we reached the aircraft.

Smith looked at me.

"So, at some point, is a man in black going to show up and put a bullet between my eyes because I know too much?"

He smiled at me and stifled a laugh. "You've read way too many books and seen way too many movies. We use a lot of contractors in this line of work. They give us the highly-desirable quality of 'plausible deniability.' Frankly, it's a business thing. If word got out that we were whacking our contractors, no one would work for us."

"That makes me feel a little better," I said. "Whenever you throw the word 'business' into the context, it puts things in perspective."

"Besides, this isn't over," he said. "That reminds me." He handed me a package. "Don't open this until you get on the ground in New Castle. Follow the instructions and be careful."

I raised my eyebrows quizzically.

"It's a government-issue Glock Model 23 with a holster that fits inside the waistband of your pants in the small of your back, two extra magazines, and fifty rounds of forty-caliber Smith and Wesson ammo. The gun and the extra magazines are fully loaded. It comes complete with a federal concealed carry permit. It might come in handy."

"Thanks," I said. "You guys didn't have to do that."

Smith nodded. "Oh, and one more thing." He handed me something else, wrapped in a well-oiled rag. "I've been meaning to get this back to you for... a while."

I unfolded the rag and looked at the item that was exposed. My mouth went dry. "Holy shit," I said after a moment. "I always wondered what happened to this."

"Now you know. It only seemed right that you should

have it."

I was dumbstruck. All I could do was extend my hand.

Smith shook it firmly. "Damn good work out there," he said.

I looked back at him. "Is that check you gave me still good?"

"It is," he replied, smiling. "You should cash it as soon as you can. Once money in our budget is spent, no one cares about it anymore. And something else you should know," he said, lowering his voice to a conspiratorial whisper, "we don't tell the IRS anything."

I laughed and walked up the air-stairs into the Citation. The captain took my bags and stowed them in the aft baggage compartment while I got comfortable in the principal seat, the first forward-facing seat on the right side of the aircraft, and buckled in.

"KILG?" he asked me, using the identifier for New Castle County Airport.

I nodded. "And step on it, please."

He smiled at me. "This is the fastest business jet in the world. We'll have you there in less than four hours."

"Cool."

"If you want anything to eat or drink, the galley is just up front here. Help yourself."

"Thanks," I said.

He went back to the air-stair, closed the door, and resumed his place in the cockpit. The engines were started and we were taxiing a few minutes later. I was asleep before we took off.

##

A taxi dropped me off in front of my townhouse several hours later. The place looked dark and empty. I paid the driver, put my computer bag over my shoulder, and pulled my roller bag behind me up the concrete stairs. After searching for my keys for a few moments, I opened the door, disarmed the alarm, and brought my bags inside. Then I locked the door behind me and left the bags in the empty foyer as I turned on a few lights downstairs. The house looked the same as I had left it, but it almost didn't seem real now.

The CIA BlackBerry suddenly vibrated in my hip holster but I ignored it. I knew what I wanted and I wanted it badly. I made my way into my dining area, walked up to my bar, and found the bottle I was looking for. It was the cask-strength Glenfarclas, sixty percent alcohol. I poured a healthy shot of the stuff and knocked it back. It exploded in my mouth with a sensation of pure malt and alcohol and left a long, lingering finish as it oozed down my throat. I could feel the calming effect of the stuff almost immediately. I refilled the glass.

"Nothing like a stiff drink after a long day, is there, TC?"

Easy, I said to myself as my pulse quickened. *Easy.* I sighed and turned around.

The lighting in the dining area was very dim. Its only illumination was the yellowish reflection of the streetlights, coming in through the gauzy curtains hanging across the sliding glass door.

I could make out the shapes of two people sitting around the end of my dining table. Then the light switch went on, and I could suddenly see there were three people in the room rather than two.

Ron Phillips stood across from me, next to the kitchen entry. He was dressed in a black turtleneck sweater and black pants, and had a nasty-looking Uzi machine pistol strapped to him. I could see the long, metal cylinder of a suppressor screwed onto the short, stubby barrel. The business end of the Uzi was loosely pointed in my direction. I guess they didn't think I was much of a threat.

At the end of the table sat Ruth Shalev, her face a mask of hate. She was dressed in a black business suit, and she, like Phillips, came equipped with a silenced Uzi machine pistol.

In her case though, the Uzi sat on the table in front of her. She had her arms crossed and if her eyes had been lasers, she would have bored two holes through me.

I expected the final person to be present, but I had hoped she wouldn't be. It was going to make things harder.

Samantha Everhart sat there, clad in a black sweater dress, which clung to every curve of her splendid upper body. Her strawberry-blonde hair was pulled back behind her head and her striking blue eyes peered at me across the few feet of my dining room. The uncomfortable look on her face told me everything I needed to know. She didn't want to be here.

"Do you have any idea just how big a pain in the ass you've been?" Ruth exploded. "Do you have any idea how much money you've cost our investors?"

"You mean how much money I've cost you," I said, fighting to keep my voice even and the maniacal grin off my face. "You don't give a shit about your investors. You're just pissed because there will be no billion-dollar payday. The irony is that you've got only yourselves to blame. If you'd conducted your little revenge mission by bombing an obscure target with non-nuclear weapons, you'd still be in business. But you couldn't leave it there. You had to do the nuke thing. And against the United States no less. Did you really think you'd get away with it?"

"We almost did," Phillips said quietly. I shook my head.

"That's your ego talking, not reality," I replied. "Your activities have been tracked for over a year now. Ever since you stole the Vipers from the Boneyard. But you know what's ironic? No one really cared until you started talking about nuking something."

I paused for effect. I wanted them to hear what I was about to say very clearly. "But that's not the reason you got your asses kicked."

"And that was?" Ruth asked.

"Burt Magnusson," I said. "Like I said, you've only got

yourselves to blame."

A vicious look passed between Samantha and Ruth.

"Well, that couldn't be helped," Ruth said. "We knew he was talking to someone and we had to do something about it."

I looked across the table at Ruth. "You're the one who killed him?" She nodded once.

"Let me guess," I said as I felt my blood begin to simmer, "after the heated discussion with him and Ron in the office, you lured him out into the magic cove and tried to fuck him into submission."

Ruth's eyes narrowed slightly. "How do you know..." she began.

"That's not the whole story," Samantha interrupted Ruth with some venom in her voice.

"Sammy!" Ruth snapped.

Samantha acted like she didn't even hear her. "She brought him out there so that we could both fuck him."

Loaded glances passed between Ruth and Phillips. For a second, I imagined there'd be quite a discussion between them later. But neither of them had a 'later.'

"We got some drugs into him and got him naked, but that's as far as it went," Samantha continued. "He kept saying something about his wife." Samantha inclined her head toward Ruth. "She even went down on him a few times to try to get him into it. But he kept pushing her away."

Phillips was glaring at Ruth now. Ruth was ignoring him and obviously trying to figure out how she could regain control of the conversation.

"So, what happened?" I asked.

"She killed him," Samantha said. "She just pulled out a 9 millimeter and killed him. While he was lying there, helpless, on the damned futon."

"Where's his body?"

"I buried it!" Ruth spat at me. "We put him in that airtight metal box and buried him in the sand, right underneath the futon."

"And that would be the same futon I fucked you on?" I said, eyeing Phillips. "Three times?"

"You told me you never slept with any of them!" Phillips hissed at Ruth.

"I lied, honey," Ruth answered impatiently. "I have needs and you're not around much. It doesn't affect how I feel about you though. I just fuck them. I don't love them."

"Except for Burt," I injected.

"Stay out of this," she snapped at me.

"No, what about Burt?" Phillips demanded.

The tense situation in my dining room had suddenly dissolved into a soap opera. I couldn't decide whether I was in more danger or less.

"You know about the assignment where they met, right?" I asked Phillips. "During the development of the Python Four?" I inclined my head toward Ruth. "She threw herself at him and he wasn't having any. It made her nuts. That's the whole reason she wanted him to do the attack planning for the unit. She wanted to have another go at him."

"You liar!" Ruth spit at me. Then she turned to Phillips. "Don't believe him Ron! Magnusson was the best candidate I reviewed. The fact that we had worked together in the past was a bonus, but that's all it was."

I laughed. "Which is why it took you so long to do anything! Do you have any idea how long he'd been passing information about you? My God, you should have heard the briefing I got when I signed up for this gig! They knew *everything* thing about you guys."

"Passing information to whom?" Ruth asked, scowling. "That's actually the reason we're here. We need to know who he and you are working for."

"Enough of the bullshit, Pearce," Phillips snapped, visibly on edge now. "You're going to tell us what we want to know. And then you're going to die, so you'll never fuck with anyone else again." He raised the machine pistol and pointed it at my chest.

"Here's a question you have to ask yourself," I said conversationally. I had both my hands on my hips and I was inching my right one back, under my coat, toward where the CIA Glock resided in its holster in the small of my back.

"Do you honestly think that an organization with the resources this one has wouldn't have anticipated you guys would show up here?" I watched their eyes closely. They were doing the math. "And by the way, Ron," I continued, "how does it feel to be the one most used in all of this? How does it feel to take orders from these two all the time? It's apparent who runs things around here."

"You son of a bitch!" Phillips spat at me. "I have my role in this operation."

"Yeah," I sneered, "as first-class bitch-boy. What do they need from you? Is it your contacts in Russia? Is that where the investor money comes from?"

"Ron!" Ruth snapped. "Don't say anything. He's trying to get us to talk! They're listening."

Phillips' eyes became hot and I saw his jaw tighten. He flexed his fingers on the Uzi.

"Target standing," I said into the hidden microphone in my collar. "Go."

There was a barely audible 'tink' sound as the CIA sniper's bullet penetrated my sliding glass door and impacted Phillips' head, spraying a gory mural of bone, brains, and blood all over my dining room wall. Phillips collapsed to the floor like he'd been instantly deflated.

"We need them alive, Pearce," said the voice in my earpiece.

Fuck that.

I leapt toward the dining room table and attempted to lift it up and over onto the two women, but I didn't make it. Ruth's hand had closed around the grip of her Uzi and she had managed to squeeze off several rounds. The gun was so quiet it didn't seem real. All I heard from it was the rapid metallic 'click-click-click' of the bolt moving back and forth. But then I heard several slugs slap into the bar behind me and the rattle of broken glasses inside. As my ears analyzed the sounds, multiple burning shafts of white-hot pain slammed into my left thigh. My leg collapsed underneath me and I sprawled onto the table.

Pop. Pop. Pop.

The muffled gun shots sounded almost comical after the mayhem of the previous few seconds. I reflexively surveyed my body to ensure I wasn't taking additional wounds from a different source. And then I looked up.

Samantha had stood and pushed herself away from the table. She had a small automatic pistol in her hand and was firing it at Ruth. Ruth was still seated and looking down at the series of small red holes that had materialized on the left side of her shoulder and chest. She raised the Uzi and began to sweep it, obviously intending to finish me and kill Samantha in the same motion.

I grabbed the edge of the table on Ruth's side and pulled my body toward her. Another white-hot spear dug into my left shoulder, but then my body was inside her arms, and my hands were on her. I grasped her clothing and used all the strength I had to pull the two of us onto the floor. As we went down, I could still hear the bolt of the Uzi cycling with its rhythmic metallic click and I could hear the thuds of the bullets impacting my ceiling and walls.

The Uzi's magazine emptied as Ruth and I hit the floor, and then I heard Sammy utter a single word.

"Oh," she said, quietly.

Ruth and I ended up face to face, inches apart, with my body resting on hers. "You bastard!" she screamed at me. "I'll fucking kill you!"

She struggled, trying to swing the Uzi and hit me on the back of the head with the thick metal silencer. I raised my left shoulder and deflected the blow, and then I shifted my weight, grabbed her upper right arm with my left hand, and leaned into it, pinning her right side to the floor. She clawed at me ineffectually with her left hand, its strength dampened by the wounds Samantha had inflicted on her.

I looked down at her and let the smile stretch my lips, watching the ire in her eyes turn into fear. I weighed nearly twice what she did. She wasn't going anywhere and. we both knew it.

"Entry team one minute," said the voice in my earpiece. I barely registered it.

The warmth took me then, seeping into me and possessing me with the comforting heat of the old rage. I was transported back to the prison house in Iraq and to my old house in Phoenix in an instant and I felt an odd sense of tranquility, like forces were aligning inside and around me. I calmly reached back to my right hip and retrieved the second item Smith had given me from my back pocket. I raised the item and rotated it in a slow circle in my right hand, allowing the oiled cloth wrapping to fall to the floor.

Ruth saw it then and the fear in her eyes became panic. She knew what was coming.

The knife was about nine inches long with a jeweled handle and a wickedly curved five-inch blade that was sharp enough to shave with. Arabic writing was etched into both sides of the gleaming steel. It looked evil and beautiful all at once.

"No!" she screamed. "Not here! Not by you! Not like this!"

My right hand flashed across her throat and then she couldn't talk any more. A thin, red line appeared across her neck, just below her Adam's apple. She grasped her throat with her left hand just as the thin line turned into a thicker one and rivulets of bubbly blood began to seep through her fingers. Her eyes looked at me with the horrified realization of someone who knows they're about to die and can't do a damn thing about it.

I couldn't help smiling at her. "I'll see you in hell, you homicidal bitch."

I heard the Uzi clatter to the floor as the life left her body and she went slack beneath me.

"Colin," Samantha's voice was barely audible.

I looked back over my shoulder to see Samantha sitting on the floor, about three feet from Phillips' corpse. She was leaning against the wall and had her hands in front of her, covering her abdomen, just below her breasts.

Blood was pouring from between her fingers. "Sammy!" I shouted. "Oh, my God, Sammy!"

I rolled off Ruth and crawled under my table over to her, my wounds forgotten. I pushed myself up into a sitting position next to her and threw one arm around her while I pushed down onto her two hands with my other hand.

"I guess...I guess I owe you an apology," she said very softly, leaning her head against me.

"No, you don't, Sammy," I replied as I held her a little more tightly. "I figured it out."

"I wasn't supposed to fall for you," she continued, almost like she was talking to herself. "I've done this sort of thing so many times before and I've never fallen for anyone. But you were too perfect for me."

She coughed blood onto our hands and it began oozing from the corner of her mouth.

"This is Pearce," I said into the mic mounted in my collar, "we need medical personnel and an ambulance, ASAP!"

"I wanted...to save...you," she said, now laboring for every word as the life ebbed out of her. "Had...a way...out...for us.

She tilted her head back and looked up at me. She smiled and I could see something in the depths of her eyes that was unmistakable. Then as I held her, I felt her body tense as she gathered her strength to speak again.

"I...loved you," she said, her voice barely a whisper." I... wasn't...trying...to...kill you. I...was trying...to...save...you."

The door to my house swung open and I could hear the thump of boots in my hallway. But all I could do was look down into the striking blue eyes which were now sightless and staring back at me.

"I know," I said to her. "I know."

EPILOGUE

Saturday, 17 October
1400 Hours Local Time
Orlando, Florida, USA

It was a bright, sunny day in central Florida when we laid Burt Magnusson to rest. Fortunately, the mid-October temperature and humidity weren't too oppressive. The USAF sent an active-duty lieutenant colonel to be the duty officer for the funeral, and he helped Mandy and the kids through the entire process. The funeral was heavily attended by Burt's family, Mandy's family, and several people he and I both had known in the Air Force.

By that time, the story of the attempted air-strike in California was all over the news, and despite the CIA's best efforts, someone had snapped a picture of me getting out of the F-16 at Edwards. It was a long-distance photo but it was a reasonable likeness and it came complete with the headline: "Hero Pilot Saves Southern California from Nuclear Strike." Fortunately, my name was never discovered. I found that I was the target of several looks and stares at the funeral and I did my best to stay in the background throughout the proceedings, an easy feat since I was moving slowly anyway.

The injuries I sustained a week ago were substantial. My left thigh absorbed three nine millimeter bullets from Shalev's submachine gun and the meaty part of my left shoulder had taken a fourth one. There probably would have been several more holes in me if I hadn't been wearing the Kevlar vest the CIA gave me. The doctors didn't want to let me out of their sight, but I fought them to be here. I had a debt to pay.

The eulogy ended. The honor guard folded the flag and handed it to Mandy. Then came the mournful strains of *Taps* on the trumpet and the 21-gun salute. After the last volley of gunfire, we heard the low rumble of jets and a four-ship of F-16s flew overhead at 500 feet, the number three man pulling up and out as they reached us, to form the classic 'missing man' formation. That was when the last tears finally hit me.

I waited until all the other mourners had filed away for the wake. Then, with the help of my newly-acquired cane, I made my way over to the open grave. Burt's coffin gleamed at the bottom. I grabbed a handful of dirt and threw it down on top of the casket.

"Rest in peace, Boomer," I said, my voice cracking. "I got them for you. I got them all. I just wish to God I'd been able to do more. Sleep well, pal."

I wiped my eyes, turned around to go, and found his wife, Mandy standing right in front of me. She stepped forward and hugged me tightly, nearly knocking me over.

"Thank you so much for bringing him back to me," she said. "Thank you so much."

I squeezed her for a minute and then tenderly pushed her away, looking down into her teary green eyes.

"It was, quite literally, the least I could do," I said.

"Can you come back to the house with us? The kids would love to spend some time with you and so would I." She looked down at the dirt for a moment. "I feel like there's so much I don't know."

"I'm sorry," I said. "I have another errand to run because of this business. But I promise I'll come see you and the kids as soon as I'm back."

She looked up at me and smiled dutifully, like she didn't believe me. "What kind of errand?"

I could have made something up, but I just didn't. "I have to go talk to some people in England. Government orders." I paused for a second. "Not to change the subject but...are you and the kids okay financially? Is there anything I can do to help?"

She laughed. "That's the least of our worries. Between Burt's life insurance, the money from...those people...and the money Smith had the government pay us, I may never have to work again. And the kids can go to any college they want."

I made a mental note to thank Smith the next time I spoke to him. "Well, at least there's that," I said, as I took her arm and walked her to her car. I wasn't sure who was walking whom.

We stopped at the door to her limo. Her youngest daughter, the one with her father's eyes, knocked on the window glass from inside and waved at me. I waved back. She giggled and disappeared into the limo's interior.

"Was that really you?" Mandy asked, looking up at me. "The guy in all the papers?"

I shook my head and smiled at her. "I only wish I was that good," I said.

##

About sixteen hours later, I stepped off a CIA Gulfstream G-550 at Farnborough in the United Kingdom. Unlike the previous day, this one was typically British, wet and breezy, with low overcast skies, dark cloudiness, and the ever-present English mist. They had parked us well away from the massive executive terminal and a dark sedan waited for me, the mist already forming a coat of moisture on the vehicle's black paint.

Brianna Blenhem waited for me at the base of the air-stair as I hobbled down it. She was smartly dressed in a gray coat over some sort of dark red dress; and she smiled at me as I alit from the steps.

"Fancy meeting you here," I said, while the flight attendant stowed my bags in the trunk of the car.

"Kim Page, MI-6, British Intelligence," she said, extending her hand. "That's my real name, actually." Her Australian accent was gone. It was pure British.

She motioned me towards the car where the driver held one of the rear doors open for me. I doffed my coat, entered the vehicle, and seated myself. The interior of the sedan was brown leather and very spacious. There was enough room behind the front seat for me to extend my legs completely. I also noticed there was a raised partition behind the driver's compartment and that all the windows were darkly shaded. I was getting the VIP treatment.

"Northumberland?" I asked "Kim" as she slid into the vehicle, took off her own coat, and fastened her seatbelt.

She looked at me quizzically.

"Your childhood home? Northumberland? I lived here for a few years. Identifying the different accents got to be sort of a hobby with me."

She nodded. "Newcastle upon Tyne. You're good."

"If that's even your real accent."

"It is."

She kicked off her high-heeled shoes and turned on the seat to face me, tucking her legs up under herself. Her dress hiked up on her thighs, exposing quite a bit of her luscious legs. Her rich, brunette hair was just slightly damp and there were a few drops of moisture on her skin. I looked into her face. Her deep, brown eyes sparkled at me and there was the slightest hint of a smile on her lips.

She's actually glad to see me. The thought warmed me a little. "So, I guess I'm all yours for the next week or so. I don't know how valuable I'll be to you. My understanding is that you guys were working the banking end of things and apparently

Everhart was the key to setting that whole part of it up."

She nodded, her face serious. "It's too bad she's dead. Samantha Everhart was the whole reason I was there. She'd been shagging senior RAF officers since the late eighties. After she left the RAF, she started making the rounds in the London banking establishment and found her way into quite a few bedrooms there, as well. Turns out she was quite the ruthless, blackmailing little bitch. We started hearing rumors of some sort of international operation she was trying to run through a few of the banks here, and that's when MI-6 got involved. I was set up to meet her, and that's what led to my being recruited to join the unit. Of course, we did have to ensure their first choice wasn't available."

I looked at her sharply.

"We gave the girl I replaced an all-expense paid trip to Bermuda," she said hurriedly, correctly interpreting my concern about the girl's disposition. "She loved it and she's still there."

There was a pause. I could feel her eyes on me.

"By the way," she said, "we heard you killed Shalev. What happened?"

I turned my head away and looked out of my passenger window at the dull green English countryside.

"Things sort of went crazy," I sighed. "It was all set up. I was wired; the place was wired; the CIA had a sniper team and an entry team in place. The plan was to look for an opening, take Phillips down, and capture the other two. Well, I thought Phillips was going to shoot me and I gave the 'go', and then all hell broke loose. The sniper nailed Phillips, and I tried to put Shalev and Everhart out of action long enough for the entry team to come in. But then Shalev shot me, and Everhart shot Shalev, and then Shalev tried to shoot both of us, and I sort of got in the middle of it all. I ended up with several of Shalev's bullets inside me, and Everhart ended up dead."

I turned my gaze inside, and looked sightlessly at the back

of the driver's partition in front of me.

"During the mayhem, I wrestled Shalev to the floor. She started struggling, and I cut her throat without even thinking about it. I don't know what came over me."

That was a lie. I knew exactly what had come over me. And I had reveled in it.

My hands started to shake as I relived the surges of emotion and adrenaline that had been coursing through me.

But then my mind turned to Samantha Everhart. The woman who had loved me. The woman who had wanted to save my life - by trying to kill me. What had she possibly seen in me that made her willing to turn her back on everything she had done? Everything she had worked for?

But, I knew the answer. A part of her had still *believed.* We had been kindred spirits. The many disappointments of life had worn us down, nearly to bitterness. But a thread of hope had remained.

And that was what had killed her.

Goddamn it, Sammy, what the hell were you thinking? What the hell were either of us thinking? Happy endings are such bullshit.

Kim looked over at me. Then she reached out and took my right hand, which had been resting on the armrest between us. She held it with both of hers and pulled it into her lap, bringing me back into the moment.

"Don't be too hard on yourself," she said soothingly, leaning the side of her head against the seat. "It's difficult to know what any of us will do in those sorts of situations."

I smiled at her. "You're awfully understanding, Miss Page." I looked down at my hand, nestled between both of hers. I could feel the warmth of her hands and the heat of her body. "So, I heard a rumor you volunteered to be in charge of my visit here and my questioning."

She nodded and smiled back at me. "That's true, actually."

"Good," I replied. "I just wanted to make sure you weren't

'under orders' again."

She flushed slightly but looked directly at me. "Well, as the agent with the most knowledge on the case, I'm the logical person to lead your debriefing. Besides, there's no one better qualified than you are to talk us through the technical and military aspects of MAG's operation. Between the two of us, we can document a lot of the internal aspects of the operation. But, having said that..." She paused for a second, as if trying to decide what she was going to say next. "I did want to see you again, Colin."

I grinned at her. "Well, frankly, I wasn't terribly keen about coming over here until I found out you'd be in charge."

She squeezed my hand. "You know," she said, looking down at our entwined hands, "Brianna *really* liked you. And she's been thinking *a lot* about the time she spent with you."

I could feel my heart lightening. I could lose myself in this young woman's body and rebuild the walls around me. I needed that.

"Is that a fact?" I asked.

"It is," said "Kim," nodding. "And it just so happens that I've arranged to have the questioning conducted in a safe house down in Devon. We'll have visitors during the days to do the questioning and record the conversations, but at night it will be just the two of us." She looked up and smiled at me sensually. "Do you think we can find something to do?"

Once again, the words 'I'd rather be lucky than good' flashed through my mind.

"Oh, I'm sure we can," I said, as we drove down the motorway into the English mist. "After all, I'm a contractor. Improvisation comes with the package. No extra charge."

COLIN PEARCE WILL RETURN
IN
THE CABO CONTRACT

FROM THE FIRST EDITION: A NOTE TO MY FELLOW VIPER DRIVERS

As much as this story is about the characters, it's also about the jet itself. My last flight in the Viper took place under the sweltering Arizona sun at Luke Air Force Base in the summer of 2001. I can still remember certain elements of it like it was yesterday. As I sat down to write this book, I wanted to draw the reader in but also not give away all of our 'trade secrets' or all the capabilities of the jet. I'll tell you up front that while I tried to keep it as 'real' as possible, literary license is a wonderful thing. Having said that, time out of the jet does things to you and I'm sure there are a few mistakes in the text. For those, 'I'll take the hit in the debrief.' So, find me on the road, point one out to me, and I'll buy you a drink. In the meantime, check six!

ABOUT THE AUTHOR

Chris Broyhill is a retired U.S. Air Force fighter pilot who flew the OV-10, A-10, and F-16 while on active duty. He holds a bachelor's degree in computer science from the U.S. Air Force Academy, a master's degree in national security studies from California State University at San Bernardino and a Ph.D. in aviation from Embry-Riddle Aeronautical University. Chris is an outstanding graduate of the U.S. Air Force Fighter Weapons School and is a National Business Aviation Association Certified Aviation Manager. Chris has flown in and led aviation organizations for over 30 years.

CPSIA information can be obtained
at www.ICGtesting.com
Printed in the USA
LVOW08s1800230518
578237LV00003B/521/P